THE HARLEQUIN

THE
HARLEQUIN

LAURELL K. HAMILTON

BERKLEY BOOKS, NEW YORK

THE BERKLEY PUBLISHING GROUP
Published by the Penguin Group
Penguin Group (USA) Inc.
375 Hudson Street, New York, New York 10014, USA
Penguin Group (Canada), 90 Eglinton Avenue East, Suite 700, Toronto, Ontario M4P 2Y3, Canada
(a division of Pearson Penguin Canada Inc.)
Penguin Books Ltd., 80 Strand, London WC2R 0RL, England
Penguin Group Ireland, 25 St. Stephen's Green, Dublin 2, Ireland (a division of Penguin Books Ltd.)
Penguin Group (Australia), 250 Camberwell Road, Camberwell, Victoria 3124, Australia
(a division of Pearson Australia Group Pty. Ltd.)
Penguin Books India Pvt. Ltd., 11 Community Centre, Panchsheel Park, New Delhi—110 017, India
Penguin Group (NZ), 67 Apollo Drive, Rosedale, North Shore 0745, Auckland, New Zealand
(a division of Pearson New Zealand Ltd.)
Penguin Books (South Africa) (Pty.) Ltd., 24 Sturdee Avenue, Rosebank, Johannesburg 2196, South Africa

Penguin Books Ltd., Registered Offices: 80 Strand, London WC2R 0RL, England

This book is an original publication of The Berkley Publishing Group

First edition: June 2007

Library of Congress Cataloging-in-Publication Data

Hamilton, Laurell K.
  The harlequin / Laurell K. Hamilton.— 1st ed.
    p. cm.
  ISBN 978-0-425-21724-5
1. Blake, Anita (Fictitious character)—Fiction. 2. Vampires—Fiction. 3. St. Louis (Mo.)—Fiction. I. Title.
  PS3558.A443357H37 2007
  813'.54—dc22   2007005971

PRINTED IN THE UNITED STATES OF AMERICA

10 9 8 7 6 5 4 3 2

To Jonathon, who never freaks about my choice of research. He took away my serial killer books, at my request. When I was ready he gave them back. He's helping me understand that just because someone else thinks you're a monster doesn't mean you are. Even if that person says they love you. Here's to finding love that builds you up, instead of breaking you down.

ACKNOWLEDGMENTS

To the Staff: Darla, Chief Operations Officer, and Lauretta, who assists her; Sherry, Chief Domestic Officer, and Teresa, who assists her; Mary, Comptroller and Grandma extraordinaire; and Charles aka Gru, Chief Security Officer. For those who are wondering, Jon's official title is Chief Information Officer.

Merrilee Heifitz, my agent, who has worked hard as we've pushed boundaries and entered new territory.

To Bev Leveto, thanks for your wonderful donation to Granite City. Hope you enjoy being a victim in this book.

To everyone at DBPro and Marvel, who helped bring Anita to life in the comic-book world. Special thanks to Les and Ernst Dabel for being gentle. Extra special thanks to our artist, Brett Booth, who did an amazing job and listened.

As always thanks to my writing group: Tom Drennan, Debroah Millitello, Rett MacPherson, Marella Sands, Sharon Shinn, and Mark Sumner. You guys help keep me going.

1

MALCOLM, THE HEAD of the Church of Eternal Life, the vampire church, sat across from me. Malcolm had never been in my office before. In fact, the last time I'd seen him, he'd accused me of doing black magic and being a whore. I'd also killed one of his members on church grounds, in front of him and the rest of his congregation. The dead vamp had been a serial killer. I'd had a court order of execution, but still, it hadn't made Malcolm and me buddies.

I sat behind my desk, sipping coffee from my newest Christmas-themed mug: a little girl sat on Santa's lap saying, "Define good." I worked hard every year to find the most offensive mug I could so that Bert, our business manager, could throw a fit. This year's mug was tame by my usual standards. It had become one of my holiday traditions. I'd at least dressed for the season in a red skirt and jacket over a thin silk sweater—very festive, for me. I had a new gun in my shoulder holster. A friend of mine had finally persuaded me to give up my Browning Hi-Power for something that fit my hand a little better and had a smoother profile. The Hi-Power was at home in the gun safe, and the Browning Dual Mode was in the holster. I felt like I was cheating but at least I was still a Browning girl.

Once upon a time, I'd thought Malcolm handsome, but that had been when his vampire tricks worked on me. Without vampire wiles to cloud my perception, I could see that his bone structure was too rough, almost as if it hadn't quite gotten smoothed out before they put that pale skin on it. His hair was cut short and had a little curl to it, because to take the curl out of it he'd have had to shave it. The hair was a bright, bright canary yellow. That's what blond hair does if you take it out of the sun for a few hundred years. He looked at me with his blue eyes and smiled, and the smile filled his face with personality. That same personality that made his Sunday morning television program such a hit. It wasn't magic, it was just him. Charisma, for lack of a better word. There was force to Malcolm that had nothing to do with vampire powers and everything to do with who he was, not what he was. He'd have been a leader and a mover of men even if he'd been alive.

The smile softened his features, filled his face with a zeal that was both compelling and frightening. He was a true believer, head of a church of true believers. The whole idea of a vampire church still creeped me out, but it was the fastest-growing denomination in the country.

"I was surprised to see your name in my appointment book, Malcolm," I said, finally.

"I understand that, Ms. Blake. I am almost equally surprised to be here."

"Fine, we're both surprised. Why are you here?"

"I suspect you have, or will soon have, a warrant of execution for a member of my church."

I managed to keep my face blank, but felt the stiffness in my shoulders. He'd see the reaction, and he'd know what it meant. Master vampires don't miss much. "You have a lot of members, Malcolm; could you narrow it down a little? Who exactly are we talking about?"

"Don't be coy, Ms. Blake."

"I'm not being coy."

"You're trying to imply that you have a warrant for more than one of my vampires. I do not believe it, and neither do you."

I should have felt insulted, because I wasn't lying. Two of his upstanding vamps had been very naughty. "If your vampires were fully blood-oathed to you, you'd know I was telling the truth, because you'd be able to enforce your moral code in entirely new ways."

"A blood oath is not a guarantee of absolute control, Ms. Blake."

"No, but it's a start."

A blood oath was what a vamp took when he joined a new vampire group, a new kiss. He literally took blood from the Master of the City. It meant the master had a lot more control over him, and the lesser vamps gained in power, too. If their master was powerful enough. A weak master wasn't much help, but Jean-Claude, St. Louis's Master of the City and my sweetie, wasn't weak. Of course, the master gained power from the oath, as well. The more powerful a vamp they could oath, the more they gained. Like so many vampire powers, it was a two-way street.

"I do not want to enforce my moral code. I want my people to choose to be good people," Malcolm said.

"Until your congregation is blood-oathed to some master vampire, they are loose cannons, Malcolm. You control them by force of personality and morality. Vampires only understand fear, and power."

"You are the lover of at least two vampires, Ms. Blake. How can you say that?"

I shrugged. "Maybe because I *am* dating two vampires."

"If that is what being Jean-Claude's human servant has taught you, Ms. Blake, then it is sad things he is teaching you."

"He is the Master of the City of St. Louis, Malcolm, not you. You, and your church, go unmolested by his tolerance."

"I go unmolested because the Church grew powerful under the previous Master of the City, and by the time Jean-Claude rose to power, we were hundreds. He did not have the power to bring me and my people to heel."

I sipped coffee and thought about my next answer, because I couldn't argue with him. He was probably right. "Regardless of how we got where we are, Malcolm, you have several hundred vampires in this city. Jean-Claude let you have them because he thought you were blood-oathing them. We learned in October that you aren't. Which means that the vamps with you are cut off from an awful lot of their potential power. I'm okay with that, I guess. Their choice, if they understand that it is a choice, but no blood oath means that they are not mystically tied to anyone but the vamp that made them. You, I'm told, do the deed, most of the time. Though the church deacons do recruit sometimes."

"How our church is organized is not your concern."

"Yes," I said, "it is."

"Do you serve Jean-Claude now, when you say that, or is it as a federal marshal that you criticize me?" He narrowed those blue eyes. "I do not think the federal government knows or understands enough of vampires to care whether I blood-oath my people."

"Blood-oathing lowers the chance of vamps doing things behind the back of the master."

"Blood-oathing takes away their free will, Ms. Blake."

"Maybe, but I've seen the damage they can do with their free will. A good Master of the City can guarantee that there is almost no crime among his people."

"They are his slaves," Malcolm said.

I shrugged and sat back in my chair. "Are you here to talk about the warrant, or to talk about the deadline Jean-Claude gave your church?"

"Both."

"Jean-Claude has given you and your church members their choices, Malcolm. Either you blood-oath them, or Jean-Claude does. Or they can move to another city to be blood-oathed there, but it has to be done."

"It is a choice of who they would be slaves to, Ms. Blake. It is no choice at all."

"Jean-Claude was generous, Malcolm. By vampire law he could have just killed you and your entire congregation."

"And how would the law, how would you, as a federal marshal, have felt about such slaughter?"

"Are you saying that my being a federal marshal limits Jean-Claude's options?"

"He values your love, Anita, and you would not love a man that could slaughter my followers."

"You don't add yourself to that list—why?"

"You are a legal vampire executioner, Anita. If I broke human law, you would kill me yourself. You would not fault Jean-Claude for doing the same if I broke vampiric law."

"You think I'd just let him kill you?"

"I think you would kill me for him, if you felt justified."

A small part of me wanted to argue, but he was right. I'd been grandfathered in like most of the vamp executioners who had two or more years on the job and could pass the firearms test. The idea was, making us federal marshals was the quickest way to grant us the ability to cross state lines and to control us more. Crossing state lines and having a badge was great; I wasn't sure how controlled we were. Of course, I was the only vampire hunter who was also dating her Master of the City. Most saw it as a conflict of interest. Frankly, so did I, but there wasn't much I could do about it.

"You do not argue with me," Malcolm said.

"I can't decide if you think I'm a civilizing influence on Jean-Claude, or a bad one."

"I saw you once as his victim, Anita. Now I am no longer certain who is the victim, and who the victimizer."

"Should I be offended?"

He just looked at me.

"The last time I was in your church you called me evil, and accused me of black magic. You called Jean-Claude immoral, and me his whore, or something like that."

"You were trying to take away one of my people to be killed with no trial. You shot him to death on the church grounds."

"He was a serial killer. I had an order of execution for everyone involved in those crimes."

"All the vampires, you mean."

"Are you implying that humans or shapeshifters were involved?"

"No, but if they had been, you would never have been allowed to shoot them to death with the police helping you do it."

"I've had warrants for shapeshifters before."

"But those are rare, Anita, and there are no orders of execution for humans."

"The death penalty still exists, Malcolm."

"After a trial, and years of appeals, if you are human."

"What do you want from me, Malcolm?"

"I want justice."

"The law isn't about justice, Malcolm. It's about the law."

"She did not do the crime she is accused of, as our wandering brother Avery Seabrook was innocent of the crime you sought him for." He called any of his church group who joined Jean-Claude "wanderers." The fact that Avery, the vampire, had a last name meant he was very recently dead, and that he was an American vampire. Vampires normally only had one name, like Madonna or Cher, and only one vamp per country could have that name. Duels were fought over the right to use names. Until now, until America. We had vampires with last names, unheard of.

"I cleared Avery. Legally, I didn't have to."

"No, you could have shot him dead, found out your mistake later, and suffered nothing under the law."

"I did not write this law, Malcolm, I just carry it out."

"Vampires did not write this law either, Anita."

"That's true, but no human can mesmerize other humans so that they help in their own kidnappings. Humans can't fly off with their victims in their arms."

"And that justifies slaughtering us?"

I shrugged again. I was going to leave this argument alone because I'd begun to not like that part of my job. I didn't think vampires were monsters anymore; it made killing them harder. It made executing them when they couldn't fight back monstrous, with me as the monster.

"What do you want me to do, Malcolm? I have a warrant with Sally Hunter's name on it. Witnesses saw her leave Bev Leveto's apartment. Ms. Leveto died by vampire attack. I know it wasn't any of Jean-Claude's vampires. That leaves yours." Hell, I had her driver's license picture in the file with the warrant. I have to admit that having a picture to go with it made me feel more like an assassin. A picture so I'd get the right one.

"Are you so certain of that?"

I blinked at him, the slow blink that gave me time to think but didn't look like I was thinking furiously. "What are you trying to say, Malcolm? I'm not good at subtle; just tell me what you came to say."

"Something powerful, someone powerful, came to my church last week. They hid themselves. I could not find them in the new faces of my congregation, but I know that someone immensely powerful was there." He leaned forward, his calm exterior cracking around the edges. "Do you understand how powerful they would have to be for me to sense them, use all my powers to search the room for them, yet not be able to find them?"

I thought about it. Malcolm was no Master of the City, but he was probably one of the top five most powerful vampires in town. He'd be higher, if he weren't so terribly moral. It limited him in some ways.

I licked my lips, careful of the lipstick, and nodded. "Did they want you to know they were there, or was that part an accident?"

He actually showed surprise for a moment before he got control of his face. He played human too much for the media; he was beginning to lose that stillness of features that the old ones have. "I don't know." Even his voice was no longer smooth.

"Did the vamp do it to taunt you, or was it arrogance?"

He shook his head. "I do not know."

I had a moment of revelation. "You came here because you think Jean-Claude should know, but you can't let your congregation see you going to the Master of the City. It would undermine your whole free-will thing."

He settled back into his chair, fighting to keep the anger off his face, and failing. He was even more scared than I thought, to be losing it this badly in front of someone he disliked. Hell, he'd come to me for help. He was desperate.

"But you can come to me, a federal marshal, and tell me. Because you know I'll tell Jean-Claude."

"Think what you like, Ms. Blake."

We weren't on a first-name basis anymore. I'd hit it on the head. "A big, bad vamp checks your church out. You aren't vampire enough to smoke him out, and you come to me, to Jean-Claude and all his immoral power structure. You come to the very people you say you hate."

He stood up. "The crime that Sally is accused of happened less than twenty-four hours after he, it, they came to my church. I do not think that is a coincidence."

"I'm not lying about the second order of execution, Malcolm. It's in my desk drawer, right now, with a driver's license picture of the vampire in question."

He sat back down. "What name is on it?"

"Why, so you can warn . . . them?" I'd almost said *her*, because it was another female vamp.

"My people are not perfect, Ms. Blake, but I believe that another vampire has come to town and is framing them."

"Why? Why would someone do that?"

"I don't know."

"No one has bothered Jean-Claude or his people."

"I know," Malcolm said.

"Without a true master, a true blood-oathed, mystically connected master, your congregation are just sheep waiting for the wolves to come get them."

"Jean-Claude said as much a month ago."

"Yeah, he did."

"I thought at first that it was one of the new vampires who has joined Jean-Claude. One of the ones from Europe, but it is not. It is something more powerful than that. Or it is a group of vampires combining their powers through their master's marks. I have felt such power only once before."

"When?" I asked.

He shook his head. "We are forbidden to speak of it, on penalty of death. Only if they contact us directly can we break this silence."

"It sounds like you've already been contacted," I said.

He shook his head again. "They are tampering with me, and my people, because technically I am outside normal vampire law. Did Jean-Claude report to the council that my church had not blood-oathed any of its followers?"

I nodded. "Yes, he did."

He put his big hands over his face and leaned over his knees, almost as if he felt faint. He whispered, "I feared as much."

"Okay, Malcolm, you're moving too fast for me here. What does Jean-Claude's reporting to the council have to do with some group of powerful vamps messing with your church?"

He looked at me, but his eyes had gone gray with worry. "Tell him what I have told you. He will understand."

"But I don't."

"I have until New Year's Day to give Jean-Claude my answer about the blood-oathing. He has been generous and patient, but there are those among the council that are neither of those things. I had hoped they would be proud of what I had accomplished. I thought it would please them, but I fear now that the council is not ready to see my brave new world of free will."

"Free will is for humans, Malcolm. The preternatural community is about control."

He stood again. "You have almost complete discretion on how the warrant is executed, Anita. Will you use some of that discretion to find the truth before you kill my followers?"

I stood up. "I can't guarantee anything."

"I would not ask that. I ask only that you look for the truth before it is too late for Sally, and my other follower, whose name you will not even give me." He sighed. "I have not sent Sally running out of town; why would I warn the other?"

"You came through the door knowing Sally was in trouble. I'm not helping you figure the other bad guy out."

"It is a man, then?"

I just looked at him, glad that I could give full eye contact. It had always been so hard to do the tough stare back when I couldn't look a vamp in the eyes.

He straightened his shoulders as if only now aware that he was slumping. "You won't even give me that, will you? Please tell Jean-Claude what I have told you. I should have come to you immediately. I thought morals kept me from running to the very power structure I despise, but it wasn't morals, it was sin; the sin of pride. I hope that my pride has not cost more of my followers their lives." He went for the door.

I called after him. "Malcolm."

He turned.

"How big an emergency is this?"

"Big."

"Will a couple of hours make a difference?"

He thought about it. "Perhaps; why do you ask?"

"I won't be seeing Jean-Claude tonight. I just wanted to know if I should call him, give him a heads-up."

"Yes, by all means, give him his heads-up." He frowned at me. "Why would you not see your master tonight, Anita? Aren't you living with him?"

"Actually, no. I stay over at his place about half the week, but I've got my own place still."

"Will you be killing more of my kindred tonight?"

I shook my head.

"Then you will raise my other colder brethren. Whose blissful death will you disturb tonight, Anita? Whose zombie will you raise so some human can get their inheritance, or a wife can be consoled?"

"No zombies tonight," I said. I was too puzzled by his attitude on the zombies to be insulted. I'd never heard a vampire claim any kinship with zombies, or ghouls, or anything but other vamps.

"Then what will keep you from your master's arms?"

"I've got a date, not that it's any of your business."

"But not a date with Jean-Claude, or Asher?"

I shook my head.

"Your wolf king then, Richard?"

I shook my head, again.

"For whom would you abandon those three, Anita? Ah, your leopard king, Micah."

"Wrong again."

"I am amazed that you are answering my questions."

"So am I, actually. I think it's because you keep calling me a whore, and I think I want to rub your face in it."

"What, the fact that you are a whore?" His face showed nothing when he said it.

"I knew you couldn't do it," I said.

"Do what, Ms. Blake?"

"I knew you couldn't play nice long enough to get my help. I knew if I kept at you, you'd get snotty and mean."

He gave a small bow, just from the neck. "I told you, Ms. Blake, my sin is pride."

"And what's my sin, Malcolm?"

"Do you want me to insult you, Ms. Blake?"

"I just want to hear you say it."

"Why?"

"Why not?" I said.

"Very well; your sin is lust, Ms. Blake, as it is the sin of your master and all his vampires."

I shook my head and felt that unpleasant smile curl my lips. The smile that left my eyes cold, and usually meant I was well and truly pissed. "That's not my sin, Malcolm, not the one nearest and dearest to my heart."

"And what would your sin be, Ms. Blake?"

"Wrath, Malcolm, it's wrath."

"Are you saying I've made you angry?"

"I'm always angry, Malcolm; you just gave me a target to focus it on."

"Do you envy anyone, Ms. Blake?"

I thought about it, then shook my head. "Not really, no."

"I will not ask about sloth; you work entirely too hard for that to be an issue. You are not greedy, nor a glutton. Are you prideful?"

"Sometimes," I said.

"Wrath, lust, and pride, then?"

I nodded. "I guess, if we're keeping score."

"Oh, someone is keeping score, Ms. Blake, never doubt that."

"I'm Christian, too, Malcolm."

"Do you worry about getting into heaven, Ms. Blake?"

It was such an odd question that I answered it. "I did, for a while, but my faith still makes my cross glow. My prayers still have the power to chase the evil things away. God hasn't forsaken me; it's just that all the right-wing fundamentalist Christians want to believe he has. I've seen evil, Malcolm, real evil, and you aren't that."

He smiled, and it was gentle, and almost embarrassed. "Have I come to you for absolution, Ms. Blake?"

"I don't think I'm the one to give you absolution."

"I would like a priest to hear my sins before I die, Ms. Blake, but none will come near me. They are holy, and the very trappings of their calling will burst into flames in my presence."

"Not true. The holy items only go off if the true believer panics, or if you try vampire powers on them."

He blinked at me, and I realized his eyes held unshed tears, shimmering in the overhead lights. "Is this true, Ms. Blake?"

"I promise it is." His attitude was beginning to make me afraid for him. I didn't want to be afraid for Malcolm. I had enough people in my life that I cared for enough to worry about; I did not need to add the undead Billy Graham to my list.

"Do you know any priests that might be willing to hear a very long confession?"

"I might, though I don't know if they're allowed to give you absolution, since technically in the eyes of the Church you're already dead. You have ties to a lot of the religious community, Malcolm; surely one of the other leaders would be willing."

"I do not want to ask them, Anita. I do not want them to know my sins. I would rather . . ." He hesitated, then spoke, but I was pretty sure it wasn't the sentence he started to use. "Quietly, I would rather it be done quietly."

"Why the sudden need for confession and absolution?"

"I am still a believer, Ms. Blake; being a vampire has not changed that. I wish to die absolved of my sins."

"Why are you expecting to die?"

"Tell Jean-Claude what I have told you about the stranger or strangers in my church. Tell him about my desire for a priest to hear my confession. He will understand."

"Malcolm . . ."

He kept walking, but stopped with his hand on the door. "I take back what I said, Ms. Blake, I am not sorry I came. I am only sorry I did not come days ago." With that he walked out and closed the door softly behind him.

I sat down at my desk and called Jean-Claude. I had no idea what was going on, but something was up, something big. Something bad.

2

I CALLED JEAN-CLAUDE'S strip club, Guilty Pleasures, first. He'd gone back to being manager there since he had enough vampires to help run the other businesses. Of course, I didn't get Jean-Claude on the phone first thing. One of the employees answered and informed me that he was on stage. I told them I'd call back, and yes, it was important, so have him call me ASAP.

I hung up and stared at the phone. What was my sweetie doing while I sat in my office a few miles away? I pictured all that long dark hair, the pale perfection of his face, and I was thinking too hard. I could feel him. Feel the woman in his arms as she clung to him. He held her face between his hands to keep the kiss from getting out of hand, to keep her from shredding her own lips against the sharp points of his fangs. I felt her eagerness. Saw inside her mind, that she wanted him to take her here and now on the stage in front of everyone. She didn't care; she just wanted him.

Jean-Claude fed on that desire, that need. He fed on it, as other vampires fed on blood. Half-naked waiters came onto the stage to help pry her, gently, from him. They helped her back to her seat, while she cried, cried for what she could not have. She had paid for a kiss, and she'd gotten that, but Jean-Claude always left you wanting more. I should know.

He spoke like some seductive wind through my mind, "*Ma petite*, what are you doing here?"

"Thinking too hard," I whispered to the empty office, but he heard me.

He smiled with at least two different types of lipstick smeared around his mouth. "You entered my mind while I fed the *ardeur* and it did not rise in you; you have been practicing."

"Yeah." It felt weird saying it out loud in the empty, dim office, especially because I could hear the hum and murmur of the club around him. The women clamoring to be next, waving their cash for him to choose them.

"I must choose a few more; then we may talk."

"Use the phone," I said. "I'm at the office."

He laughed, and the sound echoed through me, shivered down my skin, made things low in my body tighten. I drew away from him, closed the metaphysical links between us enough so I wouldn't get sucked back into his act. Then I tried to think about something else, anything else. If I'd known enough about baseball, I'd have thought about that, but that wasn't my sport. Jean-Claude didn't strip, but he did feed off the crowd's sexual energy. In another century he'd have been called an incubus, a demon that fed on lust. The thought almost pulled me back to him, but I thought, *Think about legal stuff, the law.* Something. In this century he just had to put a disclaimer in several prominent places in the club stating, "Warning: Vampire powers will be part of the entertainment. There are no exceptions. By being inside the club, you give permission for the legal use of vampire powers upon yourself and anyone with you."

The new laws that had helped make vamps legal hadn't really caught up to everything they could do. You couldn't do one-on-one mind control, though mass hypnosis was okay, because the call wasn't as deep, or as complete. One-on-one mind control meant the vampire could call people out of their beds, force them to come to the vampire. Mass hypnosis didn't work that way, or that was the theory. A vamp couldn't drink blood without getting the donor's permission first. You couldn't use vamp powers to get sex. Beyond that, the law stated that you had to notify humans in your place of business, and beyond that the law got really vague. The last no-no about no vamp powers for sex had been added only last year. It was treated like a date-rape drug, for legal purposes. Except that a vampire convicted of its use was sentenced to death, not trial or jail. Malcolm was right about the double standard. Vampires were people under the law, but they didn't get all the rights that the rest of the American citizenry got. Of course, most of the rest of the citizens couldn't tear iron bars from their sockets and use mind control to wipe people's memories. They'd been deemed too dangerous for jail after a few bloody, and very messy, escapes.

So my job as vamp executioner had been invented. I don't mean to make it sound like I was the first one with the job. I wasn't. The ones who took the job first were people who had been slaying vampires when they were still illegal, so you could kill them on sight with no legal problems. The government had actually yanked the credentials of some people who'd had a hard time understanding that they had to wait for a warrant of execution before killing anyone. They'd finally had to put one of the old-style vamp hunters in jail. He was still in jail five years later. That had sent the message they wanted.

I'd come in at the tail end of the old school, but mostly I had never killed a vampire that hadn't been covered by legal paperwork.

I glanced at my watch. I still had enough time to run home, change into date clothes, get Nathaniel, and make the movie.

The phone rang, and I jumped. Nervous, who me? "Hello?" I made it a question.

"*Ma petite*, what is wrong?" That smooth voice eased over the phone like a hand caressing down my skin. It wasn't sexual this time; it was calming. He'd picked up my nervousness. In the middle of feeding the *ardeur*, he'd missed it.

"Malcolm came to see me."

"About the blood-oathing?"

"Yes, and no," I said.

"Why yes, and no, *ma petite*?"

I told him what Malcolm had told me. Somewhere in the middle of the talk, he shut down the metaphysical link between us, shut it down so hard and so tight that I couldn't feel anything from him. We could share each other's dreams, but if we shielded hard enough, we could shut each other out. But it took work, and we didn't do it often lately. The silence when I finished was so complete that I had to ask, "Jean-Claude, you still there? I can't even hear you breathing."

"I do not have to breathe, *ma petite*, as well you know."

"It's just a saying," I said.

He sighed then, and the sound of it shivered over my skin. This time it was sexual. He could use some of his powers on me and still shield like a son of a bitch. I couldn't. When I shielded that tight, I was cut off from a lot of my abilities. "Stop that. Don't try to distract me with your voice. What is it that Malcolm can't speak of without being killed?"

"You will not like my answer, *ma petite*."

"Just tell me."

"I cannot tell you. I am under the same vow as Malcolm, as all the vampires everywhere are."

"All vampires?"

"*Oui.*"

"What, or who, could force an oath like that from all of you?" I thought about it for a second, then answered my own question. "The vampire council, of course, your ruling body."

"*Oui.*"

"So you aren't going to tell me anything about what's happening?"

"I cannot, *ma petite*."

"Well, that is just frustrating as hell."

"You have no idea how frustrating, *ma petite*."

"I am your human servant; doesn't that make me privy to all your secrets?"

"Ah, but this is not my secret."

"What does that mean, not your secret?"

"It means, *ma petite*, that I cannot discuss this with you unless I am given permission."

"How do you get permission?"

"Pray that I am never able to answer that question, *ma petite*."

"What does that mean?"

"It means that, if I am able to speak about this openly, then we will have been contacted, and we do not wish to be contacted by this."

"*This*, a thing, not a person?"

"I will say no more."

I knew I could push against his shields, and sometimes crack them. I thought about it, and it was as if he read my mind, and maybe he had. "Please, *ma petite*, do not push me on this."

"How bad is it?"

"Bad, but I think it is not our bad. I believe Malcolm will come to vampire justice for his crimes, whether we do it or not."

"So whatever, or whoever, this is, is hunting Malcolm?"

"Perhaps. It is certainly he and his congregation that have the attention."

"Would whoever this is really frame Malcolm's people and set up me and the other vamp executioners to do their dirty work?"

"Perhaps. This legal status is very new. I know some of the older levels of vampire politics are puzzled by it. Perhaps some decided to use it to their own advantage."

"I had a case of that just two months ago, where one vamp framed another for a murder of a woman. I don't want to kill someone who's innocent."

"Is any vampire truly innocent?"

"Don't give me that fundamentalist shit, Jean-Claude."

"We are monsters, *ma petite*. You know that I believe that."

"Yeah, but you don't want us to go back to the bad ol' days and have it be open season on you guys."

"No, I do not want that." There was something in the dry tone of his voice.

"You're shielding so hard, I can't tell what you're feeling. You only shield this hard when you're scared, really scared."

"I am afraid that you will pick from my mind what I am forbidden to tell you. There is no, how do you say, fudging, on this . . . rule of law for us. If you learned this secret even in my mind, by accident, it might be grounds to slaughter both of us."

"What the hell is this secret?"

"I have told you all I can."

"Do I need to sleep at the Circus of the Damned with you tonight? Do we need to circle the wagons?"

He was quiet again, then finally said, "No, no."

"You don't sound sure."

"I think it would be a very bad thing for you to sleep with me tonight, *ma petite*. Sex and dreams are the times when shields drop, and you might learn what we cannot afford for you to know."

"Are you saying that I'm not going to see you until this is resolved?"

"No, no, *ma petite*, but not tonight. I will think about our situation and decide a course of action by tomorrow night."

"Course of action? What are the possibilities?"

"I dare not say."

"Damn it, Jean-Claude, talk to me." I was a little angry, but the tight feeling in my stomach was mostly fear.

"If all goes well, you will never learn this secret."

"But it's something that the council could have sent to kill Malcolm and destroy his church?"

"I cannot answer your questions."

"Won't, you mean."

"*Non, ma petite*, cannot. Has it not occurred to you that this could be a ploy of our enemies to give them an excuse under vampire law to destroy us?"

I suddenly felt cold. "No, it hadn't occurred to me."

"Think upon it, *ma petite*."

"You mean, they send something, so that if you tell me about it, then it, or they, can kill us. You think someone on the council is counting on the fact that we're so tightly bound metaphysically that you can't keep a secret this big from me. And if I find out, it won't just be Malcolm that they'll kill, but us, too."

"It is a thought, *ma petite*."

"A very twisty-turny, underhanded thought."

"Vampires are a very twisty-turny lot, *ma petite*. As for underhanded, they would think of it as clever."

"They can think what they like, but it's a coward's way."

"Oh, no, *ma petite*, we do not want anyone on the council to put their full attention in a challenge to me. That would also be a very bad thing."

"So, what? I meet Nathaniel for our date, and I pretend we haven't had this talk?"

"Something like that, yes."

"I can't pretend that I don't know something big and bad has come to town."

"If it is not hunting us, be grateful, and do not pick at it. I beg you, Anita, for the sake of all you love, do not seek an answer to this riddle." He'd called me by my real name; it was a bad sign.

"I can't just pretend nothing is happening, Jean-Claude. Aren't you even going to tell me to be more careful than normal?"

"You are always careful, *ma petite*. I never worry that any bad thing will catch you unaware. It is one of your charms for me that you can take care of yourself."

"Even against something bad enough to scare you and Malcolm this badly."

"I trust you, *ma petite*. Do you trust me?"

That was a loaded question, but finally I said, "Yeah."

"You do not sound certain."

"I trust you, but . . . I don't like secrets, and I do not trust the council. And I have a warrant of execution on a vamp who is probably innocent. I've got a second warrant coming by tomorrow. They are both members of the Church of Eternal Life. I may not agree with Malcolm's philosophy, but his members usually stay away from killing offenses. If I get a warrant of execution for a third member of Malcolm's church this week, then it's a frame. The law, as written, doesn't give me much wiggle room, Jean-Claude."

"Actually, it gives you a great deal of wiggle room, *ma petite*."

"Yeah, yeah, but if I don't use the warrant in a timely manner, I may have to answer to my superiors. I'm a federal marshal now, and they can call me on the carpet and make me explain my actions."

"Have they done that to any of the new marshals yet?"

"Not yet. But if I've got a warrant, and other murders with the same MO keep happening, I'll need an explanation as to why I haven't killed Sally Hunter. The police, whatever the flavor, won't accept 'it's a secret' as an answer if people keep dying."

"How many humans are dead?"

"One victim per warrant, but if I hesitate on the warrants, will whoever this is escalate the violence and force my hand?"

"Possibly."

"Possibly," I said.

"*Oui.*"

"You know, this could get ugly really fast."

"You have used your discretionary powers to get warrants vacated in the past. You saved our Avery."

"He is not 'our' Avery."

"He would be yours, if you would let him." There was the faintest of tones in his voice.

"Are you jealous of Avery Seabrook? He's like only two years dead."

"Not jealous in the way you mean."

"Then how?"

"It was my blood he drank when he took oath to me, *ma petite*, but it is not me he watches. I should be his master, but I think if we both ordered him to do opposite things, I am not certain I would win the contest."

"Are you saying that my hold on him is stronger than yours?"

"I am saying it is a possibility."

It was my turn for silence. I was a necromancer, not just an animator of zombies, but a real, true necromancer. I could control more than just zombies. We were still trying to figure out how much more.

"Malcolm said he wasn't sure which of us was victim and which victimizer anymore."

"He is foolish, but not a fool."

"I think I understood that," I said.

"Then I will be plain. Go on your date with Nathaniel, celebrate your almost-anniversary. This is not our fight, not yet, perhaps not ever. Do not make it our fight, for it could be the death of everyone we love."

"Oh, thanks, and with that cheery message, I'll have no trouble going to the movies and enjoying myself." Truthfully, I felt a little silly about the whole date tonight. Nathaniel wanted to celebrate our anniversary. The trouble was, we couldn't agree on when our relationship changed from friends to more than friends. So, he'd chosen a date and called it our almost-anniversary. If I hadn't been too embarrassed, I'd have picked the first time we had intercourse as the anniversary date. I just couldn't figure out how to explain to friends why that date.

Jean-Claude sighed, and it wasn't sexual this time, just frustrated, I think. "I wanted this almost-anniversary to go well, tonight, *ma petite*. Not just for your sake, and Nathaniel's, but if he can work you through your reluctance to be romantic, then the rest of us might have a chance to celebrate special days with you, as well."

"And what date would you pick as our anniversary?" I asked, in a voice thick with sarcasm.

"The first night we made love, for that is the night that you truly let yourself love me."

"Damn it, you've thought about this."

"Why does sentiment make you so uncomfortable, *ma petite*?"

I'd have loved to answer him, but I couldn't. Truthfully, I wasn't sure. "I don't know, and I'm sorry that I'm such a pain in the ass. I'm sorry that I don't let you and the rest of the guys do all the romantic gestures you want. I'm sorry that it's so hard to be in love with me."

"Now, you are being too hard on yourself."

"I'm scared, I'm angry, I'm frustrated, and I don't want to fight with you, because it's not your fault. But now, thanks to what you just said, I don't feel like I can cancel the date with Nathaniel tonight." I thought about what I'd just said. "You bastard, you did this on purpose. You manipulated me into keeping the date with Nathaniel."

"Perhaps, but you are his first real girlfriend, and he is twenty. It is important to him, this night."

"He's dating me, not you."

"*Oui,* but if all the men in your life are happy, you are happier, and it makes my life easier."

That made me laugh. "You bastard."

"And I did not lie, *ma petite,* I would love to celebrate once a year the first night you came to me. If your first attempt at a modest celebration fails, then the larger, more romantic gestures will never come to pass. I want them to come to pass."

I sighed and leaned my head against the phone receiver. I heard him saying, "*Ma petite, ma petite,* are you still there?"

I put the receiver back to my mouth and said, "I'm here. Not happy, but I'm here. I'll go, but there won't be time to change now."

"I am sure that Nathaniel would much rather you go on this almost-anniversary than that you are dressed a certain way."

"Spoken from the man who most often dresses me in fetish wear."

"Not as often as I would like." Before I could think of a comeback, he said, "*Je t'aime,*" and hung up. *I love you,* in French, and he got off the phone while the getting was good.

3

I WAS RUNNING too late to even go home first. A phone call and Nathaniel agreed to just meet me at the theatre. There was no reproach in his voice, no complaint. I think he was afraid to complain, afraid I'd use it as an excuse to cancel the almost-anniversary. He was probably right. I was dating, at last count, six men. When you're dating that many people, anniversaries seem hypocritical. I mean, wasn't an anniversary something you did for your special someone? I still hadn't worked my way through the squirming discomfort of dating this many men. I still couldn't get rid of the idea that with six men to choose from you couldn't have a special sweetie. I was still struggling with the idea that they could all be special. When I was alone, not with any of them, not looking at them, or all covered in their metaphysical stuff, I could be all uncomfortable, and feel stupid. I felt stupid and grumpy right up to the moment that I saw Nathaniel standing just inside the doors, waiting for me.

He was five foot six and a half now. He'd grown half an inch in the last month. At twenty, twenty-one in the spring, he was growing into the broad shoulders, filling out in the way that most men do at a slightly earlier age. I actually got carded more at clubs than he did now, which irritated me, and pleased him. But it wasn't height that made me stop and stare.

I stood in the midst of the Friday night crowd hurrying around me, and for just a few minutes I forgot that something bad enough to scare Jean-Claude and Malcolm had come to town. Yeah, Jean-Claude had told me we were safe, but still, it wasn't like me to be careless in a crowd.

Nathaniel wore a leather trench coat and a matching fedora. The hat and coat hid most of him, and still managed to emphasize the body underneath. It was like hiding and asking for attention at the same time. He'd added the hat to his winter gear because without it, he had gotten recognized a few times. Customers from Guilty Pleasures had spotted him as Brandon, his stage name. Once we covered the hair, it didn't happen again.

His hair was in some kind of tight braid, so that it looked like his auburn hair was cut nice and standard short. It was illusion. His hair fell to his ankles, totally impractical, but God, it was pretty.

It wasn't just the standard *ooh, isn't he pretty* that made me stop. It was that suddenly in his new leather trench coat and hat, with his hair all covered, he looked grown-up. He was seven years younger than me, and I'd felt vaguely like a child molester when he first hit my radar. I'd fought long and hard to keep him out of the boyfriend box, but in the end, it hadn't worked. Now I looked at him like a stranger might, and realized that the only one who still thought he might be a child was me. Standing there looking like a fetish version of Sam Spade, he didn't look twenty. He looked very over twenty-one.

Someone bumped me, and that made me jump. Shit, that was too careless. I started moving, dressed in my own black leather trench coat, but no hat. I didn't do hats unless it was freaking freezing. Even with Christmas only weeks away, it wasn't that cold. St. Louis in the wintertime: freezing one day, nearly fifty the next.

My trench coat was unbuttoned from the waist up, only belted in place. It was colder that way, but I could still reach my gun. Going armed in winter was always full of fun choices like that.

He spotted me before I'd gotten through the outer doors. He gave me that smile that made his whole face glow, so happy to see me. Once I would have bitched, but I was too busy fighting off my own version of the same smile. One of my other boyfriends said I hated being in love, and he was right. It always felt so stupid, like your insurance rates should go up, because you're impaired. Romantically handicapped.

The face under the hat was too pretty to be handsome. He was beautiful, not handsome. Apparently, no matter how tall he got, or how much he muscled up, that wasn't going to change. But it wasn't a delicate face, the way Jean-Claude's was, or Micah's was; it was stronger boned than that, higher cheekboned. Something a touch more male in his face—I couldn't put my finger on it, but something—and when he looked full at you, you never thought feminine, but always male. Had that changed in the last few months? Had I not noticed that, or had it always been like this and I just was so determined to marginalize him that I couldn't let his face be more masculine than Jean-Claude's or Micah's? Did I still equate strength and being a grown-up to being male? Me, of all people? Surely not.

His smile had faded around the edges. "What's wrong?"

I smiled and went to hug him. "Just wondering if I'm paying enough attention to you."

He hugged me back, but not like he meant it. He pulled me back so he could see my face. "Why would you say that?"

I finally let myself look full into his eyes. Tonight I was so distracted by him that I'd avoided his eyes almost like he was a vampire with a gaze and I was some tourist human. His eyes were lavender—really, truly the color of lilacs. But it wasn't just the color; they were large and perfect, and crowned his face with that final touch that just made your heart hurt. Too beautiful, simply too beautiful.

He touched my face. "Anita, what's wrong?"

I shook my head. "I don't know." And I didn't. I was attracted to Nathaniel but this was excessive. I looked away so I wouldn't be staring directly into his face. What the hell was wrong with me tonight?

He tried to draw me into a kiss, and I pulled away. A kiss would undo me.

His hands dropped away from me. His voice held the first hint of anger. It took a lot to make Nathaniel angry. "It's just a movie, Anita. I'm not even asking for sex, just a movie."

I glanced up at him. "I'd rather go home and have sex."

"Which is why I asked for the movie," he said.

I frowned at him. "What?"

"Are you embarrassed about being seen with me in public?"

"No." I let my face show how much it shocked me that he'd even have to ask.

His face was very serious, hurt, ready to be angry. "Then what is it? You won't even kiss me."

I tried to explain. "I forgot everything but you for a minute."

He smiled, his eyes not quite catching up to it. "Is that so bad?"

"In my line of work, yes." I watched him try to understand. He was beautiful, but I could look at him without being stupid-faced. I moved closer to the smell of the new leather coat. I hugged him, and after a second's hesitation he hugged me back. I buried my face against the scent of leather and him. Sweet, clean, and underneath that the smell of vanilla. I knew now that it was only partially him, that some of that sweet scent was bath products and cologne, but the scent he wore didn't smell so lusciously of vanilla on anyone else's skin. One of those tricks of skin chemistry that changes the scent of the really good perfumes.

"We need to get seats." He whispered it against my hair.

I drew away from him, frowning again. I shook my head and that only partially cleared it. I reached into my coat pocket for a small, padded velvet bag. I opened it and dug the padding out until a cross spilled into my hand. It lay there silver and inert. I'd half expected it to glow, to show me that some vamp was messing with me. But it lay there, innocent and untouched.

"What is wrong, Anita?" Nathaniel looked worried now.

"I think someone's messing with me."

"The cross isn't showing it."

"You're scrumptious, Nathaniel, but it's not like me to lose focus this badly in public."

"You think Mommie Dearest is trying again?" he asked.

Mommie Dearest was my nickname for the head of the vampire council, the creator of vampire culture. The last time she'd messed with me, a cross had burned into my hand and had to be pried out by a doctor. I had a permanent scar in my left palm from it. Up to now the cross, in a bag or under my bed, had kept her at bay.

"I don't know, maybe."

"There aren't that many vamps that can get through your psychic shields," he said.

I slipped the chain over my neck, the silver glittering against the thin silk sweater.

"You sure that's enough cloth between your skin and the cross?"

"No, but I don't think it's Mommie."

He sighed and tried to keep the frown off his face. "Do you need to skip the movie?"

"No, Jean-Claude said we'd be safe tonight."

"Okay," Nathaniel said, "but I don't like the way you said that. What's gone wrong now?"

"Let's find seats and I'll tell you what little I know," I said. We managed to find two seats in the back row so my back was to a wall and I could see the rest of the theatre. I wasn't being paranoid, or at least not more paranoid than usual. I always sat in the back row, if I could manage it.

By the time the previews had finished, I'd told him everything I knew, which wasn't much.

"And that's all Jean-Claude would tell you?"

"Yep."

"Way too mysterious."

"Understatement," I said.

The music came up, the lights went down, and for the life of me I couldn't remember what movie we'd decided to see. I didn't ask Nathaniel, because it might have hurt his feelings, and besides, in moments, the question would answer itself.

4

THREE HOURS AND some change later, I knew the movie was the new version of *King Kong*. Nathaniel liked the movie better than I did. The special effects were great, but I was way ready for the ape to die long before he did. Which was a shame, since some of the movie was amazing. My cross hadn't glowed once, and I hadn't been more than normally fascinated with Nathaniel. Normally fascinated meant that sitting in date seats in the dark was intimate and fun, but it didn't make me lose control. I thought about letting my hands wander, and with the other men in my life, I might have, but Nathaniel had less inhibitions than most. I might start something I wouldn't want to finish in the theatre. Besides, you can't watch the movie and grope your boyfriend, or at least I can't.

One thing I had to do after a movie that long was take a restroom break. Riddle me this: Why is it that there is never a line for the men's room, but the women's always seems to have one? I did my bit in line, then finally got into the stall. At least it was clean.

The noise died away and let me know I was alone. Long damn line. I tucked and buckled everything back into place. One of the things I liked about shoulder holsters as opposed to carrying on the hip is that you don't run the risk of dumping the gun in the toilet. Inner pants holsters that don't go through a belt loop are some of the most precarious for bathroom use. Guns, unlike pagers, do not float.

I smoothed the stockings in place, glad that I wasn't having to struggle with pantyhose anymore. Garter and stockings really are more comfortable. The bathroom was empty as I pushed the door open. I started for the sinks when I saw the box sitting across one of them. "Anita" was printed on the box in black block letters.

That little dickens. How had Nathaniel gotten in here to leave a present? If he'd been caught in the ladies' restroom, it could have gone badly. I washed and dried my hands, then opened the box. I had to fold back layers of white tissue paper before I found a mask. It was white and would have covered everything but the eyes from forehead to chin. It was utterly plain, a blank white face staring up at me. Why would he buy me this? If it had been leather and fetish-looking, I might have guessed something more adventurous on the sexual front, but this didn't look like that kind of mask. Of course, I wasn't an expert on *that* kind of mask, so maybe that was what it was for. If so, he hadn't sold me on the idea. I didn't like masks, and I was far from comfortable with bondage and submission. The fact that I had leanings that way myself hadn't made me like it more; on the contrary, it scared me more because of it. You hate most in others what you're afraid of in yourself.

I tried to find an expression that was neutral, but pleased, and walked out carrying the box. Nathaniel was waiting against the far wall, holding both our coats and his hat. The leather hat got hot indoors. He smiled when he saw me and walked toward me with a quizzical look on his face. "Did someone leave that in the bathroom?"

I showed him that it had my name on it. "I thought you were trying to surprise me."

"You hate surprises," he said.

My pulse sped up, not a lot, but a little. I moved us so that the wall was at my back. I was suddenly looking at the people near us, looking hard; but everyone looked innocent, or at least not guilty. Couples holding hands, families with kids in tow: it all looked normal.

"What's in there?" Nathaniel asked.

"A mask," I whispered.

"Can I see it?"

I nodded.

He moved the lid and tissue paper, while I kept searching the happy moviegoers for evil intent. There was a couple staring a little too hard at us, but that could be other things.

"It looks like someone started to make a mask and stopped before they finished," he said.

"Yeah, it looks too blank."

"Why would someone give you this?"

"Did you see someone carry this in?"

"It's a big box, Anita. I'd have noticed."

"Did anyone carry in a bigger-than-average purse?"

"Not one big enough to hide this."

"You were standing right there, Nathaniel. You had to see."

We exchanged a look. "I didn't see this."

"Shit," I said low and with feeling.

"Someone was messing with you earlier, and they messed with me to get inside the bathroom," he said.

"Did you sense anything?" I asked.

He thought about it, and finally shook his head. "No."

"Double shit."

"Call Jean-Claude, now," he said.

I nodded and handed him the box so I could use my cell phone. Nathaniel wrapped the mask back up while I waited for Jean-Claude to pick up. This time he actually answered his office phone himself. "I got a present," I said.

"What did our pussycat buy you?" he asked, not offended that I hadn't said hello first.

"Nathaniel didn't buy it."

"It is not like you to speak in riddles, *ma petite*."

"Ask me what it is," I said.

"What is it?" and his voice was sliding into that blankness he did so well.

"A mask."

"What color is it?"

"You don't sound surprised," I said.

"What color is it, *ma petite*?"

"What does that matter?"

"It matters."

"White, why?"

He let out a breath I hadn't known he was holding, and spoke softly and heatedly in French for several minutes, until I could get him calmed down enough to speak English to me.

"It is good news, and bad, *ma petite*. White means they have come to observe us, not to harm us."

I moved so that my hand covered my mouth as I talked. I wanted to keep an eye on the drifting crowd, but I didn't want some human to overhear what promised to be a tricky conversation. But I didn't want to go outside until I found out how much danger we were in. The crowd was both a danger and a help. Most bad guys are reluctant to start cutting people up in a crowd. "What color would mean harm?" I asked.

"Red."

"Okay, who is *they*, because I assume this means we've been contacted by the mystery whoever."

"It does."

"So who are they, what are they? And why the hell this cloak-and-dagger shit with the mask? Why not a letter or a phone call?"

"I am not certain. They would normally have sent the mask to me, as Master of the City."

"Why send it to me, then?"

"I do not know, *ma petite*." He sounded angry, and he didn't usually get angry this easily.

"You're scared."

"Very."

"I guess we come to the Circus tonight, after all."

"Apologize to Nathaniel for this ruining his date with you, but *oui*, you must come here. We have much to discuss."

"Who are these guys, Jean-Claude?"

"The name will mean nothing to you."

"Just tell me."

"The Harlequin, they are the Harlequin."

"Harlequin, you mean like the French clown?"

"Nothing half so pleasant, *ma petite*. Come home and I will explain."

"How much more danger are we in?" The couple was still staring at us. The woman nudged the man, and he shook his head.

"White means they will observe only. This could be the only contact we have with them, if we are very, very lucky. They will watch us, then leave."

"Why tell us at all, if that's all they plan to do?"

"Because it is our law. They may pass through a territory, or hunt someone across a territory, much as you hunt wicked vampires across state lines, but if they are planning to be within an area for more than a few nights, then they are bound by law to contact the Master of the City."

"So this could be all about Malcolm and his church."

"It could."

"You don't believe that."

"It would be too easy, *ma petite*, and nothing about the Harlequin is ever easy."

"What are they?"

"They are the closest thing to police that we vampires have. But they are also spies, assassins. It was they who slew the Master of London when he went mad."

"Elinore and the other vamps didn't say that."

"Because they could not."

"You mean, if they had told anyone who killed their master, they'd have been killed?"

"Yes."

"That's crazy, they all knew it."

"Among themselves, *oui*, but not to outsiders, and once the Harlequin leave town the secrecy takes effect once more."

"So we can talk about them now, but later, when they leave, it's forbidden to mention them?"

"*Oui.*"

"That's insane."

"It is law."

"Have I told you recently that some of the vampire laws are stupid?"

"You have never put it quite that way."

"Well, I'm putting it that way now."

"Come home, *ma petite*, or better yet, come to Guilty Pleasures. I will tell you more of the history of the Harlequin when I have you safe with me. We should be safe. It is a white mask. We are expected to act as if there is nothing wrong. So I will finish my work night."

"You've fed the *ardeur*. You're done for the night."

"There are still acts to manage and my voice to lend to a microphone."

"Fine. We'll be there."

Nathaniel whispered, "They're coming over."

I glanced up to find the couple that had been staring so hard walking toward us. They didn't look dangerous, and they were definitely human. I whispered into the telephone, "Are all the Harlequin vamps?"

"To my knowledge, why?"

"We've got a pair of humans walking toward us."

"Come to me, *ma petite*, and bring Nathaniel."

"Love ya," I said.

"And I you."

We hung up so I could give my attention to the couple. The woman was petite and blond, and embarrassed and eager at the same time. The man was grumpy, or embarrassed.

"You're Brandon," she said to Nathaniel.

He admitted it, and I watched his stage smile come on line. He was happy to see her, and all the worry was just gone. He was on.

I didn't really have an "on" face. I wasn't really sure what I was supposed to do while strange women came up and said things to my boyfriend.

"But *you* were on stage, too," she said, turning to me. I'd been recognized as Anita Blake, vampire hunter, zombie raiser, but never from that one night I'd gone on stage at Guilty Pleasures. Nathaniel had picked me out of the crowd instead of some stranger. I'd agreed to it, but I hadn't wanted to do it again.

I nodded. "Once." I felt Nathaniel tense beside me. I should have just said yes. Nathaniel worried that I was embarrassed by him, and I wasn't. It was fine that he was a stripper, but it wasn't my gig. I was not nearly exhibitionist enough for it.

"I'd finally persuaded Greg to go with me to the club, and he was glad he came, weren't you?" She turned to the grumpy boyfriend.

He finally nodded, and he wouldn't look at me. Definitely embarrassed. That made two of us. None of my clothes had come off on stage, but I still didn't like being reminded of it.

"It was so erotic, what you did on stage together," she said, "so sensual."

Nathaniel said, "So glad you enjoyed the show. I'll be on stage tomorrow night."

Her face glowed with happiness. "I know. I check the website. But it doesn't mention your friend." She nodded at me. "Greg wants to know when you'll be back, don't you, Greg?" She was looking at me when she said it.

What I thought in my head was, *When hell freezes over*. I don't know what I would have said out loud, because Nathaniel saved us. "You know how you had to persuade Greg to come to the club?"

She nodded.

"I had to persuade her to get on stage."

"Really?" she said.

"Really," Nathaniel said.

Greg finally spoke. "Was it your first time on stage?"

"Yes," I said, wondering how to get out of this conversation without being rude. I'd have been rude, but Nathaniel wouldn't be. Bad for business, and rude just wasn't one of the things that he did much.

"It didn't seem like your first time," and he looked at me then. The look was the kind you never want a strange man to give you. Too much heat, too much sex.

I looked at Nathaniel. The look said clearly, *End this conversation, or I will*.

Nathaniel understood the look; he'd seen it enough. "I'm glad you enjoyed the show, and I hope to see you both again tomorrow. Have a wonderful night." He started to move away, and I followed.

Greg moved closer to us. "Will you be there tomorrow night?"

Nathaniel smiled, and said, "Of course."

He shook his head. "Not you, her. What's her name?"

I didn't want to give him my name. Don't ask me why, but I didn't. Nathaniel came to the rescue again. "Nicky."

I gave him a look, but my back was to them, so they couldn't see it. Greg said, "Nicky?"

Nathaniel took my arm and kept us moving, balancing the box in his other hand. "When she's on stage," he said.

"When will Nicky be at the club?"

"Never," I said, and walked faster. Nathaniel kept up with me. When we were clear of his, our, fans, his face showed dread. Dreading the fight that was coming.

5

I WASN'T SO angry that I forgot to check out the crowd as we moved, but I had to force the anger down to be able to see straight. I was actually more embarrassed than angry, which meant the fight could be all the worse for it. I hated being embarrassed, and usually masked it with anger. Even knowing that's what I did didn't change the fact that I did it. It just let me know why I was angry.

I actually waited until we were in the parking lot to say, "*Nicky?* What the fuck kind of name is that?"

"One I'd remember," he said.

I jerked away from him hard enough that he almost dropped the box. "I'm never going to be on stage again; I don't need a stage name."

"You don't want them to figure out your real name, do you?"

I frowned at him. "I'm in the news enough. They'll figure it out eventually."

"Maybe, but if you give them a stage name to remember, they'll think of you as a stripper, not as a federal marshal. You're embarrassed enough that Detective Arnet saw us on stage that night."

"Yes, and I'm still waiting for her to tell the rest of the police that she and I work with."

"But she hasn't," he said.

I shook my head.

"She can't admit she saw you without admitting she was there, and why," he said.

"Cops go to strip clubs all the time," I said.

"But she didn't go to see strippers, she went to see me."

That stopped me. Made me turn and stare at him. "What do you mean?"

"She came to the club on a night you weren't there. Since you've avoided the club as much as possible, that's a lot of the time. Can we have this conversation in the car?"

He had a point. I unlocked the car, and we climbed in. "Where's the other car?"

"I had Micah drop me off, so he'll have the car if he needs it. I knew you'd drive me home."

It made sense. I turned on the car so the heater would start working. I finally realized it was a little chilly. My anger had kept me warm even with my coat flapping open. "What do you mean, Arnet came to the club?"

"She paid to have a private dance."

I stared at him. "She did what?"

Detective Jessica Arnet worked on the Regional Preternatural Investigation Team, RPIT for short. It was the branch of local police that I worked with the most. I'd known she had a crush on Nathaniel, but I'd been so busy trying not to admit that I was living with a stripper that I'd kept him too much a secret. Until I brought him as a date to a wedding that Arnet was at. Then the secret was out, and she was mad at me for not telling her we were an item sooner. She seemed to feel like I'd let her make a fool of herself. She hadn't made a fool of herself, but she had come to Guilty Pleasures for the first time that one night that Nathaniel got me on stage. She was now convinced that I was abusing Nathaniel. Chain someone up on stage and hit them with a flogger a few times, and people think you're abusing them. Of course, the flogger had been Nathaniel and Jean-Claude's idea. A part of Nathaniel's regular show, apparently. What I'd done next had been all me, and Nathaniel. I had marked him, bitten him hard enough to bleed him, on stage. It had been the first time I'd voluntarily marked him like that, not just because the *ardeur* got out of control, but because he liked it, and I liked it, and I'd promised.

Arnet was convinced that I was Madame de Sade and Nathaniel

was my victim. I'd tried explaining that Nathaniel was only a victim when he wanted to be, but she hadn't bought it. I'd been convinced she would tell the other cops and out me, badly. Living with a twenty-year-old stripper with juvenile arrests for prostitution was bad enough, but getting on stage myself, well, that would have been . . . oh, hell, bad.

"How private a dance did she get?"

He grinned. "Are you jealous?"

I thought about it for a second, then had to say, "Yeah, I guess so."

"That's so sweet," he said.

"Just tell me about Arnet."

"She didn't want the dance. She wanted to talk." He seemed to think about it for a second, then added, "Okay, she wanted the dance, a lot, but she was too uncomfortable with me to ask for what she wanted. We just talked."

"About?" I said.

"She tried to get me to admit that you were abusing me. She wanted me to leave you and save myself."

"Why didn't you tell me?"

"You were already worried about Arnet telling Zerbrowski and the other cops what she'd seen. You were in the middle of some messy murder investigation. I didn't figure you needed the hassle, and I handled it."

"Has she been back?"

He shook his head.

"Tell me next time, okay?"

"If you want."

"I want."

"She can't tell on you, because she'd be afraid you'd tell them that she has a thing for your stripper boyfriend. She doesn't want to admit that what bothered her the most about the show you and I did is that she liked it."

"I didn't think Arnet swung that way," I said.

"Neither did she."

I looked at him, studied that face. There was a look on it now. "Just say it, the look in your eyes, just say it."

"You hate most in others what you don't like in yourself."

"Huh."

"What?"

"I thought something almost identical to that earlier tonight."

"What about?"

I shook my head. "Do you really think giving Greg and his girl-friend a stage name for me will keep them from making the connection to Anita Blake?"

"Yeah, I do. They'll think of you as a stripper named Nicky and that's it. You won't be anything or any more to them than that."

"Strangely disturbing, but why Nicky, why that name?"

"Because I knew I'd remember it."

"Remember it, why?"

"Because it was my name when I did porn."

I blinked at him. "What?"

"Nicky Brandon is the name I used when I did movies."

I did the long blink, the one that meant I was thinking hard, or too surprised to think. "You gave me your pornography name?"

"Half of it," he said.

I didn't know what to say. Was I supposed to be flattered, or insulted? "I declare this fight over until I figure out if we're actually fighting."

"Trust me, Anita, this isn't a fight."

"Then how come I'm angry?"

"Let's see: there's some bad vamps in town messing with us, you always hate it when fans recognize Brandon the stripper, but tonight, for the first time, you got recognized from the one time you went on stage. If you're embarrassed by my job, you're even more embarrassed that anyone would think you could be a stripper."

"I'm not embarrassed about your job."

"Yeah, you are," he said.

I started the car. "I am not."

"Then next time you introduce me to your friends, don't call me a dancer, call me an exotic dancer."

I opened my mouth, closed it, and started backing up. I wouldn't do it. He was right. I'd keep introducing him as simply a dancer. "Do you want me to introduce you like that?"

"No, but I want you not to be ashamed of what I do."

"I'm not ashamed of you, or your job."

"Fine, have it your way." But his tone said clearly that he was letting me win, but that I was wrong, and hadn't won anything. I hated when he did that. He just stopped fighting in the middle of the fight, not because he'd lost, but just because he didn't want to fight anymore. How do you fight with someone who won't fight? Answer: you don't.

The real trouble was, he was right. I was embarrassed about his job. I shouldn't have been, but I was. When he was a teenager, he'd been a runaway, and a prostitute, and on drugs. He'd been off drugs for nearly four years. He'd been out of "the life" since he was sixteen. He'd done porn, and I knew that. But I didn't dwell on it. I assumed he'd stopped doing the movies about the same time he stopped hooking, but I wasn't sure of that. I hadn't really asked, had I? He was a wereleopard, which meant he couldn't catch any sexually transmitted disease. That helped me ignore his past. The lycanthropy killed everything that could injure the host body; it kept him healthy. It made it so that I could pretend he hadn't had more sexual partners than I wanted to know about.

I was trapped at the light across from St. Louis Bread Company when I said, "Want to hear what Jean-Claude told me about the mask?"

"If you want to tell me." He sounded mad.

"I'm sorry that I'm not completely comfortable with your job, okay?"

"Well, at least you admit it."

The light changed, and I eased forward. We'd had two inches of snow, and everyone here forgot how to drive in it. "I don't like to admit when I'm uncomfortable, you know that."

"Tell me what Jean-Claude said."

I told him.

"So they may be here for Malcolm and his church."

"Maybe."

"I'm surprised you didn't demand more answers on the phone."

"I didn't know what the happy couple wanted. Jean-Claude said we're not in danger, so I hung up."

"It's not my fault that they recognized us."

"You. They recognized you."

"Fine, they recognized me." He was back to being mad again.

"I'm sorry, Nathaniel, I'm really sorry. That wasn't fair."

"No, you're right. If we hadn't been out together they probably wouldn't have spotted you."

"I am not embarrassed to be seen with you in public."

"You hate it when fans recognize me."

"I thought I was pretty cool when that woman passed you her phone number at dinner, when you were out with Micah and me."

"She waited until you went to the bathroom."

"And that's supposed to make me feel better?" I turned onto 44 and headed toward the city.

"She didn't want to intrude on our date."

"She thought you and Micah were escorts, and that I was paying you for the evening."

"The last time she saw me that's what I was doing for a living, Anita."

"I know, I know. She passed you her number because she wanted to see you again, and the old number wasn't working. You're right, she was polite about it."

"I told her I was on a date-date, and she was embarrassed."

I still remembered the woman. She'd been slender and elegant and old enough to be Nathaniel's mother. Thanks to Jean-Claude I knew clothes, and she'd been wearing expensive ones. The jewelry had been understated, but very nice. She was one of those women who headed charity balls and sat on committees for the art museum, and she'd been hiring male prostitutes young enough to be her son.

"I think what bothered me about her was that she didn't look like someone who would . . ."

"Hire an escort," he finished for me.

"Yeah."

"I had a lot of different kinds of customers, Anita."

"I figured that."

"Did you, or did you try never to think about it?"

"Okay, the latter."

"I can't change my past, Anita."

"I didn't ask you to."

"But you want me to quit stripping."

"I never said that."

"You're embarrassed by it, though."

"For God's sake, Nathaniel, let it go. I'm embarrassed about being up on stage myself. I'm embarrassed that I fed on you in public." I gripped the steering wheel so tight it hurt. "When I fed the *ardeur* off you that night, I fed off the entire audience. I didn't mean to, but I fed on their lust. I felt how much they enjoyed the show, and I fed on it."

"And you didn't have to feed again for twenty-four hours."

"Jean-Claude took my *ardeur* and shared it around among you guys."

"Yes, but he thinks that one of the reasons he was able to do that is that you fed off the crowd, and me. I loved that you marked me in front of the crowd. You know how much I loved it."

"Are you saying that if I hadn't gone up on stage and accidentally fed from the crowd, the *ardeur* would have gotten out of control in the middle of that serial killer case?"

"Maybe."

I thought about that for a second as I drove. I thought about the *ardeur* going out of control in a van full of cops, Mobile Reserve cops, our answer to SWAT. I thought about the *ardeur* getting out of control while I was in a nest of vampires that had killed over ten people.

"If that's true, then why didn't Jean-Claude try to get me down to the club again?"

"He's offered."

"I've refused."

"Yeah," Nathaniel said.

"Why tell me now?"

"Because I'm mad at you," he said. He lowered his head on top of the box in his lap. "Because I'm mad that our date is ruined. I'm mad that some metaphysical crap is going to ruin our almost-anniversary."

"I didn't plan this," I said.

"No, but your life is always like this. Do you have any idea how hard it is to have a normal date with you?"

"If you don't like it, you don't have to stay in it." The moment I said it, I wished I hadn't, but I didn't take it back.

"Do you mean that?" he asked, in a low, careful voice.

"No," I said, "no, I don't mean it. I'm just not used to you picking at me. That's usually Richard's job."

"Don't compare me with him. I don't deserve that."

"No, you don't." Richard Zeeman had once been my fiancé, but it hadn't lasted. I'd broken up with him when I saw him eat someone. He was the head of the local werewolf pack. He'd broken up with me when he couldn't handle that I was more comfortable with the monsters than he was. At the moment, we were lovers, and he was finally letting me feed the *ardeur* off him. I was his girlfriend in the preternatural community, lupa to his Ulfric, and he wasn't shopping to replace me in that part of his life. He was shopping for a completely human woman to replace me in the part of his life where he was a mild-mannered junior high science teacher. He wanted kids and a life that didn't include full moons and killer zombies. I didn't blame him completely. If I'd had an option for a normal life, I might have taken it. Of course, Richard really didn't have the option either. There was no cure for lycanthropy. But he was going to divide his life into pieces and try to keep all the pieces from finding out about the other parts. Sounded hard, hell, sounded like a recipe for disaster. But it wasn't my life, and so far he was just dating people. If he got serious about someone else, then we'd see how I felt about being the other woman.

"You missed the turn, Anita," Nathaniel said.

I cursed and braked too hard in the thin snow. I got the Jeep under control, then let us coast past our exit. I'd turn around. You could always turn around. "Sorry," I said.

"Thinking about Richard?" He tried for neutral and failed.

"Yeah."

"My fault, I guess; I brought him up."

"What's with the tone?" I asked. I turned into a section of town that was in the middle of being gentrified but hadn't quite made it yet. But we were headed back toward the riverfront.

"If Richard were a stripper, would you be embarrassed by him, too?"

"Drop this, Nathaniel, I mean it."

"Or what?" There was that first prickling run of energy over my skin. He was angry enough that it was making his beast peek out.

"You're picking on me tonight, Nathaniel. I don't need that."

"I believe that you love me, Anita, but you love me by hiding from what I am. I need you to accept who I am."

"I do."

"You tell Arnet that I'm not your victim, but you won't tie me up during sex. You won't abuse me."

"Don't start this again," I said.

"Anita, the bondage is part of who I am. It makes me feel safe and good."

This was one of the reasons I'd fought so long and hard to stay out of Nathaniel's love life. I did some stuff, nails, teeth, and I enjoyed it, but there were limits to my comfort level, and he'd been trying to push me past those limits in the last few weeks. I'd worried from the beginning that he wouldn't be happy with someone who was less into the bondage scene than he was, and that was exactly what was happening.

"In some ways you make me feel better about myself than anyone ever has, Anita, but you also make me feel bad about myself. You make me feel like an evil freak, because of what I want."

I found a parking spot just down the street from Guilty Pleasures's glowing neon sign. It was unusual to find parking this close to the club on a weekend. Parallel parking is not my best thing, so I concentrated on that, while part of me thought furiously about what to say to him.

I finally got us parked and turned off the car. The silence was thicker than I wanted it to be. I turned as far as the seat belt would allow and looked at him. He stared out the window away from me.

"I don't want to make you feel bad about yourself, Nathaniel. I love you, damn it."

He nodded, then turned and looked at me. The streetlight glittered on tears. "I'm terrified that I'm going to drive you away. My therapist says that I'm either a full partner in the relationship, or I'm not. Full partners ask for their needs to be met."

Truthfully, I'd thought his therapist would be on my side, but BDSM was no longer considered an illness. It was just another alternative lifestyle. Damn it.

"I want you to get what you need out of our . . . out of us."

"I'm not asking for that much, Anita. Just tie me up while we have sex. Then do what we would have done anyway. Nothing else."

I leaned over and brushed the tears from his cheeks. "It's not the tying up, Nathaniel. It's that once I say yes to that, what's next? And don't tell me there isn't a next."

"Tie me up, make love to me, and we'll go from there."

"That's what scares me," I said. "I say yes to this, and there'll be something else."

"And what's wrong with something else, Anita? What scares you isn't my needs, but that you might like it."

"That's not fair."

"Maybe not, but it's true. You like being held down during sex. You like it rough."

"Not all the time."

"And I don't like being tied up all the time, but I like it some of the time. Why is that wrong?"

"I'm not sure I can meet all your needs, okay? It was one of the things that worried me about us as a couple from the beginning."

"Then are you okay with me finding someone else to meet those needs? Sex with you, bondage with someone else?" He said it fast, as if he were afraid he'd lose his nerve.

I just stared at him. "Where the hell did this come from?"

"I'm trying to find out what the limits are, Anita, that's all."

"Do you want someone else?" I asked it, because I had to ask.

"No, but you have other people in your bed, and I'm okay with that, but if you won't meet my needs, then . . ."

"Are you saying that if I don't come across, you'll break up with me?"

"No, no." He hid his face with his hands and made a frustrated noise. His energy level swirled back through the car, like hot water spilling across my skin. He swallowed the power back and looked at me. He looked pained. "I need this, Anita. I want to do it with you, but I need it with someone. It's part of who I am sexually; it just is."

I tried to wrap my mind around letting Nathaniel play sex games with someone else, then come home to me. I couldn't do it. He was right; I was forcing him to share me with other men, but sharing him with another woman . . . "So what, you'd have tie-up games with someone else, then come home to me?"

"I can find a master who doesn't do sexual contact. I can find someone who will just do the bondage."

"But bondage is sex for you."

He nodded. "Sometimes."

"I can't do this tonight, Nathaniel."

"I'm not asking you to; just think about it. Decide what you want me to do."

"You're giving me an ultimatum; I don't deal well with ultimatums."

"It's not an ultimatum, Anita, it's just true. I love you, and I'm happier with you than I've ever been with anyone for this long. Honestly, I didn't think we'd still be together this long. Seven months is the longest relationship I've ever had. When I thought it would be like all the rest—a few months, then over—it wasn't a big deal. I could behave myself for a few months, until you got tired of me."

"I'm not tired of you."

"I know that. In fact, I think you're going to keep me. I didn't expect that."

"Keep you? You make yourself sound like a lost puppy that I picked up on the street. You don't 'keep' people, Nathaniel."

"Fine, pick a different word, but we're living together and it's working, and it might last years. I can't go years without having this need met, Anita."

"It *might* last years; you still talk about us like we won't last."

"Years is lasting," he said, "and everyone gets tired of me, eventually."

I didn't know what to say to that. "I'm not tired of you. Frustrated, puzzled as hell, but not tired."

He smiled, but it didn't reach his eyes. "I know that, and if I didn't feel secure enough, I wouldn't make any demands. I'd just go on being unhappy about this, but if you love me, then I can ask for what I want."

If you love me, he'd said. Jesus. "It must be true love, Nathaniel, because I'm not booting your ass to the curb for this."

"For what, asking for my sexual needs to be met?"

"Stop, just stop." I rested my forehead against the steering wheel and tried to think. "Can we please drop this for now, while I think about it?"

"Sure." His voice sounded hurt.

But his voice could sound hurt; I was out of my depth. "How long have you been saving this conversation up?" I asked, still resting against the wheel.

"I kept waiting for there to be a quiet time, when you weren't ass-deep in alligators, but . . ."

"But I'm always ass-deep in alligators."

"Yeah," he said.

I rose and nodded. That was fair. "I'll think about what you said, and that's all I've got tonight, okay?"

"That's wonderful. I mean it. I was afraid . . ."

I frowned at him. "You really thought I'd dump you because of this?"

He shrugged and wouldn't look at me. "You don't like demands, Anita, not from any of the men in your life."

I unbuckled my seat belt and slid over so I could turn him to look at me. "I can't promise that this won't eventually break me, but I can't imagine not waking up beside you most mornings. I can't imagine not having you puttering in our kitchen. Hell, it's more your kitchen than mine. I don't cook."

He kissed me and drew back with that smile that made his face shine with happiness. I loved that smile. "Our kitchen. I've never had an 'our' anything before."

I hugged him, partially because I wanted to, and partially to hide the expression on my face. On one hand, I loved him to pieces; on the other hand, I wished he had come with an instruction book. More than almost any other man in my life, he confused me. Richard hurt me more, but most of the time I understood why. I didn't like it, but I understood his motivation. Nathaniel was so far outside my comfort zone sometimes that I had no clue. That I understood vampires that had been alive over five hundred years better than I understood the man in my arms said something. I wasn't sure what it said, but something.

"Let's go inside before Jean-Claude wonders what happened to us."

He nodded, still looking happy. He got out on his side with the box in hand. I got out, hit the button to make the Jeep beep, and eased between the cars onto the sidewalk. He'd put his hat back on. Nathaniel in disguise. I put my left arm through his, and we walked over the melting snow toward the club. He was still all glowing from the "our" comment I'd made. Me, I wasn't glowing. I was worried. How far would I really go to keep him? Could I send him to a stranger for slap and tickle? Could I share him if I couldn't meet his needs? I didn't know. I really didn't know.

6

I OPENED THAT metaphysical connection I had to Jean-Claude. Opened it and thought, *Where are you?* I felt him, or saw him, or some other word that they hadn't invented yet for seeing and feeling what someone else was doing in another room. He was on stage, using that voice of his to announce an act.

I drew back enough to be solidly on Nathaniel's arm. Sometimes when I tried mind-to-mind stuff, I had trouble walking. "Jean-Claude is on stage, so we'll go in the front."

"Whatever you say," he said.

Once, in our relationship, he'd meant that. He'd been my little submissive wereleopard. I'd worked long and hard to make him more, to force him to be more demanding. Try to do a good deed and it bites you on the ass.

The bouncer at the door was tall, blond, and way too cheerful for the job. Clay was one of Richard's werewolves, and when he wasn't bodyguarding someone, he worked security here. Clay's gift was avoiding fights. He was really good at calming things down. A much more useful ability for a bouncer than brute strength. Last week Clay had been helping guard my body. No pun intended. There'd been a metaphysical accident, and it had looked for a while like I'd be turning into a wereanimal for real, so I'd had different lycanthropes with me so that whatever I changed into, I was covered. But I had gotten some control over it all, and it looked like I still wasn't going to turn furry. Clay had been one of my watch-wolves. He was happy to be off the duty. I scared Clay. He was afraid the *ardeur* would make him my sexual slave. Okay, he didn't say that exactly. Maybe it was just me projecting my terrors on him. Maybe.

His smile slipped a little when he saw me, his face going all serious. He gave me a hard look as he said, "How's it going, Anita?" He wasn't just being polite; as afraid as he was of some of my metaphysical abilities, he'd been convinced it wasn't a good idea to take all my guards off duty. He thought it was too soon.

"I'm fine, Clay."

He peered at me, leaning that six-foot frame down to my five foot three. He studied me as the crowd behind us grew to four. His gaze went to Nathaniel. "Has she really been fine?"

"She's been fine."

Clay stood up straight and motioned us through. He looked positively suspicious as he did it, though.

"Honest," Nathaniel whispered as we went by, "not a twinge of anything furry."

Clay nodded and turned to the next group. He was the gatekeeper tonight. We entered the permanent dimness of the club. The noise was soft, murmurous, like the sea. The music picked up, and the crowd noise both was drowned out and got louder. The murmur of it was drowned out with the rise of the music, but the screams and yells of encouragement were louder.

The woman behind the coat area came out, smiling. "Crosses aren't allowed in the club."

I'd forgotten I was wearing one outside my clothes; usually I just tucked it out of sight and got to avoid the holy-item check girl.

I spilled the cross inside my sweater. "Sorry, forgot."

"I'm sorry, but just hiding it isn't enough. I'll give you a claim check just like for a coat."

Great, she was new and didn't know me. "Call Jean-Claude over, or Buzz; I get a pass on this one."

Nathaniel took off his hat and gave her a grin. Even in the dim light I could see her blush. "Brandon," she breathed, "I didn't recognize you."

"I'm in disguise," he said, and gave her that look that was part mischief, part flirting.

"Is she with you?"

I was holding on to his arm—of course we were together. But I stood there and was quiet. Nathaniel would handle it. Me yelling at her wouldn't help things. Honest.

Nathaniel leaned over and whispered, "Joan thinks you're a fan that just grabbed me at the door."

Oh. I gave her a real smile. "Sorry, I'm his girlfriend."

Nathaniel nodded to confirm it, as if women claimed to be his girlfriend all the time. It made me look at his smiling, peaceful face and wonder how many overzealous fans he had. How weird did it get?

Joan leaned in to us to whisper over the rising music. "Sorry, but Jean-Claude's orders are that just because you're dating a dancer, the holy item still doesn't get inside."

On one hand, it was good that she was good at her job. On the other hand, it was beginning to irritate me.

Two of the black-shirted security people came over to us. I think the hat and coat fooled them, too. They didn't act like they recognized either one of us. Lisandro was tall, dark, handsome, with shoulder-length hair tied back in a ponytail. He was a wererat, which meant somewhere on him was a gun. A quick glance didn't show it under the black T-shirt and jeans, so it was probably at the small of his back. The wererats were mostly ex-military, ex-police, or had never been on the "right" side of the law. They always went armed.

The other security guy was taller and way more muscled. The weight lifting meant he was probably a werehyena. Their leader had a thing for weight lifters.

"Anita," Lisandro said, "what's the holdup?"

"She wants my cross."

He looked at Joan. "She's Jean-Claude's human servant. She gets a pass."

The woman actually blushed and apologized. "I'm sorry. I didn't know, and you being with Brandon. I . . ."

I held up a hand. "It's okay, really, just let us get out of the doorway." There was a crowd behind us that went out the door. Clay was peeking inside, wondering what was happening.

Lisandro helped us ease through the room away from the door, but not quite to the tables, closer to the drink area. I would have said bar area, but they weren't allowed to serve liquor. Yet another of the interesting zoning laws about strip clubs on this side of the river.

The weight lifter stayed near the door to help sort the crowd with Joan.

I could finally see who was dancing to the music. Byron was near the end of his act because he was down to a very small G-string. It left the pale, muscled body very bare. His short brown hair curled haphazardly, as if some of his customers had mussed it. A woman was stuffing money down the front of the G-string. I felt him use a small slap of power to capture her just enough to keep her hand out of his pants. It skirted the edge of legal, but the vamps had found that a tiny bit of control could keep them from getting hurt on stage. I'd seen bloody nail marks, and even a few bite marks, on Nathaniel and Jason. It was a lot more dangerous to strip for women than for men, apparently. All the dancers agreed that men behaved themselves better.

Byron writhed around the eager circle of women who surrounded the front of the stage. He laughed and joked. They ran hands over his body and rained money down on his skin. I'd had sex with him once, to feed the *ardeur*. We'd both enjoyed it, but Byron and I both agreed that it wasn't our cup of tea. That each other wasn't our cup of tea. Besides, the weight lifting helped him pass for eighteen, but he'd died at fifteen. Yeah, he was several hundred years old, but his body wasn't. His body was still that of an athletic teenager. I was still disturbed by the fact that I'd had sex with him. Also, Byron preferred men to women. He'd do bisexual, if it came his way, but he was one of the few men who spent more time ogling my boyfriends than me. I found that disturbing, too.

Jean-Claude was standing near the back of the stage, lost in shadow, letting Byron have his limelight. Jean-Claude turned to look at me, his pale face lost in the darkness of his hair and clothes. He breathed through my mind, "Await me in my office, *ma petite*."

Lisandro leaned over and whisper-shouted over the music, "Jean-Claude said to take you through to the office."

"Just now?" I asked, puzzled, because to my knowledge no one but me should have heard it.

Lisandro gave me a puzzled look back, and shook his head. "No, after you called. He said to take you back to the office when you got here."

I nodded and let him lead us to the door. Nathaniel had kept his hat and coat on. He didn't want to be recognized, for several reasons. It was rude to distract the audience from Byron's show, and "Brandon" wasn't working tonight. Lisandro unlocked the door and ushered us through.

The door closed behind us, and it was blessedly quiet. The rear area wasn't soundproof, but it was sound-muffled. I hadn't realized how loud the music was until it stopped. Or maybe that was just how bad my nerves were tonight.

Lisandro led us down the hallway to the door on the left-hand side. Jean-Claude's office was its usual elegant black-and-white self. There was even an Oriental screen in one corner that hid an emergency coffin. Sort of a vampire's version of a rollaway. Only the couch against the wall and the carpet were new. Asher and I had ruined the old stuff with sex that got so out of hand, I'd ended up in the hospital.

Lisandro closed the door and leaned against it, on this side. "You staying?" I asked.

He nodded. "Jean-Claude's orders. He wants you to have bodyguards again."

"When did he order that?"

"Just a few minutes ago."

"Shit."

"Did your beast try to rise again?" he asked.

I shook my head.

Nathaniel had set the box on Jean-Claude's black lacquer desk. He took off the hat and coat and laid them on one of the two chairs in front of the desk. "I've got to get a lighter-weight hat if I'm going to keep using it for a disguise. The leather is just too warm." He wiped a thin bead of sweat off his forehead.

"If your beast didn't try to rise again, then why are you back to needing bodyguards?" Lisandro asked.

I opened my mouth, closed it. "I don't know how much Jean-Claude will want you to know. I'm not even sure how much anyone is allowed to know."

"About what?"

I shrugged. "I'll tell you if I can."

"If you're going to get me killed, can I at least know why?"

"I've never gotten you hurt before."

"No, but we've lost two of our rats guarding you, Anita. Let's just say that if my wife ends up a widow, I'd like to know why."

I glanced at his hand. "You don't wear a ring."

"Not at work, no."

"Why not?"

"You don't want people knowing you have people that you care about, Anita. It can give them ideas." His gaze flicked to Nathaniel, just for a moment, then back to me. But Nathaniel had seen it.

"Lisandro thinks I'm a victim. That you need stronger men in your life."

I went to sit beside Nathaniel on the new white couch. He put his arm across my shoulders, and I settled in against him. Yeah, we'd been fighting, but that wasn't Lisandro's business, and it certainly wasn't his business who I dated.

"You can date who you want, that's not my beef."

"What *is* your beef?" I asked, and let my words take on that slight hostile edge that was almost always just below the surface for me.

"You're a vampire now, right?"

My, my, news travels fast. "Not exactly," I said, out loud.

"I know you're not like a bloodsucker. You're still alive and every-thing, but you gained Jean-Claude's ability to feed off sex."

"Yeah," I said, still hostile.

"Human servants gain some of their master's abilities, that's normal. You should have gained the ability to help Jean-Claude feed his hungers, but your feeding on lust isn't an extra for his energy, it's a ne-cessity for you. I heard what happened the night you tried to stop feeding it. You almost killed Damian, and Nathaniel, and yourself. Remus thinks you would have died if you hadn't fed the *ardeur*. If you hadn't fucked someone, he really thinks you might have died."

"Isn't it nice that he shared with everybody," I said.

"You can be all defensive about it if you want, but it's weird as hell. Rafael can't find anyone who's ever heard of a human servant gaining a hunger or thirst like this."

"And how weird my life has become is your business, why?"

"Because you're asking me and my people to risk our lives to keep you safe, that's why."

I gave him unfriendly face because I couldn't argue with his logic. I had gotten two of the wererats killed in the last couple of years. Killed guarding me. I guess he had a right to be pissy.

"It's your job," Nathaniel said. "If you don't like it, ask your king to change your job description."

"Rafael would take me off duty if I asked, you're right on that."

"Then ask," Nathaniel said.

Lisandro shook his head. "That's not my point."

"If you have a point, make it," I said, and let him hear the impatience in my voice.

"Fine, you're some sort of living vampire. A master vampire, because you gained a vampire servant in Damian, and an animal to call in Nathaniel."

"You're not telling me anything I don't already know, Lisandro."

"Jean-Claude chose you as his human servant. He chose one of the most powerful necromancers to come along in centuries. It was a good move to pick you. His animal to call is the head of the local werewolf pack. Richard may have his problems, but he's powerful. Again, a good choice. You both help Jean-Claude's power base. You both help him be stronger." He motioned at Nathaniel. "I like Nathaniel. He's a good kid, but he's not powerful. He gained more from you than you gained from him. The same with Damian. He's a vampire over a thousand years old, and he's never going to be a master anything."

"Have you reached your point?" I asked.

"Almost."

"You know, this is the most I've ever heard you talk at one time," I said.

"We all agreed that whoever had a chance to ask should talk to you."

"Who's we?"

"Me and some of the other guards."

"Fine, what's your point?"

"Did you have a choice about Nathaniel and Damian?" he asked.

"Do you mean, could I have chosen another wereleopard, another vampire?"

"Yes."

"No."

"Why no?" Lisandro asked.

"One, none of us had any idea that this could happen. Like you said, human servants don't gain powers like this. Two, I don't have the con-

trol over my metaphysics that Jean-Claude has. Most vamps who gain
a human servant or animal to call don't do that until they've got a few
decades, or centuries, under their belt. I got thrown into the deep end
of the pool without a life preserver. I grabbed who the power threw at
me." I patted Nathaniel's leg. "I'm happy with the choices, but I didn't
know I was choosing when it happened."

Nathaniel hugged me one-armed. "We were all surprised."

"But you have more control of it now," Lisandro said, "and you
know what's happening."

"I've got more control, yes, but as to what's happening . . . pick a
topic."

"Somehow you've got three or four different kinds of lycanthropy
inside you. But you haven't shifted into any of them."

"Yeah, so?"

"But you're starting to be attracted to the different animals, the way
you were to the wolves and the leopards. I'm just saying that if you
pick a new animal, can't it be someone powerful, instead of weak?
Why can't you choose someone who will help you power up, instead
of hurting you?"

Nathaniel shifted beside me.

"Nathaniel doesn't hurt me," I said, but part of me was thinking
about our fight earlier. There was room to get hurt, but not the kind
of hurt that Lisandro meant.

"He doesn't help you either, not the way Richard helps Jean-
Claude."

I could have argued that part. Richard was so conflicted about what
he was, and what he wanted out of life, that he crippled the triumvirate among the three of us, but if Lisandro didn't realize how reluctant
a partner Richard was, then I wasn't going to share it.

"What do you want from me, Lisandro?"

"Just, if we're going to put our bodies between you and a bullet, can
we have some input into the next animal you pick?"

"No," I said.

"Just no?" he said.

"Yeah, just no. This is so not in your job description, Lisandro, not
you, or Remus, or anyone. If you don't want to risk yourself, then
don't. I don't want anyone guarding me who feels like it's a bad idea."

"I'm not saying this right."

"Then stop saying it," I said.

"Stop explaining and just say what you want Anita to do," Nathaniel said.

Lisandro frowned, then said, "I think Joseph was wrong when he forced you to send the werelion Haven back to Chicago. Joseph keeps trying to feed you his weak-assed pride of lions, and they aren't any better than Nathaniel. No offense, even Joseph's brother, Justin, isn't that much stronger."

It had taken me a moment to remember who Haven was, because I still thought of him as Cookie Monster. He'd had hair dyed that color of blue, and had sported several Sesame Street tattoos. Haven was also an enforcer for the Master Vampire of Chicago. Haven had helped me handle the lion part of my metaphysical problem, but he'd also picked fights with three of the local werelions, including Joseph, their Rex, their leader. Haven and Richard had had a fight. Richard had kicked his ass, proving that Richard could be damned useful when he wanted to be. But also proving that Haven was way too much trouble to keep around.

"You guys all explained to me how lion society works. If someone that tough, and that powerful, had moved into town, they would have felt compelled to take over the local werelions. The first thing most takeovers do is slaughter most of the pride."

"I think you could control him."

"You saw him, Lisandro, please. He's a thug, a professional thug, with a prison record."

Lisandro nodded. "I've got a record, too, juvie, but some bad stuff on it. My wife straightened me out. I think you could do the same for him."

"What, a good woman is all a bad boy needs to straighten his life out?"

"If the woman has something that the man wants bad enough, yeah."

"What does that mean?" I asked.

"It means I saw the way he looked at you. I smelled what effect the two of you had on each other. The only reason you didn't have sex was that your head overruled the rest of you."

"You know, Lisandro, I liked you better when you didn't talk this much."

"I've seen Haven's record. He doesn't have anything on his sheet that I ain't got on mine."

That made me give him the long blink. Because I hadn't known that about him. "That would make you a very dangerous man," I said, my voice low and even.

"You've killed more people than I have."

"This conversation is over, Lisandro."

"If not Haven, then can Rafael put out feelers for some better lion candidates? Joseph is so scared that some big bad lion will come and eat his weak-assed pride that he won't ever bring anyone to town who will do the job for you."

I started to say no, but Nathaniel squeezed my arm. "Rafael is a good leader."

"He can't interview for new lions. He can bring in new rats, but it's not his place to bring in new lions," I said.

"Lisandro is right on one thing, Anita. Joseph is scared. Everyone he's thrown at you in the last few weeks has been wimpy—not just weak in power, but innocent. Your life doesn't have room for innocents."

I stared into those lavender eyes and didn't like what I saw. I was seven years older, but he'd seen as much violence as I had, or more. He'd seen what our fellow human beings could do, up close and personal. I'd solved crimes of violence, but mostly I hadn't been the victim. He'd been on the streets alone before he hit ten. Nathaniel was weak in some ways that Lisandro counted, but he was stronger than me in ways that most people wouldn't understand. He'd survived things that would have destroyed most people.

He let me see in his face what he usually hid, that I was the innocent. That no matter how many people I killed in the line of duty, I'd never really know what he knew.

"Do you think I was wrong to make Haven go back to Chicago?"

"No, he scared me, but you need a werelion, and they need to know the score."

"What does that mean?" I asked.

"Two of the lions he sent you were virgins," Nathaniel said. "You're a succubus, Anita. You don't give virgins over to something like that."

"You have to have had bad sex to appreciate really good sex," Lisandro said.

Nathaniel nodded. "That, too, but what I meant was that we haven't met a lion yet who we didn't all think was weak." He looked at the tall guard by the door. "Some of them were tough in a normal-world sort of way, but we all live in a world where guns, and sex, and violence of all kinds can happen and do. We need someone who doesn't make us all feel like we're corrupting children."

We both looked at Nathaniel.

"What?" he said.

"Is that how you really felt about all of them, even Justin?" I asked.

"Yes," he said. "Justin's idea of violence is the kind that has referees, and limits. The fact that he's Joseph's enforcer is scary for them."

"Joseph's better in a fight," Lisandro said.

"But neither of them is as good as Richard, or Rafael."

"Or your Micah?" Lisandro asked.

"I think Micah would do anything it took to keep his people safe."

"I heard that about him," Lisandro said.

Since we were talking about one of my other live-in sweeties, I wasn't sure how I felt about it. Micah and I were both very practical people. Sometimes *practical* and *ruthless* were just different words for the same thing.

"You're both saying that you don't think Joseph would do whatever it took."

"The only thing that's kept his pride safe is the fact that there just aren't a lot of werelions in this country. Cat-based lycanthropy is usually harder to catch than other kinds," Lisandro said.

"Reptile-based is harder to catch," Nathaniel said.

Lisandro nodded. "True, but there aren't a lot of lions in this country. The closest is Chicago."

"They won't be trying a takeover. Jean-Claude and I made sure of that," I said.

"But don't you see, Anita, you and Jean-Claude made sure of it, not Joseph. That makes his threat weak," Lisandro said.

"Nobody from Chicago will mess with them now," I said.

"Yeah, but if Chicago noticed they're this weak, then so will someone else."

"I didn't know we had any big prides other than these two."

"One on the West Coast, one on the East," Lisandro said.

"Is that where Joseph got his last candidate?" I asked.

"East Coast pride, yeah. But you turned him down, just like all the others."

"I can't give your leader permission to shop for lions, Lisandro. It's against the rules to interfere that much over cross-species lines."

"Not for you," Lisandro said. "Remember, Joseph asked you not to keep Haven. The moment he asked you to protect him and his pride, he asked you to interfere. You're the leopards' Nimir-Ra, and the wolves' lupa; you were nothing to the lions. Once he asked for your help, he gave you permission to mess with his lions."

"I don't think Joseph saw it that way," I said.

Lisandro shrugged. "Doesn't matter how he saw it, it's still the truth."

I don't know what I would have said to that, because there was a knock on the door. Lisandro went all bodyguardy on us. His hand went behind his back, and I knew for sure the gun was there. "Who is it?"

"Requiem. Jean-Claude requested my presence."

Lisandro glanced at me. I realized he was asking my permission. I liked him better for that. I didn't really want to see Requiem tonight. I was still embarrassed that I'd added him to my list of food. But he'd been in England, so he'd seen the Harlequin in person, and recently. He'd be helpful. Or that's what I told myself as I nodded for Lisandro to let him in.

7

REQUIEM GLIDED IN wearing a long, hooded cloak as black as his hair. He was the only vamp I'd ever met who wore a cloak like that.

Byron came behind him, carrying a towel that seemed to be full of something. He was still wearing nothing but his G-string. There was still money stuffed in it. He grinned at me. "Hi, duckie."

"Hey, Byron."

He always talked like he had just stepped out of an old British movie: lots of *loves* and *duckies*. He talked that way to everyone, so I didn't take it personally. He up-ended the towel on the couch beside me. It was suddenly raining money.

"Good night," Nathaniel said.

Byron nodded and started taking the money out of his G-string. "Jean-Claude used that sweet, sweet voice of his during my act. The pigeons always give it up for him." He slipped off the G-string, letting some bills flutter to the floor. I used to protest the nudity in front of me, but they were strippers, and after a while either you stopped being bothered by the casual nudity, or you didn't hang at the club. Nudity didn't mean to the dancers what it meant in the real world. Stripping is about the illusion that the customers can have them—the illusion of sex, not the reality of it. It had taken me a while to understand that.

Byron used the towel to dry some of the sweat off his body. He winced, and turned to show bloody scratches high on one buttock. "Got me from behind, just at the end of m' act."

"Hit-and-run, or did she give you extra money for it?" Nathaniel asked.

"Hit-and-run."

I must have looked puzzled, because Nathaniel explained. "A hit-and-run is when a customer gets an extra grope, or scratch, or something intimate, and we don't know who did it, and they don't pay for it."

"Oh," I said, because I didn't know what else to say. I didn't like watching my boyfriends being groped by strangers. It was another reason I stayed away.

"'The evening star, love's harbinger, sits before me, and does not even waste a smile upon me.'" Requiem's greeting to me. It wasn't what he always said, but it was typical. He'd started calling me his "evening star."

"You know, I looked up the quote. It's John Milton's *Paradise Lost*. I'm not sure, but I think it's your very poetic way of complaining."

He glided in, making sure the cloak showed nothing but the long oval of his face, and even that was mostly hidden by the Vandyke-style beard and mustache. The only color on him was the swimming blue of his eyes: the richest, deepest, medium blue I'd ever seen.

"I know what I am to you, Anita."

"And that would be?" I said.

"I am food." He bent over me, and I turned my face so that the kiss he gave was on the cheek and not the mouth. He didn't fight me on it, but the kiss was empty and neutral, the kind of kiss you'd give your aunt. But I'd made certain it wouldn't be more. I'd turned away first, so why did it bug me that he'd just accepted the rebuff and not tried to make the kiss more? I didn't want him pursuing me harder than he was; I'd made that clear, so why did his just accepting the cheek bother me? God only knows, because I had no idea. I was mad at Nathaniel for demanding more of me, and irritated with Requiem for not demanding anything. Even in my own head I was confused.

He glided away to sink into the empty chair near the desk. He made sure the cloak covered him completely, only the tips of his black boots peeking out. "Why the frown, my evening star? I did exactly what you wished me to do, didn't I?"

I fought not to frown harder, and probably failed. "You bother me, Requiem."

"Why?" he asked, simply.

"Why, just why, no poetry?" I asked.

Nathaniel patted my shoulder, either reminding me he was there or trying to stop me from picking a fight. Either way, it worked, because I closed my eyes and counted to ten. I wasn't sure why Requiem got on my nerves lately, but he did. He was one of my lovers. He was food. But I didn't like it, any of it. He was wonderful in bed, but . . . there was always that feeling from him that no matter what I did it was never enough. Never what he wanted me to do. There was a constant, unspoken pressure from him. I knew the feeling, but unless you were going to have a "relationship" with a man, it was a pressure you didn't deserve, or wouldn't respond to. He was food, and we were lovers; he was Jean-Claude's third-in-command. I'd tried to be his friend, but somehow the sex had ruined that. I think without the sex we could have been friends, but with it . . . with it we were neither friends, nor boyfriend or girlfriend. We were lovers, but . . . I had no words for what was wrong between us, but I could feel it, like an old ache in a wound you thought had healed.

"You told me you were tired of my 'constantly quoting poetry' to you. I'm practicing speaking simply."

I nodded. "I remember, but . . . I feel like you're unhappy with me, and I don't know why."

"You have allowed me into your bed. I share the *ardeur* once more. What could any man desire above that?"

"Love," Nathaniel said.

Requiem looked past me to the other man. There was a flash of blue fire in the vampire's eyes: anger, power. Requiem hid it, but I'd seen it. We'd all seen it.

" 'Where both deliberate, the love is slight: Who ever loved, that loved not at first sight?' "

"I don't know who you're quoting," Nathaniel said, "but Anita doesn't love at first sight, or at least she didn't me."

"He's quoting from *Hero and Leander* by Christopher Marlowe," Byron said. The other vampire was counting the money he'd rained down on the couch. He had his back to the other vampire. "And what's bothering him is that he thinks he's wonderful, and he can't understand why you don't love him."

"Do not tempt me, Byron. My anger seeks only a target," Requiem said.

Byron turned with his stacked and counted money in his hand. "I can resist anything but temptation," he said. He glanced at me. "He hates it when you quote back at him."

"Your tongue doth overstep your purpose, Byron," Requiem said, his voice purring low with warning.

"My purpose," Byron said, his gray eyes flashing with a moment of shining power like quiet lightning. He laid his money on the lacquered coffee table and turned to face the other vampire. "I want that glib and oily art, To speak and purpose not." He sat in Nathaniel's lap, putting his legs across my lap.

Nathaniel put an arm around him, almost automatically, and gave me a look. The look said, *What's going on?* but since I didn't know, I had no answers. It was like we'd stepped into a fight I hadn't known was happening. I had my hands in the air, above Byron's bare legs. I could ignore the nudity most of the time now, but not when that nudity was sitting in my boyfriend's lap and had flung itself across my legs. My ability to ignore just wasn't that good.

"What's going on?" I asked, my hands finally coming to light on Byron's bare legs, because I felt stupid keeping my hands in the air. If he'd been more on my lap than Nathaniel's I might have just dumped him on the floor, but whatever was happening he'd involved Nathaniel, too, and that meant I couldn't simply act. I had to think, too. Simply reacting was so much easier, not always in the long run, but in the short run, it felt so much better.

"Ask Byron," Requiem said. "I have no idea why he's acting like this."

I patted Byron's calf and said, "Why are you sitting in our laps?"

Byron wrapped his arms around Nathaniel's shoulders, cuddling his face next to his. He stared at me, giving me a look out of those gray eyes that made me fight off a shiver. Not a shiver of fear, but one that was all about sex. Nathaniel looked faintly puzzled as their faces pressed next to each other. It was the blatant sex look that made me slide out from under his legs and stand up. "I don't know what game this is, Byron, but Nathaniel and I don't want to play."

Byron slid off Nathaniel's lap and knelt on the far side of him, so that I could still see the two of them clearly. It was like he was doing serious flirting. Byron flirted, but not seriously, more like it was a casual hobby. There was nothing casual about the look on his face.

He slid his hand along Nathaniel's neck, then grabbed his braid. Grabbed it, and yanked Nathaniel's neck backward at a painful angle. Nathaniel's breath came in fast pants, his pulse visible like a trapped thing in his throat.

My gun was just in my hand. I didn't remember drawing it. I didn't remember aiming it. My own pulse was hammering in my throat. Years of practice had a gun pointed at Byron's face. He was staring at me, his gray eyes straight on, face still serious, but not threatening. I didn't know what was going on, but whatever it was, someone was going to get hurt if it didn't stop.

"Let him go," I said, and my voice was as steady as the gun pointed at his forehead. I had a sense of Lisandro moving away from the door, coming toward us. I wasn't sure if I wanted the interference, or even if I needed it.

"He doesn't want me to let him go, do you, Nathaniel?" Byron's voice was very careful, even, as if he finally realized that his game could turn deadly.

Nathaniel's voice came strangled with the angle of his neck, and the force of the vampire's hand on his hair, but what he said was, "No, no, don't stop."

I finally let myself glance at Nathaniel. I didn't normally look away from someone I was pointing a gun at, but there was no sense of menace to Byron. Whatever we were doing, I wasn't sure it was about violence. Nathaniel's hands were gripping Byron's arm, but not like he was trying to stop the vampire from hurting him, more like he was just holding on. But it was the look on Nathaniel's face that made me lower the gun to point at the floor.

Nathaniel's lips were half parted, his eyes fluttering closed, his face slack with pleasure. His body was tense with anticipation. He was enjoying the pain, enjoying being manhandled. Shit.

Byron let go of Nathaniel abruptly, almost with a throwaway gesture. Nathaniel fell back onto the couch, gasping for breath, his eyes rolled back into his head behind fluttering eyelids. His spine bowed, throwing his head back, making him writhe against the back of the couch.

Byron stood there and watched him. "Duckie, this much reaction, you have been neglecting your boy."

He was right. I'd have liked to argue it, but he was right. The proof of neglect was writhing on the couch in some sort of ecstasy that I couldn't even begin to understand. I liked a little force now and then, but it didn't do this for me. Nathaniel began to grow quiet, eyes still closed, and a smile on his face. I understood for the first time that the violence could be sex for him, really, truly could.

I looked at Byron. "And your point?" I was pretty sure I knew what the point was, but I'd be damned if I'd help him make it.

"I heard rumors that you weren't doing dominance and submission with the boy, but I didn't believe it. I mean, how can you be with Nathaniel and not do BDSM? Bondage and submission is the boy's bread and butter."

I nodded, and put my gun up. "Do you know how close you came to getting yourself shot?"

"I did once I saw your gun pointed at my face." The joking was gone again, so serious, and then he smiled. "So exciting."

"Are you saying you got off on the fact that I damn near shot you?" I laughed a little at the end, but it was a nervous laugh.

"Not got off the way that Nathaniel does, but I like to be dominated sometimes." He sat down on the couch, squeezed between Nathaniel and the couch arm. He wrapped his arms around Nathaniel's shoulders again, though he was sitting on his knees so that he couldn't put their faces next to each other. Nathaniel cuddled in against him, a peaceful look on his face. It creeped me out. But he cuddled Byron's arms tighter around him, as if he were his favorite teddy bear. He'd never liked Byron that much, and now just a little abuse and he was his best buddy. I did not get it, I just didn't.

Byron hugged him back and stroked the side of his hair. "I'm a switch, Anita, in every sense of the word."

I frowned at him. "*Switch* means bisexual, right?"

"There's another meaning for it, duckie."

"Just tell me, Byron. I'm not very good at subtle."

"It means that I'm both a sub and a dom."

"Submissive and dominant," I said.

He nodded.

"What are you offering?" I said.

"I could help you tame your kitty-cat here."

"How?" I let the word hold all the suspicion it could.

He laughed. "You can put so much menace and doubt into one word, duckie."

"Answer the question," I said.

"Feed the *ardeur* on me and Nathaniel, while I abuse him. If this is a preview, the energy will be amazing."

"And what do you get out of it?"

"I get to have sex with you, duckie."

I shook my head. "Try again, Byron. You like boys a lot more than you like girls."

"I get to have sexual contact with Nathaniel."

I felt my eyes narrow at him. "You've never acted like Nathaniel was your type before."

"I know that he's unhappy, and I want my friends to be happy."

"That's not all of it," I said.

"Don't know what you mean, lover." He settled into the corner of the couch. Nathaniel and he cuddled like they had done it before, though I didn't think they had.

"He's doing it for my benefit," Requiem said.

I looked at the other vampire, who had never moved from his chair. "Explain," I said.

"Tell her, Byron, tell her why you're offering."

"Where has all your poetry gone, Requiem?" Byron asked.

" 'In chains and darkness, wherefore should I stay, And mourn in prison, while I keep the key?' " Requiem said.

"That's better," Byron said. "Have you thought about ending it all, duckie? Is the fact that Anita doesn't adore you that painful to you?"

Requiem just stared at him, and something in that look made Byron shiver. I wasn't sure if it was a shiver of fear or of other things. If he wasn't afraid, he should have been. I'd never seen Requiem look at anyone with that coldness before.

"This has the smell of something that will get out of hand and get people hurt. Since part of my job is to protect everyone who could get hurt, talk to me," I said.

Byron looked at me. "Nathaniel needs his pain, Anita. I'll help you give it to him, while you're in the bed with us. You get to supervise but you don't have to do the dirty work."

"Did Nathaniel talk to you about this problem?"

"I know what it's like, Anita, to want a certain kind of touch and be denied it. I spent centuries being given to masters that didn't give a damn what I wanted or needed. You love Nathaniel and he loves you, but eventually, needs left unanswered can curdle love like milk left to spoil in the sun."

"So this little demonstration is out of the kindness of your heart," I said, and let my tone say how little I believed that.

"He's tried to tell you, duckie, but you didn't understand."

"I'm not sure I understand now," I said.

"But did it help, my little show?"

I wanted to say no, but it would have been a lie. Most vamps could smell or feel a lie, so why bother? "Hate to admit it, but yeah, it helped. Don't pull shit like this again, but you've made your point."

"Have I?" he said, sliding lower on the couch, so that he and Nathaniel were more intertwined. If it bothered Nathaniel to be that up close and personal with a naked man, it didn't show. Okay, a naked man who wasn't one of our sweeties. Had just a little hair pulling made him like Byron that much? Was Nathaniel's need that great, or had I just neglected his needs that much?

Byron hadn't done anything that I wasn't willing to do. He hadn't done anything bad. Would it be so bad to just tie Nathaniel up and have the sex we would have had without the tying up? Was that so awful? I looked at the two men, cuddled together, the look of peaceful contentment on Nathaniel's face, and realized that I'd been arrogant. I'd assumed that if our relationship ended, it would be me doing the ending. That I'd dump him for being too needy, or too something. In that instant I realized that he might dump me for simply not trying hard enough to meet his needs. The thought made my chest tight. I loved him, I really did. I could not imagine my life without him. So what was I willing to do to keep him? How far would I go, and did I need help to get there? I'd had sex with Byron once before. I'd fed the *ardeur* off him. Could Byron teach me how to dominate Nathaniel? Maybe, maybe not. But his little show had proved one thing: that I needed someone to show me how Nathaniel worked. I would never have dreamed that simply pulling his hair, putting a little force behind it, would get such an amazing reaction out of him.

"You look like you're thinking too hard, lover."

"I'm thinking about your little show; isn't that what you wanted?" I asked.

"I wanted it to excite you, but that's not excitement in your eyes." It was his turn to frown.

"She is not easily captured," Requiem said.

"She likes two men at once."

"Not just any two men," Requiem said, "just as she does not prefer just any single man."

"You're talking about me like I'm not here; I really hate that," I said.

"Sorry, duckie, but I was hoping that the sight of Nathaniel and me together would do something for you."

"It puzzled me."

Byron laughed, and it made his face look younger, gave you a glimpse of what he might have been at a human fifteen when a vampire found him and made sure he'd never see sixteen. "Puzzlement wasn't exactly what I had in mind."

I shrugged. "Sorry."

He shook his head. "Not your fault, dearie. I don't do it for you."

"I don't do it for you either," I said.

He laughed again. "The sex was lovely."

"But you'd have liked it better if it had been Jean-Claude."

A look slid through his eyes. He actually looked down, lowering his eyes in a show of coyness to hide the look. When he raised his gaze to me again, it was that smiling blankness that he hid behind. "Jean-Claude loves you, duckie; he's made that abundantly clear."

I might have asked what he meant by that, but the door opened and the vampire in question glided through. His clothes had just looked dark in the club; his usual black. The clothes were black, but they weren't usual.

He was wearing a tuxedo complete with tails—though once you made it out of leather, was it still a tuxedo? Braces like silk suspenders slid over the bare flesh of his chest. I stared at that bare skin the way some men stare at a woman's breasts. It wasn't like me. I mean, it was a nice chest, but to stop there and not look at his face was just wrong. Because as nice as the chest was, the face was better. I raised my gaze to that face. The hair fell past his shoulders in black curls. The line of his neck was encircled with a black velvet ribbon and a cameo I'd bought for him. Up to the kissable curve of his mouth, the curve of his cheek like a swallow's wing, all grace and . . . Swallow's wing? What the hell did that mean? I would never have described anyone's jawline like that.

"*Ma petite*, are you well?"

"No," I said, softly, "I don't think I am."

He moved closer and I had to move my eyes upward, had to meet that midnight blue gaze. It was like back at the movies when I'd first seen Nathaniel. I was too fascinated, too taken with him. I actually had to close my eyes so the vision of him didn't distract before I could say, "I think someone's messing with me."

"What do you mean, *ma petite*?"

"You mean like at the movie theatre," Nathaniel said. His voice was closer than the couch. He must have moved toward us.

I nodded, eyes still closed.

Jean-Claude's voice came from right in front of me. "What happened at the theatre?"

Nathaniel explained. "She had to get her cross out before it got better."

"But I'm wearing my cross now," I said.

"It's inside your shirt now. It was in plain sight before," Nathaniel said.

"That shouldn't matter unless the vampire is in the room with me."

"Try bringing it into the light," Jean-Claude said.

I opened my eyes a crack, glancing at him. He was still heartrendingly beautiful, but I could think again. "That shouldn't matter for this." I stared up into his face, straight into those wondrous eyes. They were just eyes, beautiful, captivating, but not literally. "It's gone again."

"What's going on, duckies?" Byron asked. He walked up to us, looking from one to the other.

"Lisandro, leave us," Jean-Claude said.

Lisandro seemed to think about protesting, but he didn't. He just asked, "Do you want me to stay on the door, or go back to the club?"

"The door, I think," Jean-Claude said.

"Don't our guards need a heads-up?" I asked.

"This is not the business of the rodere."

"Lisandro raised a point before you came in, that if we're going to endanger them, they have a right to know why."

Jean-Claude looked at Lisandro. It was not a completely friendly look. "Did he?"

Lisandro gave him a flat look back. "I was talking about when Anita picks another animal to call, nothing about your orders, Jean-Claude."

"All that concerns *ma petite* concerns me." There was a dangerous purr to his voice.

Lisandro shifted a little and visibly let out a breath. "No offense, but don't you want her to pick a stronger beast next time? Someone who will help your power base?"

Jean-Claude stared at him, and Lisandro fought to both look at the vampire and not look—a trick that I'd mastered over the years, but was glad I'd become powerful enough to give up. So hard to be tough when you can't look someone in the eyes.

"Is my strength the concern of the rats?" Jean-Claude asked.

"Yes," Lisandro said.

"How?" One word, flat and unfriendly.

"Your strength keeps us all safe. The wererats remember what St. Louis was like when Nikolaos was Master of the City." Lisandro shook his head, face darkening. "She didn't protect anyone or anything but the vampires. You think about the entire preternatural community, Jean-Claude."

"I think you will find it is *ma petite* who thinks of such things."

"She's your human servant," Lisandro said. "Her actions are your actions. Isn't that what the vampires believe, that their human servants are just extensions of their masters?"

Jean-Claude blinked and moved farther into the room, collecting me by the hand as he moved. "A pretty conceit, but you know that *ma petite* is her own person." His hand in mine felt solid, real, and the world was suddenly safer. Just the touch of his hand and I felt more myself.

"Whatever or whoever is messing with me is still here," I said, "around the edges somehow, but still here."

"What do you mean, *ma petite*?"

"When you touched me, I felt more solid. Your touch chased back a fuzziness I didn't even know was there."

He drew me in against his body, so that it was almost a hug. I caressed the butter softness of his leather lapels. "Is that more solid still?" he asked.

I shook my head.

"Try touching skin to skin," Requiem said.

He had stayed in the chair by the desk. We'd moved until we were close to him, not intentionally, at least not on my part.

I kept one hand in Jean-Claude's, but the other I put against his bare chest. The moment I touched that much of his skin, it was good. "Even better," I said. I traced my hand over the smooth, firm muscles of his chest. I traced the cross-shaped burn scar. Better still.

"Why did you want to speak to Byron and me, Jean-Claude?" Requiem looked up at us, his face fighting for blankness but failing around the edges. He reclined in the chair, body at ease, but his eyes gave him away: tight, careful.

"You've seen this before, haven't you?" I asked.

"Once," he said, his voice more neutral than his eyes.

"When?" I asked.

He looked at Jean-Claude. "The wererat should leave."

Jean-Claude nodded. "Go, for now, Lisandro. If we can tell you more, we will."

Lisandro looked at me as he left, as if he thought I was the one most likely to tell him the truth later. He was right.

8

Byron looked at all of us. His usual joking face was utterly serious. "Someone talk to us poor little peons, please."

"Did you receive a gift?" Requiem asked.

"*Oui.*"

"What kind of gift?" Byron asked.

"A mask," Jean-Claude said.

Byron paled; he'd fed tonight so he had enough color to do it. "No, no, fuck me, not here, not again."

"What color was it?" Requiem said in a voice that had fallen away to emptiness, the way some of the old vampires could do.

"White," Jean-Claude said.

Byron relaxed so suddenly he almost fell. Nathaniel offered him a hand that he took. "I'm all weak-kneed, duckies. Don't scare me like that. White, we're safe with white."

Nathaniel helped him back to the couch, but didn't stay by him. He moved back toward us.

"What color did your master in England get?" I asked.

"Red first, then black," Requiem said.

"What does red mean?" I asked.

"Pain," Jean-Claude said. "It is typically a bid to punish a master, to bring him to heel. The council does not use the Harlequin lightly."

The name fell into the room like a stone dropped down a well. You strained to hear the splash. I leaned my face in against Jean-Claude's chest. There was no heartbeat to hear. He would breathe only when he needed to speak. I raised my head away from his chest. Sometimes it still disturbed me to lay my ear against a silent chest.

Byron broke the silence. "Red means they fuck with you."

"Like someone has been doing tonight?" I asked.

"Yes," Requiem said.

"And black?" I asked.

"Death," Requiem said.

"But doesn't white mean they just observe us?" Nathaniel said.

"It should," he said. I'd begun to dread when Requiem answered in short, clipped sentences. The poetry might occasionally get on my nerves, but the short, choppy words meant something had gone wrong, or he was pissed, or both.

"You said you'd explain more about them when I got to Guilty Pleasures. Well, I'm here. Explain."

"Harlequin is now merely a figure for jest. Once he was, or they were, the Mesnee d'Hellequin. Do you know what the wild hunt is, *ma petite*?"

"The wild hunt is a common motif all over Europe. A supernatural leader leads a band of devils, or the dead, with spectral hounds and horses. They chase and kill either anyone who crosses their path, or only the evil, and take them to hell. It depends on who you read whether it's a punishment to join the hunt, or a reward. It's usually considered really bad to be outside when the hunt goes by."

"As always you surprise me, *ma petite*."

"Well, it's such a widespread story that there has to be some basis for it, but it hasn't been seen for real since the time of one of the Henrys in England. I think Henry the Second, but I'm not a hundred percent on that one. Usually the leader of the hunt is some local dead bad guy, or the devil. But before Christianity got hold of it, a lot of the Norse gods were said to lead it. Odin's mentioned a lot, but sometimes goddesses like Hel, or Holda—though Holda's version gave gifts as well as punishment. Some of the other hunts did, too, but generally it was really bad to get caught, or even see them ride by."

"Harlequin is one of those leaders," Jean-Claude said.

"That's a new one on me, but then I haven't read up on it since college. I think the only reason it stuck with me is that it's such a wide-spread story, and it stops abruptly a few hundred years ago. Almost every other legend that has that many witness stories is true. Or at least that's what I've found. So why did it stop? Why did the wild hunt just stop riding, if it was real?"

"It is real, *ma petite*."

I looked at him. "Are you saying it was vampires?"

"I am saying that the legend existed and we took advantage of it. The Harlequin adopted the persona of the wild hunt. For it was something that people already feared."

"Vampires scare people already, Jean-Claude. You guys didn't need to pretend to be Norse gods to be frightening."

"The Harlequin and his family were not trying to frighten people, *ma petite*. They were trying to frighten other vampires."

"You guys already scare each other; Mommie Dearest proves that."

"Early in our history, Marmee Noir decided we were too dangerous. That we needed something to keep us in check. She created the idea of the Harlequin. As you say, *ma petite*, there were so many wild hunts over the face of Europe, what was one more? Vampires begin life as people, and the idea of the wild hunt was something many already feared."

"Okay, so what does this fake wild hunt have to do with us?"

"They are not fake, *ma petite*. They are a supernatural troop that can fly, that can punish the wicked and kill mysteriously and quickly."

"They aren't the original wild hunt, Jean-Claude; that makes them fake in my book."

"As you will, but they are the closest thing that vampires have to police. They are taken from all the major bloodlines. They owe allegiance to no one line. They are called upon when the council is divided. They are divided about us, about me."

"What do they do, exactly?" Nathaniel asked.

"Disguise and subterfuge are their meat and drink. They are assassins, spies of the highest order. No one knows who they are. No one has ever seen their faces and lived. They come to us masked if they mean us no harm. Masked in the manner of Venice when the rich and powerful wore masks, caps, and hats, so all looked alike, and none could be distinguished from the other. If they appear before us in those costumes, then they are merely here to observe. If they appear in the masks of their namesakes, then it could go either way. They could be merely observing, or they could mean to kill us. They would wear their namesakes, both to hide their faces and to let us know that if we do not cooperate they could turn deadly."

"What do you mean, namesakes?" I asked.

"There is only one Harlequin at a time, but there are other Harlequin as a group name. Whatever names they had once, they have adopted the names and masks of the commedia dell'arte."

"I don't know the term," I said.

"It was a type of theatre that flourished before I was born, but it gave rise to many characters. The women were not originally masked on stage, but there are those among Harlequin's band that have taken female personas; whether they are actually women or only seek to confuse the matter is open for debate, but does not truly matter. As for namesakes, there are dozens, but some names have been known for centuries: Harlequin, of course; Punchinello; Scaramouche; Pierrot or Pierrette; Columbine; Hanswurst; Il Dottore. There could be dozens more, or a hundred. No one knows how many are in the Harlequin's raid. Most of the time they will only appear in nearly featureless masks of black and white. They will simply say, 'We are the Harlequin.' The best possible scenario is that we never learn who individually has come to our city."

"How serious a breach of vampy etiquette is it that we get a white mask but they're acting like it's red?" I asked.

Jean-Claude and Requiem exchanged a look that I couldn't read exactly, but it wasn't good.

"Talk to me, damn it," I said.

"It should not be happening, *ma petite*. Either this is an attack by some other vampire powerful enough to fool us all, or the Harlequin are breaking their own rules. They are deadly within their rules; if the rule of law were to break down . . ." He closed his eyes and hugged me, hugged me tight.

Nathaniel came to stand beside us, his face uncertain. "What can we do about it?"

Jean-Claude looked at him, and smiled. "Very practical, *mon minet*, as practical as our Micah." He turned to look at Requiem, whose smile had vanished. "Is this how it began in London?"

"Yes, one of the Harlequin could increase our emotions of desire.

But only emotions we already owned. It was very subtle at first, then worsened. Truthfully, what has happened tonight to Anita went unnoticed among us. It simply seemed to be couples finally deciding to consummate their friendships."

"How did it worsen?" Nathaniel asked.

"I don't know if it was the same vampire, but they began to interfere when we used the powers of Belle's line. Making the lust go terribly wrong."

"How terribly?" I asked.

"The *ardeur* at its worst," he said.

"Shit," I said.

Nathaniel touched my shoulders and Jean-Claude opened his arms to pull the other man into our embrace, so that he hugged us both, and I was firmly in the middle of them. It was as if I could finally catch my breath. "Better and better," I said.

"The more you touch your power base, the more surety you have against them, at first," Requiem said.

"What do you mean, 'at first'?" I asked.

"Eventually, our master was tormented by them no matter who he touched. Whatever he touched turned ill, and whatever touched his skin was poisoned."

"Poisoned with what?" I asked.

"They turned our own powers against us, Anita. We were a kiss made up almost entirely of Belle Morte's line. They turned our gifts against us so that the blade bit deep, and we bled for them."

"They didn't torment Elinore and Roderick," Byron said from the couch.

The three of us looked at him, still clinging to each other.

"Not true. She was bothered at first like all of us. So smitten with Roderick she couldn't do her job."

"But, how did you say it, when the madness overcame us, they were spared," Byron said. There was a tone to his voice that held anger, or something close to it.

Jean-Claude hugged us both, and Nathaniel hugged back until it was hard to breathe, not from some vampire trick, but from the strength in their bodies. Jean-Claude eased away, and Nathaniel did the same. Jean-Claude moved us to the desk edge. He leaned upon it, drawing my back in against his body. He held a hand out to Nathaniel and drew him to the desk. Nathaniel sat on the desk, his feet dangling in the air. But he kept his hand in the vampire's, as if afraid to let go. I guess we all were.

"What do you mean, madness?" I asked.

"We fucked our brains out, dearie."

I tried to think of a polite way to say it.

Byron laughed. "The look on your face, Anita. Yes, sex is our coin, and we did a lot of it, but you want to have a choice, don't you?" He looked past us to Requiem. "You don't like having your choices taken away, do you, lover?"

Requiem gave him a look that should have stopped his heart, let alone his words, but Byron was already dead, and the dead are made of stouter stuff than the living. Or maybe Byron just didn't care anymore. "Requiem found that men were on the menu, didn't you, lover?" There was a purring insolence in his voice, bordering on hatred.

I got the implications; they'd become lovers after the Harlequin messed with them all badly enough. Requiem didn't do men, period. Belle had punished him over the centuries for refusing to bed men. To refuse Belle Morte anything was never a good idea, so he'd been serious about saying no. Someone on the Harlequin's team was very good at manipulating emotions. Scary good.

I hugged Jean-Claude's arm tight to me and reached out to Nathaniel. I ended up touching his hip, just running my hand lightly along it. Shapeshifters were always touching each other, and I'd begun to pick up the habit. Tonight I didn't fight it.

"You are never to speak of it," Requiem said, his voice low and very serious.

"How much does it bother you to know that I've had sex with Anita, too?"

Requiem stood in one swift motion, the black cloak swinging out, revealing that he wasn't wearing much under the cloak.

"Stop," Jean-Claude said.

Requiem froze, his eyes blazing with blue-green light. His shoulders rose and fell with his breathing, as if he'd been running.

"I believe that lust is not the only emotion the Harlequin can incite," Jean-Claude said.

It took Requiem a moment, and then he frowned and turned those sparkling eyes to us. "Our anger."

Jean-Claude nodded.

The light began to fade, like light moving away through water. "What are we to do, Jean-Claude? If they do not even observe their own rules, we are doomed."

"I will ask for a meeting with them," he said.

"You'll what?" Byron said, his voice squeaking just a little.

"I will ask for a meeting between them and us."

"You do not seek the Harlequin out, Jean-Claude," Requiem said. "You hide, cowering in the grass, praying that they pass you by. You do not invite them closer."

"The Harlequin are honorable. What is happening is not honorable behavior."

"You are mad," Byron said.

"You think one of them is disobeying the rules," I said, quietly.

"I hope so," Jean-Claude said.

"Why hope so?" I asked.

"Because if what is happening is being done with the full weight and approval of the Harlequin behind it, then Requiem is correct, we are doomed. They will play with us, then destroy us."

"I don't do doomed," I said.

He kissed the top of my head. "I know, *ma petite*, but you do not understand what force is against us."

"Explain it to me."

"I have told you, they are the bogeymen of vampirekind. They are what we fear in the dark."

"Not true," I said.

"They're bloody frightening, lover," Byron said. "We do fear them."

"The bogeyman of all vampires is Marmee Noir, Mommie Dearest, your queen. That's who scares the shit out of all of you."

They were quiet for a heartbeat or two. "Yes, the Harlequin fear the Queen of Darkness, our creator," Jean-Claude said.

"Everyone fears the dark," Requiem said, "but if the Mother of All Darkness is our nightmare, then the Harlequin are the swift sword of the dark."

Byron nodded. "No arguments from me on that one, duckie. Everyone fears her."

"What are you suggesting, *ma petite*?"

"I'm not suggesting anything. I'm saying, I've stood in the dark and seen her rise above me like a black ocean. She's invaded my dreams. I've seen the room where her body lies, heard her voice whisper through my head. Tasted rain and jasmine choking on my tongue." I shivered and could almost feel her moving restless in the dark. She lay in a room with windows, and they kept a fire below her, a continuous watch. She'd fallen into a "sleep" longer ago than most of them remembered. Once I'd thought they watched to celebrate her awakening, but I'd begun to realize most of them were as afraid of her as I was, which meant they were scared shitless. Marmee Noir liked me for some reason. I interested her. And from thousands of miles away, she messed with me. She'd made a cross melt into my hand. I'd have the scar until I died.

"Speak of the devil and you bring him closer," Requiem said.

I nodded and tried to think of something else. Oh, yeah, I knew what to think about. "The Harlequin are just vampires, right, which means they're subject to your laws, right?"

"*Oui.*"

"Then let's use the law against them."

"What do you propose, *ma petite?*"

"This is a direct challenge to our authority. The council has forbidden any Master of the City to fight in the United States until the law decides whether you guys are staying legal or not."

"You're not suggesting that we fight them?" Byron said.

"I'm saying that we act in accordance with the law," I said.

"Don't you understand, Anita," Byron said, "the Harlequin are who we turn to when the bad things happen, sort of. They are the police for us."

"When the police go bad, they aren't police anymore," I said.

"What are they?" he asked.

"Criminals."

"You cannot seriously suggest that we are to fight the Harlequin?" Requiem said.

"Not exactly," I said.

"What exactly then?"

I looked up at Jean-Claude. "What would you do if someone powerful moved in on us like this?"

"I would contact the council in hopes of avoiding open war."

"Then contact them," I said.

"I thought not everyone on the council liked us," Nathaniel said.

"They do not, but if the Harlequin are breaking the law, then that would take precedence over more petty concerns," Jean-Claude said.

"Have you forgotten how petty the council can be?" Requiem said.

"*Non*, but not all on the council have forgotten what it means to live in the real world."

"Which council member will you contact first?" Byron asked.

There was a knock on the door. All of us with heartbeats jumped. Nathaniel gave that nervous laugh, and I said, "Shit."

Lisandro's voice: "There's a delivery for you, Jean-Claude."

"It can wait," he said, his voice showing some of the strain.

"The letter with it says you're expecting it."

"Enter," Jean-Claude said.

Lisandro opened the door, but it was Clay who walked in with a white box in his hands. A box just like the one I'd found in the restroom. I think I stopped breathing, because when I remembered to breathe, it came in a gasp.

Clay looked at me. "What's wrong?"

"Who delivered this?" Jean-Claude asked.

"It was just sitting by the holy-item check desk."

"And you just brought it in here," I said, my voice rising.

"No, give me some credit. We checked it out. The note says Jean-Claude is expecting it."

"What is it?" I asked, but was afraid I knew.

"A mask," Clay said. He was looking at all of us now, trying to see why we were so upset.

"What color is it?" Jean-Claude's voice was as empty as I'd ever heard it.

"White."

The tension level dropped a point or two.

"With little gold musical notes all over it. Didn't you order it?"

"In a way, I suppose I did," Jean-Claude said.

I stared up at him and moved away enough so I could see his face clearly. "What do you mean, you suppose you did?"

"I said I wanted to meet with them, did I not?"

"Yeah, but so what?"

"That's what this mask means, *ma petite*. It means they wish to meet, not to kill us, or torment, but to talk."

"But how did they know what you'd said?" Nathaniel asked.

Jean-Claude looked at me, and there was something in that look that made me say, "They're listening to us."

"I fear so."

"When was the mask delivered?" Requiem asked.

Clay was still looking at us, as if waiting for us to throw him a clue. "We're not sure. I went on break about thirty minutes ago. It must have come while I was off the door."

"How long have you been back on the door?" Jean-Claude asked.

"Maybe five minutes."

"They were listening," Requiem said.

"They knew what Jean-Claude was going to say," Byron said, and his voice held more panic than most vampires would have shown. He just couldn't quite keep all the emotion out of his face and voice.

"What is going on?" Clay asked.

"Something big and bad has come to town," Lisandro said. "They won't tell us about it, but they'll expect us to fight it, and die because of it." His voice sounded bitter.

"What are the rules about telling our soldiers about . . . them?" I asked.

Jean-Claude took in a deep, deep breath, and shook, almost like a bird settling its feathers. "Mutable."

"Mutable—oh, it depends."

He nodded.

Then I had a smart idea. "I believe we'd know if someone was listening in on us metaphysically, especially another vampire."

"They are very powerful, *ma petite*."

"Lisandro," I said.

He came to his version of attention; he gave me all his concentration. There was a demand to his dark eyes. If I widowed his wife, he wanted to know why. I thought he deserved to know why, but first things first. "I need this room swept for bugs."

"What kind of bugs?"

"Anything that would let someone listen to us."

"You think they are relying on technology, *ma petite*?"

"I don't believe that any vampire could spy on us like this without our sensing it."

"They are very powerful, *ma petite*."

"They are fucking ghosts, lover," Byron said.

"Fine, they're ghosts, but it doesn't do any harm to look for technology. If the room is clean, then we can blame it on spooky stuff, but let's look for tech first."

Jean-Claude looked at me for a long moment, then nodded. "It would be interesting if they used listening devices."

"Did you look for bugs in London?" Nathaniel asked.

Byron and Requiem exchanged a look, then both shook their heads. "It never occurred to us, duckies. I mean this is the bloody . . ." Byron licked his lips and stopped himself before saying their name, just in case. "They are ghosts, bogeys, walking nightmares. You don't expect the bogeyman to need technology."

"Exactly," I said.

"What's that supposed to mean?" he asked.

"It means that most vampires don't use technology much. If these guys use it a lot, then it would seem like magic, if you didn't know what it was."

"Any sufficiently advanced technology is indistinguishable from magic," Requiem said.

I nodded.

He stared at me. "My evening star, you are full of surprises."

"I just don't think like a vampire."

"Does Rafael have someone he trusts to clean a room of such things?" Jean-Claude asked.

"Yes," Lisandro said.

"Then do it."

"How soon do you need it?"

"We said we wanted to meet with them a minute or two ago, and the mask arrives with the invitation," I said.

"So, like yesterday," Lisandro said.

"Or sooner," I said.

He nodded. "I'll make the call." He hesitated at the door. "I'll put someone on the door, and I'll use a phone outside the club."

"Good thinking," I said.

"It's what I do." Then he was gone.

"Where do you want this?" Clay asked, motioning with the box.

"Put it on the desk with the other one, I guess."

He put it beside the first one. Jean-Claude didn't seem to want to touch it. I was the one who opened it and found the white mask staring sightless up at me. But this one looked more finished, with gilt musical notes decorating the face. I touched a note and found it was raised above the rest of the mask. The note with it said only, "As you requested."

"Is there writing inside the mask?" Jean-Claude asked.

I lifted it out of the tissue paper. Inside the smooth bow of the mask was writing. "Do not read it out loud, *ma petite*."

I didn't, I just handed it to him. Inside the mask was written "Circus of the Damned," and a date that was two days away. The date was written backward with the day first, then the month, then the year like they wrote it in Europe. They'd chosen one of Jean-Claude's own businesses for the meeting. Was that good, bad, or neither? Did it mean we had home-court advantage, or that they were planning to torch the place? I wanted to ask, but didn't want our enemies to hear the question. If we did find bugs in this office, we'd have to look everywhere. All the offices, all the businesses, my house, all of it.

I was praying we found bugs, because the alternative was that these vamps were so good that they could plant psychic bugs inside our brains. You could find and destroy mechanical shit in the rooms; if they were good enough to use magic inside our heads, then we were fucked. We'd die when they wanted us to die, or we'd live, and either way it would be their idea, and not ours. I never thought I'd pray to have our offices turn out to be bugged. Funny, what turns out to be the lesser evil some nights.

9

DAWN HAD COME and all the vampires were asnooze in their coffins when I finally got a few minutes to try Edward again. I'd called twice while Lisandro's experts searched everything. They had found bugs, but not where they were listening to us, like listening posts. Hours of work later and we were clean. We actually got lucky. The bugs weren't the smallest and latest cutting-edge technology. Which meant they needed to be close to the clubs to hear. Probably something mobile like a van, the experts said. The tech was good, but not the latest and greatest. Which probably meant the Harlequin didn't know how to hack phone lines and computer systems. Probably. But even the listening devices we found were pretty high tech for a bunch of ancient vampires. Made me wonder what other wonders of modern technology they might be willing to use. Most vamps relied on vampire powers. I wasn't sure the Harlequin did. In fact, I was betting they didn't. Ancient vampires and armed with modern shit; it just wasn't fair.

I wanted to even those odds, so I was in Jean-Claude's bathroom with my cell phone, trying one last time to reach Edward.

I dialed the number, and had almost given up when I heard the phone click over. The voice that answered the phone was thick with sleep. For a second I thought it was Edward, so I said, "Edward?"

The voice cleared a little and said, "Anita, that you?" The voice was male, but definitely not Edward. Shit.

Edward was engaged to a widow with two kids. Lately when I wanted to be sure I'd get him the first time, I called Donna's house, not his. They weren't officially living together, but he spent more time at her place than at his own. "Hey, Peter, sorry, forgot the time difference."

I heard some movement, as if he'd rolled over and taken the phone under the covers with him. "It's all right. What's up?" His voice had spent the last year breaking and finally settled into a deeper bass that still startled me sometimes.

"I just need to talk to Ted," I said, hoping he hadn't heard the Edward earlier.

"It's okay, Anita," and he gave a laugh that still held a lazy edge of sleep. "I know who Edward is, but you're lucky I answered the phone. Mom or Becca would have asked questions."

This was the first I knew that any of Edward's new family knew his secret identity. I wasn't sure how I felt about Peter knowing, or about any of them knowing. They knew what he did, sort of, the legalish parts, but they didn't really know who Edward was, or at least that's what I had believed until now.

I checked my wristwatch, which had gone on along with a robe. I did quick math in my head and said, "Shouldn't you be getting ready for karate class?"

"They're painting the dojo." he said.

I would also have asked why he had a phone in his room, but he wasn't my kid. I mean, sixteen was a little young for your own phone, wasn't it?

"I placed first in the karate tournament last Saturday," he said.

"Congratulations," I said.

"It's not like real fighting, not like you and Edward do, but it's still cool."

"I've never won first place in a martial arts tournament of any kind, Peter. You're doing good."

"But you have a black belt in judo, right?"

"Yeah."

"And you're training in other martial arts, right?"

"Yeah, but . . ."

"A tournament is just kid stuff, I know, but Edward says I have to wait until I'm at least old enough to sign up for military service before he'll take me on anything real."

I did not like the sound of that at all. "Eighteen, right."

"Yeah"—he sighed so heavily—"two years." He made two years sound like forever. I guess at sixteen it is.

I wanted to tell him that there were other lives to live that had nothing to do with fighting, guns, or violence. I wanted to tell him that he couldn't follow in his almost-stepfather's footsteps, but I couldn't. It wasn't my place to say it, and Peter wouldn't have listened anyway. I was in the same business as his "dad," so I was cool, too.

"Is Ted there?"

"Anita," and he sounded chiding, "I know his real name."

"Yes, but you're right, I should never have said Edward when calling this number. It should be Ted until I'm sure who I'm talking to. I'm practicing."

He laughed again. I didn't think I was that funny. "Ted's here." I heard that slide of cloth again. "Though at eight on a day we don't have school, Mom and Ted are probably still in bed." He must have rolled over to look at a clock.

"I didn't mean to call this early," I said, "I'll call back later."

His voice sobered. "What's wrong, Anita? You sound all stressed."

Great, I couldn't even control my voice enough to fool a teenage boy. Truth was, I'd finally realized that I wasn't just asking Edward to come hunt monsters, I was asking him to leave his family to come hunt monsters. Edward used to live to find bad things that could test his skills. He lived to be better, faster, meaner, quicker, more deadly than the monsters he hunted. Then he'd met Donna, and suddenly he had other things to live for. I wasn't sure he'd ever walk down the aisle with her, but he was the only father the kids had, and the only husband Donna had. Her first husband had been killed by a werewolf. An eight-year-old Peter had picked up his father's dropped gun and finished off the wounded shapeshifter. He'd saved his family while his father's body was still twitching on the floor. In some ways Edward fit in just fine. Edward picked Becca up from ballet class, for God's sake. But . . . but what if I got him killed? What if I got him killed and Peter and Becca lost another parent because I was too chickenshit to handle my own mess?

"Anita, Anita, are you there?"

"Yeah, yeah, Peter, I'm here."

"You sound strange, like, scared almost."

Peter was too damned perceptive for comfort sometimes. "I just . . ." Oh, hell, what could I say that would fix this? "Let Edward sleep in, don't wake them."

"Something's wrong, I can hear it in your voice. You called because you're in trouble. That's it, isn't it?" he asked.

"I'm not in trouble," I said. In my head, I added, *yet.*

Silence on his end of the phone for a heartbeat. "You're lying to me." He sounded accusatory.

"Well, that's a hell of a thing to say," I said, with as much indignation as I could muster. I wasn't lying, not really, I was just fudging the truth. Okay, fudging like double chocolate with three kinds of nuts, but it still wasn't completely a lie.

"Your word, your word of honor," he said in a very serious voice. "Tell me you didn't call to get Edward's help with some nasty monster problem."

Shit. "You know you're being a pain in the ass here," I said.

"I'm sixteen. I'm supposed to be a pain in the ass, or that's what Mom says. Give me your word that you're not lying to me, and I'll believe you. Give me your word, and I'll believe everything you've said, and I'll hang up, and you can go back to not being in trouble."

"Damn it, Peter."

"You won't give your word and then lie, will you?" His voice held question, and almost wonderment, as if he didn't quite believe it.

"No, not as a general rule, no."

"Edward said you wouldn't, but I wasn't sure I believed him. But you really won't, will you?"

"No," I said. "Happy now?"

"Yes," he said, though his voice didn't sound exactly happy. "Tell me what's wrong. Why do you need Edward's help?"

"I need to talk to Edward, but I won't tell you why, or what it's about."

"I'm not a baby, Anita."

"I know that."

"No, you don't," he said.

I sighed. "I don't think you're a baby, but you are a kid, Peter. You're grown-up for sixteen, but I'd like to keep some of the darker shit away from you until you reach at least eighteen. If Edward wants to share with you later, that's his lookout."

"You might as well tell me, Anita. If I ask, he'll tell me."

I hoped he was wrong, but was afraid he was right. "If Edward wants you to know, he'll tell you, Peter. But I am not going to tell you, and that's final."

"Is it that bad?" he asked, and I heard the first thread of worry.

Shit, again. I just couldn't win conversations with Peter. I'd only had a handful of them lately, but he always seemed to talk me into a box. "Get Edward on the phone, Peter, now."

"I can handle myself in a fight, Anita. I can help."

Shit, shit, and double shit. I was not going to win this conversation. "I'm hanging up now, Peter."

"No, Anita, I'm sorry, I'm sorry." And his voice went from that cynical grown-up to an almost childlike panic. The panic had worked better before his voice deepened. "Don't hang up, please, I'll get Ted." The phone hit wood so hard, I had to put the phone away from my ear. He came back on, saying, "Sorry, dropped the phone. I'm getting dressed. I'll go knock on their door. If it's bad enough for you to call Edward, then you need to talk to him. I'll stop being a kid and just get him for you." He was a little angry with me, but mostly frustrated. He wanted to help. He wanted to grow up. He wanted to fight for real, whatever the hell that meant. What was Edward teaching him? Did I really want to know? No. Would I ask? Yes, unfortunately, yes. God, I did not need another problem on my plate right now. I thought about trying to lie to Edward, say I'd just called up to chat about the latest issue of *Mercenaries Quarterly*, but if I wasn't up to lying to Peter, Edward was absolutely out of my weight class.

10

I SAT ON the edge of the bathtub, waiting for Edward to come to the phone. I'd insisted on privacy for the phone call, though I'd told Jean-Claude and Micah who I was trying to call. Jean-Claude had said only, "Help would not be unwelcome." The comment said, clearly, that he was worried. The more worried I realized he was, the more worried I got.

I heard noise over the phone, movement. The phone was picked up, and I heard Edward's voice say, "Hang up the other extension, Peter." A second later he spoke directly into the phone. "Anita, Peter said you needed help, my kind of help." His voice was that empty-middle-of-nowhere accent. It was his normal voice; when he was playing Ted Forrester, good ol' boy, he had a drawl.

"I didn't say I needed help," I said.

"Then why did you call?"

"Can't I just call to chat?"

He laughed, and the laugh was strangely familiar. I realized it was an echo of Peter's laugh earlier, or maybe Peter's laugh was an echo of Edward's. They weren't genetically related, I knew that, so what was with the laugh? Imitation, maybe.

"You would never call me just to chat, Anita. That's not what we do for each other." He laughed again, and murmured, "Called to chat," as if the idea were too ridiculous for words.

"I do not need you to be condescending, thanks anyway." I was angry and had no right to be. I'd called him, and it was me I was angry at. I was wishing I hadn't called—for so many reasons.

"What's wrong?" he asked, not taking offense. He knew me too well to let a little angry outburst bother him.

I opened my mouth, closed it, then said, "I'm trying to decide where to start."

"Start with the dangerous part." There, that was Edward, not *start at the beginning*, but *start with the dangerous part*.

"I did call for backup, but I have other backup already. It's not you, but it's not a bunch of amateurs either." I was being honest. The were-rats were almost completely ex-military, ex-police, or ex-criminals. Some of the werehyenas were the same flavor of professional. I had help. I shouldn't have called Edward.

"You sound like you're trying to talk yourself out of asking me for help," he said, and his voice was curious, not worried, just curious.

"I am."

"Why?"

"Because Peter answered the phone."

There was a sharp intake of breath. "Hang up the phone, Peter," Edward said.

"If Anita's in trouble, I want to know about it."

"Hang up the phone," he said, "and don't make me ask again."

"But . . ."

"Now."

I heard the phone click.

"Well," I said.

"Wait," he said.

I sat on my side of the phone in silence, wondering what we were waiting for. Finally Edward said, "He's off."

"Does he listen in on phone conversations a lot?"

"No."

"How do you know he doesn't?"

"I know . . ." He stopped himself, and said, "I don't think he does. I think you're a special case for Peter. He's in Donna's old room. I told him he could keep the phone if he behaved. I'll talk to him."

"If he's in Donna's old room, where are you and she sleeping? Not that it's any of my business," I added.

"We put a master suite on the house."

"Have you moved in, then?"

"Pretty much."

"You sell your house?" I asked.

"No."

"I guess Batman can't sell the bat cave."

"Something like that." But his voice, which had started a little friendly, was not friendly now. It was empty, the old pre-Donna Edward talking to me. He might be talking about domestic bliss and raising teenagers, but he was still the coldest killer I'd ever met, and that person was still in there. I wasn't sure whether I couldn't bear the thought of him watching Becca at ballet class, or would have paid to see him sitting with all the other parents waiting for their leotard-clad darlings.

"If I lied well enough I'd just make something up and hang up."

"Why?" he asked, in that empty voice.

"Because Peter answering the phone made me realize that it's not all fun and games anymore. If I get you killed, then they lose another father. I don't want to have to explain that to Peter, or Donna, or Becca."

"But especially Peter," he said.

"Yeah," I said.

"Since you can't lie to me, just tell me, Anita." His voice was a little softer now, a little feeling to it. Edward liked me; we were friends. He'd miss me if I were gone, and I'd miss him, but there was still a little question on whether one day we'd find ourselves on the opposite sides of a problem, and have to finally see which of us was the better man. I was hoping that day would never come, because there was no way for me to win the fight now; dead or alive, we'd both lose.

"Do you know what the Harlequin are?" I asked.

"French clowns?" he said, and let himself sound puzzled.

"Do you know them in any other context?"

"Twenty questions isn't like you, Anita; just talk."

"I just wanted to see if I was the only vampire hunter extraordinaire who was totally in the dark about this. It makes me feel a little better that you don't know about them either. Apparently Jean-Claude is right; they really are a big, dark secret."

"Talk," he said.

I talked. I told him what little I knew about the Harlequin and his band. It really wasn't that much.

He was quiet so long that I said, "Edward, I can hear you breathing, but . . ."

"I'm here, Anita. Just thinking."

"Thinking what?" I asked.

"That you always let me play with the best toys." And his voice wasn't empty now, it was eager.

"And what if these toys finally manage to be bigger and badder than you and me?"

"Then we die."

"Just like that," I said. "You wouldn't have regrets?"

"You mean Donna and the kids?"

"Yes," I said, and I stood, starting to pace the bathroom.

"I would regret leaving them."

"Then don't come," I said.

"And if you get killed, I'd always believe that I could have saved you. No, Anita, I'll come, but I will bring backup."

"Not anyone too crazy, okay?"

He laughed, that chuckle of true delight that I'd heard maybe six times in the entire seven years I'd known him. "I can't promise that, Anita."

"Fine, but Edward, I'm serious. I don't want to get you killed on them."

"I can't stop being who I am just because I love Donna, Anita. I can't stop being what I am because I've got the kids to think about."

"Why not?" I asked, and I was thinking of a conversation Richard and I had had when we thought I was pregnant. He'd expected that if I were pregnant I'd stop being a federal marshal or vampire hunter. I hadn't agreed.

"Because it wouldn't be me, and they love me. Donna and Becca may not know everything that Peter does about me, but they know enough. They know what I had to do to save the kids when Riker took them."

Riker had been a very bad man. He had been doing illegal archaeology digs, and Donna's amateur protection group had gotten in their way. It actually hadn't been Edward or me that first got the kids on Riker's radar. Nice to know we weren't completely to blame for what happened. Riker had wanted me to do a certain spell for him, which truthfully I hadn't been necromancer enough to do, but he wouldn't believe me. He tortured the children to get my, and Edward's, cooperation. Six-year-old, now eight-year-old, Becca had gotten a badly broken hand. Peter had been sexually molested by a female guard. We'd had to watch on videotape. We'd killed Riker and all his people. We rescued the kids, and Edward had made me give Peter my backup gun. Edward decided in that moment that if we lost, he preferred Peter to be killed resisting, rather than taken again. I hadn't argued, not after what they'd done to him. I had watched Peter empty my gun into the body of the woman who'd hurt him. He'd kept dry-firing into her body until I wrestled the gun away from him. I still saw his eyes when he told me, "I wanted her to hurt."

I knew that Peter had lost some of his innocence the night his father died and he had to pick up a gun to protect his family. He'd taken a life, but I think he thought it was killing a monster, and that didn't really count. Hell, once I'd thought the same thing about monsters. Killing the woman who had hurt him had taken more from him, a bigger piece of his soul. I couldn't even imagine how big a piece the sexual abuse stole away. Had it been better for him to have his revenge so quickly? Or had it cost him more?

I'd told him the only truth I had that night: "You killed her, Peter. That's as good as revenge gets. Once you kill them, there isn't any more." Revenge was always the easy part; the hard part was living with it afterward. Living with what you'd done. Living with what they'd done to you, or those you loved.

"Anita, are you there? Anita, answer me."

"Sorry, Edward, I didn't hear a damn thing you said."

"You're a thousand miles away inside your own thoughts. That's not a good place to be in the middle of a firefight."

"It hasn't come to a firefight yet," I said.

"You know what I mean, Anita. I have to round up my backup and arrange transport. That'll take a day or so. I'll be there as soon as I can, but you need to watch your back until I get there."

"I'll do my best not to get killed before you get here."

"This isn't funny, Anita. You seem seriously distracted."

I thought about it for a moment, then realized what was wrong. I was happy for the first time in my life. I loved the men I was living with. I, like Edward, had a family to protect, and mine wouldn't be tucked safely in New Mexico while we cleaned this up. "I just realized that I've got my own family here, and I don't like them being on the firing line. I don't like that a lot."

"Who are you worried about?" he asked.

"Nathaniel, Micah, Jean-Claude, all of them."

"I'm looking forward to meeting your new lovers."

It took me a minute to realize. "You've never met Micah and Nathaniel. I'd forgotten that."

"Jean-Claude can handle himself, Anita, as well as anyone in this situation. It sounds like the shapeshifters have you covered for now. Micah is head of the local wereleopards. He didn't get the job on his winning personality. He's a survivor and a fighter, or he'd be dead already."

"Is this supposed to be a pep talk?" I asked.

He gave a sound that was almost a laugh. "Yeah."

"Well, you suck at it."

He laughed then. "Which of your lovers is cannon fodder, Anita? Who are you really the most worried about?"

I took a deep breath, let it out slow, and said, "Nathaniel."

"Why him?"

"Because he's not a fighter. I've taken him to the gun range and he knows the basics." Then I remembered a moment when Chimera, a very bad guy, had come to town. I remembered an ambush, when Nathaniel had been with me. I'd forgotten. He'd killed someone, and I'd forgotten. I hadn't even thought how it might have affected him. Some leopard queen I was. Fuck.

"Anita, you still there?"

"Yeah, I just remembered something that I guess I was trying to forget. Nathaniel shot someone, killed him to save me. One of the were-rats had gotten killed, and he picked up the guy's gun and used it just like I'd taught him." I was suddenly cold down to my toes. All the awful things that people had made Nathaniel do over the years while he was on the street, and it had been me that forced him to kill. He'd done it out of love, but motive didn't change the end product. Someone was still dead.

"He'll do, Anita." There was a tone to Edward's voice, approval maybe.

"You know, I hadn't thought about what he'd done until just now. What kind of person forgets that?"

"Did he seem messed up about it?"

"No."

"Then let it go," Edward said.

"Just like that," I said.

"Just like that."

"I'm not good at letting go."

"No, you're not."

"How much does Peter know about your real life as assassin to the undead and furry?"

"That's my call, Anita, not yours." His voice wasn't friendly now.

"I'd love to argue, but you're right. I haven't laid eyes on Peter since he was fourteen."

"He turned fifteen that year."

"Oh, so not two years since I saw him but more like a year and a half. That gives me so much more room to bitch at you for introducing him to the scary stuff."

"I'm just saying that he wasn't a kid when we met him. He was a young man, and I've treated him like one."

"No wonder he adores you," I said.

It was Edward's turn to be quiet.

"I can hear you breathing," I said.

"You know how I said we don't chat?"

"Yeah."

"I finally realized, just now, you're the only person I can talk about this with."

"What, Peter?"

"No."

In my head I went through the list of things that Edward could only talk to me about; nothing came to mind. "I'm all ears."

"Donna is pushing for kids."

That stopped me. It was my turn to be at a loss for words. I managed to stumble out some words, the wrong words. "Really? I mean, I guess I thought she was too old to start over."

"She's only forty-two, Anita."

"I'm sorry, Edward. I didn't mean it that way, I just never saw you with a baby."

"Ditto," he said, and he sounded angry now, too.

Worse yet, I felt my throat closing tight, my eyes burning. What the fuck was wrong with me? "Do you ever wish you had a life where you could see babies and shit like that?" I asked, and fought to keep the sudden rise of emotion under check.

"No," he said.

"Never?" I asked.

"You thinking about a baby?" he asked.

Then I told him something I had never expected to tell Edward. "I had a serious pregnancy scare last month. False positive and everything. Let's just say it made me reassess some parts of my life."

"The biggest difference between us, Anita, is that if I have a baby with Donna, she carries it, not me. You would have a lot more trouble doing it."

"I know, the whole girl thing."

"Are you seriously thinking about babies?"

"No, I was relieved as hell when I found out I wasn't pregnant."

"How'd your lovers take it?"

"You know, most normal people would call them boyfriends."

"No one woman could date as many men as you have in your life, Anita. You can fuck them, but you can't date them. I'm having enough trouble having a relationship with one woman; I can't imagine juggling a half dozen of them."

"Maybe I'm just better at relationships than you are," I said, and my voice was not friendly. I wasn't close to tears; I had the beginnings of a nice anger warming me up.

"Maybe; girls usually are better at it."

"Wait a minute. How do you know how many men I'm sleeping with?"

"You and your little harem are big news in the preternatural community."

"Are we?" and I let it be hostile.

"Don't be that way; I'd be bad at my job if I didn't listen to my sources. You want me good at my job, right? Ted Forrester is a legal vampire hunter, a federal marshal, just like you." It had creeped me out when I'd discovered Edward had a badge. It just seemed wrong. But too many of the vampire hunters had failed the firearms test; for the newer ones, too many hadn't made it through the more detailed training. The government had turned further afield to get enough vampire hunter/federal marshals to cover the country. Edward had been grandfathered in on the firearms training, no sweat. But the fact that Ted Forrester had stood up to government scrutiny meant either that Edward had some high-placed friends or that Ted Forrester was his real identity—the name he'd gone into the military with, his actual true name. I'd asked him which it was, and he wouldn't answer. Of course Edward wouldn't answer. Such a mystery man.

"I don't like being spied on, Edward, you know that." Did Edward know about the *ardeur*? How long had it been since I'd filled him in on the metaphysics in my life? I couldn't remember.

"How did your lov . . . boyfriends take the news of the almost-baby?" he asked.

"Do you really care?"

"I wouldn't have asked if I didn't care," he said, and that was probably absolutely true.

"Fine," I said, "pretty well. Micah and Nathaniel were ready to re-arrange their lives to play daddy and nanny, if I decided to keep it. Richard proposed, and I turned him down. Jean-Claude seemed like he always was: cautious, and waiting for me to decide what wouldn't piss me off." I thought about that. "I think Asher was pretty sure it wasn't his, so he didn't offer too much comment."

"I knew you were living with Micah and Nathaniel. But when did Jean-Claude start sharing you with other vampires? I didn't think master vamps shared well."

"Asher is sort of an exception for Jean-Claude."

He sighed. "Normally I'd enjoy playing with you, Anita, but it's early, and I know you've had a hard morning."

"What's that mean?" I asked, and I couldn't keep the suspicion out of my voice.

He made a sound halfway between a chuckle and an *mmm* sound. "I'll tell you the rumors I've heard, and you tell me how big a lie they are."

"Rumors," I said. "What rumors?"

"Anita, thanks to my new status I hang with a lot of creature killers. You're not the only one who's got ties to the monsters in their town. Admittedly, you have the most . . . intimate ties to them."

"And that means what?" I asked, and didn't try to keep the irritation out of my voice.

"It means no one else is fucking their local Master of the City."

Put that way, it was hard to argue with the intimate part. "Fine."

"The Harlequin only come if you've gotten high enough on the radar to attract the council's attention, for good, or not so good, right?"

"Yeah," I said.

"I could just ask you what you've been doing, you and your vampires, that has attracted their attention, but I think it'll go quicker if I ask which rumors are true. I need to get off the phone and start gathering backup. The backup may take longer than transport or the weaponry."

"Ask," I said, not sure I wanted him to ask at all.

"That Jean-Claude has become his own bloodline and broken from his old mistress."

I was surprised, very surprised. "How the hell did that rumor get started?"

"We're wasting time, Anita, true or false?"

"Part true. He is his own bloodline. That makes it so he doesn't have to answer to his old mistress, but he hasn't broken with Europe. He's just stopped being Belle Morte's beck-and-call boy."

"That you've got a string of lovers among Jean-Claude's vamps and the local shapeshifters."

I really didn't want to answer this question. Was I embarrassed? Yes. "I don't see what my love life has to do with the Harlequin coming to town."

"Let's just say that the answer to this question will decide me on whether I ask something else, something I didn't believe. Now I'm beginning to wonder."

"Wonder what?" I asked.

"Answer the question, Anita—do you have a string of lovers?"

I sighed and said, "Define *string*."

"More than two, three, I guess." He sounded uncertain.

"Yes, then."

He was quiet for a second, then continued. "That Jean-Claude makes everyone, male or female, fuck him before they can join his kiss."

"Not true."

"That he makes the men fuck you?"

"Not true, and someone's having a better fantasy life with my life than I am."

He gave a small laugh, then said, "If you had told me no on the first question, I wouldn't even ask this next one, but here it is. That you're some kind of daywalking vampire that feeds off sex instead of blood. I don't believe that one, but I thought you might be interested in what some of your fellow monster hunters are saying about you. I think they're just jealous of your kill count."

I swallowed hard, and went back to sit on the edge of the tub.

"Anita," he said, "you're awfully quiet."

"I know."

"Anita, it's not true. You're not a daywalking vamp."

"Not the vampire part, not exactly."

"How not exactly?"

"Do you know the term *ardeur*."

"I know the French word, but that's not what you mean, is it?"

I explained, briefly, as coldly as I could, just the facts, what the *ardeur* was.

"You have to fuck people every few hours, or what?"

"Eventually I die, but before that I start draining the life out of Damian and then Nathaniel."

"What?"

"I have a vampire servant and an animal to call."

"What!" I'd never heard him sound so astonished.

I repeated myself.

"There isn't even a rumor about this, Anita. Human servants can't have vampire servants; it doesn't work that way."

"I know that," I said.

"Nathaniel is your animal to call?"

"Apparently."

"Does the council know this?"

"Yep."

"Well, shit, no wonder they sicced their dogs on you. You're lucky they didn't just kill you."

"The council is divided on the appropriate action to take about Jean-Claude and us."

"Divided how?"

"Some of them want us dead, but it's not a majority vote. They can't agree."

"So the Harlequin come to break the tie, is that it?" he asked.

"Maybe; honestly, I'm not sure."

"Is there anything else you've done that might make them decide to kill you quicker, like before I can get there?"

I thought about the fact that I might be a panwere. I thought about a lot of things, then sighed. Then I thought of one thing that we'd done that might bother the other Masters of the City in the United States enough to cry for council help. "Maybe."

"How 'maybe'? Anita, can you wait for me to get backup, or do I need to get a plane and get my ass to St. Louis? That's what I need to know."

"Truth, Edward, I don't know. Jean-Claude and I did something back in November that was pretty powerful. It might be enough to scare the Harlequin."

"What did you do?"

"We had a little private get-together with a couple of the visiting Masters of the City. The two that Jean-Claude calls friends."

"And," he said.

"And Belle Morte interfered from all the way in Europe. She messed with me and the Master of Chicago."

"Augustine," he said. "Auggie to his friends."

"You know him?"

"Of him," Edward said.

"Then you know how powerful he is."

"Yes."

"We rolled him, Edward."

"Rolled how?" he asked.

"Jean-Claude and I fed off him; we both fed the *ardeur* off him. We fed on him, and through him we fed on every person he had brought to our lands. We did this massive feed on them all. It was an amazing power rush, and all of us, vamps, beasties, anyone tied to either Jean-Claude or me by metaphysics, gained power from it."

"I'll contact the backup I want; they can join me later. I'll be on the ground in"—he paused as if checking his watch—"four hours, five at the outside. I'll be in St. Louis before sundown."

"You think it's that serious?" I asked.

"If I were a vampire, and you had a vampire servant, I might kill you just for that. But if you guys rolled Augustine, one of the most powerful masters in this country, then yeah, Anita, they'll be nervous. I'm just surprised the Harlequin didn't hit St. Louis earlier."

"I think they needed the excuse of Malcolm and his misbehaving church. The council is truly divided about Jean-Claude and his power base. I think maybe the council wouldn't agree to let the Harlequin near us, but now that they're here checking out the Church of Eternal Life, well, two birds with one stone."

"Sounds reasonable," he said. "I'll be there as soon as I can, Anita."

"Thanks, Edward."

"Don't thank me yet."

"Why not?"

"I'll see you in a few hours, Anita. Watch your back like a son of a bitch; if these guys are masters they may have wereanimals and humans to do their daywalking. Just because the sun is up doesn't make you safe."

"I know that, Edward. I probably know that better than you do."

"Maybe, but be careful until I get there."

"I'll do my best." But I was already talking to an empty phone line. He'd hung up. I hung up, too.

11

NATHANIEL WAS ASLEEP in Jean-Claude's red silk sheets. Jean-Claude himself was in Asher's room for the day, but he'd made a point of telling me he'd had the sheets changed to red because the three of us look so lovely against red. Micah's eyes caught the light from the partially opened bathroom door. His curly brown hair was a heavy darkness around the delicate triangle of his face. The door was our version of a night light here, since there was no bedside lamp, and the other light switch was across the room by the door. Micah's eyes caught that faint glow and glittered with it. His eyes were leopard eyes, or looked like leopard eyes. A doctor had told him that the optics were still human, but the eyes themselves weren't. Splitting hairs, I guess. Chimera, the same bad guy who'd made the ambush that caused Nathaniel to pick up a gun and shoot for real, had also forced Micah into animal form so long that he couldn't come all the way back. His eyes were never human. I'd asked him once what color they'd started as, and he'd said brown. I couldn't picture it. I couldn't picture his face with anything but the green-gold of the eyes he'd come to me with. They were simply Micah's eyes; anything else would have made it the face of a stranger.

His voice was quiet, that voice you use when you're trying not to wake someone in the room. "What did he say?"

"He'll be here in four or five hours. His backup will be following."
I came to the edge of the bed.

"What backup?"

"I don't know."

"You didn't ask."

"No." Truthfully, it had never occurred to me to ask.

"You trust him that much?" Micah asked.

I nodded.

Micah rolled under the red silk so he could reach my hand. He tried
to draw me onto the bed, but in a silk robe, on silk sheets, I'd learned
better. They were too slippery. I took my hand back and undid the
robe's sash. He lay back and watched me with that look a man can
get—the look that is part sex, part possession, part just male. It's not a
look that has much to do with love, not the kind that includes hearts
and flowers anyway, but it has everything to do with being together,
being real. Edward was right. Micah was my lover. Not my boyfriend.
We dated. We did movies, theatre, picnics even, at Nathaniel's insis-
tence, but in the end what had drawn us together had been sex. Lust
like a forest fire that could have burned our lives down around our
ears, but instead had saved us. Or that's how I felt. I hadn't really asked
him in so many words.

"Serious face," he whispered.

I nodded and let the robe slip to the floor. I stood in front of him
naked and had the feeling I'd had from almost the first moment, that
my skin was thick with need. He reached for me again, and this time I
let him help me climb up on the big bed. The bed was big enough that
he could draw me down beside him without either of us touching
Nathaniel's sleeping form.

In November, when Jean-Claude and I had rolled Augustine of
Chicago, we'd also figured out something else. My instant lust for
Micah, and his for me, had been vampire powers. Not Jean-Claude's,
or Augustine's, but mine. My vampire powers, mine and mine alone.
My powers may have started with Jean-Claude's marks, but they had
mutated with my necromancy and become something else, something
more. I was like a vampire of Belle Morte's line, and all of her line had
powers dealing with sex and love, though not real love, not usually.
That was beyond most of Belle's line. My version of her *ardeur* allowed
me to see the strongest need in someone's heart, and my own, and

meet those needs. When Micah had come to me, I'd needed a help-mate, someone to help me run the shapeshifter coalition that we'd just established. Someone to help me with the wereleopards that I'd inherited when I killed their old leader. I'd needed help and someone who didn't see my cold-blooded practicality as a bad thing. Micah had met those needs, and I had given him his greatest wish, to have his own wereleopards safe from Chimera, the sexual sadist who had taken them over. I'd killed Chimera, freed them all, and Micah had moved in with me. Just like that. It had been so unlike me, and in November we'd realized why; my own vampire tricks had made us a couple.

Micah was under the silk and I was on top of it. His hands danced down my body as our lips found each other. We must have moved too much because Nathaniel made a small noise. It made us freeze in mid-motion and look at him. His face was still peaceful, eyes still closed, his hair a gleam in the near dark.

Vampire powers had made Nathaniel my animal to call, and made us love each other, too. It was real love, true love, but it had begun with vampire mind tricks. But Belle Morte's powers cut both ways. As Auggie had said, "You can only cut someone as deep as you're willing to be cut." Apparently, I'd been willing to be cut to the heart.

Nathaniel stirred in his sleep again. His face flexed, frowned. He made another small sound. It was his bad dream sound. He'd had more nightmares of late. His therapist said it was because he felt safe enough with us to explore his deeper pain. We were his safe haven. Why did safety raise all the shit deeper? It seemed like it should have been the other way around, didn't it?

We reached for him at the same time—Micah's hand going for the bare paleness of his shoulder, my hand going for his cheek. We stroked him wordlessly. Most of the time petting him in his sleep was all it took to chase the bad things away. Real-life bad things weren't so easy.

There was a soft knock on the door. We both looked toward it and Nathaniel stirred, one arm pulling out of the covers. He blinked awake, his eyes confused, as if he expected to be somewhere else. He saw us and visibly relaxed. He smiled, and said, "What is it?"

I shook my head, still lying pressed in Micah's arms. Micah said, "Don't know."

I called, "What?"

It was Remus, one of the ex-military werehyenas. They'd been hired after Chimera nearly destroyed the bodybuilders and martial artists of the hyenas. As Peter had said, it wasn't real. The hyenas had liked showy muscle that had never seen real battle. They'd learned that just because muscle is pretty doesn't mean it's the real deal. "It's the Ulfric. He wants in."

Ulfric, wolf king, Richard Zeeman was at our door. The question was, why? I wanted to ask what he wanted, but he might take it wrong, so I looked at Micah.

He shrugged, lying back, one arm still curved around me, holding me along the line of his body. I stayed propped up so I could see the door, and so most of my nakedness was covered. Richard was my lover, but he didn't share nearly as well as everyone else did. I wouldn't get out of bed for him, but I wouldn't make it as bad as it could be by flaunting either. No matter what I did, we'd probably end up fighting. When we weren't having sex, that's what we did. We fought and had make-up sex, and he let me feed the *ardeur* off him. It wasn't much of a relationship lately.

"Anita"—Richard's voice—"let me in."

"Let him in, Remus," I said.

Nathaniel rolled onto his back so that the covers pooled at his waist, and the expanse of his upper body was naked to the light that came in through the door as Richard came inside. He hesitated at the door, watching us in the rectangle of light from the hallway. His hair had finally grown out enough to go a little past his shoulders in heavy chestnut waves. His hair looked black with a nimbus of gold around it now, but his hair was brown with highlights of gold and copper when the light hit it just right. He was wearing jeans and a jean jacket with a heavy wool collar. He had a small suitcase in one hand. He set it down on the floor as he came through the door.

I caught a glimpse of the guards in the hallway as he shut the door. Claudia, wererat and one of the few other women who carried a gun besides me, looked a question at me. I shook my head. It was my way of saying, *Let it go*. I wasn't sure it was a good idea, but I couldn't figure out a way to refuse him access to the bedroom without starting a fight. I didn't want to start the fight.

"May I turn on the light?" he asked, very polite.

I looked at the other two men. They nodded, and shrugged. "Sure," I said.

I was left blinking into the sudden glare. It wasn't that bright a light, but after almost complete darkness it seemed bright. When my eyes adjusted I could finally look at Richard. He was as he had always been: six feet one inch of handsome masculinity. Perfect cheekbones and a nearly permanent tan showed that somewhere back in all that Dutch blood was something darker and less European. I'd always bet on American Indian, but they actually didn't know. He was almost heartrendingly handsome. So why hadn't my new vampire powers made us the perfect couple, too? Because for my abilities to work you had to know what you wanted, what you really wanted. Richard didn't know that. He was too conflicted, too full of self-loathing, to know what his heart's desire was.

He looked at the coffin that sat near the far wall, closer to the door than to the bed. "Jean-Claude?" He made it a question.

"Damian," I said.

He nodded. "So if you start draining him of life you'll be able to check on him." Richard had actually carried Damian's nearly lifeless body to me once, so I could save the vampire.

"Yes." I pulled up the sheet so that my breasts were more covered. It bared a little more of Micah's chest, but that was okay. His body was already blocking all but the upper curve of my hip from Richard's sight. Covered was better until I knew what Richard wanted.

"Where's Jean-Claude sleeping?"

"Asher's room," I said.

He had left his suitcase by the door, but he was in the middle of the floor, halfway between the door and the bed. He licked his lips and wouldn't quite look at us. He was nervous—why?

"Jason has his new girlfriend bunking with him."

"Perdita, Perdy," I said. She'd come to us from the master of Cape Cod. She was a mermaid. A real live mermaid. The first I'd ever met. Though I'd never seen her look anything but human. I was told she really could be part fish, but I'd never seen it.

Richard nodded.

Micah moved against me and let me know he'd thought of something. Oh. "Do you want to stay here with us?" Micah asked.

Richard closed those perfectly brown eyes, the color of milk chocolate. He took a deep breath, let it out slow, then nodded.

We all exchanged a look, which was almost finished by the time he opened those eyes. We must have looked surprised, though, because he said, "I'm a shapeshifter; we like big puppy piles for sleeping."

"Most of you guys do," I said, "but you've never willingly slept with me and any of the other guys."

"This is who you are, Anita. This is who we both are." He shoved his big hands into his jacket pockets and looked at the floor. "I was on a date when I got the call that some insanely powerful vampires are in town." He looked up, and his face held that anger that he'd gotten from me through Jean-Claude's vampire marks. He shared my rage at the world, and it had made him even harder to deal with. "I had to call it an early evening, and I couldn't explain to her why."

"We had to cut our date short, too," Nathaniel said.

Richard looked at him; it was not an entirely friendly look, but his words were civil. "You guys were trying to celebrate some kind of anniversary."

"Yes," I said.

"Sorry it got ruined."

"Sorry your date got cut short," I said. My, we were being terribly polite.

"They found bugs in my house, Anita. My dates, my phone calls, everything recorded." He rocked on the heels of his boots.

"I know," I said. "Same for us."

"The Circus is the most secure place we have, so I'm here for the duration."

"Scary," I said.

"The scary part is that I might be endangering the kids I teach. If it's not fixed by Monday, maybe I should take a leave of absence."

He seemed to be asking my opinion and I didn't know what to say, but Micah did. "We've all been blindsided by this. Let's get some sleep."

Richard nodded his head, a little too rapidly, a little too often. There were guest rooms in the underground. There was even a couch big enough for him to use in the living room. So why was he here?

"I can stay?" He asked it without looking at us.

"Yes," Micah said.

"Yes," I said, my voice soft.

He looked up. "Nathaniel?"

"I'm not dominant to anyone in this room; I don't get a vote."

"It's polite to ask," Richard said.

"Yes," I said, "it is. I appreciate it."

"So do I," Nathaniel said, "but you don't have to ask. It was your bed before it was ours."

That seemed a little impolitic, but strangely Richard smiled. "Nice of someone to remember that." But he didn't sound angry as he said it. He picked up his suitcase and started walking toward the bed. He walked past the bed, and we all watched him. He put the suitcase down beside the armoire in the corner that held extra clothes for all of us. He knelt, opened the case, and began to unpack. He took his jacket off first and put it on a hanger in the armoire. Then he took out shirts, socks, and underwear and put them in the drawers. He unpacked as if we weren't there. We all exchanged looks again. This was too weird, entirely too civilized for Richard. The other shoe had to drop soon, and all hell would break loose, wouldn't it?

Micah moved the covers, letting me know to get off them enough to get under them. He was right; discretion was the better part of valor. We were all three under the red silk sheets when Richard finally finished putting everything away—including one trip with a toiletry kit to the bathroom. He left the door wide open so he had plenty of light, then walked to the light by the door and turned it off. It was so normal, it scared me. I hadn't seen him this reasonable in months, maybe years. My shoulders and arms were tight with tension. It felt like the quiet before the storm, but I couldn't tell if the tension was just me projecting. Richard and I could share each other's dreams, let alone thoughts, but right now he and I were shielding so tight that nothing got through. We were separate from each other metaphysically, or as separate as Jean-Claude's marks would let us be. It was safer that way.

Richard walked to the bed, his eyes downcast, not looking at us. He sat down on the bed near me. The three of us scooted back a little to give him more room. He must have felt the bed move, but he ignored it. He pulled off his boots and let them fall to the floor, then socks. He took off his T-shirt and I was suddenly looking at the muscled expanse of his naked back. His hair caressed the edges of all that bare skin.

I fought the urge to touch him. I was afraid of what would happen. Afraid that he would take it wrong.

He had to stand up to undo his belt, unbutton the fly. The sound of the buttons coming undone jerked things low in my body. Richard had been the man who taught me the joys of button-fly jeans.

Micah's arm curled around my waist, drawing me in closer to his body. Was he jealous?

Richard hesitated. As a shapeshifter nudity should have been second nature, maybe first, but he didn't like being nude in front of my other lovers. He just didn't. He stripped the jeans down in one motion. If he'd been wearing underwear, he wasn't now. The sight of him nude did what it always did: it made me catch my breath and think about touching him. All Richard had to do to win any fight with me was to strip. I just couldn't argue with him when he looked so scrumptious.

He let the jeans hit the floor, then turned toward the bed. His eyes were still downcast, his hair spilling forward around his face. He finally looked up, and our eyes met. I didn't try to keep my face blank. I let him see what I thought of him beautiful and nude before me. Even with Micah's body pressed against me in the bed, Richard was still beautiful.

He smiled, half shy, and half the old Richard. The Richard who had known how much I loved him, and how much he meant to me. He lifted the covers up and slid under them. He was tall enough that he had no trouble getting into the bed without help. "Scoot over . . . please," he said.

Micah scooted, moving me with him a little. Richard slid into the space we'd made. I felt the bed move, which meant Nathaniel had moved, too. The bed wasn't a king-size, it was an orgy-size bed. We'd had more people than this on it at the same time, sometimes even for sleeping.

Richard scooted down until he was almost pressed to the front of my body, but not quite. Micah's hand was still around my waist. "I'm not sure where to put my hands," Richard said.

Micah laughed, but it was a good guy laugh. "I know what you mean."

"Where do you want to put them?" Nathaniel asked.

I glanced over my shoulder and found that Nathaniel was peering over Micah's more slender body at us.

"I'm nervous, tired. I want to be touched and held."

"You're a shapeshifter," Micah said. "We all like skin contact when we're shaky."

Richard nodded. He was propped up on one elbow, and he made even Nathaniel look small. Richard was one of those large men who didn't seem that large until moments like this; then you appreciated the full physical presence of him. "I brought wolves with me. They're in one of the guest rooms. I could have my puppy pile. I didn't have to come here for that."

I swallowed hard enough that it hurt.

Micah said, "Then why are you here?"

"I'm tired of running from myself."

I wasn't sure that answered the question, but Richard seemed to think it did, and I felt Micah nod behind me. "Stop running."

"I'm not sure I know how."

It was like I wasn't there, as if whatever issues they were discussing had less to do with me than with the two of them. Maybe the three of them—or did Nathaniel feel as left out as I did?

"This is a good start," Micah said.

Richard nodded, then finally gave me the full attention of those eyes. Those eyes that I once thought would be the eyes I woke up with every morning. Lately he hadn't slept over much. "I don't know how to do this."

"Do what?" I whispered.

"I want to kiss you, but I don't want to have sex with everyone in this bed."

I wasn't sure if he meant he didn't want to have sex while the other men were in the bed or if he didn't want to actually have sex with them. I was pretty sure both were true.

"I've been wanting to touch you since you took off your shirt," I said. There, that was the truth. Maybe if we told the truth we'd be okay.

He smiled, and it was Richard's smile. That smile that he sometimes gave that let you know he really did know how lovely he was to look at. He usually came off humble, but then he had that smile.

He leaned in toward me, his hands still chastely to himself. Our lips touched, his hair spilled along my cheek. Micah's hand eased from around my waist, letting me know I could move where I wanted to move. Or that's how I took it. I let my hand rest against the swell of Richard's chest. His hand cupped the side of my face. We kissed, and his lips were still as soft, as full, as kissable as they had always been. My hand slid down the curve of his chest to his waist. He pulled me in against his body, and the kiss grew to something fuller, deeper. My body fell against his, my hand tracing across his back, not sure whether to touch lower. His body was already growing with need. I wanted to react to that need, but he'd said he didn't want to have sex with all of us in the bed, and no one was leaving.

He drew back from the kiss, breathless, panting, eyes laughing. "God, how do you do that to me?"

My own voice came breathy. "You, too."

He laughed, then his gaze slid past me to the other men. His eyes darkened for a moment. "I can't, I can't, not yet."

"Truthfully, Richard, this is more than I ever thought you'd do with Micah and Nathaniel."

He nodded. "Me, too."

"Would it totally spoil things if I asked what changed your mind?" Nathaniel asked it. I'd wanted to ask it, but I wouldn't have.

Richard looked across the bed at the other man. "It's none of your business."

"No, it's not," Nathaniel said.

Richard bowed his head, then nodded. "Okay, I love Anita. I'm trying to learn to love all of her, even the part that wants to live with two other men." His eyes were uncertain, a little angry.

Nathaniel said, "My therapist told me that if I'm an equal partner in our relationship I need to ask for what I want. Did yours tell you that you need to resolve your feelings about Anita?"

Richard ignored the question. "What did you ask Anita? What aren't you getting from her?"

"I'll answer yours, if you'll answer mine."

Richard nodded, as if that was fair. "Yeah, my therapist says I have to either come to terms with Anita's life, or move on."

"You know I'm into the bondage and submission scene?" Nathaniel said.

I wanted not to be naked in the bed with them while they had this conversation, but if they could be honest, I could lie there and let them do it. "I know. Raina talked about you a lot." Raina had been the old lupa of the wolf pack. She'd taken Richard's virginity and trained Nathaniel to be a good little pain slut.

Micah and I looked back to Nathaniel. It was like a therapy tennis match.

Nathaniel nodded. "Anita won't do it with me, and I want her to."

"She's not much more comfortable with that side of herself than I am," Richard said.

"I know," Nathaniel said.

"Did she agree to do it?"

"Not yet."

"Are you going to leave her if she doesn't come across with it?"

Micah and I lay back between them, feeling superfluous.

"I've asked permission to have someone else abuse me, but save sex for Anita."

Richard looked at me, finally, and I wished he hadn't. "You really know how to pick them, don't you?"

"What's that supposed to mean?" I asked, but it was hard trying to sound indignant naked in a bed with three men.

Richard laughed, a good, open laugh. He kissed me hard and fast. I lay there and frowned at him. "It means let's go to sleep."

He settled on his side, facing me. I hesitated a second, then turned onto my other side. It started a chain reaction with Micah and Nathaniel following suit. It took us a while, but finally we were all settled. Richard's body spooned along the back of mine, Micah against me, and distant Nathaniel against him. My hand went over both of them, so I could still touch Nathaniel. Richard had the hardest time figuring out where to put his arm. He finally seemed to think, *To hell with it*, because he let his arm follow the line of mine, so he was both holding more of me and helping me hold the other two men. For sex, it would have been fun, but for sleeping, I thought I'd have trouble relaxing. But either it had been a long night, or the sensation of being held between Richard and Micah's body was more comforting than I realized. Nathaniel went to sleep first, as he always did. Micah and Richard went at almost the same time. Sleep wrapped over me, Richard's breath warm against my neck.

12

I WOKE IN a tangle of bodies. I was on my back with Micah and Richard half on top of me, as if even in their sleep they had fought over who would touch the most of me. The scent of their skins had mingled into a rich perfume that tightened my body. But I was still pinned and not comfortable at all. I was so tangled that I couldn't even rise enough to see Nathaniel on the far side of Micah. I thought the uncomfortable position had been what woke me; then I caught movement at the foot of the bed. I held my breath. Was it one of the guards? Somehow I knew it wasn't.

The faint light from the half-open bathroom door didn't really show me anything. It was almost as if the light were being sucked at by the dark, as if eventually the darkness would swallow the light completely. My pulse was thudding in my throat, so hard I could barely breathe past it, and swallowing hurt. I knew who was in the dark, and I knew I dreamed. But just because it's a dream doesn't mean it can't hurt you.

"What is that?"

I screamed, a short, sharp scream. I was looking into Richard's face. He was awake. He started easing up to sit, and I moved with him. He tried to shake Micah awake, but I didn't bother. I'd had this dream before.

"Wake them up," he whispered, eyes searching the darkness.

"Her animals to call are all cats; they won't wake."

"Who . . . Marmee . . ."

I stopped the words with fingers against his lips. "Don't," I whispered. I don't know why we were whispering. She would hear us. But there's something about being in the dark when you know the predator is out there, that makes you whisper. You try to be small and quiet. You pray that it passes you by. But this wasn't a predator, exactly; this was the entire night, given life and substance, and a mind. I smelled jasmine and summer rain, and other scents of a land that I had never seen except in vision and dream. The land where Marmee Noir had begun. I had no idea how old she was, didn't want to know. I was a necromancer. I could have tasted her age on my psychic tongue, but I didn't know if I could swallow that many centuries. I feared I'd choke.

"Necromancer." Her voice eased through the night like a sweet-scented wind.

I managed to swallow past the beating of my heart. "Marmee Noir," I said, and my voice was only a little hoarse. It was better with Richard beside me, awake. His arm wrapped around me as if he felt it, too, that together we were more here. Maybe our accidental sharing of dreams, Richard and me and Jean-Claude, had a purpose. One we just hadn't understood until now.

I leaned into the curve of Richard's body, and his arm tightened. My hand on his bare chest let me feel the beat of his fear against my palm.

The darkness gathered, almost the way light will narrow down to a point of brightness, except this was darkness compacted, squeezed down as if a small black hole were forming in front of our eyes. The black hole took on the vague shape of a woman in a cloak.

I thought, very carefully, in my head at Richard, "Don't look at her face."

"I know the rules," he said out loud. He had heard me; good, great. Mind-to-mind talking was still not my best thing in dream or out of it.

"Do you truly believe that not looking upon my face will save you?"

Great, she read minds, too. I'd had much lesser vamps be able to do it. I shouldn't have been surprised.

"Tell me again why Micah and Nathaniel won't wake?" Richard asked, his voice soft, but not a whisper anymore. It was too late for whispering. She'd found us.

"Necromancer," she said.

"Cats are her creatures to call, all cats, so she can keep them out of the dream. Jean-Claude was with me last time and she was able to keep him out, too. She doesn't do wolves."

"Your wolf will not save you this time, necromancer."

"How about mine?" Richard said, and a low growl trickled out from between his lips. It raised the hair on my arms, and that part of me where the beasts waited, stirred. The best I can describe it is that the place is like a cave where my animals wait. They walk up a long corridor to get to me. Since they're inside me, that can't exactly be right. But it's the visualization that works for me.

In dream, though, the wolf inside me could come out and play. My wolf was pale, white and cream with a black saddle and marks on her head. She crouched in front of me and joined her growl with Richard's. I dug my free hand into her fur and found it like last time: soft, coarse. I could feel the vibration of the growl through my hand, feel the muscle and meat of her body. She was real, my she-wolf. She was real.

Richard stopped growling and stared at the wolf. She turned eyes that were brown and glowing to him. My eyes when vampire powers had filled them. They stared at each other, then she turned back to the darkness. When Richard looked down at me, his eyes were the amber of his wolf.

"Your master has left you both with the last piece undone," she said. Her voice floated around the almost-body she'd formed from the shadows. She came to the foot of the bed.

The wolf crouched, and growled, that sound that was absolutely serious. It was the last warning sound before violence.

She didn't try to touch the bed. She actually stopped moving. I remembered seeing her body in that distant room jerk when my wolf bit her in dream last time. Had it hurt her enough to make her hesitate? Had it hurt her enough to make a true threat? God, I hoped so.

"You can still be enslaved to any master stronger than he, and there is no one stronger than me, necromancer."

I clung to the wolf's fur and Richard's body. "I believe that last part, Marmee Noir."

"Then why has your master left this door open?"

The question puzzled me.

"I do not know that expression on your face. I have been too long without humans."

"I'm puzzled," I said.

"I will help you not be puzzled, necromancer. I came tonight to make you mine. To shatter your triumvirate and make you my human servant. I do not need to share blood to own your soul."

I was trying to breathe past my pulse again, and having trouble doing it.

"You won't touch her," Richard said, and his voice sounded gravelly, the beginnings of the change in the sound of his words.

"I think you are right, wolf. I think it would be a battle with you by her side. I am not ready for battle, not yet. But there are others who know what Jean-Claude has not done."

"Who?" I managed to ask.

"Do I need to say the word?" she asked.

I opened my mouth to say it, but Richard said, "It's against your laws to say it out loud. A killing offense, Jean-Claude said."

She laughed, and the darkness tightened around the bed like a giant's fist. You knew, could feel, that it could crush the bed and everyone on it, if it wanted to. "That is not the trick I have come to play, wolf, but fine: Harlequin. They know you are not safe. They know that I am close to waking. They fear the darkness."

"Everyone's afraid of you," I said. The wolf had begun to relax under my grip. You could only hold on to emergency mode for so long. Apparently, we were talking, not fighting. Fine by me.

"True, and I would have taken you tonight. I planned on it."

"You said that already," Richard said, his voice a little more human, but sullen.

"Then let me not repeat myself, wolf." Her anger was not hot, but cold, as if an icy wind danced across my bare skin. Richard shivered beside me. I didn't think I'd have to caution him to be nice. That flex of power explained it nicely. "By tomorrow they will be upon you, and I do not want them to have you."

"Have me, how?" I asked.

"I will allow Jean-Claude to have you, because you are already his. But no one else. I would prefer you were my human servant, but Jean-Claude is acceptable. No one else, necromancer. I will destroy you before I allow the Harlequin to make you their slave."

"Why do I matter to you?"

"I like the taste of you, necromancer," she said, "and no one else can have you. I am a jealous Goddess, and I do not share power."

I swallowed past the lump in my throat. I nodded as if that made sense to me.

"A parting gift, necromancer, wolf." The shadowed form vanished, but she wasn't gone. The darkness suddenly had weight and grew thicker, as if the night itself could become so thick it would eventually crawl down your throat and choke you. She'd done almost exactly that to me before. The scent of jasmine and rain was thick on my tongue.

The wolf growled and Richard echoed her. "Can you bite that which you cannot find?" Her voice echoed from everywhere and nowhere. "My mistake was trying to be too human for you. I do not repeat mistakes."

The wolf crouched, but Marmee Noir was right, there was no body to bite here now. I had to find a way to visualize a target for my wolf. I struggled to believe that my wolf could bite the night itself.

Richard grabbed my shoulders, turned me to him. His eyes were still amber and inhuman. He kissed me. He drew back enough to say, "I can taste her power in your mouth."

I nodded.

He kissed me again, and this time he stayed with our mouths pressed together. He poured that warm, rising energy that was shapeshifter into me. He pushed it into me through our mouths, his hands, our bodies. I kept my grip on my wolf, but the rest of me I gave to Richard, and gradually I could taste pine, and leaf mold, rich and thick and foresty. I smelled the musk of wolf fur. I smelled pack. I smelled home, and the last taste of jasmine vanished under the taste of Richard's power, Richard's wolf, and finally, at the end, simply the taste of Richard. The sweet, thick taste of his kiss. The dream ended with a kiss.

13

I WOKE ON the floor of Jean-Claude's bedroom with Nathaniel staring down at me. I glanced to my right and found Richard on the floor with Micah beside him. There were guards in the room, and the smell of burning.

Richard's first words were, "You all right?"

I nodded.

His second words were, "What's burning?"

"The bed," Micah said.

"What?" I asked.

"The cross in its bag that you have underneath your pillow got hot enough that it set the pillow on fire," Micah said.

"Shit," I said.

Claudia appeared above me with a fire extinguisher in her hands. "What the hell happened, Anita?"

I stared up at her, and there was a lot of her to stare up at. She was one of the tallest people I'd ever met, and lifted weights in a serious fashion. Her black hair was in its usual tight ponytail, her face free of makeup, and still strikingly beautiful.

"That bitch queen vampire came again, didn't she?" Remus said.

I tried to sit up, but if Nathaniel hadn't caught me, I'd have fallen back to the floor. The last time I'd fought off the darkness, I'd been damn near killed by my own beasts trying to tear their way out of my human body. Apparently today I'd just be weak. I could live with that.

Remus was standing scowling at the foot of the bed. He was tall, muscled, and blond, but his face was a crisscross of scars, as if he'd been badly broken and put back together again. When he was angry enough, his face mottled, and you could see the pale lines against the flushed skin of his face. He almost never made eye contact with anyone. I think because he didn't want to see in others' faces what they thought of his own. But when he got upset enough he'd meet your eyes, then you could see how lovely the eyes were, all green and gray with long lashes. Tonight I got a good dose of the eyes.

I leaned into the warm curve of Nathaniel's body and said, "Yeah, it was the Mother of All Darkness."

"At least your beasts aren't trying to tear you apart this time," Claudia said.

"Yeah," I said, "at least."

Then I felt something stirring inside me, as if something big and furred had brushed the inside of my body. "Oh, shit," I whispered.

Nathaniel leaned in and sniffed just above my face. "I smell something. Cat, but it's not leopard." He closed his eyes and breathed in deep. "It's not lion."

I shook my head.

Richard said, "She said it was a parting gift."

I looked inside myself, in that place where the beasts waited. There was a gleam of eyes, then a face came out of the shadows. A face the color of night and flame: tiger.

"Oh, shit," I said louder, "tiger."

"Crap," Claudia said.

To my knowledge there was only one weretiger in the entire St. Louis area. Christine worked as an insurance agent and was miles away. She'd never get here in time for me to share my beast with her and keep it from tearing me apart. Either Marmee Noir had decided it was time for me to finally be a shapeshifter for real, and she'd chosen tiger, or she meant to kill me. If she couldn't have me, no one could. Possessive bitch.

But I was better at controlling the beast than I had been the last time she tried this. I called the other animals. We could play metaphysical tag for a while, at least. The black panther looked frail compared to the great striped beast. The wolf growled and flared its ruff of fur. The tiger stared at them, waiting. The lioness came from the darkness last, almost the same size as the tiger. They were animals that should never have met in the wild, never have tried their great strengths against one another. But the inside of my body was a lot weirder than any zoo. The beasts stared at the newcomer, and we waited. By calling them all at once, I kept myself from trying to turn into any single one of them. But eventually my body would choose, and when that happened there had to be a weretiger in the room.

"Call Christine," Micah said. He'd helped me learn this control. He knew what I was doing.

"Jean-Claude warned me that Anita might be collecting more kitty-cats," Remus said, "so we went shopping." He turned to one of the guards by the door. "Go get Soledad. We need her ASAP."

The man went out the door at a jog. Remus turned back to me. "She'll do what needs doing."

"She's a wererat?" I managed to say.

"She's pretending to be one of Rafael's rats, but she's a tiger. We had to promise to keep her secret before she'd agree to stay in town."

"She's probably running from an arranged marriage. Tigers are weird about keeping it in the family," Claudia said.

"What?" I said.

"We'll explain later, promise," Claudia said.

Remus said, "Most of the solo tigers I've met all hide what they are really well. Most of them can even hide their energy enough to pass for human."

I wanted to look at Richard, but didn't dare. Even the thought made the wolf stand up straighter and think about coming closer. Once Richard had played human for me, and I'd been fooled. I buried my face against Nathaniel's arm, smelled his leopard, and the wolf quieted, but the leopard began to pace.

I still didn't have a werelion to call my own. I wasn't even sure we had a lion in the place tonight, but I should have known that Remus and Claudia would think of it. "We better send for the lions, too," she said.

Remus just looked at the door. One of the other guards opened the door, then hesitated. "Which one?"

"Travis."

The guard went. I would have protested the choice, but of the few lions we had he was probably one of the best. None of the local lions really appealed to me—they were too weak. My lioness didn't want food, she wanted a mate. I'd worked hard not to give her one. Eventually she'd pick one whether I liked it or not. Or that was the prevailing theory. Since what I was doing metaphysically was pretty much impossible, it was just a theory. None of us truly knew how all this was going to turn out. I sat in Nathaniel's arms and tried to think evenly about all the beasts. But Nathaniel was too close, and the scent of his skin too real. The leopard turned and began to pace up that corridor that led to pain.

I gripped Nathaniel's arm. "I can't hold them."

Richard crawled to me and put his arm by my face. The musk of wolf was there, to slow the leopard and send it circling around, not trying to come out. But now the wolf paced toward the light. Not good.

Travis got there before Soledad. His blond-brown curls were tousled from sleep, his face still not wholly awake. He was wearing the bottoms of a pair of cotton pajamas, and nothing else. They'd dragged him from bed with no time to do anything. He was a college student and I wondered briefly if his Rex, lion king, had made him stay here with us instead of going to class.

He knelt by my legs and didn't even react to the fact that I was nude. Either the guard had explained the problem or he could feel it. His sleepy face began to clear, and an intelligence that was both too acute and one of his best features began to fill his gold-brown eyes. He held his wrist out to me, and the lioness began to pace. The three of them played tag with my beasts. As one moved, they traded whose skin I was smelling. But it would not last; eventually my body would pick someone.

The tiger moved up, and there was no tiger to smell. But the others distracted me, calling their beasts, keeping us playing our metaphysical musical chairs, except I was the chair.

I waited for the tiger to try to tear me apart as the other three beasts had done periodically, but the tiger sat there, waiting. Wolf, leopard, lion; the three men played me like a game of tag, putting their bare skin close enough for me to smell it, touch it, and the tiger waited. Then a thing happened that had never happened before with any of the other beasts—the tiger began to fade; like some monstrous version of the Cheshire cat, it began to fade in pieces. I settled back in Nathaniel and Richard's arms, with Travis kneeling beside us. Travis was close, but not as close as the other two. My mistake. The tiger fading had made me let my guard down. Big mistake. The leopard and wolf paced around each other. The lioness saw her opportunity and charged past them, up that long black tunnel inside me. The leopard and wolf were still circling each other. The lioness didn't care about them. She just wanted to be real.

Richard put his wrist near my face, but it was too late for simple measures. The lioness hit my body as if it were a wall. It felt like a small car crashed into me from the inside. The impact jerked me off the floor, tore me out of their surprised hands. My body hit the floor and they tried to cradle me, but it was too late. The lioness stretched inside my body, trying to fit all that huge cat inside me. There was no room. I was too small. The lioness was trapped, trapped in a small, dark space. She reacted like any wild animal; she tried to destroy the trap. Tried to claw and bite her way out of it. The trouble was, my body was what she was trying to tear her way out of.

I shrieked, while the muscles in my body tried to tear themselves off my bones. You try to forget how much it hurts, and then it's happening and you can't forget. Can't think, can't be, can't do anything but hurt!

Weight, pressing me down, hands holding my wrists on the floor. Something pinning my lower body. I opened my eyes and found Travis above me. The lioness screamed her frustration, because she'd seen him before. She didn't like him. She didn't want him. Travis tried to grab my face in his hands, tried to take my beast into him, but the lioness was too close to the surface, and we agreed on one thing. Travis was weak. We didn't want him.

I bit him, sank teeth into his wrist. The lioness meant it to chase him away, and so did I, but the moment that hot blood spilled into my mouth, all I could taste was lion. I could taste Travis's beast in his blood and that was enough. I looked up at him with his blood spilling out of my mouth, and I shoved my beast into him. I gave the lioness what she wanted. I gave her a body that could make her real. The lioness spilled out of me in a rush of heat and power that felt like it was taking my skin with it. I screamed, and Travis's screams echoed mine.

One minute Travis was staring down at me, the next second he exploded, bits of skin and meat and liquid spraying over me. A lion rose above me, shaking its maned head, staggering as it straddled me, as if even in lion form he hurt. He made a sound halfway between a roar and a moan, and fell to his side beside me. I lay there, my body aching from my toes to the roots of my hair. God, I hurt, but it was fading, a bone-grinding ache, but it was fading. As it faded, I was able to pay attention to the fact that I was covered in that clear, warm goo that shapeshifters seem to lose instead of blood when they change. The more violent the change the more of it there seems to be. I'd given my beast to Travis, and even though it wasn't exactly my beast, it was as if my lioness did go to him, for a while. The pain faded enough so I could think about something else, and the first thought was that when Haven had taken my beast, he hadn't been weakened by it. Hell, Nathaniel, Micah, even Clay and Graham didn't collapse like Travis did. He was weak. I needed someone strong.

Then I had other things to worry about, because the wolf decided she wanted a chance. She ran up that tunnel like a pale ghost. I had time to say, "Wolf," then she hit me, and I was back to writhing on the floor.

I reached out, and Richard was there. He wrapped his arms around me, held me tight while my body tried to tear itself apart. He pinned my face with one strong hand. He called his beast. His power hit mine, and it felt like my blood was boiling. I shrieked, tried to tell him to stop. He leaned in to kiss me, while his power combined with mine to boil me alive. I tried to give him my wolf, but I couldn't. It couldn't get past the weight of his power.

His power began to push my beast back like boiling water pushing a forest fire back. It worked, but it felt like my skin was singeing and smoking as he forced my beast back. He drove it back to that place deep inside me. He drove it back, and it went whimpering. I whimpered with it, because it felt as if my body had been burned with power. I tried to look down at my body, and the world swam in streamers of color and nausea. I'd seen Richard force people to swallow their beasts before, but I'd never known that it hurt.

When my vision cleared, Richard was smiling down at me. He looked pleased. "I wasn't sure it was going to work," he said, and there was strain in his own voice as if it had cost him something, too.

I whispered in a voice that was broken from screaming, "That hurt."

His smile faded around the edges, but I didn't have time to worry about his hurt feelings, because the leopard spilled up into me like poison trying to find a way to drip out of my skin.

Nathaniel's arms found me, but Micah took me from him. Micah wrapped his arms around me, pinned me to his body. My leopard knew his, knew the smell and taste of it. The energy went into him like a huge hot breath. It washed over his human body, and fur followed the power, like turning a shirt inside out. Micah was one of the smoothest shifts of any wereanimal I'd ever seen. Only Chimera had changed more easily and less messily than he did.

I was left clasped to the front of his furred body. Held by a body that was half man and half leopard. Travis had only two shapes: lion and human. Every other wereanimal in the room had three: animal, human, and half-and-half. Once I'd thought you had to be powerful to do the half-human form. But I'd been spending too much time around really powerful wereanimals. Now, I thought that only the weak couldn't do it.

I let Micah hold me, but I was too weak to hold him back. He laid me gently on the floor and lay down on his side beside me, propped up on one elbow. I stared up into his black-furred face, a strangely graceful mix of cat and human. His eyes looked just as at home in this face as his other one. They were both Micah to me.

"Did you do that to make a point?" Richard's voice, angry.

Micah looked up at him and spoke in that gravelly purr that he had in this shape. "What point would that be?"

"That I caused her more pain making her swallow her beast than you did by taking it."

"I took her beast because I'm not powerful enough to make her swallow it, and because being forced to swallow it can hurt, a lot."

"So I cause her more pain, and you come off the hero."

If I hadn't been exhausted, and aching from head to toe, I'd have told Richard to stop it, not to fight, but I was too tired. He'd slept over. He'd helped me with Marmee Noir. It had all been going so well. I didn't want it to go badly. Damn it, damn it.

"I called her leopard, instead of letting Nathaniel do it, because I can do this." He moved away enough so he wasn't touching me, and then it was like magic. It was as if the black fur were tiny flames that spilled off and blew away in the wind of his power, and everywhere the black blew away there was skin underneath. Everyone else looked as if they were being torn apart and remade, or pulled inside out when they shifted. The best you could hope for was to have the other body melt away and the beast, or the human, pull itself out of the other form. But Micah, Micah just changed. One minute leopardman, the next human again. If I hadn't seen Chimera shift from one form to the other like water spilling back and forth between hands, I'd have said Micah was the best at shifting I'd ever seen.

Micah looked up at Richard. "Nathaniel would have been trapped in leopard form for hours."

I couldn't see Richard's face because I was turned to Micah, and it seemed like too much effort to turn my head the other way. But I heard the disbelief in his voice. "It's supposed to cost if you change back before six hours, sometimes longer. Aren't you exhausted?"

"No," Micah said.

"Are you disoriented at all?"

"I wouldn't want to jump to my feet, but give me a few minutes and I'll be fine."

"I've never seen anyone who can shift back and forth like that."

"I've seen one other who was better," Micah said.

"Who?"

"Chimera," and just saying it caused Micah's face to take on that serious, sorrow-filled expression that I knew too well.

I reached up to touch his arm. I'd have liked to touch his face, but those extra inches seemed too much effort. He smiled down at me, as if he knew what even that small effort had cost.

A woman's voice said, "If this guy could change shape easier than that, I'd have liked to meet him."

Soledad came to stand over us. She wasn't as tall as some of the guards, well under six feet, but from flat on the floor, she looked tall enough. She was slender but curvy, with hair cut boy short and dyed a shade of yellow that didn't occur in nature. With the hair you'd expect more makeup, but she usually did lipstick and just enough liner to accent her brown eyes. She stared down at me with that look she usually had, like she thought something was funny and would laugh any minute. I'd realized a few days ago that it was her version of a blank face.

I might have asked her what she was thinking, staring down at me, but the tiger flashed inside the darkness in me. *No, please, no,* I thought.

Soledad stared down at me. The smile slipped away from her face, and I saw something I hadn't expected for a moment: fear. I might have asked what she was afraid of, but the tiger started racing up that long dark hallway inside me. I reached up to her.

She hesitated.

Claudia said, "Do your job, Soledad."

She leaned over to take my hand, saying, "In this world I would rather live two days like a tiger than a hundred years like a sheep."

I might have asked what she was quoting, but the moment her hand touched mine, the tiger sped up. It bounded down that hallway, and I braced for the impact.

14

THE IMPACT NEVER came. The tiger hit my skin, my body, and kept going. I didn't give my beast to Soledad; it just washed out of me and into her. It didn't hurt me; it was as if all that went down my hand to hers was power. It just happened to look like a tiger. I wasn't sure that was it at all because Soledad didn't change shape. She half-collapsed around me, catching herself with her free hand so she didn't fall on top of me. Her breath came in sharp pants, as if something hurt, but I wasn't feeling it. I was just holding her hand and watching her face.

She managed to whisper, "You don't hold tiger inside you."

"I think you're right," I said. My voice still sounded hoarse from all the screaming, but at least I could talk above a whisper.

"What's wrong?" Claudia asked from behind us.

"I think Marmee Noir couldn't turn me into a tiger," I said. I kept looking at Soledad's face, though. She still looked hurt. I asked, "Are you all right?"

She nodded, but her lips were pressed in a tight, thin line. I think she was lying to me about being all right.

"I think she's hurt," I said.

Claudia knelt beside us. "Soledad, are you hurt?"

She shook her head.

"Tell me you aren't hurt," Claudia said.

Soledad just kept shaking her head. Claudia helped the other woman to her feet, and Soledad's knees wouldn't hold her. Claudia had to catch her, or she'd have fallen to the floor. Remus came on the other side of her and helped ease her to the edge of the bed. He asked, "What's wrong with her?"

"I'm not sure," Claudia said.

Soledad found her voice. "That was not a weretiger."

I tried to sit up, and Micah had to help me. Richard moved in on the other side to help me sit between them. "It was Marmee Noir," I said.

"Who?" Soledad asked.

"The Mother of All Darkness, the queen of the vampires."

"It smelled like tiger, not vampire," she said.

"Tigers are one of her animals to call," I said.

Soledad shook her head and leaned against Claudia for a moment. "All right, I admit it, I don't feel so good."

"Why didn't she bring her beast?" Nathaniel asked.

"Anita isn't a weretiger, so the tiger couldn't be as real as the rest of the beasts," Micah said.

"What do you mean?" Richard asked.

"We'd been wondering if Anita is picking up beasts because she survived attacks, or if it's vampire powers, and she'll collect animals to call as if they are types of lycanthropy. I think this answers the question. She's never been attacked by a weretiger, and Chimera didn't hold tiger as one of his shapes."

"So why try to call tiger?" Richard said. "Why not call one of the cats Anita already has?"

"I don't know," Micah said.

I had a thought. "She's been inside my head deep enough to know that I didn't think we had a tiger nearby. She said she wanted to make me hers, but if she couldn't have me, then . . ."

"She meant for the tiger to tear you apart," Richard said, softly.

"Or she was trying to make you a tiger from a distance," Soledad said. "I don't think she knew what would happen. I don't think she cared what would happen. The power that brushed me didn't think like a tiger."

"What did it think like?" I asked.

"A serial killer, a butcher. Tigers only hunt when they're hungry. This thing hunts because it's bored."

"Yeah," I said, "that sounds like Mommie Dark. Sorry you got a taste of her, Soledad."

She gave a weak smile. "My job to take the hits for you, right?" But she was pale, and looked as close to fainting as I thought I'd ever see one of the guards.

"Chimera might not have been a tiger," Remus said, "but he did hold hyena, snake, and bear, at least those three more. Why doesn't Anita react to them, too?"

Micah shrugged. "She's never been attacked by them. She seems to need to be bled by an animal first." He stroked his hand down my bare back. It reminded me that we were nude, but strangely because everyone else treated it like it was nothing, so could I.

Richard settled in closer to my other side, as if that one touch of Micah's made him have to touch me, too. Or maybe he was just nervous and letting himself take comfort. I looked for bad motives for Richard. I didn't mean to do it, but he'd hurt me so badly and so often that I finally realized I looked for the negative in him, not the positive. I took a deep breath in and let it out slow.

"You all right?" Remus asked, but his eyes did a slide to each side of me, as if he knew what was wrong.

I nodded, and the movement was too fast. I ached, but it was sharper than that. The pain would fade, but damn, I didn't know how the real wereanimals did it. Changing completely had to hurt worse than this in-between stuff.

Remus asked, "Do you know why you don't react to all of Chimera's animal forms?"

"Jean-Claude thinks maybe I need a vamp with that animal to call to mess with me before the beast rises."

"So a combination of the attacks you've survived and vamp powers," he said.

"Something like that," I said.

Richard moved his hand across my shoulders, drawing me in against his body, and away from Micah. I tried not to tense up, but failed. He stopped in midmotion and just kept his hand on me. The movement that had been so natural was suddenly awkward. Awkward moments when I'm naked make me want clothes.

"Then you should react to us, the hyenas, because we're Asher's animal to call and he has messed with you, Anita. Messed with you so much he almost killed you."

I tried not to think about Asher, tried not to dwell on what we had done together the last time we'd been allowed alone together. His bite was orgasmic; combine that with actual sex and it was an experience you'd give your life for, and I'd almost done just that.

Micah touched my shoulder. "Anita, don't."

I jumped and looked at him, startled. He was right, I'd almost thought too hard about Asher. Just the memory could come back and duplicate the pleasure, at the most inopportune moments, or the most embarrassing. I shoved thoughts of Asher and his hair like spun gold as far away as I was able. But he never seemed to be too far from my thoughts lately, not since the night that we'd both gotten so caught up in his ability to bring pleasure. . . .

Micah grabbed me, hard, and turned me to look at him. "Anita, think about something else."

I nodded. "You're right, you are right."

"You're still having flashbacks to that night?" Richard made it a question.

I nodded.

He touched my back again, tentatively, gently. Not trying to move me away from Micah, but just touching me. That I could deal with. "Hard to compete with someone who can make you orgasm just from remembering."

I turned and looked at him. He looked away, as if he wasn't certain I'd like what I saw on his face. I already knew he was jealous of the other men. I couldn't even blame him, I guess. He let all that heavy hair fall forward, to help hide his face. It wasn't as long as Asher's hair, but the gesture was similar. Asher used his hair to hide the scars that the old Inquisition had given him centuries ago when they'd tried to burn the devil out of him with holy water. Was Richard mimicking that hiding gesture on purpose, or by accident?

Travis, the lion, gave a gasping breath. It turned my attention to him and away from Richard. Micah let go of me so I could run my hand down the soft furred side of the lion. Travis's lion was a pale straw gold. He rolled over on his stomach and looked at me with a perfect lion face, but the look out of that face wasn't lion. The look said, clearly, that there was still a person in there. Lions just didn't give you that disgusted look.

"I'm sorry it hurt," I said.

He shook his head hard enough to fluff his mane. It was dry. I never understood that, but though changing shape was wet work, the product at each end was always mostly dry. The floor or bed would be wet, people around them could be wet, but they were dry. I'd asked all the lycanthropes in my life how that worked, and they didn't know either.

"I'll take Travis to find food," Nathaniel said. He stood there, still nude, still covered in some of the gunk that had managed to miss the lion.

"You'll need to shower," Micah said.

"I'll catch one in the group showers."

Nathaniel was quietly counting himself out for the morning feed—morning sex. It occurred to me then that I hadn't fed last night before bed. The *ardeur* hadn't risen, and we hadn't woken it on purpose.

I looked toward Damian's coffin, but the bed blocked my view. "Shit," I said, softly.

"Jean-Claude says that you can practice going longer between feedings," Nathaniel said.

"But I have to feed now." I sounded disappointed and couldn't help it. Having sex when you wanted to was one thing; being forced to have sex because you might die was different. I didn't like to be forced to do anything, even things I enjoyed.

"I'll take Travis to the food area, and I'll clean up." He looked at the two men still beside me. I caught a quick flash of feeling. He was out of here. He could stand his ground when he needed to, but Nathaniel didn't really like to play the king-of-the-hill games, especially when I was the hill. He knew it pissed me off, so he opted out most of the time. Micah, too, sometimes. They lived with me, which meant they had to understand me better than some of the other men in my life. Okay, better than Richard. There, I'd said it, at least in my head. He usually turned everything into a pissing contest. Trouble was, I felt like I was the one getting pissed on.

"Who did you feed on last?" Richard asked.

"Me," Micah said, and looked at the other man.

They had a moment where they just looked at each other, and like last night in the bed, I felt superfluous. "I don't know how to do this," Richard said.

"Just say it," Micah said.

"I don't want to have to ask your permission to have sex with Anita."

Micah laughed then, a sharp, surprised burst of sound. "I can't believe you said that."

"Well, I don't," Richard said.

"It's not my permission you need, Richard," Micah said.

Then Richard seemed to get it, because he looked at me. He actually had the grace to look embarrassed. "I didn't mean it that way."

"How did you mean it?" I asked, and tried to keep the words as neutral as I could.

"I'm trying to get along with the other men in your life. I don't know how to do that, Anita. I want to ask you to feed on me, but I feel like I have to ask for everyone's okay, not just yours; am I wrong?"

I felt my face soften. He was trying so hard. I touched his hair. There was an edge of drying goop in it. I guess I was a bigger mess since Travis had been practically on top of me when he shifted. Violent shifting is always messier. "We need to get cleaned up," I said.

He gave me uncertain eyes.

"I'll go with Nathaniel to the showers," Micah said, standing up. He petted Travis's back. "Come on, ol' lion, we'll get you fed."

Micah bent over and gave me a quick kiss and a reassuring smile. He did his best to let me know it was all right with him. One of my favorite things about Micah was that he usually made things better, easier, not worse.

He walked out with the huge, slinking form of the lion on one side and Nathaniel on the other. Nathaniel blew me a kiss from the door, but didn't try for a kiss on the lips. I wasn't sure why, but I'd have liked the kiss.

Richard touched my arm, gently. It made me look at him. Whatever he saw on my face didn't make him happy. His eyes showed it. Since I didn't know what was in my eyes, I couldn't change it. Whatever he saw on my face was what was there to see.

He gave a smile that left his eyes sad. "Let's use the bathtub and clean up." He looked down, his hair sliding around his face. He took a breath deep enough that it moved his shoulders up and down. "If that's all right with you."

I touched his arm. "A nice hot bath would help with the aches. Does it hurt this much to shift completely?"

Richard frowned, thinking, then shook his head. "No, I mean it hurts while you're doing it sometimes, but with practice, no. You seem to be stuck at the early stages when it hurts the most."

"Great," I said.

I heard water running in the bathroom. Remus or Claudia had sent someone in to start the bath. The tub was big; it took a while to fill.

Richard stood up and offered me a hand. He'd moved so that I had his body in profile—the smooth, strong line of his hip to stare at instead of other things. I appreciated the modesty. Sometimes when he wasn't modest, I just didn't think very clearly. Of course, it wasn't just his manhood that made me go *wow*. I stared up the line of his body, from feet, to the muscled swell of calf, thigh, the tight curve of his ass, the waist that led up to the swell of that chest, those shoulders. He held one muscled arm down at me, and I followed that arm to the face. That face. It wasn't just that he was handsome, or that his newly long hair framed it all, but the eyes. Pure brown, deep, rich, and full of a weight that was just Richard. A weight of personality and strength that once I'd thought would be enough to sustain me. I saw all of it in seconds, so that I was able to not just give him my hand in his, but wrap my other hand around his wrist. A wrist thick enough that I couldn't hold it between thumb and forefinger. He was just too big. He pulled me gently to my feet.

It hurt to stand, and I swayed, clutching at him. He put his other hand at my back to steady me. "Let me pick you up, Anita, please." He knew I didn't like to be carried. It made me feel weak, but tonight I hurt, and I knew that it would mean something to him to do it.

I whispered, "Yes."

He smiled, that smile that brightened his whole face. He picked me up in his arms, and I cuddled in against the strength of him. Just holding me in his arms, I could feel the potential in his body, so strong.

I let my head rest in the curve of his shoulder and didn't fight the fact that I was small in his arms. Once it had bothered me, but some part of me had grown up, or accepted it. Maybe I just didn't need to be the biggest, baddest ass in the room anymore. Maybe I was finally old enough to let someone else be the one in charge. Maybe.

I draped an arm around his neck and breathed in the scent of him. It loosened something tight and frightened in the center of my being. It felt a little like the rabbit was cuddling with the wolf, but if a lion can lie down with a lamb, why not?

15

ONE OF THE younger guards was bent over the tub. I couldn't remember his name in that moment. He looked up and seemed startled, as if he hadn't expected us. "Remus told me to fill the tub." He sounded a little breathy. I remembered his name then: Cisco. He was eighteen, and I'd declared him too young to guard my body. But it hadn't been his age alone that had made me suggest he go elsewhere. He'd had problems around the sex and me. Apparently he was getting his second chance to see if he could be cool around the sex.

"We'll take it from here," Richard said.

"Remus was really clear that I am to follow every order exactly."

I sighed. "Cisco, just go."

He took his hand out of the water, shaking droplets off it. "Okay." His eyes were too wide, his face too bothered by us. He was a wererat; no lycanthrope should have this much problem around nudity. But it wasn't the nudity, I didn't think, but the fact that we were going to have sex. That bothered him. I'd declared that I was a twenty-one-or-older zone. Cisco's face made me think I needed to make that rule stick.

I got a flash of the gun at his hip as he moved past us. Remus said Cisco had one of the best scores on the firing range of any guard. But high scores weren't the only thing you needed to be a bodyguard.

The bathroom door closed, firmly. Richard stood there, holding me as if it were effortless, as if I weighed nothing and he could have done it all night. Sometimes it bugged me to know how much stronger the men were than I was, but not this morning. This morning it seemed comforting.

"Can I say something without you getting mad?" Richard asked.

I tensed, I couldn't help it. "I don't know."

He sighed, but he said it. "Cisco seems too young to be doing this."

"I agree."

He moved his head against the top of mine, as if he'd glance down at me if my face was where he could have seen it. "You agree?"

"Yeah, he's been weird around me since . . ." I didn't say it out loud, because I didn't want to upset Richard either. But Cisco had been in the room when I'd had sex with London, one of our British vamps, for the first time. Cisco had had trouble not seeing me as a piece of ass since that moment. He was young, young in ways that weren't just about how old he was. "Since he saw some stuff," I finished, and hoped Richard would let it be.

He did. He carried me to the edge of the tub. The water was very loud, rushing into the huge tub. Jean-Claude had explained to me that the swan spout that filled it was hooked up to a system that filled the tub extra fast. I had a tub almost that big at home, and apparently my system was like his, a quick fill. Since I had bought the house with the tub and system in place I hadn't realized there was anything special about it. High-tech tubs, who knew? Richard hugged me, and again I got a flash of that amazing strength. "I want to check the water, but I'm really enjoying carrying you."

"Me, too," I said.

He rested his face against my hair. "Really?"

"Yes," I said, and I would have whispered it, except the water was loud enough that true whispering wasn't possible.

He stepped into the water with me in his arms. I laughed and lifted enough to see his face. "Shouldn't you check the temperature first?"

The look on his face made the laughter leak away. Eager, amazed, just so many emotions. Lately when we'd been together the only thing I'd seen in his face had been lust. We'd both shut down our emotions, kept ourselves safe. It had had that feel of sex at the end of a relationship, when sex is all you have left, and it isn't enough.

"The temperature's fine," he said, his voice soft. He knelt down, still holding me. He folded all that six feet and change down into the water, and just above his waist the water hit me. It was warm, almost hot. The water slid over my body like another set of hands, gliding, exploring. He was right, the temperature was fine.

He whispered against my hair, "How much do you hurt?"

"I ache all over."

"We'll get cleaned up first, then let your body soak in the water. Hot water helps." He kissed my forehead, then lowered us both down into the water, so that he was almost floating with me held across his chest. He let go of me with one arm, so he could half-swim, half-pull us to the water faucet. My legs trailed out into the water, but the rest of me was held tight to his chest. He sat down against the side of the tub. The water came to his upper chest, which meant it was almost chin deep to me. He kept me pinned to the front of his body, and I was okay with that. Touching was good.

"Enough water?" He made it a question.

"Yes," I said.

He reached back and turned off the water, then settled down with me cuddled against the front of his body. The height difference was enough that to keep my chin above water I couldn't cup my body against anything but his chest and stomach, with the rest of my body mostly floating. It was probably just as well; if too much of him touched me, I tended to get distracted. We were going to let some of the aches and pains drift away before we got distracted. He kissed the side of my face, and I settled into his arms, and the warm, warm water.

It was relaxing, or should have been, but there was a kernel of me that couldn't relax completely. What was wrong?

"What's wrong?" Richard asked.

"Nothing."

"You're tense."

I sighed. "I don't know."

His hand slid down the side of my body to cup my hip. "It seems like unless we're having sex, you get tense when we're alone."

"I don't mean to," I said.

He wrapped his arms around me and forced my body lower as he rose, so that certain parts of his anatomy were touching me. He wasn't as hard as he got, but even partially erect he was a special treat. The feel of him pressed to the back of my butt felt wonderful. It made me writhe against him, which made his body react, growing, moving against my body. It was all involuntary, and I loved knowing that I affected him like that. He pushed against me, and it brought a small sound from my lips.

"So quick, so eager. God, I do love that about you." He whispered it against my face.

"I wanted to make love to you months before you'd say yes."

"I was afraid." He nuzzled my neck, biting just a little.

That little biting made me writhe more. The aches and pains were starting to fade under the first wave of endorphins, those happy little chemicals. "Afraid of what?" I whispered.

He bit harder, and my spine bowed with it. "You."

"Why?"

He cupped his mouth around the side of my throat and bit down. I cried out for him; my nails clawed at his arms. I finally had to say, "Enough, enough."

He eased back and turned me in the water so that I was facing him. He drew me in against the front of his body, and he was hard and eager now. The feel of him against the front of my body made me cry out.

He cupped my ass, pressed me harder against the front of him. I pushed at his body, almost like I wanted to get away, but that wasn't what I was thinking. It was just almost too much, for some reason. The feel of him so eager, so big, trapped between our bodies. It was almost too much.

He shuddered, head back, his voice panting, "God, Anita, God, I love the way you react to me. I do love it!"

I wrapped my body around him, pressed the length of him against the most intimate part of me. It made me cry out and press myself tighter against him.

He pushed me against the side of the tub and moved his hips away enough to try to angle himself for my opening. I didn't protest, until the tip of him started inside and my body let me know that the combination of water—which is not a lubricant—lack of foreplay, and his size meant this wasn't going to work.

I half-patted, half-slapped his chest. "Too big, you're too big."

"The water," he said, breathy. He leaned his hands on the sides of the tub, face down, the head of him still inside me. "If you release the *ardeur*, we can do it."

"But I'll be sore afterward, and so will you."

He moved his hips a little, and the sensation, even tight, made me catch my breath. "Not too sore," he said.

"Yes," I said, "trust me. I don't want to be walking funny tomorrow."

He raised his head enough to frown at me. "We've never done it before like this—how can you be so sure?"

Shit. I stared up at him with his body halfway inside mine and didn't know what to say. The truth was Micah and I had done it, but that seemed impolitic, to say the least, in this moment. I tried to think of something that wouldn't make him feel bad. But I waited too long.

He said, "Just say it, Anita, just say it."

"I want to make love with you, Richard. I don't want to fight."

He pulled back enough so he wasn't inside me anymore. He stayed with his arms on either side of the tub, framing me. The look on his face was cautious now, almost as if he were steeling himself for bad news. It wasn't the look I wanted on his face right now.

"Say it, Anita." His voice sounded tired.

"I tried it with someone else."

"Why did it hurt?"

"Don't make me say this, Richard, please."

"Say it," and his voice was harsher now.

I sighed. "Fine, because he was too big for it not to hurt."

"Who?"

"Don't do this, Richard."

"Who?" This time it was a demand.

I gave him angry eyes. "Who do you think?"

"I don't know; you've added at least two men to your list, and I've never seen either of them erect."

I ducked under his arm and half-swam to the other side of the tub. "Tell me what you want me to say, Richard."

"Is it your two new vampires?"

"Are you wanting to know how you measure up to Requiem and London? Is that what you're actually wanting to know?"

He nodded. "Yeah, I guess I do."

I crossed my arms under my breasts, the water helping, since they floated. "I cannot believe you're asking this."

"It's an easy question, Anita."

"Do you actually want to know if you're bigger than they are?"

"I'm so jealous of them that I can't see straight, so yeah, I want to know. I want to know that I'm still the best-endowed man in your bed."

"You know, I don't actually get out a ruler and measure everybody."

"So they are big."

"Jesus, Mary, and Joseph." I covered my face with my hands. "No, no, they aren't as well endowed as you are. Happy?" I lowered my hands and found that it wasn't a happy look on his face.

"Then who is?"

I'd managed for months not to have this discussion, this specifically, with anyone. Of course, it would be Richard who pushed it. "Micah, okay? Micah."

"Is that why you love him?"

"Jesus, no, Richard, you should know better than most that a really big cock is not enough to win my heart."

"Then why him? Why are you living with him and not me?"

I sighed. We weren't going to have sex. We were going to have therapy. Sweet Mary, Mother of God, I did not want to do this. "Don't do this, not now, not today."

"I need to understand what went wrong before I can move on, Anita. I'm sorry, but I do."

I shook my head and tried to settle into the water, but it wasn't soothing anymore. It was just wet. "Fine. Do remember, I'm living with Nathaniel, too. You always seem to forget him, or discount him."

"He's not dominant, Anita. In the world of wereanimals that makes him discountable."

"But in the world of my affections, Richard, he is not discountable."

"I don't understand."

"I know you don't, and I'm sorry you don't, but it's still the truth. I'm living with Micah and Nathaniel, not just Micah. The fact that Nathaniel isn't a dominant doesn't make me love him less."

"How can you sit there, like this, and tell me you love someone else? Don't you know how much that hurts me?"

"You wanted this talk, not me. I wanted to make love. I wanted to clean up, feed the *ardeur*, and be together, but you had to get all hung up on the size of everyone's equipment. I know it's a guy thing to worry about that, but this wasn't the time to bring it up."

"You're right, it was stupid, but I'm stupid around you, Anita. You make me say things, do things, that I know are bad for the relationship."

"I don't make you do anything. You choose to say and do things that spoil stuff. Your choice, not mine."

"Fine, you're right. I choose to say and do this shit. I could have let it go and we'd be having sex right now, and it would be great sex. But I really do want to know what Micah has that I don't. What magic does he have that made you move him into your house, live with him, when you wouldn't do it for me?"

God, we were going to do the big fight. *The fight.* I did not want to do this, ever, but I especially didn't want to do this with the Harlequin in town, and heaven knew what nasty surprises headed our way. "Jean-Claude explained to you that it was partly vampire powers that drew Micah and me together."

"You're a succubus, a vampire that feeds on sex; yeah, he told me." I saw something on his face. "You don't believe him."

"I don't believe it's permanent. I think if you could get enough space between yourself and Jean-Claude's power, it would go away."

"Richard, this isn't Jean-Claude's power anymore; it's mine."

He shook his head, his arms crossing over that lovely chest. "You aren't a vampire, Anita. You can't have vampire powers. They're still part of the triumvirate we have with Jean-Claude."

"Richard, this is real. You can't wish it away."

"What, that you're some kind of sex-crazed demon? I don't believe that. It's more of Jean-Claude's power, or Belle Morte's, or even Marmee Noir. Jesus, Anita, you have had so many vampires running through your mind, you don't know what is you and what is them any-more."

There was some truth to what he was saying, but . . . "Richard, I have forged a triumvirate of power with Nathaniel and Damian. That's me, not Jean-Claude. That's real."

He shook his head again. "There's got to be a way to undo it."

I just stared at him. This was not the talk I thought we'd be having. "Richard, I am a succubus, me, not Jean-Claude, not Belle Morte, not Mommie Dark, me."

"Humans can't be succubi."

"Maybe not, but then humans can't have a vampire servant or an an-imal to call, and I have both of those."

"Because you're Jean-Claude's human servant."

"Richard, you saw what happened when I tried to undo that connection. I would have died and taken Nathaniel and Damian with me."

He settled back into the water, giving me angry eyes. "Jean-Claude told me the theory. That your version of the *ardeur* helps you see the deepest desire in someone's heart and grant it, and make them into what you most need. Micah needed his people safe; you killed Chimera for him. You needed what from Micah?"

"A helpmate, a partner, someone to help me run the furry coalition, and help me run the wereleopards that I'd inherited when I killed their old master."

"I could have been your partner," he said.

"You didn't want to be my partner. You want your own life, not to be just an adjunct to mine."

"What does that mean? That I won't give up my job for you?"

"That I needed someone to do the coalition full time, and you have your career."

"That can't be all Micah is to you."

"He's there for me, Richard. He's there for me and the people I love. He doesn't fight me all the time. He says yes more than he says no."

"And I just say no."

"Sometimes."

"Nathaniel needed to belong to someone; now he belongs to you. I get that. But what did he do for you?"

"I needed a wife," I said.

"What?"

"I needed a 1950s wife to make my life run smooth. I needed someone to be my wife, and he's really good at it."

"And I want you to be my wife, is that it?"

"Something like that, yeah."

"Why didn't your *ardeur* look into my heart and see what I most needed, and make us into the perfect couple, too?"

"I thought Jean-Claude explained all this to you."

"I asked him why not me, and he said the power was unpredictable. But that wasn't the truth, was it?"

"Not all of it," I said, and cursed my vampire lover for being a chickenshit.

"Tell me all of it," Richard said.

"Micah knew what he wanted: his people safe at any cost. He said from the moment he came to me that he'd do anything, be anything, to be in my life. The *ardeur* made that happen for him. Nathaniel wanted a home and to be loved for himself, not just for sex, and the *ardeur* made that happen. Both of those desires are very clear. Do you know what you want most, Richard? Do you have one single heart's desire?"

"I want you."

I shook my head. "That's not your deepest darkest wish, Richard."

"I should know what my deepest wish is, Anita."

"Richard, if a genie appeared before you right now, what would you wish? Really, truly, if you could have anything, what would it be?"

"You."

"Liar," I said.

He sat up, and that otherworldly energy swirled through the room. "How dare you?"

"Richard, be honest with yourself. What would you have if you could have anything, no matter how impossible?"

He blinked at me, and the energy level in the room seeped away. He stared at me. "I don't want to be a werewolf."

"That's your deepest wish, Richard, and the *ardeur* can't give you that. I can't be that for you, so the *ardeur* doesn't work between you and me, because what you want most doesn't have anything to do with sex and love."

He stared at me and sat back in the water, almost like he was faint. "Oh, my, God." He whispered it.

"We thought at first you were just too conflicted for the *ardeur* to pick and choose, but I was the one who figured it out."

"You're right," he said. A look of soft horror covered his face. He looked at me, and such pain filled his eyes. "I did this to myself."

I shrugged.

"I was so afraid I'd become a monster that I took the inoculations against lycanthropy. That's how I caught it."

"I know," I said softly.

"And I lost you because I hate what I am more than I want you."

"You haven't lost me, Richard."

He looked at me, and I had to fight to keep meeting that look. "You'll never be just mine. We'll never have a life together."

"We can be part of each other's lives, Richard."

"Not in the way I want."

"Maybe not, but, Richard, don't throw away what we have. Was it so bad last night, sleeping with all of us? Was that so awful?"

"No," he said, "and if I hadn't been in bed with you, then Marmee Noir could have done something awful to you. You need me to protect you."

"Sometimes, yes."

"But I can't live with two other men, Anita. I can't share my bed with them every night. I just can't."

My eyes felt hot, my throat was tight. Damn it, I would not cry. I managed to say, "I know."

"Then where do I fit in your life?"

"Where do I fit in yours?" I asked.

He nodded. "That's fair." But that was all he said.

I sat on my side of the tub feeling lost and horrible. Only Richard could make me feel this bad; only he managed to cut me this deep. Damn it.

I felt Nathaniel like a distant tug. He wasn't feeling well, which meant that Damian, in his coffin, would be feeling worse. Damian hadn't woken for the day yet, and I needed to feed the *ardeur* before he tried to wake. Jean-Claude had explained to me that if one morning I didn't have enough energy to make Damian's body wake, he would never wake again. He would simply remain dead, forever.

"I've got to feed, Richard, now. Nathaniel is starting to feel bad, and I won't risk killing Damian."

Richard nodded. I expected him to say he'd get someone else for me to feed on, but he didn't. "We need to do enough foreplay so you can feed from me."

"We're fighting, that's not good foreplay."

"Are you saying you don't want to be with me now?" He said it low, careful, as if he were balancing a world of emotions on a very thin stick. One wrong comment and the stick would break and the world would fall. Shit.

"I'm saying I don't have time for lengthy foreplay. I need to feed, right away. I'm trying not to cry; that's not conducive to sex. Not for me, at least."

"I'm sorry, Anita."

"Don't be sorry, Richard. Fix it. Fix yourself, fix us, or don't fix us. But whatever you're going to do, we need to do it now. I won't risk lives because we're having another fight."

He nodded his head as if that were fair. Maybe it was. He started moving toward me through the water.

"What are you doing?" I asked, and sounded suspicious.

"I want you to feed off me, Anita."

"I'm pissed and hurt, and that doesn't lead to sex for me."

"If I leave you'll still be pissed and hurt. You'll still have trouble concentrating on the sex, won't you?"

I couldn't argue his logic. I almost said, *But the others are smaller than you*, and this is one situation where bigger isn't better. But I didn't say it out loud. I didn't want to hurt him that badly. I also knew that if Richard and I couldn't come to some kind of understanding, one day we'd be finished as a couple. He'd always be Jean-Claude's wolf to call. He'd always be bound to us in a triumvirate of power, but we'd be broken up. It would be like being trapped in a relationship with someone you'd divorced but could never completely get rid of. A little slice of hell, that.

He was kneeling in front of me, the water just above his waist. The edges of his hair were wet, but the top was still dry, and still held some of the slick stuff that had gotten on us when I ripped Travis into his animal form. Truthfully, a little mess wasn't enough to take away from how handsome he was, but the constant fighting was. The picking at it all, and his deep unhappiness with being a werewolf, that was unattractive. I gazed up at him, all that way to the nearly heart-stopping face, so handsome. Handsome enough that I'd have been embarrassed around him in high school. But handsome and well-endowed wasn't enough to keep letting him hurt me like this. I stared up at him, and for the first time my heart did not leap up, and neither did my libido. I was tired of the fighting. I was tired of his inability to accept our reality. He didn't believe I was a succubus. He thought it was something that would go away if we got me away from Jean-Claude. Didn't he understand that there was no going away from Jean-Claude, not for either of us? His comments said no, he didn't understand that, and that made me sad.

He stood up. He stood up with water dripping down his body. I was suddenly staring at a certain part of his anatomy with water drops decorating it. We all have our weaknesses, and one of mine was water. Richard had dated me long enough to know that. He was betting that seeing him wet was enough to distract me from being mad at him. I had a moment to decide to hold on to that angry sadness, or do what I wanted to do. Do what the suddenly rapid pulse in my neck wanted to do. I felt Nathaniel sway against a wall. I went to my knees, steadied my hands against the warm, wet sides of Richard's thighs, and lowered my mouth to his body.

16

I LICKED THE water off him with the tip of my tongue. I drank water from the looseness of his body, licking water from the testicles where they hung so heavy and large. I licked and drank the water until his body lengthened and hardened. I couldn't reach the tip of him now, not without wrapping my hand around the base of him and lowering all that hardness toward my mouth. He made small noises for me, and when I gazed up his body, the eyes that looked back had changed to wolf amber. Sex was supposed to be about losing control, but all lycanthropes could never completely lose control—because to lose control for them meant to change shape. At least once a year some new lycanthrope lost control and cut up a lover during sex. Sometimes the lover survived, sometimes they didn't, sometimes they got to be furry, too.

I drove my mouth over him until my lips met my own hand. I used the hand to squeeze and pulse around him, but it also kept me from having to try to take all of him in my mouth. I could deep-throat, but it wasn't always the most comfortable position, not with someone Richard's size. I could raise the *ardeur* and do it, do it all, but . . .

I rose off his body, enough to talk. "I'd raise the *ardeur* and finish like this, but you're too strong. You keep me out except during intercourse."

He looked down at me, and it was almost a look of pain. "I want you to do whatever you want to do."

"Will you lower your shields and let me feed?"

"I'll try."

I shook my head and squeezed him tight at the same time. It threw his head back, made his hands reach to empty air for something to hold on to. He liked to hold on to things when we did this. But his hands found only air, and he looked down at me with a shudder that ran up the length of his body. Just feeling him shudder in my hand brought a cry from me. "God, Richard, God!"

He reached down and grabbed my arms, pulled me up out of the water. I had to let go of him as he came out of the water with me in his arms. He threw me onto the marble around the tub edge. It was cold and hard, and I started to protest. Richard's fingers found my opening. He shoved his finger inside me, and just doing oral sex on him made me wet, but the water had kept me tight. Even one finger seemed big. He moved it in and out and around, and I cried out for him.

He put two fingers inside me, and he actually closed his eyes, concentrating, searching, until he found that spot, no bigger than a fifty-cent piece, that spot just inside and to the front of the opening. He found it, and flicked his fingers back and forth across it. There hadn't been enough foreplay for a full-blown G-spot orgasm, but it still felt good, so good. It made me spread my legs wider for him, made me angle my hips for him. He took that for the invitation it was, and drove his fingers inside me harder and faster, until I cried out for him again.

"You're wet," he said, in a voice that was a little strangled with need.

I nodded, breathless.

He started to angle himself to enter me, but I put a hand on his chest. "Condom."

"Shit," he said, but he went to his knees and riffled through the pile of towels behind us. Condoms lived in the bathrooms and bedrooms of any place I was alone with the men. The pregnancy scare in November had made me unwilling to count on just the birth-control pill. He was cursing under his breath by the time he got the condom on, but he turned back to me, his body hard, eager. Just the sight of him like that, knowing what we were about to do, made things low in my body tighten. Small orgasms before he even entered me.

Even wet and eager, he had to work himself inside me. I writhed around him, just from the feel of him working his way inside. I gazed up at him, let my eyes see his face, the wolf eyes in his face as he fought himself, his arms supporting him above me, so that most of his body was above me, so that I could see him as he pushed his way into me.

"Feed, Anita, feed, please."

A *please* like that usually meant that a man was close. I called the *ardeur* to life. I called it, like coaxing a spark to life, to flame, to burn. The power spilled over me, through me, and into him. The *ardeur* poured over us in a warm wash of power. It opened my body to him so that he could push in and out of me. I could watch him in the mirrored walls around us, his body above mine, pushing in and out, in and out. He knew with the *ardeur* on us he didn't have to be careful, and he wasn't. He pushed all that length into me as hard and fast as he could. He grabbed my hips, lifted my lower body off the marble, held me in his big hands as he pounded himself into me, so hard and fast that our bodies made a wet, thudding noise. The end of him found the end of me, so that each stroke hit as far into my body as it could, and still he came in and in, so hard, so fast, he was almost a blur in the mirrors. He wasn't human, and he had speed and strength that wasn't human. Once he'd worried that he'd hurt me, but we'd found that I wasn't human-fragile anymore. We'd found that Richard could be as rough as he wanted, and he wouldn't break me. He was that rough now, then he found a new speed, a new hardness. It was as if he'd always been holding back, and I just hadn't known it. Faster, harder, until he was a blur in the mirrors, pounding himself inside me, until I cried out, orgasming around him, body spasming. I felt his body spasm inside me, felt his body buck against mine. All movement ceased, his head flung backward, eyes closing. His fingers dug into my ass, holding us both in that moment, as his body spasmed and went inside mine, with him buried as deeply inside my body as was possible to be. In that frozen moment, as our bodies rode each other, the *ardeur* fed. I fed. I fed on Richard's energy, fed on the part of him that was wolf, and human. I fed on all of him, took in every last delicious inch of his power, as I took in every last delicious inch of his body. When he let himself go like this, he gave so much energy.

He lowered me back to the edge of the marble tub. He slid out of me, and even that made me writhe. He collapsed onto his side, because there wasn't enough room for his shoulders otherwise. He lay gasping with his head near my waist. I managed to move my hand enough to touch his hair, but that was all I could manage. My pulse was still thundering in my ears.

He found his voice first. "Did I hurt you?"

I started to say no, but the endorphins were fading around the edges. There was already an ache beginning between my legs. To Micah I would have said, *A little*, but to Richard I said, "No." He had more issues than Micah did.

I felt his hand slide clumsily over my thigh, as if he couldn't quite make his hand work just yet. He brushed between my legs. I said in a voice that was half-laughing, "Not again, not yet."

He raised his hand so I could see that he had blood on his fingertips. "Did I hurt you?" His voice sounded surer of itself and less postcoital.

"Yes, and no," I said.

He managed to raise himself up on one elbow. "You're bleeding, Anita. I hurt you."

I looked at his fingertips. "A little, but it's a good hurt. I'll remember what we did with every ache."

His face closed down, and he stared at the blood on his fingertips as if it were an accusation.

"Richard, it was wonderful, amazing. I didn't know you'd been holding so much of yourself back."

"I should have kept holding back."

I touched his shoulder. "Richard, don't do this. Don't make it bad when it was good."

"You're bleeding, Anita. I fucked you so hard you're bleeding."

I thought of one thing to say, but wasn't sure if it would make things better or worse.

He moved away from me to sit on the edge of the tub with his legs dangling over the side. He washed the blood away.

"I'll be all right, Richard, honest."

"You can't know that," he said.

I rose, and I ached, deep inside my body. Maybe more than normal. I rose enough to see the blood on the marble, but there wasn't much of it. "If this is all the blood, then I'll be fine."

"Anita, you've never bled after sex before."

Truth time; I prayed that it was the right choice. "Yeah, I have."

He looked at me, frowning. "No, you haven't."

"Yeah, I have, just not with you."

He started to say, "Who . . . Micah?" He said the word like he wasn't happy to say it.

"Yes."

"This much blood?" he asked.

I nodded and sat up; now that the endorphins were leaving at a rapid rate, the marble felt cold. I held my hand out to him. "Help me back into the tub."

He took my hand almost automatically, as if he did it because it was there more than because he wanted to. He helped me slide back into the tub. I made a small pain noise. I was hurt, no doubt about that, but I wasn't broken. I'd had this hurt before with Micah. I didn't want it this rough every night, but I could do it, and when it was the right time, it was amazing.

"Has he hurt you this badly before?"

"It isn't hurt the way you say it, Richard. I'm not hurt, I hurt; it's not the same thing."

"I don't see the difference."

I lay back in the water, easing into it, letting the abused parts of my anatomy relax a little at a time. Strangely, the ache inside me was the only ache. The muscle soreness was gone, washed away on a wave of sex and the *ardeur*. Good for that.

"I wanted to fuck you, Anita. I wanted to fuck you as hard and fast as I could, and I did."

"Didn't it feel wonderful?" I asked.

He nodded. "It did, but if I hurt you, then think what I could do to someone who doesn't have vampire marks to make them harder to hurt. Think what I could do to a human woman."

I settled back into the water enough to wet all my hair, then sat up so I could look at him. He looked so sad, lost. "I've heard the stories, Richard. Broken pelvises, crushed organs, women and men who needed surgery to put themselves back together."

"When we're with humans we always have to be careful of them."

"So I've been told."

"I didn't know if you could take this, Anita. I didn't know if I would break you. The thought that I might fuck you until I pushed my way into parts of your body that should never be touched, excited me. I didn't want to do it, but the possibility of it excited the hell out of me. How sick is that?"

I blinked at him, not sure what to say. "I'm not sure it's sick at all. You didn't do it. You just thought about it. The thought excited you, but you didn't rip me apart to make it come true. I think maybe it's like a lot of violent fantasies: if the reality happened, it wouldn't be sexy at all, but the thought of it, a violent thought in the middle of sex, can drive the sex to the next level."

"Weren't you afraid of me?"

"No."

"Why not?"

"I trusted you not to hurt me," I said.

He took off the condom and said, "There's blood on the condom."

"I'm not hurt, Richard, or at least no more than I wanted to be." Truthfully, maybe I was more hurt than I wanted to be. A pleasant ache between the legs was fine, but I was starting to hurt somewhere close to my belly button. That usually meant you'd overdone it. But I couldn't say that to Richard.

He looked at me. "You flinched just now."

I closed my eyes and floated back in the water. "I don't know what you're talking about," I said.

I felt the water move, knew he'd gotten in the tub. I sat up, but he was already standing over me. There was something menacing about the way he loomed over me. Most of the time I could ignore how physically large he was, in every way, but sometimes, like now, he made me see it. He wasn't trying to be intimidating, or I didn't think he was. Not on purpose, anyway.

That otherworldly energy began to flow off him as if the water were getting reheated. I moved so I was sitting against the side of the tub. Standing up wouldn't help; he'd still loom over me. Besides, my stomach, or rather lower things, were beginning to cramp. I wasn't entirely certain I could stand up without bending over. That wouldn't help the situation. Was I hurt? Was I really hurt? Not a question I wanted to have to ask.

"You're hurt, really hurt, aren't you?"

His question was a little too close to what I'd just thought. We could accidentally share thoughts and feelings. I fought to put the shields back in place. Sex can bring them crashing down.

He knelt in the water, putting an arm on either side of me. He leaned in, the heat of his power beating against my body. It made things low in my body tense, and that hurt. I fought not to make little pain sounds. I managed not to, but Richard put his face against the side of mine and whispered, "Are you hurt?"

"Please, Richard." I whispered it.

"Are . . . you . . . hurt?" His power pulsed through me, and this time I made a small sound, but not a good one.

"You're going to raise my wolf if you don't control your power better." I said it through gritted teeth. One, I was hurting; two, I was getting angry.

He leaned in against my face and drew a deep breath. He was smelling my skin. His power was like a warm, wet heat pushing against me. I was shielding as hard as I could against him, his power, all of it. I thought of rock, stone walls to hide behind and put them in his metaphysical way.

He spoke against my cheek, his breath hot on my skin. "Pain has a smell to it, did you know that?"

"No. Yes." I'd smelled it myself once, twice, when the beast was first prowling around inside me.

"Are . . . you . . . hurt?" He said each word, slowly, carefully, his lips brushing against my cheek as he spoke.

Another cramp hit me, and I fought not to bend over my stomach. I fought to sit in the water, with him pressed against me, and not react. He'd implied he could smell I was hurt. Most lycanthropes can smell a lie. I said the only thing I could say: "Yes."

He kissed my cheek and said, "Thank you." Then he stood up and climbed out of the tub. He reached for one of the towels in the pile that always seemed to be in the bathroom.

"Where are you going?" I asked, though frankly I was ready for him to go.

"Away from you," he said.

I let myself fold over the next cramp. I didn't fight that it hurt. He wanted to be a bastard, fine. When I looked up again, he had the towel wrapped around his waist. He'd swallowed all that otherworldly energy, as if when he covered his nakedness, he'd covered more than just his body.

"I'll send for a doctor."

"No, not yet."

"Why not yet?"

"Because it may pass."

He frowned at me. "You sound like you've done this before."

"I've had cramping before—not this bad, truthfully—but it faded."

"Micah." He said the name like it was a curse.

"Yes." I was tired of protecting Richard's ego. Frankly, in that moment, I was tired of Richard.

"He always gets there before I do."

"There isn't a single thing that Micah got to do that you didn't have the chance to do first."

"My fault again," he said.

"Your choices," I said. I couldn't keep the strain out of my voice. Fine, let him know how much I was hurting.

"I love that," he said.

I frowned up at him, my hands pressed over my abdomen. "What?"

"That sound in your voice, I love it. The last time I heard it was in Raina's voice."

I frowned harder. "What are you talking about?"

"You know that she was a sexual sadist, and God knows she was, but she also liked pain. She liked rough sex from both sides; dishing it out and being the dish."

I couldn't frown harder so I said, "I actually did know that. I have some of her memories, remember."

"That's right, you carry her munin, her ghostly memory."

The munin were the ancestral memories of the werewolves. When a wolf died, they ate a little bit of the deceased and made them a permanent group memory. For real, not just ritual—though most werewolves couldn't "talk" as directly as I could with Raina's munin. It was supposed to enable you to access memories, get advice, but Raina had done her best to try to possess me for real. I had almost complete ability to keep her contained inside me. She wasn't like the beasts, or the *ardeur*. Raina was something I could keep caged. Using her powers, that was chancier.

"You used her to heal the cross burn in your hand. Maybe you could use her to heal yourself now?"

I looked at him. The cross-shaped burn on my hand was a shiny, permanent scar. Raina's ability to heal was something I had retained.

It had been one of the reasons that Richard had made her munin, instead of leaving her body to rot. She'd been a sexual sadist and tried to kill us both, but she had been powerful. So I could sometimes use her abilities to heal myself and others, but the cost was always high. I could cage her inside me, ignore her, but if I let her out, well, she demanded payment. Her payment was usually painful, or sexual, or both.

I shook my head. "I don't think that would be a good idea right now."

"Have you ever seen memories of her and me together?"

"Some. I try to steer clear of them."

"The last time I was able to do what we did today was with her." He looked at me, his face almost peaceful, waiting.

"You miss her."

"I miss some things about her. Remember, Anita, I was a virgin. I didn't understand how unusual what she was teaching me was."

"Nothing to compare it to," I said.

"Exactly."

"There are other sexual positions where you can be as rough as you want, and I won't hurt this much afterward, Richard. Part of it is that you don't do it this rough during the *ardeur*. The *ardeur* steals my ability to guard myself."

"Don't you understand, Anita? I hate, and I love, that I hurt you. I love the sound of strain in your voice. I love the thought that my body did this to you. That just flat does it for me. That I was so big, so powerful, so violent, that you're hurt inside. You're right, if I hurt you enough for hospitals, it wouldn't be fun. That I wouldn't enjoy. Raina tried to get me to enjoy that level, but for that she had to turn to Gabriel."

Gabriel had been in charge of the local wereleopards before I had to kill him. He'd being trying to rape and kill me, on film, at the time. Raina had been offstage urging him on. They'd made a lovely couple, in that lower-circle-of-hell sort of way. I'd sent them to hell together on the same night; talk about a double date.

"Yeah, Gabriel liked it serial-killer bad."

"So did Raina," Richard said, "though not her body, not for the worst of it."

"I'm told a good dominant in the bondage and submission scene never asks of their sub what they aren't willing to do to their own body."

"That's the rule," Richard said, "but we both know that Raina wasn't a good dominant."

"No," I said, "she wasn't."

"The cramping easing?" He made it a question.

"Yeah, how did you know?"

"Your face is smoothing out. You're not clutching as much at your stomach. And I watched Raina work through the same kind of pain, a lot. She said one of the things she liked about me was that I could be as rough as she wanted in exactly the way she wanted it."

"For future reference, don't ever fuck me this hard in that position again, okay?"

He nodded. "What position do you like?"

I opened my mouth, closed it. Tried to think of how to phrase it. "I don't like it this rough on a nightly basis. After a session even close to this rough, it takes a day or two to feel like doing it again."

"You'll have to feed the *ardeur* in a few hours."

"There are gentler ways to feed it, Richard."

"Not with Micah there isn't."

"Well-endowed doesn't mean you can't be gentle, Richard."

He nodded. "You're right."

We stared at each other a moment. Something on his face made me say, "Raina really fucked you up, didn't she?"

He nodded. "Yes, she did. When she found out I enjoyed it rough, she wanted to make sure I'd never be able to get my needs met anywhere but with her. She meant to keep me, Anita, and if she hadn't tried to include Gabriel, I might have stayed with her."

"No, you wouldn't have," I said.

He gave me sad eyes. "How can you be so sure?"

"Because you're a good person, and if it hadn't been Gabriel it would have been someone or something else. Raina couldn't resist pushing people past their boundaries. She'd have kept pushing until she broke you; it's what she did."

He nodded and took in a breath deep enough that it rocked his broad shoulders. "I'll clean up in the group showers."

I wanted him to go, but . . . He'd tried so hard. He'd actually saved me from Marmee Noir. "You can clean up here."

He shook his head. "No, I can't."

The way he said it seemed odd. "Why not?"

"Because I like the idea I hurt you. I like it a lot. I don't trust my-self not to hurt you again."

"I'd say no, Richard. You respect *no*."

He nodded. "But I also know the effect we have on each other. I don't trust myself not to try to seduce you again, so that I can push myself inside you while you're still bleeding from the first time." He closed his eyes and a shudder ran down him from head to feet. I didn't think it was because he was repulsed by what he wanted to do; no, it was a shudder of anticipation. He was being honest with me, with himself, about what he wanted.

"I like it rough sometimes, Richard, but not that rough. Sorry."

He nodded and gave me a sad smile. "Raina helped me enjoy inter-course too rough for anyone else. She made Nathaniel like pain in a way that most people wouldn't even survive."

"I know."

He shook his head. "No, you don't. You think you know, but you can't imagine it. I saw some of what she taught him to enjoy."

"He doesn't talk like you ever saw him with her," I said.

"Blindfolds, earplugs, nose plugs; you can't see, hear, or smell who's in the room. She invited me over once, tried to get me to help her, but torturing was never anything I liked. Raina found that disappointing."

I swallowed and tried to think of something useful to say; nothing came to mind. "I don't know what to say to that."

"I don't know why I told you that. Did I want to shock you? Did I want you to think less of Nathaniel? Less of me?" He shook his head and started for the door again.

I was ready for him to leave because I didn't know what to do with the mood he was in, and I really didn't want more sex. The hard cramps had passed, but I was hurting, and would be for a while.

He stopped with his hand on the doorknob. "Do you realize that most of the men in your bed are ones that she was with?"

"I hadn't thought about it."

He turned and looked over his shoulder at me. "Jean-Claude was with her and Gabriel; it was the price she demanded from him. You know she made Jason a werewolf?"

"Yeah." I'd actually shared that memory with Jason. She'd tied him to a bed and cut him up while she fucked him. She hadn't cared whether he lived or died. I'd been inside her head on the memory, and she hadn't cared. She really was serial-killer material, because her pleasure had meant more to her than Jason's life.

I got a whisper through my head. "Think harder, Anita."

I shivered, and that made my lower body hurt. "Go, Richard, go, okay?"

"What's wrong?"

"I think I need not to think about her so hard."

"She talked to you?"

I nodded.

"You think you have her under control, and maybe you do, but you might just think on this. Jean-Claude, me, Jason, Nathaniel, all of us were hers first. Maybe there's a reason you're attracted to her old lovers." With that very unsettling thought, he left, closing the door behind him. I was happy that Richard was doing therapy; it was helping, honest. The trouble was, he seemed to want me to do therapy with him, and that I wasn't ready for.

17

I DID A quick cleanup, and then realized I had no clothes in the bath-room. My robe was lying in a heap beside the bed. Great. I wrapped the towel more securely around my hair, then wrapped one of the bigger tow-els around my body. One of the good things about being short was that the towel covered me from armpits to ankles. The funny thing was that almost no matter who was in the other room, they'd probably seen me nude at least once. I should have just walked out and gotten my clothes out of the armoire and ignored everybody. But I couldn't do it. I just couldn't do it. I wasn't that comfortable around my own nudity. There were days when I was pretty sure I'd never be that comfortable.

Worse yet, my gun was outside in the bedroom. My clothes I could live without, but that I'd left my gun in the other room said just how much Richard affected me. He made me forget myself, even the parts of me that almost no one else could drive from my mind. For some reason I just couldn't go out there unarmed, I don't know why. I just couldn't do it. I was still aching all the way up to almost my belly but-ton. The cramping had mostly stopped, but I was feeling stupid and vulnerable. I wanted a gun. It would make me feel better. There, that was the truth. I'd started hiding guns in the places where I spent a lot of time. They were for emergencies. This wasn't an emergency, but . . . hell with it, it was my gun. If I felt the need, screw it.

I knelt down by the sink and opened the cabinet doors. I had to reach back and up into the plumbing to find it, but there was my Firestar duct-taped among the pipes. There'd been a couple of times when I'd been separated from my carry guns and needed a gun. So I'd given into my paranoia and hidden a few around. The Firestar wasn't my main backup gun anymore, so it lived here as the ultimate hideaway. I brought the gun out into the light and laughed. There was writing on the tape. It read, "Anita's gun," in Nathaniel's handwriting. He'd been with me the day I did it. Apparently he'd added his own little touch when I wasn't looking. He'd handed me the pieces of tape. Had he written on it then, and I just hadn't noticed, or had he come back later? I'd ask him.

It left me smiling and shaking my head as I took the tape off the gun. I'd have put it in my pocket, if I'd had one. The gun was very visible against the white towel. I tried the grip in my hand, squeezed it a little. A tightness in the center of my body eased. What does it say about your life when a gun makes you feel this much safer?

I checked to make sure the gun was still loaded, because any time a gun has been out of your sight, you damn well better check. Never trust anyone else that a gun is either loaded or unloaded; check it yourself. Gun safety 101.

Towel tucked tight under my arms, and gun in hand, I opened the door. I thought for a moment the bedroom was empty, but then Clay and Graham stood up near the fireplace. They'd been sitting in the room's only chairs.

"Clay, shouldn't you be in bed somewhere? You just got off work at Guilty Pleasures." I looked at the bed and found it stripped down to the slightly singed mattress. My gun had been there somewhere.

As if he read my mind, Clay said, "Your gun is in the bedside table."

I didn't check to make sure he was telling the truth. One, I trusted Clay; two, I had a gun in one hand and the other hand helped hold the towel in place. I was armed and out of hands. "Thanks, but why aren't you in bed?"

"After they found the bugs in all the businesses, Jean-Claude asked us to do double shifts." He ran his hand through his short blond curls. Early twenties looked better on no sleep, but he still looked tired.

"Don't I even get a hello?" Graham asked. I looked at him and couldn't fight a frown. He was about the same size as Clay: six feet tall, but his shoulders were much broader. Graham was muscled in a way that only serious weight lifting would give you. His black hair was so long on top that his dark eyes peered out from the hair. The bottom of his hair was freshly shaved, very short, so that it looked like two different haircuts put together. He wasn't wearing the black T-shirt that was standard bodyguard wear. He was wearing red. The red shirt was a new addition to the bodyguard uniform. Most of them were still in black, some with the appropriate club name and "Security" written on them, or just plain black. Red meant the guard was okay with being emergency food for the *ardeur*. It had been Remus's idea originally. He'd come up with it after I'd nearly killed Damian, Nathaniel, and myself from not feeding the *ardeur* enough. I thought the red shirt idea was a joke until the first guard showed up wearing one.

Strangely, since the red shirt policy went into effect, I'd gained a much better control over the *ardeur*. Let's hear it for fear, embarrassment, and sheer stubbornness. Graham had been trying to get into my pants for months, so no big surprise that he volunteered. What creeped me out was some of the other guards who'd done it. Men I hadn't known thought of me in a sexual way. I mean, it's one thing to suspect a man lusts after you, but absolute confirmation, well, that made me uncomfortable.

"Hey, Graham, nice shirt," I said, and I was happy that it sounded hostile.

"Why are you mad at me? It's not my rule. Be mad at Remus, or Claudia, or Jean-Claude. It's their rule that you are not to be alone in a room unless accompanied by a man willing to feed the *ardeur*."

"Since when?" I asked.

"Since this mysterious bad guy came to town. No one's giving details, but apparently the people who give us orders are worried that the bad guys will use magic to make the *ardeur* go out of control. So you have to have food at all times." He didn't sound happy about it. Maybe my being pissy was finally rubbing off on Graham. Good.

"We're short of red shirts today, Anita," Clay said.

"Why?"

"Because the guard is doubled around all of Jean-Claude's businesses. He's having to renegotiate with Rafael and Narcissus for more people."

"I guess we pay more money, we get more men," I said.

The two men exchanged a look. "Maybe," Clay said.

I was getting cold standing there in nothing but a towel, so I went to the armoire for clothes. "What else could they be negotiating for except money?" I said. I stared at the double door of the armoire, because the towel was slipping, and I had a gun in the other hand. I'd never been good at getting a towel to stay fastened. It wasn't like both of the men hadn't seen me naked. But . . . damn it.

"Power," Clay said. "Everyone wants a closer tie to Jean-Claude now that he's his own vampire bloodline. And Narcissus is seriously freaked that Asher's new animal to call is hyena."

"Freaked how?" I asked. I tucked the arm with the gun tight on the towel and tugged on the door of the armoire. It stuck.

"We're wolves, not hyenas, so this is all secondhand," Clay said. "Narcissus wants guarantees that Asher won't try to run his clan."

I finally got the door opened; yea for me. "Asher isn't powerful enough to do that."

"Maybe," Clay said, "but Narcissus is worried about it. He wants to negotiate now before it's an issue."

I had black jeans in hand, but I really needed the second hand to get the other clothes.

"Oh, for God's sake," Graham said. He stalked toward me. He was angry enough that as he got closer I got little bits of it, like embers from a fire hitting my skin. He grabbed the edge of the jeans in my hand. I held on. We glared at each other. "I'll just hold the clothes for you, Anita. That's it, okay?"

It was a reasonable idea. It was helpful. So why didn't I want to do it? Because Graham seriously bugged me. His persistent pursuit of sex with me, with no pretense of emotion, let alone love, really hit my buttons wrong. Of course, if he'd lied about me being the love of his life, that would have pissed me off more. God. I let go of the jeans. I took a deep breath, let it out slowly, and said, "Thank you."

Graham blinked down at me as if I'd never said *thank you* to him before. Maybe I hadn't. Shame on me then. He put his life on the line to keep me safe. So he was a lech; at least he was an honest lech.

I looked up at him. This close I could see the slight uptilt of his brown eyes. His mother was Japanese, which got him the hair and eyes. The rest of him looked like his blond and blue-eyed father had cloned himself. Meeting his parents by accident one night hadn't made me like him better. In fact it had made it worse. His parents seemed like good people. Would they be ashamed to know how much of a horndog their only child was? It seemed likely.

I shook my head and turned back to the armoire. I'd concentrate on getting dressed. That would help me feel better. I always felt better with clothes on. Grandma Blake's influence. There was a woman who thought naked meant bad.

I was getting low on shirts here. My choices were black or red. Black made me look like one of the bodyguards, and red, well, red looked like all the red shirts were my people, like a special Anita Blake uniform. I picked up one of the black shirts, put it back, picked up a red shirt, put it back.

"Anita, just pick a shirt," Graham said.

"I hadn't realized until this moment that my normal off-duty clothes are the same as the uniform for you guys."

"Why is that a problem?" he asked.

"I don't know," I said, and that was the truth.

"Then pick red. I promise that just because we're dressed like we match, it's not a date, okay?" He finally sounded angry.

I sighed. "I'm sorry that it bugs me that the red shirts mean that people want to fuck me. It does bug me. It really does."

"The color of my shirt didn't change anything about how I interact with you," Graham said. "I've been honest from the beginning about what I'd like to do."

I nodded. "You know, Graham, I was just thinking that. You've been honest. I say I like honest, but I guess I don't like honest past a certain point." I grabbed the red shirt. I needed to grow up about this issue and buy some different-colored clothes. I added jogging socks and black jogging shoes to the pile in Graham's arms. I did the mental list and finally realized I didn't have any underwear in the pile. I opened the bottom drawer in the armoire. Strangely, there was plenty of lingerie. Jean-Claude had gotten me to the point where I didn't own any simple underwear. Everything had lace, or fishnet, or something on it. I had learned to buy two to three pairs of the panties to one matching bra. You could wear bras longer than underwear.

I finally stood up with bra and panties in hand. I started to put them on the pile, but caught Graham's look. I'd picked a red bra to go under the red shirt. It was one of the thinner red baby-doll tees, so I'd picked something that wouldn't show through. The bra and panties were both red satin. The bra was a push-up bra because it got my breasts up and out of the way of my shoulder holster, or rather out of the way of drawing the gun. A moment ago I hadn't thought a thing about it. I'd picked what worked under the shirt. Now, I was suddenly very aware that the underwear was nice underwear.

I met Graham's eyes, and there was such heat in them. It was written all over his face that he wanted to see me in the bra and panties. Bare on his face, in his eyes, that he'd give a great deal to see me in the lingerie, and do something about it.

Heat washed up my face. I blushed embarrassingly easily sometimes. This was one of those times. If he'd been one of my boyfriends, I'd have reacted to that look, that demand. We could have gone into the bathroom and let that heat wash over both of us, maybe. But he wasn't my boyfriend, and his wanting to fuck me wasn't enough reason for me to fuck him. When I'd had the pregnancy scare last month, the fact that I hadn't had sex with Graham, that he wasn't on the maybe-daddy list, had filled me with such relief that I knew he wasn't going to be one of my sweeties. The pregnancy scare had put a lot of things in perspective. I was now back to looking at men thinking, if I got pregnant by accident, how big a disaster would it be? Maybe a few months from now I wouldn't be so freaked, and that wouldn't be a question that I thought of so strongly. Then again, maybe it still would be. I had had a false positive on a pregnancy test. It had scared the hell out of me.

I looked up into his face. He was handsome. There was nothing wrong with him, exactly, but I still remembered how happy I was that he wasn't on the list of men who might have made me pregnant. If you get knocked up, it should be by someone who's at least a good friend, and Graham wasn't even that. He was my bodyguard, and he'd been emergency food, but he wasn't my friend. He wanted to fuck me too badly to be my friend. Any man who would rather have sex with you than anything else is never going to be your friend. Friends want what's best for you more than they want sex. Graham's priorities were there on his face, in his eyes, in the tension of his body as he held my clothes.

"You're blushing," he said, and his voice sounded hoarse.

I nodded and looked down, away from that look. Maybe the blushing would stop if I wasn't meeting his eyes.

He touched my face, the barest tips of his fingers on my chin. "After everything I've seen you do with all the other men, you're blushing because I'm looking too hard at you." His voice was softer now.

"You think I can't be embarrassed, because I'm a whore."

"Not true." He tried to turn my face up to his. I stepped back from him so he couldn't touch my face.

"Isn't it?" I asked, and this time the face I gave him held the beginnings of anger.

"I see you with the other men and I want you—why is that wrong? I've watched you have sex with multiple men while I'm in the room. What am I supposed to think?"

"Oh, Graham." This from Clay. He'd stayed on the far side of the room, out of it, but those two words let me know that Clay got it. Clay understood the mistake that Graham had just made.

"I can fix that, Graham."

"Fix what?"

"Fix it so you're not conflicted anymore about me."

"What are you talking about?" The fact that he hadn't realized where I was going was also a point against him. He wasn't a quick thinker.

"You're off my detail."

He clutched the clothes to his oh-so-broad chest. "What do you mean?"

"I can't guarantee that the *ardeur* won't get out of hand and I'll lose control enough to fuck in front of my guards again. Since it bothers you so much, Graham, I can fix it so you never have to watch again."

"I don't . . ." The first hint of unhappiness came over him. He finally saw where we were going.

"You are off my detail. Put my clothes in the bathroom on the edge of the sink and go find Remus or Claudia. Tell them that you need to be replaced. I'm sure that there are places you can guard that will be far enough away from me."

"Anita, I didn't mean it the way . . ."

"The way it sounded," I finished for him. "Yeah, you did."

"Please, Anita, please, I . . ."

"Put the clothes in the bathroom and go tell someone that you need to be replaced. Do it now."

He looked behind him at Clay. Clay put his hands up in a push-away gesture, as if to say, *Don't look at me.*

"This isn't fair," Graham said.

"What are you, five? Fair, fuck fair. You just said out loud that watching me fuck other men makes you want to fuck me. I can fix that. You don't have to watch anymore."

"Do you really think any man who's watched you fuck someone didn't want to be that man? All of us think the same thing. I'm just honest about it."

I looked across the room at Clay. "That true, Clay?"

"Oh, please, do not drag me into this."

I gave him a hard look.

He sighed. "No, actually, that's not how all of us feel. For myself, I'm scared shitless of your idea of sex. The *ardeur* scares me."

"How can you say that?" Graham asked. He turned toward the other man with my clothes still clutched in his big arms.

"Because it's the truth, Graham, and if you would think with something higher than your belt buckle you'd be scared, too."

"Scared of what?" Graham said. "It's the most mind-blowing sex that any vampire line can give a mortal. I've had more of a taste of it than you have. Trust me, Clay, if she'd ever fed off you, even a little, you'd want more."

"That's exactly what scares me," Clay said.

I had a thought, a bad one. I had fed on Graham in small ways when the *ardeur* was new. I'd given him the smallest taste of it that I could. We had never been naked together. We had never touched each other in any area that was considered sexual. But just because I thought it hadn't been enough contact to addict him to the *ardeur* didn't mean I was right. The *ardeur* could act like a drug, and I'd learned through some of the vampires that how easily addicted to it you were varied from person to person. Had I addicted Graham to the *ardeur* without meaning to? Was his reaction to me my fault? Shit.

Graham turned back to me with my clothes crushed against his chest. He looked panic stricken. "Please, Anita, please, don't do this. I'm sorry, okay, I'm sorry." His eyes glittered through the fringe of his hair. I think he was on the verge of tears. I was reminded that he was under twenty-five by a few years. He was so physically big that sometimes you forgot how young he was. We were only about four or five years apart, but his eyes showed that he was younger than I had been at the same age. I wanted to touch his arm, comfort him, apologize to him. Tell him I hadn't meant this to happen. But I was afraid to touch him. I was afraid I'd make things worse somehow.

"Graham," and my voice sounded gentle, a voice for soothing frightened children and ledge jumpers, "I need you to find Remus or Claudia and bring them to me, okay? I need to talk to them about some of the things that happened last night. Can you do that for me? Can you find one of them and bring them to me?"

He swallowed hard enough that it sounded painful. "You won't kick me off your detail?"

"No," I said.

He nodded too fast, too often, over and over. He actually started for the door with my clothes still in his hands. It was Clay who took the clothes from him. When the door closed behind him, Clay turned to me. We stared at each other.

"He's addicted, isn't he?" Clay asked.

I nodded. "I think so."

"You didn't know either?"

I shook my head.

"You look pale," he said.

"You, too," I said.

"You haven't fed that much from him, right? I mean, you didn't even get naked together, right?"

"No, we didn't."

"I thought it took more than that to addict someone to it."

"So did I," I said.

Clay seemed to shake himself, like a dog coming out of water. "I'll put your clothes in the bathroom for you. I'll call Claudia and tell her we need a new red shirt."

"I think once she sees Graham she'll figure it out."

"He hid it pretty well, Anita. I think by the time he finds them, he'll have his shit together. It may not show."

I nodded. "You're right."

"I mean, he has a radio on him, too. He didn't think to use it."

"The radios are new," I said.

"The wererats have been handing the radio setups to some of the guards. When they found all the high-tech listening devices, I think they decided that we needed to go higher-tech ourselves."

"Sounds reasonable," I said. I felt Jean-Claude wake. Felt it like a hand caressing my body. It caught my breath in my throat.

"What's wrong?" Clay asked.

"Jean-Claude's awake."

"Good."

I nodded. Good was right. I let Jean-Claude feel how much I wanted him to be with me. I wanted him to hold me and tell me it was all going to be all right. In that moment, I wanted him to comfort me, even if it was all lies. Graham's face had been all the truth I wanted for a little while.

18

I WAS DRESSED by the time Jean-Claude knocked on the bathroom door. His "*Ma petite*, may I come in?" was uncertain of its welcome. I guess he thought I'd blame him for the *ardeur* having addicted Graham. There'd been a time, not too long ago, that I might have. But it was too late for blame. Blame wouldn't fix it, and I wanted it fixed. I wanted Graham free of the *ardeur*, if we could manage it. I'd freed others of the *ardeur*, but they'd been completely rolled by it. I'd never had anyone this addicted from such a small piece of it. Or maybe I had, and they were hiding it, too? God, I wish I hadn't thought of that.

"*Ma petite?*"

"Yes, I mean, come in. God, please come in."

The door opened. He stood framed for a moment before I flung myself onto him, burying my face against the furred lapels of his robe. I clutched at the heavy black brocade, pressing myself tight against him. His arms enfolded me, lifted me off the ground and moved us both inside the room. One arm held me close, the other hand reached back and closed the door behind us. The move was so fast I didn't have time to protest or think about it.

He let my feet touch the floor. "*Ma petite, ma petite*, what is so very wrong?"

"Me," I said. "I'm wrong." I spoke calmly, I didn't yell, I just happened to be talking with my face against his robe.

He drew me away from him enough for him to see my face. "*Ma petite*, I felt your distress, but I do not know what has caused it."

"Graham is addicted to the *ardeur*."

"When did this happen?" he asked, his face gone to careful blankness. He was probably unsure what expression wouldn't upset me.

"I don't know."

He studied my face, and even that careful blankness could not hide his concern. "When did you give Graham a stronger taste of the *ardeur*?"

"I didn't. I swear, I haven't touched him again. I've worked really hard not to touch him." The words came faster and faster, until even to me it sounded hysterical, but I couldn't stop.

Jean-Claude put a finger on my lips and stopped all the protest. "If you have not touched him again, *ma petite*, then he cannot be addicted to the *ardeur*."

I tried to say something, but he kept his finger touching my mouth. "The fact that Graham wants you is not proof of addiction, *ma petite*. You underestimate the pull of your sweet self."

I shook my head and moved my face back so I could speak. "He's addicted, damn it. I know the difference between lust and addiction. Ask Clay if you don't trust me." I pulled away from him; it didn't feel comforting to touch him anymore.

"I trust you, *ma petite*." He was frowning now.

"Then take my word for it. Graham is addicted, and I don't know when it happened. Do you understand? I've avoided him. I've done everything I can to keep him away from the *ardeur* and still let him be a bodyguard. Today I tried to fire him from my guard detail."

"What did he say to that?"

"He was panic stricken. He was nearly in tears. I've never seen him like that. He only calmed down when I told him I wouldn't replace him on my detail."

"The *ardeur* is not so easily caught, *ma petite*. The few touches that Graham has had are not enough to addict him."

"I saw it!" I was pacing the room now.

"I think you need a cross, *ma petite*."

"What?" I asked.

He went to the door, opened it. "Could you please get one of the extra crosses out of the bedside table?"

I caught a glimpse of myself in the bathroom mirror. The red shirt seemed to blaze against my pale skin and dark hair. The scarlet seemed to be some sort of accusation like a scarlet woman, the scarlet letter. The last thought stopped me, as if the hysteria had hit a stumbling block. I could think for a second. Scarlet woman, the Scarlet Letter; this wasn't me thinking. Shit. I was being messed with.

My gun and holster were still beside the sink; I hadn't had time to put it on before Jean-Claude came. I put my hand on the butt of the gun and squeezed. That was me; I was me. The gun wasn't a magical talisman, but sometimes all you need to get someone out of your head is to remind yourself who you are—who you really are, not who they think you are, or who they think you think you are, but you, the real you. The gun in my hand was me.

"*Ma petite*, I would prefer you step away from the gun until you are wearing a cross."

I nodded. "I'm being messed with, aren't I?"

"I believe so."

"It's daylight, early daylight. If the vampires that are messing with us are in town, they shouldn't be able to do this."

"They are the Harlequin, *ma petite*; now you begin to see what that means."

I nodded again, clutching at the gun as I'd cluthced at Jean-Claude earlier.

"*Ma petite*, if you would step away from the gun?"

"The gun is helping, Jean-Claude. It's reminding me that all the hysterics isn't me."

"Humor me, *ma petite*."

I looked at him. His face was still that beautiful blankness, but there was a tension to his shoulders, the way he held his body. Clay was behind him in the doorway, and he wasn't even trying to hide that he was worried. "I've got the cross," he said.

I nodded again. "Give it to me."

He glanced at Jean-Claude, who nodded. Clay walked forward with his hand in a fist. "You may want to step outside, Jean-Claude," he said.

"I cannot leave you alone with her."

"Won't the cross react to you?"

"*Non*, for I am doing nothing to her."

I held my left hand out toward Clay. "Just give me the cross."

"By the chain," Jean-Claude said.

"Good thinking," I said. "I don't need another cross-shaped burn scar."

Clay held his fist out to me, then opened it so that the cross dangled from a thin gold chain. If a vampire had been in the room causing trouble, that would have been enough to make the cross glow. Hell, even in Clay's hand, it might have glowed. The cross just hung there. Were we wrong? Was I wrong?

"Touch only the chain, *ma petite*. Caution is better."

If he hadn't repeated that, I might have just grabbed the cross, but at the last second I touched the chain. Clay let it go, and it swung, delicate and golden, in my hand. For a heartbeat, I thought we'd been wrong. Then the cross burst into a brilliant yellow glow. I had to turn my eyes away from it. I had a thought of what it might be doing to Jean-Claude, but I could see nothing past the golden light. I called to him. "Jean-Claude!"

A male voice that I wasn't sure of said, "He's out of the room. He's safe."

I yelled, "Clay, Claudia!" I wanted a voice I knew out of the brilliant yellow light.

Claudia's voice, a little farther away. "Clay got Jean-Claude out."

With that worry out of the way, I could concentrate on the other problem. If the vampire that had been messing with me was in the room, then the cross would have driven him away. Hell, when Marmee Noir messed with me, a cross like this had driven her away. So why wasn't this working on the Harlequin?

The chain grew warm in my hand. If this kept up it would get hot. Shit. If I threw the cross down, it would stop glowing, but would the vampire attack again? Would he enter my mind again, without my knowing it? God, these guys were good. Scary good.

"Anita, what can I do to help?" The man's voice again. I recognized the voice now: Jake, one of our newer bodyguards.

"I don't know," I said. I yelled it, as if the light were sound and I was having trouble hearing over it. I prayed, *Help me, help me figure this out.* I don't know if it was the prayer, or if the prayer helped me think;

chicken/egg, I think, but I knew what to do. With the cross blazing in my hand I could feel the vampire, now that I thought to look for it. I was a necromancer, and that meant I had an affinity with the dead. I could feel the other's power like a seed in my back. As if he'd marked me somehow. That seed had let him inside me over and over since the movies last night. I wanted that seed gone.

I thrust my power into that spot, but I should have known better. With Jean-Claude's power I might have just ripped it out of me, cast it aside, but my power was different. My power liked the dead.

I touched the mark the vampire had made in my body. I didn't understand how he'd done it, and I didn't care. I wanted it gone. But the moment my necromancy touched it, it was as if a door blew open inside my head. I caught a glimpse of stone walls and a male figure. I smelled wolf. I tried to see clearly, but it was as if darkness ate at the edges of the picture. I concentrated on that image, willed it to be clear. Willed the man to turn and show me . . . He turned, but there was no face. I was looking at a black mask with a huge false nose. I thought for a moment I could see his eyes, then the eyes filled with silver light, almost a soft light. Then that soft, silver light shot out of the mask and slammed into me. I came back to myself airborne, falling. I didn't even have time to be afraid.

19

I HAD A blurred image of black marble, glass. A second to realize that I was about to hit the mirrors around Jean-Claude's tub. I tried to both tense and relax for the impact. A dark blur passed me, and when I smacked into the mirrors, there was a body behind me. A body that wrapped itself around me and took the impact as we hit the glass and the wall underneath. I heard the glass break, and we slid in a heap at the edge of the tub. I lay there, stunned, breath knocked out of me. It suddenly seemed very important to hear my own heartbeat. I blinked at nothing for a moment or two. Only when the body under me groaned did I turn my head enough to see, in the mirrors that weren't cracked, who I'd landed on. Jake lay in a heap against the spiderweb cracks of the glass. He was one of the newest members of Richard's pack, though not new to being a werewolf, and had only been a bodyguard for a few weeks. His eyes were closed; blood trickled down from his short, dark curls. He wasn't moving. I gazed up, past us, and saw that some of the jagged pieces were missing. There was a huge piece that sparkled as it moved away from the wall and begin to fall toward us. I grabbed Jake and pulled with everything I had. I pulled like I didn't expect him to move, but I forgot that I was more than human strong. I pulled, and he moved, moved so hard and sudden that we ended up in the bathtub. I was suddenly underwater with his weight on top of me. Before I could panic, he startled awake, grabbing my arms, and jerked us both to the surface. We came up gasping, as the glass tinkled like sharp raindrops where we'd just been lying.

"Shit!" This from the doorway.

I blinked water out of my eyes to see Claudia in the room. There were more guards crowding in behind her. Claudia strode into the room and lifted me bodily out of the tub. Other hands lifted Jake. He fell to his knees when they got him out. It took two of them to carry him into the bedroom. I walked on my own, but Claudia kept her hand on my arm. I think she expected me to collapse, too. Other than being wet, everything seemed to be working. But I didn't bother telling her to let go of me, with the grip she had. . . . Call it a hunch, but she wouldn't have done it anyway. I'd learned to argue carefully with Claudia; it upped my chances of winning the arguments.

Claudia half-led, half-pulled me into the bedroom. The room was nearly black with bodyguards. A handful of red shirts stood out like berries in a muffin—though "muffin" didn't quite cover the level of adrenaline-charged readiness. There was so much tension it felt as if I should have been able to walk across it. Some of them had guns out, pointed at the floor or ceiling.

I stood there dripping wet, searching the crowd for Jean-Claude. As if she understood what I was doing, Claudia said, "I sent Jean-Claude outside. He's safe, Anita, I promise."

Graham stepped out from the crowd. "We thought it might be a plot to hurt him." He looked and sounded fine now. There was no sign of the earlier panic.

"How you feeling?" I asked.

He gave me a puzzled grin. "Shouldn't I be asking you that?"

A chill ran through me that had nothing to do with standing wet in the colder air. "You don't remember, do you?"

"Remember what?" he asked.

"Shit," I said.

Claudia turned me toward her. "What's going on, Anita?"

"Hang on a minute, okay?"

Her grip on my arm tightened enough that it hurt. She probably could have crushed it if she'd been this muscled and human, but combine the workout with being a wererat and she was very strong.

"Watch the grip, Claudia," I said.

She let me go and wiped her hand against her jeans to get rid of the water. "Sorry."

"It's okay," I said. A sound of ripping cloth took my attention from Graham. Jake was on his knees by the armoire. Someone had ripped his shirt down the back. The bare back was bleeding, a lot. Cisco, one of the youngest of the wererats, was picking glass out of that once-smooth skin. Jake was a werewolf, and he was this hurt. It meant that if it had been my back, I'd be going to the hospital.

"Thanks, Jake," I said.

"Just doing my job, ma'am." His voice hesitated at the end as Cisco and another guard started picking glass out of him.

"Did anyone check his scalp for glass?" Claudia asked.

No one said yes. She called out, "Juanito, check him for glass."

Juanito was another newer guard. I'd been introduced to some of them when the word went out that we needed more men, but the tall, dark, handsome man was a stranger to me. I'd nodded at him, that was about it. At least Jake had been here a few weeks. Juanito meant "little Juan," but he didn't match his name. He was six feet at least, slender but muscular. He was not a little anything, as far as I could tell.

"I'm not a medic," he said.

"I didn't ask," Claudia said.

He just stood there staring at her, clearly not happy.

"I gave you an order. Follow it," she said. I hadn't heard that tone in Claudia's voice often. If I'd been him I'd have done what she said.

He moved to the kneeling werewolf and started picking through the wet curls. He didn't do it like his heart was in it, though. Cisco and the other guard seemed to be taking their job seriously.

Graham brought a large towel from the bathroom and started picking up the bloody pieces of glass that were already on the floor. Cisco and the others started dropping the glass onto the towel. It looked like red rain and sharp little pieces of hail.

"How bad is Jake hurt?" I asked Claudia.

"Not bad, but we don't want the skin healing over the glass."

"That happen often?" I asked.

"Often enough," she said.

I looked back at the men and found that Jake's back was smoothing even as I watched. "Is it just me or is he healing fast even for a shapeshifter?"

"It's not just you," Claudia said. "He heals faster than almost anyone I've ever met."

The three guards were searching frantically along his body, trying to stay ahead of his skin as it flowed over the wounds. Juanito had gotten over his reluctance and was now searching Jake's hair with fumbling fingers, desperately searching through the curls. "I'm not going to get them all! He's healing too fast!"

"The glass you miss, you get to cut out," Claudia said.

"Shit," he said, and worked faster.

Jake made almost no sound while everyone picked at his wounds. He stayed silent and motionless under their hands. I'd have been cursing and at least flinching.

Graham had apparently picked up all the stray glass he could find, because he wiped his fingers on the towel and stood up.

"Graham, you wearing a holy item?" I hoped he'd say no.

"No," he said.

Relief flooded through me, and I shivered. I was cold from the wet clothes and the reaction to the accident. No, not accident. The Harlequin had tried to kill me. Fuck. I hadn't understood; even with everyone's warnings, I hadn't understood. I was like a kid who'd poked a kitten with a stick and found a tiger staring at me.

"Talk to us, Anita," Claudia said.

There were so many people in the room that they couldn't all know about the Harlequin. How to explain without overexplaining? "The bad guys messed with Graham, a lot, and he doesn't remember it."

"What are you talking about?" Graham asked. "No one's messed with me."

"Ask Clay," I said. "He saw it, too."

Claudia hit the radio in her hand and called for Clay to join us when he could. Then she turned to me. "From the top, Anita, all of it."

"I can't give you all of it until I talk to Jean-Claude."

"This cloak-and-dagger shit is getting old." This from Fredo: slender, not too tall, and dangerous. He was the only wererat who carried a gun sometimes but preferred knives, lots of them.

"For me, too," I said, "but you guys have to know about Graham now, not later."

"We're listening," Claudia said. She was very serious, almost threatening. She didn't like the cloak-and-dagger stuff either. I didn't blame her.

I told them, though I toned it down for Graham's embarrassment's
sake.

Claudia said, "A vampire, in daylight, from a distance, messed with
Graham?"

"Yes," I said.

"That shouldn't be possible," she said.

"Not in daylight, from a distance, no, it shouldn't be."

"You're telling me as a vampire executioner that you've never seen
anything like this?"

I started to say no, then stopped. "I've had a few Masters of the City
mess with me from a distance when I was sleeping, and in their territory."

"But that was at night," she said.

"True," I said.

We stared at each other. "Are you saying these guys . . ." She
stopped herself.

I waited for her to finish; when she didn't, I said, "Holy objects need
to be mandatory for everyone."

"It didn't help you much just now," she said.

"It kept them from messing with my head as bad as they messed
with Graham's. He doesn't even remember."

"I know you wouldn't lie," Graham said, "but because I don't remember, I don't believe it."

"That's what makes vampire mind tricks so dangerous," I said.
"That very thing. The victim doesn't remember so it didn't happen."

Jake's voice came with only a slight edge of strain to it. "What did
you do to get the cross to do that?"

"It wasn't the cross," I said.

There was a flash of blade as Juanito searched Jake's dark curls for
the right spot. Apparently they were going to have to cut some of the
glass out. I wanted to look away, but I couldn't let myself do that. Jake
had gotten hurt because of me. The least I could do was watch the
cleanup.

"What was it, then?" he asked, the last word hissed as the blade cut
into his scalp.

"I . . . I'm not sure how to explain it."

"Try," he said, through gritted teeth.

"I tried to fight back with my necromancy and they, he, didn't like it."

Juanito shook the piece of glass onto the bloody towel, then turned back to search through the now-bloody curls.

"He?" Claudia asked.

"Yeah, definitely he."

"Did you see him?" Jake asked, and his breath went out sharp as another piece of glass went on the towel.

"Not exactly see, but I felt him. The energy was definitely male."

"How was it male?" Jake asked, his voice thin with pain.

I thought about it. "I thought I saw a male figure for an instant, and the . . ." I almost said *mask* and stopped myself. "But that could have been illusion. Except that the power felt male."

"What else did you get?" His body shuddered as Cisco worked on his back, apparently finding more glass he'd missed. Crap.

I answered, though I probably shouldn't have, but he'd taken my hit. I felt like I owed him. "Wolf, I smelled wolf."

He cried out under the knives. "That hurt!"

"I'm sorry," Cisco muttered. "I'm really sorry."

Juanito said, "Got it." He raised bloody fingers from Jake's hair. Something glittered in his hands that wasn't the knife. "That's the last of it, all I can find."

"Hope I can return the favor sometime," Jake said.

"If I apologized like Cisco, would you be less pissed?"

"Yes," Jake said.

"Fine, I apologize."

"I accept it."

Cisco moved back from him and laid something that looked like solid blood on the towel. "That's it for your back, too."

"Thanks," Jake said. He tried to get to his feet, but fell against the armoire so hard it shuddered. Hands reached to help him, covering his arms in bloody prints of his own blood.

He pushed them away. "I'm all right." Then he fell to his knees.

"Help him," Claudia said.

Cisco and Juanito reached for him again. Jake waved them away.

I walked the few feet to them. I knelt in front of Jake, so that I could meet his eyes without him straining. He rolled brown eyes up to me. His normally handsome face seemed strained and tired. He was a little too masculine handsome for my tastes. I liked men a little softer looking, but I could still appreciate the view. Except now the view was hurting too badly to be admired.

"I'd be in the hospital or worse now, Jake. Thank you."

"Like I said, it's my job," but his voice was strained.

"Let them help you, please."

He looked at me for a long moment. "What do you think the wolf smell meant?"

"I think it was the vamp's animal to call. Some vamps smell like their animal."

"Most vampires smell like vampires to me," he said.

"I've met a couple that smelled like their animals to call." I didn't add out loud that those had been Auggie, Master of Chicago, and Marmee Noir. Auggie was about two thousand years old, and Mommie Dearest was older than dirt. Which put this vampire in very powerful company.

"You're thinking something, what is it?" he asked.

I might not have answered him, except he'd gotten himself hurt protecting me. It made me feel guilty. "That the only two vamps I've ever known who smelled that much like their animals were Auggie, Master of Chicago, and the Mother of All Darkness."

"I've heard of Augustine, but the Mother of All Darkness, I'm not sure who that is."

"She's the Mother of All Vampires," I said.

His eyes widened, then flinched. "Powerful shit."

"Yeah," I said, "powerful shit. Let them take you to the doc, okay?"

He gave a small nod. "Okay."

Cisco and Juanito picked him up under the arms. They did it like he wasn't tall and muscled, and weighed at least two hundred pounds. Super-strength did come in handy. He got his feet sort of under him as the guards parted and let them through. By the time they had the door, Jake was almost walking upright. Almost.

20

THIS TIME I chose a black shirt, because my last clean bra was hanging up to dry in the bathroom. I was never entirely comfortable without a bra. I wasn't sure whether the fact that the black baby-doll shirt was tight enough that it helped support my breasts was a good thing or not. I think I would have preferred the shirt to be looser. Tight felt better, but it looked like I'd done it on purpose, rather than just running out of clothes. Also, braless the shoulder holster fit, but if I had to draw the gun I'd brush the edge of my breast. It was a small irritation, but it could make you hesitate for a second. Sometimes a second was enough to get you killed. I stood in the bathroom, grumpy and uncomfortable. It was like my skin was too small. Itchy with embarrassment and swallowed anger. I searched myself, with the same "eyes" that let you see images in your head, for that spot where the Harlequin had marked me. It was gone, but I could still see the spot like a bruise. A metaphysical bruise, as if their touch had hurt me in a way that would last.

I dried my hair a little more with a towel and actually scrunched some hair-care product in the curls. I was half embarrassed that I used stuff on my hair, but Jean-Claude had convinced me there was no shame to a little pampering. It still felt girlie to do it. Should you be worried about your hair frizzing when you wear a gun at least twelve of any given twenty-four hours? Seemed like you shouldn't.

There was a soft knock on the door. "What?" I asked, and even to me it sounded angry. Shit.

"I'm sorry, Anita, but Jean-Claude sent me to check on you."

"Sorry, Clay, it's just been one of those days already."

"Breakfast is waiting in the living room," he said through the closed door.

"Is there coffee?" I asked.

"Fresh, from the guards' break room."

I took in a deep breath, let it out, and went for the door. Coffee. Everything would be better after coffee.

I expected Graham to be with Clay, but it was Sampson. He wasn't a guard. In fact, he was sort of a visiting prince. He was the eldest son of the Master Vampire of Cape Cod, Samuel. Their vampire group wanted a closer tie with us, and one way to do that was for Sampson to audition as my new *pomme de sang*—apple of blood, like a kept mistress. It had been Nathaniel's job until he moved up the power structure to my animal to call. Now I needed a new snacky bit, whether I liked it, or whether I didn't. The *ardeur* needed more food. So far I'd managed to avoid having sex with Sampson. Since he was almost as embarrassed about the whole situation as I was, well, it hadn't been that hard to avoid. It wasn't that he wasn't handsome. He was tall, broad-shouldered, with a fall of dark curls that were identical to his father's. He even had his father's hazel eyes. In fact, he was one of those sons who looked like the father had cloned himself, except he was a few inches taller, and somehow softer. But then Samuel was over a thousand years old. You didn't survive that long in vampire society by being soft. You certainly didn't rise to be Master of the City by being soft, and you sure as hell didn't stay there by being anything but hard.

Sampson smiled at me, and it was a nice smile, boyish, a little bashful. He was wearing a white button-up shirt with the sleeves rolled back and the collar loose. The shirt was untucked over dress slacks. He was barefoot. His mother was a mermaid, a siren, and it made Sampson react more like a shapeshifter sometimes. He didn't like shoes, though he did like clothes better than my furry friends. Maybe water is colder?

"We're shorthanded, remember?" Clay said.

"I remember." Though I didn't sound happy about it.

"Am I that big a disappointment?" Sampson asked, but his smile widened, and his eyes twinkled with it. He never seemed to take my bad moods personally. Of course, I'd met his mother, Thea. She was like the ocean: calm one minute, rising up to kill you the next. I think she'd sort of broken him to the thought that women were moody.

"Thanks for volunteering to be food so the red shirt guards could be elsewhere," I said, and my voice sounded nicely dry and sarcastic.

"I heard you'd already fed the *ardeur*," he said.

I nodded.

He held his arm out to me. "Then allow me to escort you to your master, and real food."

I sighed, but I took his arm. Sampson was supposed to have been a short-term loan. To the larger vampire community he was here to try out for the position of *pomme de sang*. That was half the truth. The other half was that his mother was a siren, and the last of her kind. She was a genetic queen among the merfolk, magical, powerful, and most of that magic was sexual in nature. All mermaids could be alluring to mortals, but sirens could force you to wreck your ship. They could call you down to the sea and drown you and you'd enjoy it. They were sort of like master vampires, except more specialized, and more rare. Like I said, Thea was the last of her kind, unless her sons could be brought into their full power.

Problem was, the only way to bring a siren into their power was sex with another siren. Since Thea was the last of her kind and her sons were the last potential of her bloodline, well, it was all too Oedipus Rex for comfort.

She actually had no problem with doing the job herself. She'd been worshipped as a goddess once a few thousand years ago. Gods and goddesses married each other all the time, or at least fucked. But Samuel, though a thousand years old, was more conventional. He told her if she approached Sampson again for it, he'd kill her. Furthermore, if she approached their seventeen-year-old twin sons at all, he'd kill her. Again, so Greek tragedy. But if their sons could be as powerful as Thea, or even close, then suddenly Samuel's family would rule the East Coast. They just would. They were our allies and friends. Jean-Claude had called Samuel friend for a few centuries. Them powerful didn't seem like a bad idea.

The idea was that the *ardeur* might be similar enough to siren power that I might be able to bring Sampson into his sirenhood. If I could, great. If I couldn't, then Thea had promised to leave her sons alone and accept that she was the last of the sirens. That her sons being half human, or half vampire, depending on how you looked at it, meant they weren't mermaid enough to be what she was. See why I'd agreed to keeping Sampson around for a while? I mean, I was like their only chance to avoid a family tragedy of epic proportions. But it still made me feel squeachy.

But I slid my left arm through his arm. I let him lead me to the door, with Clay ahead of us doing the bodyguard thing. Though, frankly, since I was the only one armed, I didn't feel all that protected. The only wolf I'd seen with a gun had been Jake. Jake had a military background, so Richard had given him permission to carry weaponry. I'd asked Richard's permission to take some of the wolf guards to the shooting range and see who could handle a gun. He'd said he'd think about it. I had no idea why he had a problem with the werewolves being armed, but he was Ulfric, wolf king, and his word was law. I was lupa, but in wolf society that's more like an uber-girlfriend. It's not a queen, and it's not equal. I preferred leopard society; it was less sexist. Nimir-Ra truly was equal to Nimir-Raj.

We were still in the stone corridor, with the draped walls of the living room in sight, when I heard enough voices to know it was a lot more than Jean-Claude waiting for me. Clay lifted to one side the heavy spill of drapes that made up the living room walls so Sampson and I could enter.

Jean-Claude and Richard had to turn on the couch to look as we entered. Jean-Claude's face remained pleasant and welcoming as he stood. Richard's face clouded over, his gaze flicking to Sampson on my arm. Richard fought to control his emotions, the effort visible on his face and in the set of his shoulders, the way his hands flexed. I appreciated that he was trying.

I appreciated the effort enough that I let go of Sampson's arm and went to Richard. I leaned over the couch and kissed him on the cheek. He looked surprised, as if it had been a long time since I had kissed him first. There were, after all, so many choices. Micah stood across the room, setting his plate down on the glass coffee table with the rest of the food that someone had brought into the underground. Nathaniel was sitting on the floor by the table. He smiled at me, but he stayed where he was. He'd wait his turn for his greeting. I went to

Jean-Claude next because he was closest. If we were doing formal we did the greetings more formally, but at breakfast with just us we tried not to sweat the niceties. Sampson had been raised in a kiss of vampires that did it old-school, which meant they all did the Miss Manners version, vampire style, no matter the hour or the event. By those rules I'd already made three mistakes. One, I had let go of Sampson's arm. You stayed on your escort's arm until someone more powerful got you off that arm, or until your escort introduced you to someone he was willing to give you up to. Two, I'd greeted someone in the room before I'd greeted the Master of the City. Three, I'd greeted a were-animal ruler before greeting the highest-ranking vamp in the room. Old-school meant that no one was more important than the vampires. The exception to this rule at Sampson's home was his mother, Thea. Technically she was Samuel's animal to call, but if Sampson's father had any weakness it was Thea, so you ignored her at your peril. She was queen to Samuel's king no matter what vampire rules said.

Jean-Claude was in one of his very formal white shirts, with a real cravat held in place with a silver and sapphire stickpin on his chest. He'd even put on a black velvet jacket with matching silver buttons. It was very militaristic. The shirt I'd seen before, or one like it; the jacket was new—to me, at least. I hadn't seen it yet, but I was pretty sure somewhere in the underground there was a huge room full of nothing but Jean-Claude's clothes. The pants were actually cloth but fit tighter than any dress slacks I'd ever seen. The tight pants smoothed into thigh-high boots that were black and leather and had silver buckles up the side of them from ankle to midthigh. He was way too dressed up for just a family breakfast. When he drew me into his arms, the curls that brushed my face were still damp from the shower. If he took the time to bathe, he'd take the time to dry his hair.

"You seem tense, *ma petite*," he whispered into my own damp hair.

"You're way too well dressed for breakfast, and your hair is still damp, which means you dressed in a hurry. Why the rush?"

He kissed me gently, but I didn't close my eyes or relax into the kiss. He sighed. "You are too observant for comfort at times, *ma petite*. We were going to allow you to finish your breakfast before we discussed business."

"What business?" I asked.

Micah came up beside us. I went from Jean-Claude's arms to his, and found that Micah, too, was too dressed up. He was in charcoal-gray dress pants and a pale green silk shirt, tucked into the pants. He was even wearing shiny dress shoes that were a few shades darker than the pants. Someone had French-braided his still-damp hair, which gave the illusion that his hair was very short and close to his head. It left his face bare so that all I could see was how very pretty he was. The bones of his face were damn near feminine. Somehow with some of his curls to distract the eye you didn't notice it as much. The green shirt made his chartreuse eyes green, green like seawater with sunlight through it, swimmingly green with gold light caught in it.

I had to close my eyes to say, "What business?"

"Rafael has requested a breakfast meeting," Micah said.

That made me open my eyes. "Clay told me Rafael was wanting something other than money for the extra guards."

Micah nodded.

"Rafael is our ally and our friend, right? Why are you guys dressed up and all serious?" I looked around the room. When I caught sight of Claudia, she looked away. She looked uncomfortable, as if whatever Rafael wanted embarrassed her. What the hell could it be?

Nathaniel came to us, his ankle-length hair unbound and still heavy with water. He'd dried it, but it just took a while for that much hair to dry completely. This wet, the hair looked closer to a simple deep brown than the nearly copper auburn that it was. He was still carrying the couch cushion he'd been balancing his plate on, though the plate was on the table. He carried the cushion in front of his waist and groin. All I could see below the cushion was a pair of cream-colored leather boots that hit him midthigh.

"What aren't you wearing behind that cushion?"

He threw the cushion behind him with a flourish and a grin. He was wearing a G-string that matched the boots, and that was it. I'd seen the outfit before, but never this early in the morning. "Not that I don't appreciate the view, because I do, but isn't it a little early for fetish wear?"

"All my dress shirts here are silk. My hair's so wet it would stain them." He pressed himself into my arms, and my hands curved under all that heavy hair and found it was still very wet, so wet that the skin of his naked back was cool and slightly damp to the touch. He was right, silk would have been ruined. My hands curved lower until I found the round, tight bareness of his buttocks. He flexed under my hands and I had to close my eyes and take a breath before I could say, "Why are you wearing this for a meeting with Rafael?"

Micah answered, "We thought it might remind Rafael what exactly being close to us means. Rumor has it, he's vanilla."

I stepped back from Nathaniel, because I had trouble thinking when I was touching any of my men naked. "Say that again."

Richard's voice, so unhappy that I knew the news was bad. "Rafael wants you, too?"

"I'm lost," I said.

"Rafael has put himself forward as a candidate to be your new *pomme de sang*," Jean-Claude said, his voice as bland and emptily pleasant as he could make it.

I just gaped at him. I couldn't even think of anything to say.

Nathaniel touched my chin and closed my mouth, gently. He kissed my cheek, and said, "It's okay, Anita."

I swallowed and stared into that peaceful face. He smiled gently at me. I shook my head. "Why would he ask this? Rafael doesn't do anything without a reason."

Claudia cleared her throat sharply. We all turned to her. She looked as embarrassed as I'd ever seen her. "He's afraid that Asher's ties to the werehyenas will make them have closer ties to Jean-Claude and you than we do, the rats."

"He's my friend," Richard said. "I am not friends with the werehyenas' leader."

"But Rafael isn't friends with Jean-Claude, or Anita. It's just a business arrangement with them. Asher is their lover, and his animal to call is the hyena now, so that makes the hyenas more essential to your plans than us."

"The rats are our allies and friends," I said, "and nothing personal to the hyenas, but I trust the rats a heck of a lot more one-on-one as guards than most of the hyenas."

Claudia nodded. "With a few exceptions the hyenas are amateur muscle, and Rafael doesn't recruit amateurs."

"You guys are important to us, Claudia. Where the hell did Rafael get the idea that we'd dump him for Narcissus?" I asked.

She shrugged those wonderfully muscled shoulders as much as the muscles would allow. "He wants a closer tie to Jean-Claude, that's all I know."

I looked at Jean-Claude and Richard. "I don't have to do this, right?"

"No, *ma petite*, you do not, but we must hear his case for it. I agree with not doing it. I think the other wereanimals would take it badly if you made someone's king your new *pomme de sang.*"

"The other wereanimals are already jealous of Anita's ties to the wereleopards and the wolves," Sampson said. He'd walked around us to help himself to food and to take one of the chairs by the fireplace. I'd sort of forgotten he was there. He had that ability to blend into the woodwork when he wanted to. Not magic, just tact.

"What do you mean?" I asked. "Those are our animals to call. We're supposed to have a tighter bind to them."

"True, but you, Anita, carry the strain for lion and at least one other lycanthrope strain. There are those among the community who believe they know why the doctors can't identify that fourth strain in your body." He took a bite of croissant, and I was suddenly hungry. With all that was happening, my stomach rolled and let me know there were other hungers besides the *ardeur.*

"What's their theory?" I asked. I went to the table and started putting food on one of the white china plates. We had take-out food every morning, but by God we ate off real plates with real silverware. Though the silverware was actually gold-plated, so that there was no problem with everyone using the utensils. Real silver can burn the skin of a lycanthrope. Not burn as in blister, but burn as in itch and hurt.

"Chimera attacked you in lion form, which explains the lion lycanthropy, but he was also a panwere. You've discussed that you may be able to add new types of lycanthropy until you shapeshift for the first time, haven't you?" Sampson asked.

"Yeah, we've discussed it, as a theory," I said.

"Some in the shapeshifter community would like you to try to take on as many of their beasts as you can before you shift, so that they'll have a tighter alliance with Jean-Claude."

I looked at Claudia. "Is that true? Have people been suggesting that?"

"There has been talk."

"Is that really what Rafael wants?" I asked. "I mean, he knows that Richard and I don't want to put him in my bed, but is that just a ruse? He offers sex, I say no, and then he does a counterproposal of what . . . trying to give me rat-based lycanthropy?"

"I'm not sure what he plans to say," she said.

I looked at Sampson. "How do you know all this?"

"I was raised in what amounts to a royal court, Anita. You live and die on your intelligence information."

"I've noticed that Sampson has an almost uncanny ability to elicit confidences," Jean-Claude said.

"You rolling them with mermaid tricks?" I asked.

He shrugged and took another bite of croissant.

"Using mind tricks on people without their permission is punishable by law," I said.

"The law actually states that it's illegal to use vampire tricks, telepathy, or witchcraft to elicit information without permission. I'm not using any of the three."

"I could make a court case that mermaid power is a form of telepathy."

"But I'm not reading their minds; they're volunteering information to me. That's not telepathy at all. Besides, this isn't a court case, this is about how to swim through the rocks in your path."

"And you have a suggestion," I said, and let it sound as suspicious as I wanted it to.

He laughed and wiped his hands on the white napkin in his lap. "You can avoid the sex question by saying that I'm the next candidate, which is true. I can simply not give up my place as next in your bed. Their king knows I am the eldest son of another Master of the City, and I have prior claim to your affections."

"And it will get you in her bed sooner," Richard said; he sounded suspicious, too.

Sampson gave him a patient look with just an edge of impatience. "I have been here for months and not pushed my claim. Partly because, until Anita tries to bring me into my siren abilities, my mother will leave my brothers alone. I'm not at all convinced that the *ardeur* is similiar enough to my mother's powers that Anita can awaken me to that other power. If I sleep with Anita and it doesn't work, then my family is back to the same problem."

"Your mother promised that if I couldn't bring you into your sirenhood, she'd accept that she was the last siren, and she'd leave you and your brothers alone."

He laughed and shook his head. "She's not human, Anita, or a vampire; her word doesn't mean what you think it means. She wants us to be sirens, and I don't believe she'll accept your failure gracefully. But as long as I'm here trying, then she'll wait."

"And she'll leave your little brothers alone," I said.

He nodded. "But my mother won't wait forever, Anita. One of the reasons she traded Perdita to you as a blood donor was so Perdy could keep an eye on me."

"She's a spy?" I made it a question.

"I know she's enjoying dating your Jason, but yes, she's a spy. My father will accept and encourage that I've been a gentleman about everything, but my mother will lose patience with it."

"We can send Perdita back when you go," Richard said.

"She's spying on me, not on you."

"Your mom doesn't trust you not to fudge on this," I said.

"No, she doesn't. She knows how much I want to avoid her doing anything that will force my father to kill her. He adores her, but if she forces sex on me or my brothers he will do what he vowed. He will slay the woman he loves above all others. It would destroy him, and our family."

"You have been most patient," Jean-Claude said.

I wanted to argue, but couldn't. I nodded. "You have been."

"So just like that he gets to fuck you," Richard said.

I sighed. "You've done so well today, Richard. Don't spoil it."

"And how would you feel if I picked one of the women here in the underground to have sex with while you fuck Sampson?"

I looked at him. I thought of several things to say, none of them helpful.

"You wouldn't like it, would you?" he said.

"No," I said, not sure what else to say.

"Then don't expect me to enjoy sharing you."

"I don't expect you to like it, Richard. I don't think Jean-Claude likes it either, or Micah." I looked at Nathaniel. I both frowned and smiled.

"I like sharing," he said, with a smile.

"Good for you," Richard said. "I don't."

"You're having sex with the human women you're dating," I said.

"Some of them, yes I am."

"You're doing that by choice; I'm doing this because I have to."

"You'll still enjoy it," he said.

"Would it make you happier if the sex were bad?"

"Yes." He stood up, and let me finally see that he was wearing nice jeans and a red T-shirt. He'd probably refused fetish wear, and I didn't think he had any dress clothes here. "Yes, it would make me feel better if I didn't know you'd enjoy it."

"I don't know what to say to that, Richard, I really don't."

"I'm not having sex with anyone but Anita, and I don't have a problem with this," Micah said.

"No, of course you don't, because you're perfect," Richard said.

Micah looked at me, as if asking how much fight to have.

"Don't fight," I said. "Let's eat, then we'll talk about what to say to Rafael."

"And just because she says 'don't fight,' you won't fight, will you?" Richard asked.

"Usually, no," Micah said.

"Sometimes, Micah, I hate you," Richard said.

"Right back at you," Micah said with a smile.

Richard's power slapped along my skin like tiny bites of heat. But Micah was closer, and when his power flared, too, it was like standing too close to an open oven. "Stop it, both of you."

"*Mon chat, mon ami*, we do not have time for this."

"I am not your friend," Richard said. "I am your wolf to call, but that does not make us friends."

Jean-Claude took a deep breath, let it out, and went very still. Still in that way that the old ones could go, so that you felt if you looked away they'd vanish, even though they were standing right there. His voice when it came was neutral, pleasant, in an empty, impersonal way. "As you like, Richard. *Mon chat*, and *mon lupe*, we do not have time for this."

Richard turned toward him, his power filling up the room like hot bathwater that had gotten out of hand. You thought you were having a nice relaxing bath, and suddenly you were drowning. My pulse sped up, and the wolf inside me stirred.

I closed my eyes and started breathing, deep and even, breathing from the soles of my feet to the top of my chest. Deep cleansing breaths, to still that movement deep inside me. To isolate me from what Richard was doing. It was his power, not mine. I did not have to respond to it. Part of me believed that, but part of me knew better. His power and mine had married too tightly.

"Don't call me that," Richard said.

"If you are only my wolf to call and you are not my friend, then what else can I call you?" Jean-Claude's voice was very flat when he said it. I realized suddenly that he was angry, too. Angry at Rafael? Angry at the Harlequin? Angry at everything?

"Not that, not just wolf."

"You take insult where none is intended, but if you will find insult where none is meant, then perhaps I should try harder to insult on purpose."

The sound of the heavy outer door banged loud in the charged silence. It made me jump. "Rafael is here," Claudia said. Her voice managed to sound relieved and worried all at the same time, as if she was happy to cut the fight short, but worried what her king would do.

Richard was glaring at Jean-Claude, and the vampire was finally letting his anger show on his face when Rafael walked through the far drapes. Rafael was tall, dark, and handsome. There was absolutely nothing wrong with the six-foot, darkly Hispanic man in his nicely cut business suit. He'd left the tie off, so that the white dress shirt framed the hollow of his neck like an invitation. That last thought didn't sound like my own. I glanced at Jean-Claude, wondering if it was his. He'd fed on someone's blood today, I could tell that much, but I knew that sometimes he lusted after powerful blood the way that other men lusted after pretty women. What I hadn't known until that moment was that he lusted after Rafael as food.

Another surprise was behind him. Louie Fane, Dr. Louis Fane, teacher of biology at Washington University, and live-in boyfriend of one of my best friends. Ronnie, Veronica, Sims would probably have told me *boyfriend* sounded too junior high school. She'd have probably preferred the term *lover*, but it was my interior dialogue so I could use the words I wanted. Besides, Ronnie's continuing campaign to make her and Louie's relationship about sex and not emotion was her problem, not mine. Though sometimes she made it mine.

Louie was five foot six, slender, but not weak looking. Today his arms were covered, but when they were bare fine muscles played in his forearms. His hair was straight and dark, and cut short, freshly so, because I'd seen him only last week and it had been past his ears; now it wasn't. His face was softly squared, almost the only hint that his mother had been from Ecuador. That and the black eyes, darker even than my own.

I was surprised to see Louie. Don't know why; he was Rafael's second-in-command. How did a mild-mannered college prof get to be second banana in an animal group made up mostly of mercs and ex-criminals? By being smart, and not nearly as soft as he looked.

"Rafael, King of the Rodere of St. Louis, welcome," Jean-Claude said. The formality of the greeting set the tone.

"Jean-Claude, Master of the City of St. Louis, I am honored that you have invited me into your home." His gaze went to Richard. "Ulfric of the Thronnos Rokke Clan, friend and ally, thank you for seeing me so early in the day."

I was close enough to hear the sharp intake of breath, and I thought Richard would say something that went with that almost violent breath, but he let the air out slowly. It shuddered a little on its way out, and he spoke almost normally. "Rafael, King of Rats, friend and ally, there's plenty of food, help yourself."

"Thank you," Rafael said, and some tension I hadn't realized was there went out of his broad shoulders, as if he'd worried about Richard's reaction, too.

Louie went to Richard, and they did that guy handshake/hug, where you grip forearms and sort of bump shoulders. I heard him say, "Sorry about this."

If Richard said anything, I didn't hear it because Micah was talking to Rafael. "Are the leopards so unimportant that you do not even greet their king or queen?"

Of all the people in the room, I hadn't expected problems from Micah. From the look on Rafael's face, him either. "I meant no disrespect, Nimir-Raj."

"Yes, you did," Micah said.

"Micah . . . ," I said.

He shook his head at me. "No, Anita, we can't let an insult like this go. We can't."

Richard said, "You finally find something worth fighting for, Micah?"

He gave Richard a cold look. "What would you do if Rafael had ignored you and greeted every other leader in the room?"

Anger flashed over Richard's face, then smoothed out. "I wouldn't like it."

"Jean-Claude, you need to teach your cats better manners," Rafael said.

That got my attention, and not in a good way. I moved to stand by Micah. Nathaniel moved up with us, though a little behind us. We were king and queen; you didn't stand in front of the royalty, even if you were living with them.

"We aren't pets," I said.

"You are Jean-Claude's human servant, and the leopards have no connection to the Master of the City except through you, Anita. They are not linked directly to the vampires of this city."

I felt movement around us as the bodyguards shifted nervously. Rafael didn't even look at them. I did. I looked at Claudia, and she actually blushed. "Whose side are you on if the flags go up?" I asked.

"Do you actually believe you could challenge me?" Rafael said, and he sounded amused. I ignored him and kept my gaze on Claudia. Micah had his attention on Rafael, and I knew he'd let me know if I needed to look at the big man.

"Come on, Claudia, Fredo, talk to me. You're our bodyguards, but he's your king. If it goes bad, can we depend on you, or not?"

"They are my people," Rafael said. "They owe their loyalty to me."

I finally looked at him. It was not a friendly look. "Then they need to leave this room, now. We need hyena and wolves in here, now."

"They are no match for my people," Rafael said.

"Maybe not, but at least I can trust who they'll jump for."

Clay had hit his radio and was relaying my request.

Rafael looked at Jean-Claude. "Are the leopards in charge here, Jean-Claude? It is what I had heard, but I had not believed it." He had turned away from us as if we didn't matter.

I had a horrible urge to draw my gun, but knew I'd never get it out in time. Not with Claudia and Fredo in the room. And besides, I wouldn't really shoot him over an insult, and you never draw a gun unless you're willing to use it. I wasn't willing to use it, but I was really wanting a way to wipe that arrogance off Rafael's face.

Wolves and hyenas spilled into the room, at a run. We now had more of our people in the room than we did wererats. The tightness in my stomach eased a little.

"Rafael," Richard said, "why are you doing this?"

"Doing what?" he asked. "Treating the leopards as the lesser power they are supposed to be?"

Richard let his face show the surprise he felt. "Are you purposefully trying to bait Anita?"

"I have come to negotiate with the Master of the City and his triumvirate of power. His animal to call and his human servant."

"I'm also the leopard's queen, and they are my animal to call," I said. "You can't insult one half of my power base while you try to negotiate with the other."

"Exactly," Rafael said.

"What?" I asked.

"You have made your point, Rafael," Jean-Claude said.

I looked from one to the other. "Not to me, he hasn't."

"I'm confused, too," Richard said.

"I have worked for years to build the wererats into a force to be reckoned with, bargained with, a force not to be treated lightly. Though I may dislike Narcissus, he, in his own way, has also built the werehyenas up into a force to be reckoned with." He motioned at us, the only three leopards in the room. "The leopards were the playthings of the wolves when Raina was their lupa. Gabriel, the leader of the leopards, was her pawn. Then Anita killed both of them. She became lupa to the wolves and tried to protect the leopards. I was happy that the leopards had a true protector, someone who did not just use them. No group deserves the treatment that they suffered at Gabriel's hands." He walked toward us, slowly, nothing menacing in that movement, but I fought an urge to step back. Somehow I wasn't sure I wanted him that close to me, to us.

Rafael spoke as he moved calmly toward us. "Then Anita became more than just a human with extraordinary powers. By all accounts she may truly be a shapeshifter one of these moons."

"So what?" I asked. "So what if I finally turn furry for real?"

"Leopard is not Jean-Claude's animal to call, it is yours. Yet you are not a vampire. You are leopard queen, but not a wereleopard. The wolves' lupa, but not a werewolf. Now the lions are yours to call. If Joseph and his pride would only give you someone worthy to choose, you would have another animal to bind to you. The lions are weaker even than the leopards, but if you find a mate among

them, they will move up, they will be powerful, and they do not deserve it."

I was beginning to see what his point was, and I even understood
why he'd put himself forward as food. "You do everything according
to the rules," I said, "and then this metaphysical wild card comes out
of nowhere and suddenly animal groups that are weak by your standards have more ties to Jean-Claude. The leopards are a small group,
but they're intimate with the vampires, so they're powerful. You think
the same thing will happen with the lions."

"Yes," Rafael said.

"You are serious about being Anita's *pomme de sang*," Richard said,
"because it's the only way you can see getting closer to the power
structure."

Rafael nodded and looked at the other man. "I am sorry, my friend,
but if I cannot guarantee my people's safety through strength of arms
and traditional methods, then I am willing to whore myself for their
safety."

"I do not hold the leopards above you in esteem," Jean-Claude said.

"If there was a choice between saving the rats and saving the leopards, who would you choose?"

"There will not be a choice like that," Jean-Claude said.

"Perhaps not, but there might be a choice between the hyenas and
the rats. Narcissus is not my friend, and now Asher's animal to call is
his people."

"Asher is not master here," Jean-Claude said.

"No, but you love him, have loved him for centuries. That is a powerful bond, Jean-Claude. If Asher whispered sweetly enough, would
you deny him and his animals? Or would you side with him over my
people?"

"Are you planning on challenging the hyenas to a war?" Jean-
Claude asked it almost jokingly. But I knew that tone of voice; it was
the tone he used when he was worried he was right.

"No, but we are not animals, any of us," Rafael said.

"Our master would not start a war with you, rat king." This from
Remus.

Rafael shook his head. "You are one of the reasons that I fear a war,
Remus. When your Oba, your leader, was only recruiting martial
artists and weight lifters, pretty muscle that had never known a real

fight without referees, I did not worry, but you are the real thing, Remus. He has hired several ex-military, ex-police."

"He did that because of what happened when Chimera took over his men," I said. "Narcissus learned the difference between a bouncer and a soldier. He learned it the hard way. He lost a lot of his men to Chimera."

"And you killed Chimera for him," Rafael said, giving me all the attention of those dark eyes.

"I killed him for all of us. He wouldn't have left the rats alone either."

Rafael came to stand in front of us. I fought the urge to grab Micah's hand. Rafael hadn't done anything threatening, just being six feet tall and standing over us. Usually tall didn't intimidate me, but there was something about him today. Something bad.

"We were too powerful for Chimera to attack, and he did not hold rat lycanthropy in his body."

"He tried to take over several groups that he didn't hold the lycanthropy for," I said.

"If I had any liking for men, I'd offer myself to Jean-Claude and be done with it."

I didn't even try to keep the shock off my face. I did grab Micah's hand, as if the world had gotten shaky and I needed something to cling to. Rafael did not say things like this.

"But men do not interest me, so I do the next best thing. I offer myself to you, Anita. Because you protect those in your bed. And something about you brings power to your lovers. I do not understand it, but Nathaniel is the perfect example of one of the least wereanimals becoming something so much more, just because of you, Anita."

Nathaniel moved to touch my shoulder. I jumped, then eased into the touch, and a little away from this strange version of Rafael. He was afraid. I could feel it.

"What has Narcissus done to make you think your rats are in danger?" Jean-Claude said.

Rafael glanced at him. "What have you heard?"

"Nothing. I give you my word of honor that I have heard nothing, but you are cautious and thoughtful. This is not like you, Rafael; only something serious, and dangerous, could make you come to us like this." Jean-Claude sat down on the couch and said, "Sit with us, eat, and tell us what Narcissus has said or done to make you willing to say such things to *ma petite*."

Rafael closed his eyes, his hands in fists. "Your word of honor that you don't know. Then it can't be true."

"What cannot be true, *mon ami*? Talk to us. We are allies and friends; posturing and threats do not become us."

Micah pulled me away from Rafael and closer to the food. We weren't backing away from the rat king; we were just going to eat. Sure, but it saved face, and I was hungry. No matter what emergency was happening, I still hadn't even had coffee. One of the side effects of the *ardeur* and the almost-lycanthropy was that I couldn't not eat. Not without consequences, like sex I'd regret later, or having my body almost tear itself apart because it couldn't decide what animal it most wanted to be.

We actually got everyone settled with food, and Rafael stopped being all strange and scary. He sat on the love seat with Louie, with his guards at his back. We took the couch. It was big enough that everyone but Nathaniel had a seat. He curled up at my feet and made the scanty leather outfit work for him. The only one in the room who knew how to be more seductive at the drop of a hat was Jean-Claude, and he was all business. Though to him, sometimes seduction was business, but not this morning.

I nibbled on a croissant and a variety of cheese and fruit, and for the dozenth time wondered how to put a real kitchen into the Circus underground. Breakfast takeout was too damn limited. But the coffee was good. I sipped it black, because the first cup should always be black. It's the morning slap in the face that lets you know you're awake.

"Now," said Jean-Claude, "Rafael, my friend, talk to us. What has Narcissus said or done to alarm you so?"

"He said that he would offer himself to Anita as a *pomme de sang*, and with that, and his tie to your love, Asher, he would be the second most powerful animal group in St. Louis, after the wolves."

"He said this to you?" Jean-Claude asked.

"Not to me personally, no."

"Then how did you hear of it?"

"One of my rats likes the way that Narcissus makes love. Narcissus is beside himself now that Asher's animal to call is hyena. He had offered himself to Asher as Asher's animal to call, and been turned down."

News to me, I thought.

"Asher was flattered," Jean-Claude said, "but we both felt it would make the other groups nervous if Narcissus was so honored."

I fought not to look at Jean-Claude, because shouldn't someone have mentioned it to me? I sipped coffee and tried to keep my face blank, not always my best thing. I drank the coffee too fast to enjoy it, but it kept me from giving anything away, or I hoped it did.

"But Asher goes to Narcissus's club, and he enjoys the entertainment," Rafael said.

Narcissus's club was a bondage and submission club, and *entertainment* could cover a lot of ground. I hadn't known that Asher was going over there. I know that it feels good to be around your animal. I liked being around the leopards, and the wolves, and even the lions. But . . . it was like a lot was happening and I'd been out of the loop. I didn't like that.

"Asher enjoys what the club has to offer, but he has turned down Narcissus's more personal offers, again because he thought other animal groups might take it badly if he were to show such favor to Narcissus," Jean-Claude said.

"Narcissus seems to think that it's only a matter of time before Asher gives in to his charms."

"He does not know Asher as well as he believes," Jean-Claude said.

"Asher enjoys the bondage," Rafael said.

Jean-Claude shrugged, that wonderful Gallic movement that meant everything and nothing. Which meant Rafael might be right. Again, news to me. What else was my vampire "master" keeping from me?

"If Narcissus can seduce your Asher, he will do so. He will try to seduce you," Rafael said.

"Narcissus has tried to seduce me in the past. He failed," Jean-Claude said.

"He says the old Master of the City, Nikolaos, gave you to him several times. He has bragged of your body and what he did to it." Rafael studied Jean-Claude's face as he said it, as he'd studied mine. It looked like he was even making eye contact, not always wise with a vampire.

Jean-Claude gave him a lovely, blank face. "He has not bragged to you."

"You are certain of that?" Rafael said.

"Very. He had a tendency to talk during . . . during. He might have talked of me while he was doing similar things to someone else. In fact, I would be surprised if he had not. He enjoyed comparing and contrasting his lovers, and his victims."

"So you were his lover?"

"No, I was his victim. Nikolaos gave me to him with no safe word, no way to stop him from doing what he wished with me, except my own poor art of persuasion."

Rafael laughed, an abrupt and unhappy sound. "'Poor art,' false modesty from what I hear. Narcissus would give a great deal to have you back as his . . . victim."

"So he has said."

"He seems confident that Asher is the key to your bed. And if not Asher, then Anita. He believes sincerely that he will find a way to your libido again through them."

Finally something I could address without revealing that I wasn't entirely sure what was happening with Asher and the hyenas. "You don't have to worry about me and Narcissus. He's really not my cup of tea."

Rafael nodded, his face still serious. We couldn't seem to get a smile out of him this morning. "Am I your cup of tea, Anita?"

I felt Richard stiffen beside me. I glanced around him to Jean-Claude. "Can I talk plainly without upsetting the political apple cart here?"

"Talk, and we shall see."

Not a rousing endorsement, but I'd take what I could get. "You're handsome, and if it was a date, we could talk, but you want to skip to sex, and I'm just not that casual about it."

He gave me a look. It was a very judgmental look. I gave him an unhappy look back.

"Yeah, I have a lot of lovers, but they aren't casual lovers, Rafael."

He let out a breath, sipped some coffee, then said, "Perhaps not, but there is something about being your lover that seems to up the power level of every man that you . . . give yourself to."

"Not true," I said.

"Name a single lover you have had who has not gained power from it."

"I can name three: London, Requiem, and Byron," I said.

"The first two were master vampires before you slept with them. It's hard to judge how much power they arrived in St. Louis with, and how much they may have gained. Byron you slept with only once. Once doesn't seem to be enough." He sat his coffee down on his plate. "Fine, your regular lovers gain power."

"I think you overestimate me."

Rafael handed his plate to Louie, who stood and put it on the coffee table, as if he'd been told to do it. Rafael looked at me. He looked at me as if he would see through me to the other side. It was a look to study, weigh, and measure a person. I tried not to squirm under that gaze, but it was hard work.

"What?" I asked.

He looked at Jean-Claude. "She doesn't know, does she?"

"I am not certain that I know what you mean," Jean-Claude said.

"Jean-Claude, every lover Anita has gains power. Asher was a master vampire in name only, almost, but since he's been in her bed he's gained enough power to have his own territory if he didn't love you both too much to leave. Nathaniel was everyone's victim; now he is becoming someone to be reckoned with. You, personally, have gained more power than you ever dreamed."

"And you believe that it is *ma petite* who has given me power, not that I have shared my power with her?"

"She has her own triumvirate of power, Jean-Claude. Her own vampire servant in Damian."

"I am not the power behind the throne, Rafael. Trust me, Jean-Claude is plenty powerful enough for both of us."

"He is, but he gained most of that power after you became his lover."

"I gained powers after he made me his servant," I said, "not the other way around."

"I've been talking to some of the wererats in Europe," Rafael said. "They speak of your Belle Morte, the creator of your bloodline. They say that she could give power to her lovers, if she chose."

"Belle Morte does not choose to share power with anyone," Jean-Claude said.

"No, but she can; through sex, she can make her lovers more powerful. Legend has it that once she made kings and emperors through her touch. She changed the face of Europe through her bed."

"She ruled from her bedroom, that is true, but not in the way you think. She chose only the powerful, only those who could give her something she wanted. And I did not gain power in her bed. I was her pawn for centuries. As was Asher."

"Masters of the City often kill their own vampire children if they become too powerful, true?" Rafael said.

"Some do."

"But isn't it strange that so many of the vampires who were nearly powerless around Belle Morte have gained power the longer they are away from her?"

"What are you saying, Rafael?"

"I have heard rumors that some masters can retard the powers of their followers."

"Some can, but I do not believe Belle is one of them."

"Why not?"

He gave that shrug again.

Frankly, the rats were a little too well informed for comfort. I'd seen a master vampire gain new powers once in America and far enough away from his old master. But I wasn't sure it was on purpose; I'd actually begun to wonder if some powerful masters gave off a sort of hormone that retarded the power of those around them. No way to test it, but I'd seen some of what Rafael was saying.

"There are rats in every city," Sampson said, and like last time it was as if we'd all forgotten him.

Rafael nodded. "There are."

I had this image of hundreds of rats scampering in the walls, hearing things, and what they heard, the rat king heard. Did it work that way? For real? I wanted to ask, but in this mood, I wasn't sure how he'd take the question.

"I am the son of two powers, but you did not concern yourself that you had insulted me,"\ Sampson said.

"I don't know what you are to Jean-Claude and Anita."

"So you would ignore me, and see if it got a reaction?"

Rafael nodded.

"I am the next lover in line for Anita."

"Why have you waited so long?"

"It is the lady's privilege to keep a man waiting."

They were supposed to be talking about me, but it was like I was missing the conversation, or not truly understanding it all.

"Would you allow me to jump ahead of you in line?"

Sampson shook his head. "No."

He looked at Jean-Claude. "Is this your final word, that the sea king's son is more important than I am, than my rats are, to you?"

"That is not what is being said here, Rafael," Jean-Claude said.

"I believe that any animal that comes to your bed, or Anita's bed, is more important to you, Jean-Claude. Deny it if you like, but the proof is in the pudding, eh?"

"The proof is in the eating of it," Jean-Claude said, "for all puddings look sweet."

"Do I or any of my people look sweet to you?" he asked.

I felt Claudia's reaction from across the room. A flare of power, like a metaphysical slap to remind us how really powerful she was. That one splash of heated energy said loud and clear that it didn't matter how tasty anyone thought she was, she wasn't playing.

Rafael let out a careful breath and rotated his neck, as if that slap of energy had been more energetic the closer you'd been to it. "I would not force any of my rats into someone's bed. But if some would choose it, would you take them as blood or flesh donors?"

"Define *flesh*," I said.

"Sex," he said.

Richard shifted beside me on the couch. "The rats don't give blood to anyone. It was one of your first rules as king. Nikolaos tortured you because you forbade your rats to feed her vampires."

"She was unstable, and farther away from her was safer for my people. Closer to Jean-Claude seems safer."

"You'd really let your rats be blood whores?" Richard sounded almost shocked.

"I would."

"You think that if some of your rats come into our bedrooms, your people will be that much safer?" Micah asked.

"If our positions were reversed, what would you do?"

"Not this," Richard said.

"I am asking the Nimir-Raj," Rafael said.

Richard shifted uncomfortably on one side of me while Micah seemed to settle back more comfortably. "I've already done what you're suggesting."

Rafael nodded. "You offered yourself to Anita and Jean-Claude and now your pard, though one of the smallest groups in the area, is one of the most secure groups in all of St. Louis. How many of your leopards donate blood to the vampires?"

"Most of them."

Rafael spread his hands, as if to say, *See?*

I wanted to argue with them, but I tried to be honest. Was his reasoning sound? Through us, Micah was in charge of the furry coalition hotline, which meant he was beginning to be the go-to guy for most of the lycanthropy community. He was the liaison between us and the larger community. His television time was even going up. He gave good sound bite.

The leopards had fewer members than almost any other group, yet no one messed with them. Because I, or Jean-Claude, or our people, kept killing anyone who fucked with them.

I looked at the rat king. "Damn," I said, softly.

"Yes," he said.

I glanced down the couch at Richard and Jean-Claude. "He's not wrong, is he?"

"I cannot argue with some of his reasoning," Jean-Claude said.

"No," Richard said, "he's not right."

"I didn't say he was right, Richard, just that he's not wrong," I said.

"That makes no sense. If Rafael isn't wrong, then he has to be right." Richard turned his body so he was facing me, and blocked my view of Jean-Claude—those broad shoulders of his getting in the way.

"He's right that our lovers are safer. He's wrong if he thinks we'd leave the rats out to dry if someone threatened them."

"You are tied to us only by money and contracts," Rafael said. "I would feel better if you were tied with more intimate things."

"You have our word that we will honor our treaty with you," Jean-Claude said.

"But you have a treaty with the hyenas, as well, and I do not believe that Asher will keep refusing the bounty that Narcissus is shoving at him."

"Do not make the mistake of thinking Asher is weak. He is not," Jean-Claude said.

"You are in love with him; you do not see him clearly."

"I could say to you that you are not in love with him, and you do not see him clearly because of it."

"Order him not to be intimate with the hyenas and I will be content with it."

"I would rather not give such an order," Jean-Claude said.

"You have no right to ask that of Jean-Claude, or Asher," Micah said.

"What would you do if you were me, Nimir-Raj?"

"I would have offered myself less confrontationally. If refused, I'd have offered others of my people until some became food and hopefully one, or more, would catch someone's eye for sex."

"Am I going about this wrong?"

"Yes."

"It is an area of politics I am unprepared for," Rafael said. "Teach me, Micah. Help me."

Micah sighed. He scooted to the edge of the couch and looked past Richard to Jean-Claude. "What do you want me to do?"

"Help him, if you can."

Micah leaned back and looked at me. He just looked at me, and the look was enough between us. I shrugged and said, "Help him, I guess."

Micah settled back against the couch and put an arm across my shoulders, which made Richard move a little farther away. I don't think Micah meant to make Richard move. I think he wanted to touch me, and after last night there'd been the possibility that Richard wouldn't mind an accidental touch. But apparently Rafael's issues had raised some of Richard's own. Hell, it had raised some of mine. I just wasn't sure which ones yet.

"Blood donors would be welcome," Micah said, "and some of your rats have already offered to feed the *ardeur* for Anita."

"But she has touched none of them," Rafael said.

"You haven't sent her anyone she likes enough, yet."

"Help me pick them."

"Guys," I said, "guys, I am still sitting right here, okay? Don't talk about me like I'm not here."

"Then you pick," he said.

I slumped and let my hair hide my face. Shit. "That isn't what I meant."

"She likes pretty men," Richard said, "and that's not what you hire for."

I looked up at him, sitting right beside me, talking about what kind of man I liked. "I thought you'd be having a fit about this," I said.

He frowned, but said, "I don't like it, but Rafael is right, about us keeping our lovers closer and safer."

"If you care for someone enough to have sex with them, then you're supposed to take care of them," I said.

"Exactly," Richard said. "It's how you feel about it."

"And what's wrong with the way I feel about it?"

"Nothing," he said, "but it means Rafael is right. You do take care of your lovers. You just do."

"Don't you?" I asked.

He looked surprised for a second, then gave a smile that left his eyes tired and more cynical than I'd ever seen him. "No, sometimes it's just about fucking."

I gave him wide eyes.

"I'd love it to always be hearts and flowers, but the one woman I love more than any other doesn't want me, so what am I supposed to do while you sleep with six or seven other guys? Wait my turn? Watch?"

We had company, or I might have pointed out to him that he had watched before, and he had waited his turn, and he'd even helped Jean-Claude make love to me. But we had company, and I didn't want to fight with him.

"So you don't take care of everyone that comes to your bed?"

"I take care of my wolves, but if they aren't pack, sometimes the sex proves that it won't work."

"So you break up with them after the sex?"

"Sometimes."

I gave him a look.

"You know who I keep comparing them to, Anita."

It wasn't my fault that I didn't want to marry Richard. I was allowed to want the men I wanted, and love who I wanted. "So it's my fault that you're sleeping around, and that you've turned into one of those men who break up with a woman after one night of sex?"

He gave me a long look out of those chocolate-brown eyes. "If the shoe fits . . . ," he said, with an unpleasant smile.

I guess we were going to fight after all. "It isn't me you keep comparing everybody to, Richard, it's Raina."

He actually blushed under the permanent tan of his skin. It was maybe the second time I'd ever seen him blush. "Don't, Anita."

Micah had gone very still beside me, as if he were wondering if he should take his arm out from between us.

"You back off of me, and I'll back off of you," I said.

"Richard," it was Louie, "we had this talk, remember?"

Richard stood up, and his power washed around the room like a wind from the mouth of hell. It actually hurt where it touched. "I remember the talk." He stared down at me, and there was such hatred on his face. "I tried last night, Anita, I really tried."

My throat was tight, and my eyes burned. I was already regretting what I'd said, would have done anything to take it back. "I know you did, Richard." My voice sounded small.

"But it's never enough, is it?"

I took a deep breath and stood up. We faced each other. I wanted to run away, but I stood there and watched the hate and pain on his face, the way his big hands kept flexing into fists. His anger breathed through the room like some sort of invisible burning beast.

"I don't know what to say, Richard."

"What would be enough?" he asked.

"What?" I asked.

"What would be enough? Move in with you and Micah and Nathaniel? Move in here with you and Jean-Claude? What do I have to do to win with you, Anita?"

"It isn't about winning, Richard. God, don't you understand that?"

"No," he said, "I don't." He pointed at Jean-Claude. "Him I get. I feel his pull, too. He's my master, too." He pointed at Micah. "But him, I don't get him. He's in my place in your life, don't you understand that?"

I nodded, and tried to breathe past the tight burning in my throat and eyes. I would not cry, damn it. "I understand that," I said.

He pointed at Nathaniel, who'd gone very still beside the couch. "How can you share her with that?"

It was Micah who figured out that he was the one Richard was talking to. "Nathaniel is not a *that*, Richard." Micah's voice held a thread of anger.

"Do you fuck him? Do you let him fuck you? Or do you just fuck Anita at the same time?"

The unshed tears were going away on a hot wave of anger. I fed the anger, embraced it, called it sweet names, because I'd rather fight than cry.

"The way you and Jean . . . ," I started to say.

Jean-Claude called the fight. He called it with a push of power that staggered both of us. I nearly fell, and Richard looked ashen. We both turned and looked at the vampire. His eyes were glittering blue pools, like the night sky was on fire.

"Enough of this." His voice whispered through the room like an echo of bats, bouncing off the curtains.

I knew he was our master, but I'd never felt him do anything like this to us. Never felt him simply throw his power into us and stop us in our tracks. I hadn't known he had it in him.

"We are in danger here, do you not understand that? Most of our guards are wererats. If Rafael pulls them out, we do not have enough guards to keep ourselves safe." He uncurled from the couch and walked toward us, his long black curls moving in the wind of his own power.

We watched him come toward us like small birds that wanted to fly from the snake, but couldn't make ourselves move.

"I am sorry, *mon lupe*, that you wish her to marry you and abandon the rest of us. I am sorry, *ma petite*, that you still love him, and that some part of you wishes you could do exactly what he wants. I am sorry that I have bound you together into such pain. But there is no time for this. We need Rafael and his people. He knows that, or he would not have come like this." Jean-Claude stood in front of us, and his power pushed so that I swayed in the wind of it. I knew he'd gained in power, but I hadn't understood, until that moment, just how much. "I will pick a blood donor among the rats. I will urge others of my vampires to do the same. You, *ma petite*, must choose one of his people for food. You must embrace Sampson, or do something for him that will allow his honor to step aside and let you take one of the wererats ahead of him as food for your *ardeur*."

He stopped in front of us, close enough that he could have touched us. For the first time in years, I prayed that he wouldn't touch me. If he did, I'd do anything he asked.

He touched Richard's arm, and he shuddered under that light touch. He closed his eyes and swayed. I touched Richard's other arm, and I thought, *No. No, don't do this.*

My necromancy opened inside me in a rush that left me wide-eyed, open-mouthed. Because it wasn't just my necromancy. I felt it like an offering to Jean-Claude. If he could figure out how to use it, it was his to command while he touched us.

Richard breathed, "Don't, please, don't."

I wasn't sure which of us he was talking to. I stared at Jean-Claude, and felt my eyes go. I saw the room through that vampiric flame, but it wasn't someone else's powers taking over my eyes, it was me. If there'd been a mirror I knew my eyes would have been filled with a black-brown light of my own eyes, as if I were the vampire.

Richard collapsed to his knees between us, with our hands still on his arms. He whispered, "Oh, God." I looked down at him, and he gazed up at me with eyes turned to brown flame. Not my fire taking over him, but his own true brown eyes turned to vampire fire.

21

RICHARD WAS STARING at himself in the bathroom mirror. His big hands clung to the marble sink edge as if he were trying to leave an imprint of his hands on the stone. I'd tried to be comforting. I'd tried to be reassuring. Nothing I said had helped. Jean-Claude had been with us, but Richard truly didn't want to talk to him. He seemed to blame Jean-Claude for this new sign that his humanity was slipping away.

"The glow will fade, Richard," I said, not for the first time. Since he wouldn't let me touch him, I was left to lean against the far side of the sink and wall, arms crossed under my breasts. I'd already checked on my bra that was hanging by the towels. It was still too wet to wear.

He shook his head. "This is what my eyes would look like if I were the vampire."

I wasn't sure it was a question, but I answered it anyway. "Yes."

He looked at me, and it was unsettling to see his tanned and very alive face set with eyes that I'd only seen in the faces of the undead. It didn't match, that life and those eyes. His fear came off him in waves, so that his power bit and flitted against my skin like hot ash from a windy fire.

"You're not afraid of this. Why, why aren't you afraid of this?" he asked.

I shrugged and tried to put into words something I was trying not to think about. "I'm treating this the way I treat an emergency in the middle of a police investigation, Richard. You don't get too hung up on the horrible details or you stop being able to function. You keep moving forward, because you have to."

"This isn't your job, Anita. This isn't my job!" The air was suddenly close and hot. I was bathed in his power, and it was hard to breathe past it. The wolf that was always inside me now, stirred.

"You're going to raise my wolf, Richard."

He looked away from me, and nodded. "Mine, too."

The wolf began to pad up that metaphorical corridor inside me. I shivered and started to back away toward the door. I needed out of this hot bath of power. "You're the Ulfric, Richard. Control yourself."

He turned and looked at me through a curtain of his own thick hair. His eyes were still glowing, but now they were wolf amber, like twin suns in his face. A low, threatening growl trickled from his lips.

"Richard," and it was a whisper.

"I could make you change," he said in a voice that was more growl than word.

"What?" I whispered.

"I can force my wolves to shift. I can smell your wolf, Anita. I can smell her."

I swallowed a lump that hurt and bumped into the door. It made me jump. I hadn't realized I was that close to it. I reached back for the knob, and Richard was suddenly there, towering over me. I hadn't seen him move. Had I closed my eyes for a second? Had he played with my mind? Or had he just been that quick?

His power pressed against me like a hot mattress, like I was being suffocated by it. I managed to breathe out his name. "Richard, please."

He leaned over me, lowered that handsome face with those sun-drenched eyes to my face. "Please what? Please stop, or please don't stop?"

I shook my head; I couldn't get enough air to speak. My wolf hit the surface of my body and the impact of it drove me off my feet. Richard caught me, hands on my arms, kept me on my feet. The wolf inside me started digging; it wanted out!

I tried to scream, and it was as if with every breath I was breathing in more of Richard's power. He jerked me off my feet, wrapped me against his body. I could feel something moving low in my stomach; I swear I could feel the wolf's claws digging through my flesh, trying to meet Richard's body. It was trying to get to him, trying to answer the call of its Ulfric.

The pain was incredible; it was like being ripped apart from the navel outward, like some horrible parody of giving birth. I screamed, not with air, but with my mind. I sent every metaphysical ability I had, and screamed for help.

I heard voices shouting on the other side of the door, but it was as if voices didn't mean anything to me anymore. As if it were just noise. But I could smell Richard's skin, smell the musk of the wolf inside him. He lowered his face to mine, and I smelled my skin through his mind. Soap, shampoo, the hair-care product, but underneath that was me, my skin, my scent. He drew a sharper breath, cupping his hand against my skin so the scent blew back into his face. He drew it in as if it were the sweetest of perfumes; wolf. I smelled of wolf, and forest, and pack.

The door shuddered against my back. Something heavy thudded against it. Richard picked me up, arms around my thighs, putting my upper body by his face. He didn't ask in words; he asked with his eyes, with his power, with that smell of wolf. He asked me to come to him. He called to that part of me that had stopped scratching, and was listening, smelling him. He called to the wolf inside me, in ways that my human brain couldn't even begin to understand. I was still too human to answer him in the way he wanted. Still too human, still too . . . human.

But the wolf wasn't human, and it answered him. It threw itself against the wall of my body, as if I were a door and all it had to do was get through it. It threw itself against my flesh, so that it staggered Richard backward into the room as he tried to hold me, while the wolf tore at me. His power pressed down my throat like a hand that was trying to help the beast, and stole my air, my words.

It was as if hot, burning liquid ran through my veins. I burned with it, but I knew what that heat was: beast, wolf. I knew now why the lycanthropes ran hot close to the moon; they were burning up with their beast. It was a new pain, a pain that my wolf and I shared, as if she was burning up, too.

I didn't know the door had burst inward. The first hint I had that the guards were in the room was them standing around us. I couldn't hear anything but the pounding of blood and heartbeats in my head. They pulled at Richard, tried to tear me out of his arms, and he wouldn't let me go. Finally a fist smashed into his face, blood ran in a crimson wash, and his beast poured over him, and me.

The fire poured out from underneath my nails. I raised my hands in front of my face, wondering how fire was pouring out from underneath my nails, but it was blood. Blood pouring like burning rain from underneath my nails.

Richard's body like thick water against me, fur flowed, muscles shifted, and it was as if his beast was tied to mine, so that as he shifted, he was dragging my wolf with him. Dragging it in blood and fire, out of my body. I would have done anything, agreed to anything, if the pain would only stop. I wasn't thinking that if I shifted, I would lose my leopards. I wasn't thinking that if I shifted Richard would win. I wasn't thinking anything but *Make it stop, please, God, make it stop!* If someone had said the only way to make it stop was to be a wolf, I wouldn't have argued. I'd have grabbed it. Just make it stop!

I felt Jean-Claude's power, felt it like a cool soothing wind. I still hurt; the wolf was still there trying to fit all that tooth and claw into my smaller body, but it was better. I could hear again, and what I heard was chaos. Screams, shouts, Claudia's voice above the rest, "Ulfric, don't do this!"

Jean-Claude's voice floated through my head, and through Richard's, because Richard had tied us that close. "My marks keep her human, Richard; all you can do is destroy her."

Richard bellowed, "She's mine!" He was standing over me. I didn't even remember being on the floor. Richard wasn't human anymore. He was that movie wolfman, except that his fur was the color of cinnamon, and he was very male, not that smooth sexless Barbie-doll look from the movies. From my angle everything about him looked monstrously large. Partly the angle, and partly the pain.

The wolf inside me stretched my body, trying to force claws out from under my nails. Trying to stretch more body out than I had to give it. I had air now, thanks to Jean-Claude, and I used it to scream. I finally screamed the pain, shrieked it, and somehow it helped. I was still human, I could still speak. I screamed, "Nooo!"

Clay appeared above me, face scared. "Give me your wolf, Anita."

A clawed hand appeared and jerked him back, out of sight. Richard had pulled him back. "No," he growled, "no, my pack does not stop this."

"Not your pack," Jean-Claude's voice now, in the room somewhere, "my pack, for all that is yours is mine; by vampire law, they are my wolves, not yours."

I turned my face and saw him in the doorway. He stood there, beautiful, cold, his eyes glittering with that cool fire. I reached out to him with my bloody hands. I screamed, "Help me!"

Richard was suddenly airborne. Too quick for the bodyguards, too quick for anyone. He hit Jean-Claude, and they both rolled out of sight into the bedroom beyond.

Clay was back at my side. He was bloody, and I couldn't tell if he was wounded or had just gotten blood on him. "Give me your beast," he said.

He was disobeying a direct order from his Ulfric. But in that moment I didn't care. I grabbed his arm, and he pressed himself to my mouth, let me kiss him. More than ever before I felt the wolf pour out of my mouth. I choked on fur and blood and things that couldn't be real. I choked, and Clay stayed pinned to me while his body struggled to get away. He forced himself to stay against me, forced his body to take my beast, but it hurt too much not to struggle. I knew now just how much it hurt, and I was sorry, but I didn't stop.

His body exploded above mine; wet, thick things covered my eyes, and only my hands told me that fur and muscle were above me now. My body still ached, but the wolf was gone, gone like a hole in my heart, an empty space where something should have been.

Someone else's hand smoothed the gunk from my eyes so I could blink up into Rafael's face. He was crying. I'd never seen him do that. It scared me. What would make Rafael cry? What was happening?

Gunshots exploded in the other room, so loud, so horribly loud. I sat up and fell back down. "Help me," I said to Rafael.

He picked me up, as if I were a child, and carried me to the other room. I didn't protest, I would have been too slow; but what I saw in the bedroom said that we'd all been too slow.

The first thing I saw was Jean-Claude sitting on the floor, his white shirt in bloody tatters, blood trickling from his mouth. The guards were standing in a semicircle with guns out. Richard's wolf form was crouched at the center of that circle. I could see his heart thudding frantically in the open air. It was a killing wound, but he still crouched there, growling at them. I could see him about to spring, and I knew that the guards wouldn't let that happen. It was one of those moments when everything slows down, when the world becomes crystal-edged, the colors brighter, the edges of everything sharper; you see everything in painful clarity. Seconds to see my world about to go up in flames.

Jean-Claude's voice whispered through my head, "I am sorry, *ma petite*, there is no time." I thought he was apologizing for the fact that they were going to shoot Richard, until I felt his power. It didn't wash over me, it didn't press against me like Richard's had; his power simply was there and did what it wanted. I felt it almost like a series of tumblers in a lock: *click*, and he took Richard's blood lust, like a cup in his hand; *click*, and he turned that blood lust into another kind of lust; *click*, and he spilled it into me.

There was a blink, where I saw Richard's head go down, watched his body begin to change back to human. Knew they wouldn't have to shoot him now. A blink, to be relieved, then the *ardeur* ripped through me as surely as the beast had done earlier. My body forgot that it hurt. My body forgot that it was bloody and aching. My body forgot everything except one thing. The *ardeur* did what it always did: it washed over the man I was touching and carried him away with me. I was already on the floor with him on top of me before I remembered who I'd be looking up at. Rafael, the rat king, who was going to get to be food after all.

22

RAFAEL CARRIED ME out to the hallway with my legs wrapped around his waist, my arms around his shoulders, my mouth feeding at his. He stumbled at the door and almost fell, having to catch his hands on the doorjamb. He put a hurried hand around me, but he was in no danger of dropping me. He'd have had to pry me off him for me to fall. I was drowning in the taste of his mouth, the scent of his skin. He smelled smoky, not like cigarettes, but wood smoke, and salt, like some food that had been smoked and salted, until the meat was flavored and tender and so ready to eat. I felt his need. I just knew that it had been a long time for him. So much need, so much power, so long denied. He was a feast waiting to be eaten. The last wasn't my thought. We fell against the wall outside the door. The sensation of him falling against me, bruising me into the wall, made me cry out. He leaned heavier against me and even through our clothes I could feel him hard and ready. I cried out again and pressed myself against him, but there were too many clothes in the way. I moaned into his mouth, too eager for words.

Rafael tore himself from my lips. He used one hand to keep my face from touching his so he could look into my eyes. "Your eyes," he whispered, "like blue fire." Blue, but my eyes were brown, I thought. Then Jean-Claude's power washed the hesitation away. He filled my head as he filled my eyes. It was my mouth but Jean-Claude's words that said, "A fire that burns just for you, Rafael, just for you." In that moment it was true. We wanted only Rafael, needed only him.

I felt him fall into our eyes. There was a moment when he swayed forward, his hand catching on the stone wall behind me. He stared into our eyes, and his face didn't smooth out and become empty, waiting for orders like every other vampire victim I'd seen—no, his face filled with need, want; months, years, of denial, all there in his face and a heartbeat later it was in his hands where they tore my shirt. His mouth fed at my breasts, biting, sucking, rough enough that he drew back and tried to fight clear of our power. A small spark inside him was afraid he'd hurt us. We laughed, and it was an odd mixture of Jean-Claude and me, so that for a moment my laugh slithered over Rafael's body and made him shiver. I bit his neck, sudden and sharp, digging my teeth into that smooth, dark flesh. He balled his hand in my hair and pried me off him. His neck bled where I'd bitten him. He drove his mouth into mine, so hard that teeth grazed on teeth. He kissed me with tongue and lips until he ate the taste of his own blood from my mouth.

He ripped my jeans apart at the seam. My body jerked with the strength of it. The sensation of the heavy cloth tearing around my body brought a small noise from me. My panties ripped and again the feel of it made me cry out. I ground myself against the front of him, but all I could touch was cloth. That hard, eager flesh was still out of reach.

I cried my frustration and he fumbled at his belt, one-handed. He was making small, frustrated noises by the time he got the belt open, the pants unbuttoned. But I was too tight against him for him to unzip.

"Climb me," he said, in a voice choked with need.

I managed to say, "What?" before his hands showed me what he wanted. He lifted me up a little higher on his body. I used my hands and arms on his broad shoulders to help climb a little higher. I wrapped my legs higher on his body, so he was left to unzip without seeing what he was doing, his hands feeling around my naked ass as he tried to free himself of his pants. He made a sound that was half shout and half word. I think the word was *Please*, but I wasn't sure.

The tip of him brushed along my bare skin, and I let my body slide those few inches lower, so he could guide himself to my opening. It was not a good angle for the first time; we didn't know the exact angle to have without being able to see what we were doing. He made a small inarticulate sound, then I felt the head of him enter me. I froze with him barely breaking the surface of my body. Froze so he could push his way inside. He hesitated in the middle of that first thrust, stopped with most of him still outside me. His body shuddered, his hands balancing against the wall, and the other hand finally free to touch my body again. His eyes closed as he traced his hand up my nearly bare back. He whispered through gritted teeth, "So tight, so wet. I won't last long."

Normally, longer was better, but in that moment I knew that we needed to feed. Jean-Claude let me know that we needed this energy. We needed him to give us what he had to give.

"Fuck me," I said, and drove my body down the length of his, and found there was even more of him than I'd thought. When he was pressed as tight as I could make him, it was my turn to close my eyes and shudder. My turn to whisper, "Fuck me, Rafael, feed me, fuck me, Rafael, feed me!"

With every word I drove my body up and down on his, drove him in and out of me. The angle was not the best for me to move without his help, but with the last word, he used his hands to cup my ass and drive my body into the stone wall with one hard thrust of his body. He drove himself into me over and over, grinding me into the stones, and the roughness of the stones. It was what I wanted, too.

I wanted him to take me, to drive all that need, all that denial into my body. The *ardeur* tried to feed, but he was a king and it could not get past his shields. A tiny thought of panic from Jean-Claude, quickly swallowed, but he was urgent that we break Rafael. I might have protested, but the *ardeur* was all I could feel, and it wanted to break him.

Rafael was so hard, so very hard, the kind of hard a man only gets when he's denied himself a very long time. He drove all that hard, long length into and out of me, fast and faster, hard and harder. His breathing changed, and I said, "Yes, yes, please, Rafael, please."

Part of that *please* was, *Please let us feed, let us in, drop all that protection, let us in, let us in.* I tried to find a rhythm, but his body, his hands, pinned my lower body against the wall. He would do the work; he didn't want the help. Thrust after hard thrust and I felt my body filling up with the pleasure of his body pounding inside mine, his hands so strong, pinning me, his body as hard and eager inside me as any man I'd ever felt. And just like that, the pleasure took me, brought me, brought me screaming, clawing, biting. Brought me writhing and dancing around him. He cried out and his body gave one last deep thrust that made me scream again. He shivered against me, eyes fluttering, and his shields crashed down. The *ardeur* fed on his body, on the warmth of him inside me, on his need, and his release. In the midst of that pleasure that made me tear Rafael's skin and cry out as his body spasmed inside mine, I felt Jean-Claude.

He'd chosen Rafael because he was king and through their king we could feed on his people. Jean-Claude reached through Rafael's body, our bodies, to the wererats. As we'd fed once on Augustine and his people, now we fed on Rafael and his. I felt Claudia stagger, felt Lisandro fall to his knees, felt the wererats try to run, or fight, or keep us out, but they couldn't. They'd given their protection over to their king; when he fell, they were ours. Ours for the taking, ours for the raping, ours for the eating. We fed, and fed, and fed; some faces I knew, some faces I didn't. They became a blur of startled eyes and up-turned faces. We fed on them all.

Rafael felt what was happening and tried to protect them, to fight us, but it was too late. His body was married to mine and all that hard-won control was gone inside my body in the feel of his hands on me.

Jean-Claude took that power and threw it into our vampires, all those in the city who owed their life spark to his power as Master of the City. He forced them all awake, some ten hours or more earlier than they'd ever woken from death. I didn't understand why he'd used the power for that, until when the last vampire had come clawing to wakefulness, he let the power go back to him, and Richard, and he let me feel how terribly hurt they were. He'd used the power to force the lesser vampires awake, because if he lost consciousness he was afraid he would drain them of power and they would all die for good. He was afraid that he would drain them dry through his ties as Master of the City, in much the same way we'd been able to feed on Rafael's rats, except the vampires would die.

I couldn't breathe, my heart was touching stone, and I couldn't breathe. Richard's body, oh, God, oh, God, he was dying. Jean-Claude tried to heal him, and that forced me to feel what Richard's claws had done to the vampire's body. His heart stuttered, hesitated. Sweet Jesus, no, Richard had stabbed him in the heart. Jean-Claude fed the power we'd taken into their injuries, and it should have been enough, but it was as if there was something in Richard's injuries that ate the power, but didn't heal him. I saw something like a shadow on Richard's back.

Jean-Claude whispered, "Harlequin."

We were dying; my chest squeezed tight and tighter. I couldn't breathe. I only half-felt when Rafael lowered me to the floor and tried to get me to say something to him. I used my last bit of air to whisper, "Help us."

Rafael said, "Anything." His shields were still down. I took their energy again, but not to feed, to strike out.

Jean-Claude cried out in my mind, "*Non, ma petite.*" But it was too late; with my last thought, before darkness swallowed us all, I took the power of Rafael and the wererats and I struck out at that phantom on Richard's back. If I could have thought clearly, I might have thought, *Die*, but the darkness was eating us, and all I had time to do was strike. I saw her—no, them—two cloaked figures in a dark room, a dark hotel room. Two white masks lay beside them on the bed. One sat, the other knelt behind her. They were both petite and dark-haired. They looked up, startled, as if they could see me and what came with me. I got a good look at the pale, upturned faces, the long brown hair, one a shade darker than the other, one with brown eyes, one gray, both glowing with power. They'd combined their powers; somehow they'd combined to hit us. I don't know what they saw, but they both cried out. The kneeling one tried to shield the other with her body, and then the power hit them. It sent them crashing to the floor, and into the nightstand. The lamp fell over on top of them and shattered. It knocked over the phone and a notepad. I read the name of the hotel on the notepad. I knew where they were. They fell into a heap and didn't move again. My last waking thought was, *Good*.

23

PAIN, PAIN, AND lights stabbing into my eyes. Voices: "I've got a pulse!" "Anita, Anita, can you hear me!" I wanted to say yes but I couldn't remember where my mouth was, or how to use it. Darkness again, then pain shot through the dark again. I came to, my body convulsing on a gurney. There were people all around me. I should have known one of them, but I couldn't remember who she was, only that I should have remembered who she was. My chest hurt. I smelled burning, something was burning. I saw those little flat paddles I'd had used once before on my chest. I realized I was what was burning. The thought didn't mean much to me. I wasn't afraid, or even excited. Nothing seemed real. Even the pain in my chest was fading. The world started going gray and soft around the edges.

Someone slapped me, hard, across the face. The world was real again. I blinked up into the face of the woman I should have known, and didn't. She yelled my name, "Anita, Anita, stay with us, damn it!"

Everything went soft again; the gray ate the world like mist. Someone hit me again. I blinked up into the woman's face again. "Don't you die on me, damn it!" She hit me again, and the world hadn't even gone gray.

I knew her now. Doc Lillian. I tried to say, *Stop hitting me*, but I couldn't seem to figure out how to say the words. I did my best to frown up at her, though.

A man's voice said, "She's stable."

Lillian smiled down at me. "You're breathing for three, Anita. If you keep breathing, they won't die."

I didn't know what she meant. I wanted to ask, *Who won't die?* Then something cold and liquid seemed to flow through my veins. I'd had something like it before, and my last thought before a different kind of darkness took me was, why was Lillian giving me morphine?

I dreamed, or maybe I didn't. But if it was heaven, it was too scary, and if it was hell, it wasn't quite scary enough. I was at a ball, everyone in glittering clothes, centuries before I was born. Then the first couple turned to me, and they were masked. Everyone was wearing the Harlequin's white masks. I stumbled back from the dancers and found that I was wearing a silver-and-white dress that was too wide to be graceful, and too tight through the ribs to let me breathe well. One of the couples bumped me and my heart was suddenly in my throat. My chest was tight and tighter, as if some huge fist were crushing my ribs. I fell to my knees and the dancers moved wide around me in a spill of skirts and petticoats. Their dresses brushed me as they whirled faceless around me.

A voice came to the dream, Belle Morte's purring contralto: "*Ma petite*, you are dying."

The hem of a crimson dress was at my hands. She knelt beside me. She was still the brunette beauty who had nearly conquered all of Europe once. All that dark hair piled atop her head, leaving her neck in that pale, white curve that we'd always loved. *We* . . . I tried to feel the rest of that *we*, but where Jean-Claude should have been was awful blankness.

She leaned over me as I fell to the floor. "He is almost gone, our Jean-Claude," she said. Her amber-brown eyes didn't seem worried. She was simply making an observation. "Why do you not ask for my help, *ma petite*?"

I wanted to say, *Why would you help us?* but there was no air to say anything. My spine tried to bow in the tightness of the corset, as I gasped like a fish left to die on the shore.

"Oh," she said, and with a flick of her will the dream changed. We were in her bedroom, on her huge four-poster bed. She knelt above me, with a huge knife in her hand. The world was going gray. I wasn't even afraid.

My body jerked, the corset gave, and I could suddenly breathe a little better. My chest still hurt, and I breathed too shallowly, but I could breathe. I looked down to find that she had cut the bodice of the dress all the way through the corset, so that there was a line of bare skin from my neck to my waist. She laid the knife beside her knees and spread the stays of the corset a little wider, as if she meant to skin me out of the dress, but she went back to kneeling beside me, in her red, red dress. Her skin seemed to glow against the crimson cloth.

"What happens in my dreams can be very real, *ma petite*. Corsets here made your breathing there harder. You don't have enough breath to spare."

"What's happening?"

She lay down beside me, her head on the pillow I was lying upon. A little too close for comfort, but I didn't have the energy to spare for moving. "I felt Jean-Claude's light snuffed out."

"He's not dead," I whispered.

"Can you sense him?"

It must have shown on my face, because she said, "Shhh, you are correct, he is not gone completely, but he is close to the edge. You are keeping him, both of them, alive. You and your second triumvirate of power. Something Jean-Claude did in this new emergency has taught you better control of the power between you and your other triumvirate; your kitty and your vampire."

I swallowed, and it hurt, though I couldn't remember why it should. "Nathaniel, Damian." I was feeling a little better, well enough to be afraid. I'd almost drained both of them to death once, or twice.

"Do not fear for them. They are well enough, but they are feeding for you, giving you their energy as they are supposed to do in emergencies," she said, and stroked my forehead, tracing down the edge of my jaw. It was an idle movement, like the way you'd stroke the curve of a couch you were sitting on. "The masks of the Harlequin were in your mind, *ma petite*. Have they come to your territory?"

I wanted to tell her to stop calling me *ma petite*, but air was precious, so I answered, "Yes."

"Show me," she said.

Not *Tell me*, but *Show me*. I said, "How?"

"You are of Belle Morte's line. How do we trade power?"

I frowned up at her.

"Kiss me, and but think of it, and I will know what you know."

I don't know if I would have kissed her voluntarily, because I didn't get a chance to decide. She pressed those ruby lips to my mouth, and I was suffocating again. I couldn't breathe. I pushed at her, and she thought inside my head, "Think of the Harlequin." It was as if it were an order, and my mind did what she asked.

I thought of the meeting with Malcolm and his fear. I went back through the date with Nathaniel and the mask in the bathroom. The second mask with the musical notes on it, and the meeting planned. The mark on me, and the scent of wolf, and Jake keeping me safe. Then the last memory, where I saw my men dying, and the ghost on Richard, and the feeding with Rafael. She slowed the memory there, lingering on the rat king's powers, then let the memories go back to speeding along, and using Rafael's power to attack the one that had attacked us. It was the last memory that she slowed down completely. She stared at the pale faces of the vampires, the long dark hair, the glowing eyes, brown and gray respectively. Belle Morte studied the faces of the other vampires. She whispered, "Mercia, and Nivia." The memory ended, and Belle Morte was simply lying beside me, propped on the pillows.

I whispered, "You know them."

"Yes, but not that they were Harlequin. It is a deep, dark secret who is, and who is not, one of them. They are spies, and secrecy is their life blood. By their hands the Harlequin have broken their most profound taboo."

"What taboo?" I asked.

"They are neutral, *ma petite*, utterly neutral, or how can they dispense justice? Did they give you a black mask? I did not see it in your memories."

"No, only the two white."

She laughed, and her face shone with joy. My heart hurt, but not from a physical blow. It hurt the way it sometimes does when you see someone you once adored do something to remind you why you loved them, and you know that that laugh will never again be for you.

"They have broken the law then, the law they swore to uphold. Unless they deliver the black mask, they are not allowed to bring death. For Mercia and Nivia, it means true death, but for their fellow Harlequin it means something worse."

"What?" I asked.

"Disbandment. They will be no more, and those who are not killed will be forced to go back to their bloodlines, their old masters. To be neutral the Harlequin are freed of their ties to their creators. They are a law unto themselves, but if they are breaking the law, then they will be broken."

"Why does that"—I had to draw a breath to finish—"make you so happy?"

She pouted out that full lower lip and said, "Poor thing, so hurt. I will help you."

"Appreciate the offer, but"—and I had to work for breath—"help us, why?"

"Because you alive are witness enough to destroy the power of the Harlequin."

"Why," breath, "do you care?"

"They were once the private guards of the Mistress of the Dark. She is waking, I know that now."

"But when she wakes," breath, "she won't have them."

"*Precisement,*" Belle said.

"But you need me, us, alive."

"Yes," she said, and she looked at me the way that a hawk must look at a wounded mouse, eager, anticipatory.

"Make you mad?" I whispered, and had to cough. It wasn't my throat that was closing off. I didn't think it was Jean-Claude's. Something bad was happening to Richard.

"I don't hate you, *ma petite,*" she said. "I don't hate anything that is useful to me, and you are about to be very useful, *ma petite.*"

"Anita," I whispered.

"Anita, Anita," she purred as she leaned our faces closer, "if I want you to be my *ma petite,* you will be. Jean-Claude is near death and he protected you from me. I will save you all, but I will do it in a way that you will not like." She leaned our faces close, and the hand that had been caressing my face was suddenly firm and solid as metal against my cheek, keeping me turned toward that lovely face. She began to lean in for a kiss.

I spoke before our mouths touched. "A win-win situation, for you."

"Oh, yes." She whispered it against my lips, then kissed me. But she didn't just kiss me, she opened the *ardeur* between us. One moment all I could think about was breathing, *Just keep breathing,* and that I really didn't want her to touch me, and the next she was kissing me, and I was kissing her back.

My hands slid over that satin dress, and the body underneath, and my hands knew that body—though my hands were smaller than they should have been. Jean-Claude's memories kept getting in the way, coloring what was happening. When her mouth found my breast, and sucked, it startled me, because the body I was remembering didn't have breasts. She bit me, driving dainty fangs around my nipple. It made me cry out, brought my body writhing off the bed. She raised a bloody mouth and smiled at me, her eyes filled with amber light. She climbed my body and pressed that bloody mouth to mine. I kissed that mouth as if it were air, and food, and water, all rolled into one. I marveled at how small her mouth was, how dainty. How I'd longed to kiss this mouth again. I knew in this moment what I had never known from Jean-Claude, how much it had cost him to leave her. They say that once you love Belle Morte you never stop, and I knew in that kiss, with her body on top of mine, that it was true. He still loved her, would always love her, and nothing would change that, not even me.

The *ardeur* started to feed then, at that bloody kiss, but this was Belle Morte, the creator of the *ardeur*. You did not feed from her and stop. You fed until she stopped you.

The knife cut us out of the dresses, and where it nicked the skin we licked and drank each other's blood, and it didn't seem wrong, or a bad thing to do. The taste of her blood was sweet, and slow, and I knew that vampire blood was not a meal, but it could be foreplay.

I ended up on top of her, and my body kept forgetting that it wasn't male. I pressed her to the bed, with my body between her legs. But I could not do what I was remembering. I swore in frustration, because more than anything in the world in that moment I wanted to pierce her body. I wanted to plunge parts that I did not have into parts of her that I did.

She lay underneath me with that dark hair spilling around her body, across the silk of the pillows. Her lips parted, her eyes filled with that eager light. I knew what she was, knew it better through Jean-Claude than most. I knew that she would slit my throat and make love in the blood while I died, but in that moment with her looking up at us, I didn't care. I just wanted her to keep giving us that look.

She laid me back against the sheets and began to kiss her way down my body. I watched her eyes roll up, watching my face, as she licked, and bit, and drew small pinpricks of blood where dainty fangs pierced too close. It wasn't my memory that made me writhe at the sight of her over my groin. At first, it felt wrong, because I was expecting a different sensation, but Belle had spent two thousand years learning about pleasure, and she knew this pleasure, too. I gazed down at her with her mouth between my legs, and her tongue found me, traced me, licked me, and finally she sucked me, lightly at first, then deeper and deeper, until fangs bit deep as she sucked me, and I wasn't certain if it was the pleasure that brought the orgasm, or the pain. The *ardeur* fed, and fed, and fed.

I screamed, and writhed, and clawed at the pillows, and only after I lay back boneless, eyes fluttering blind with pleasure, did she raise her face from my body.

She stared up at me with eyes that glowed so bright, she looked blind with power. She laughed, and the sound trailed down my body and made me cry out again. "I do see what he sees in you, *ma petite*, I truly do. I have fed you enough to keep you all alive, but Mercia and Nivia, and any of the Harlequin that took part in this, will have to kill you before you can testify against them. They will not know that I know."

I tried to say, *tell people*, but my mouth couldn't work quite yet. Hell, if there'd been an emergency I couldn't have rolled off the bed, and it wasn't the medical emergency part that kept me lying there. It was a few thousand years of practiced sex that made me lie there and look at her, or try to look at her. The world was still white-edged with orgasm.

"I believe that they have allies for their illegal activities among the council, so I must go slowly here, but you need to be well there." She smiled at me, and it was the smile that Eve must have used in the Garden of Eden; *Want a bite of apple, little girl?* "I will send a call out to my bloodline in your territory. Jean-Claude is still too hurt to stop it. I will talk to them as of old, before they had Jean-Claude's new power to hide behind. When you wake, you will need powerful food for the *ardeur*. You must share that power with Jean-Claude and your wolf."

I managed to whisper, "I don't know how to do that."

"You will," she said, and she came to straddle my body, leaning in until our lips met. I could taste my body on her mouth. We kissed, and the dream broke, and I woke, with the taste of her kiss on my lips.

24

I WOKE GASPING in a room that was too bright, too white. There was something in my arm that hurt when I tried to move it. I couldn't think where I was, couldn't think about anything but the smell and taste and feel of Belle Morte. I woke crying her name, or trying to. My voice was a harsh croak of sound.

Cherry's face appeared beside the bed. Her ultrashort blond hair and overly dark Goth makeup couldn't quite hide the fact that she was pretty. She was also a registered nurse, though she had lost her job at the local hospital when they found out she was a wereleopard. "Anita, oh my God, oh my God."

I tried to say her name, and couldn't make words.

"Don't try to talk. I'll send for the doctor." She got me water and one of those bendy straws, and let me take a minute sip. I heard a door open and close, running feet getting farther away. Who had she sent for the doctor?

Cherry's eyes were shiny, and only after her eyeliner began to run in black tears down the pale makeup did I realize she was crying. "They say it's waterproof, but they so lie." She let me have another sip of water.

I managed to croak, "Why does my throat hurt?"

"I . . ." She looked solemn again. "We had to intubate Richard."

"Intubate?" I made it a question.

"Put a tube down his throat. A machine is doing his breathing for him."

"Shit," I whispered.

She wiped at the black tears again, smearing them worse. "But you're awake, you're all right." She nodded, over and over, as if that would make it more true. I was almost sure that away from me, her leopard queen, she was more controlled as a nurse, but she sure did cry easily for a medical professional.

There were soft footfalls, and Doctor Lillian was at my bedside. Her graying hair was in a careless knot at the back of her neck, with strands of hair flying about her slender face. Her pale eyes smiled along with her lips. Relief was plain on her face for a moment.

"Did you slap me?" I asked.

"I didn't think you'd remember that."

"You did slap me, didn't you?"

"It was a close thing, Anita. We almost lost you all."

"Cherry says Richard is hooked up to machines, that he's not breathing on his own."

"That's right."

"Shouldn't he have healed by now?"

"It's only the night of the same day, Anita. You haven't been out that long."

"It feels longer."

She smiled. "I'm sure it does. I think now that we've got his body breathing, he will heal, but if we hadn't been able to keep his heart and lungs going . . ."

"You're worried."

"His heart stopped, Anita. If he were human I'd be worried about brain damage from lack of oxygen."

"But he's not human," I said.

"No, but he is very hurt. He should heal perfectly, but in truth, I've never seen a lycanthrope come back from an injury this severe. His heart was pierced by a silver bullet. It was a killing shot."

"But he's not dead," I said.

"No, he's not."

I looked up at her. "Jesus, you don't give good medical blank face either."

"Jean-Claude is in a sort of coma. Asher tells me that it is a type of hibernation while he heals himself, but truthfully, vampire medicine is confusing. They're dead, so how unhealthy can they be? We hooked him up to brainwave monitors, and that's letting us know he's still in there."

"But if you didn't have the monitors?" I asked.

"I'd think he was dead," she said.

"We're not dead."

She smiled. "No, you're not. Nathaniel has been eating for five, and he's still lost two pounds in less than a day. Damian has taken more blood than any vampire should be able to hold, and still he feeds. Asher says they are helping fuel the three of you."

I nodded, remembering what Belle had said. "He's right." I thought about letting my thoughts of Nathaniel and Damian find them for me, let me see them. But I was afraid I'd mess it up. Afraid that somehow I'd cut off the energy they were feeding us, or take too much. Apparently it was working, and I was simply grateful that it was working the way it was supposed to. Belle had said that I'd learned from Jean-Claude how to do it, but she was wrong. I think Jean-Claude had done it for us before he passed out, because I had no idea how it was working. I very carefully didn't make my shields between me and the boys any stronger, or weaker. I just tried to maintain. It was working; don't fuck with it.

"The vampires are worried that if the lesser vamps go to sleep for the day, Jean-Claude is so injured that he won't have enough energy to wake them again."

I nodded and swallowed past a sore throat that wasn't my sore throat, but it felt like it. Like I was trying to swallow past something huge and hard, and plastic. "Richard is awake enough to feel the tube in his throat, because I can feel it."

"I don't know if that's good news or bad, Anita. It will be a while before his body catches up with the machines, I think."

"We need Jean-Claude awake before dawn, awake enough so he doesn't drain the little vamps to death," I said.

She looked at me very seriously. "That is what the vampires have been discussing."

I felt vampires. I felt them outside the door. I heard voices arguing, men arguing. I said, "Tell the guards to let Asher and the others in."

She looked a question at me, but went to the door. But seeing who came through the door first made me smile, and somehow I felt it would all work out. We would be safe, because Edward was here.

25

HE SMILED DOWN at me, shaking his head. Standing there, looking down at me, he looked pleasant, and like the end product of a few generations of WASP breeding; blond hair, blue eyes, maybe a little short at five foot eight, but he would have fit in in so many places. Then the polished charm began to melt away, like magic. I watched the real Edward fill his eyes and turn them from warm to cold as a deep winter sky. The color of his eyes was the same, but the look in them wasn't. The face was still and showed nothing. If I hadn't had vampires to compare with, I'd have said Edward gave better empty face than anyone I knew.

Once, seeing Edward at my bedside would have meant he'd come to kill me. Now, it meant I was safe. We were all safe, or as safe as we could be. Edward couldn't do much about metaphysical powers, but I trusted him to take care of the Harlequin's weapons and fighting skills. The magic was my department, but no one did armed combat better than Edward.

"Hey," I said, and my voice still sounded dry.

His lips twitched. "Couldn't stay alive for just a few more hours, huh?" His voice held an edge of the smile that had been there, then settled to that empty middle-of-nowhere voice, no accent, no hint of where he'd started life.

"I'm alive," I said.

"They had to restart your heart twice, Anita."

Lillian, who had made herself scarce, came to stand beside him. "I'd appreciate it if you didn't scare my patient."

"She likes the truth," he said, without even looking at her.

"He's right, doc," I said.

She sighed. "Fine, but let's ease her into it; she's been mostly dead all day."

It took me a second to realize she'd made a joke. Edward gave her a look, then turned back to me. "According to the vamps, we don't have time to ease you into it."

"Tell me what's been happening," I said.

"There's too much, Anita. If I tell you everything, it will be dawn and your little vampires will be dead for good."

"Tell me what I need to know, then," I said.

"Jean-Claude used a lot of energy to wake every vamp in the city before he passed out."

"I was there when he did it."

"Don't interrupt," and he was way too solemn for my comfort. "The vamps and shapeshifters came up with a plan that they think will net the most power for you to feed into Jean-Claude and Richard in the shortest amount of time."

"Why are you telling me this? Why not Asher, or . . ."

"You interrupted," he said, eyes cold, and face still so serious.

"Sorry," I said.

Lillian made a noise that made us both look at her. "You said she'd take the news better from you, but I didn't believe you. I believe you now."

He gave her a look.

"Sorry, I'll stand over here and stop wasting time." She moved away from us.

He continued, "I don't like the plan and you're going to hate it, but I've listened to their reasoning and it's the best plan we've got."

I raised a hand.

He actually smiled, but it never quite reached his eyes. "Yes."

"You think it's a good plan?" I asked.

"I couldn't come up with a better one."

I looked at him. "Really?"

He nodded. "Really."

The fact that he couldn't come up with a better plan said a lot. Said enough that I didn't argue. "Okay, tell me the plan," I said.

"You feed the *ardeur* on the head of another animal group, and take their energy the way you did the wererats'." He didn't flinch or hesitate, even though he'd only known about the *ardeur* for a few hours. He'd landed in the middle of a crisis of metaphysical proportions and it hadn't fazed him, or if it had, it didn't show. In that moment I loved him, in a guy-buddy sort of way. He'd never fail me, or fuck with me, and I loved him for it.

"Which animal group?" I asked.

"The swans," he said.

I gave him surprised face. "Say again?"

He smiled, that cold smile, but it was a real smile; he was amused. "I take it the swan king is not your buddy."

"Not in that way. He and all the heads of the animal groups have been over to the house for dinner, but . . ." I shook my head and swallowed past that feeling of something in my throat that wasn't there, like a phantom pain. "I've never thought of him in that way, and there are larger, more powerful groups in St. Louis than the swans."

"You knocked most of the wererats cold when you fed on their king," Edward said.

"I did what?"

"You heard me."

I remembered Jean-Claude's voice in my head, saying no when I went back for that last bit of energy from Rafael. "I didn't mean to," I said.

Lillian peered around Edward's shoulder. "You're just lucky I was one of the few who didn't go down."

"Why didn't you?"

She looked thoughtful, and sad, and then shook her head. "I don't know."

"We don't have time to worry about the *why*," Edward said.

"Agreed," Lillian said.

I just nodded.

"The wererats still aren't a hundred percent, Anita. You did a real number on them. We can't afford for you to do the same to the werehyenas."

"Not a problem. Narcissus is sooo not on my to-do list."

His lips twitched, almost a smile, and then he gave in and laughed. "I've met him now, and . . ." He just shook his head, and said, "I wouldn't want to do him either, but he did come through for us. He let us have all the werehyenas that we asked for."

A thought occurred to me. "If most of our muscle were knocked out, why didn't the Harlequin attack us?"

He nodded. "I don't know why they didn't attack."

"They're supposed to be this uber-fighting team. Sort of you as a vampire—they should have attacked."

"Asher and the other vampires have speculated a lot why the Harlequin didn't push the advantage. I'll tell you all of it later, but right now . . ." He made a movement as if he'd take my hand, and then his hands fell back. "Do you trust me?" he asked.

I frowned at him. "You know I do."

"Then I've got the defenses covered, Anita. But only you can channel enough energy to Jean-Claude to keep the little vampires alive."

I wanted to ask so many things, but he was right. I had to trust Edward to do his job, and I did, but . . . "There aren't that many swanmanes in the city," I said.

"We asked the werelions first, but their Rex refused."

"Joseph refused to help us?" I was shocked, and let it show.

"Yes."

"We've bent over backward for the lions. Hell, I saved his life once, or twice."

"His wife said he wasn't having sex with anyone but her."

"This isn't about sex, Edward."

He shrugged.

"The lions would let the vampires die." I said it out loud, because I needed to hear it. I couldn't quite believe it.

"That's how I'd take it," he said.

We looked at each other, and I felt my eyes go as cold as his. I think we were thinking the same thing. The lions would suffer for this. Ungrateful bastards.

"Less than two hours, Anita," he said.

I nodded. "Which means we don't have time to be wrong, Edward. Are the swans enough energy?"

"Donovan Reece is the king of every swanmane in this country."

"I know. He has to travel from group to group, looking in on them, settling problems. He's also begun talking to other cities about how well our furry coalition is doing here. He's not trying to start another coalition, just talking about it. We've actually had some phone calls from other cities, wanting details about how it works."

"A politician," Edward said.

I nodded. "Being swan king is an inborn power; I think you actually do come with the skills you need. Donovan says that usually a swan queen is born in the same generation, so they rule together, but for whatever reason there was no baby born with the birthmark, or the power to help him. It means he has double the duty."

"He says that he leaves his swan maidens in the care of your leopards when he's gone for a while."

I nodded. "There's only three of them in town."

"They've stayed over at your house," Edward said.

"Yeah."

"Why?"

"They need someone to look after them sometimes."

"Donovan said that, that you took care of his people. He says you rescued them once, and almost got killed doing it."

"Yeah," I said.

"He says that if you risk your life for his people, he would do the same for you, so what's a little sex between allies?"

"He didn't say that last part," I said.

Edward grinned and shook his head. "Okay, but he did say, 'I would risk my life for Anita and her people. This is a small thing you ask of me.'"

"That sounds like Donovan," I said.

"He's offering to let you feed on every swanmane in the United States. There's maybe one to six in most major cities."

"I had no idea there were that many of them."

"I don't think anyone did but Donovan. He gave up a lot of intelligence, Anita. He didn't make me promise not to use it against him if I got a contract from someone who wanted me to go swan hunting."

"Edward . . ."

He held up a hand, stopping me. "I'll promise you, if you ask."

We looked at each other a second, and then I said, "Promise me you won't use anything you've learned against any of the animal groups."

"I won't hunt any more swans," He said.

"No, Edward, I mean it. You're going to have to learn things about vampires and the shapeshifters that you could use against them. I need your word of honor that what you learn won't come back to haunt them, or me."

His face went to that cold, empty look. It was almost the look he used when he killed, except for a hint of anger in his eyes. "Even the lions?" he asked.

"They're members of our coalition."

"That mean they're off limits?"

"No, it means we have to kick them out of the coalition before we do anything to them."

He smiled then. "So honorable."

"A girl's got to have standards," I said.

He nodded. "As long as the lions answer for it, I'm cool."

"One crisis at a time, but yeah, they'll answer for it."

He gave that cold, pleased smile. It was Edward's usual smile, the real one. The smile that said the monster was home, and happy to be there. I didn't need a mirror to know that the smile I gave back was almost a match for it. I used to worry about becoming like Edward. Lately, I counted on it.

26

WHATEVER WE WERE going to do with the local lion pride had to wait. One emergency at a time. Funny how when Edward comes into my life, or I come into his, we're almost always running from one emergency to the other. The difference this time was that the emergency couldn't be handled at the point of a knife or gun barrel. A flamethrower wouldn't even help, though Edward had probably brought one. How would he get it through airport security? It's Edward; if he wanted to, he'd manage to get a Sherman tank through security.

I had less than two hours to feed. Less than two hours to keep Willie McCoy, with his loud suits and louder ties, alive. The love of his life, Candy, tall and blond and gorgeous, and so in love with the small, not-so-handsome vampire. I thought of Avery Seabrook, who I'd stolen away from the Church of Eternal Life. Avery with his gentle eyes, so newly dead that even to me he still felt alive sometimes. I thought of so many of the lesser vamps who had jumped ship from Malcolm's church to us in the last few months. I couldn't let them die, not if I could save them. But I so didn't want to have sex with Donovan Reece.

There was nothing wrong with him. He was tall, pale, and handsome in a preppy, clean-cut sort of way. He was an inch shy of six feet, broad shoulders tucked into a baby-blue sweater that complemented a milk-and-cream complexion so perfect it looked artificial, but it wasn't. The faint pink blush on his cheeks was just his own blood flowing under that white, white skin. He was as pale as a Caucasian vampire before they'd fed. But there was nothing dead about Donovan. No, there was something incredibly alive about him, as if at a glance you could tell that his blood ran hotter. Not hot as in passion, but hot as in hot to the touch, as though if you spilled it into your mouth it would be hot, like sweet, metallic cocoa.

I had to close my eyes and hold up a hand before he got right beside the bed. I spoke with my eyes still closed. "I'm sorry, Donovan, but you hit the radar as food."

"I'm supposed to be food."

I shook my head. "Not food for the *ardeur*, but food-food. I'm wondering what your blood would taste like going down."

"I was afraid of this." A female voice. I opened my eyes to see Sylvie, Richard's second-in-command, his Freki. She was a little taller than me, short brown hair, a face that could be pretty in makeup, but she usually didn't sweat it, so that your eyes had to adjust to the plainness of her eyes and skin before you could realize that she was pretty just as she was. With the right makeup, she'd have been beautiful. I wondered if people thought that about me sometimes. Since I was wearing a hospital gown, and probably looked like shit, who was I to comment?

Sylvie filled the room with a prickling run of energy. She was small and female and had managed to fight her way to second-in-command of a large pack of werewolves. She'd have probably been in charge if I hadn't interfered a few times. Richard could have beaten her physically, but Sylvie had the will to win, the will to kill, and there are fights when that will win the day over superior strength. Then, a while back, Richard had called her challenge, and he had hurt her, badly. He'd proven that he had the will to back the strength. On one hand, I was glad; it meant the question was answered. On the other hand, it had cost Richard a piece of himself that he'd never get back. I mourned that piece of him, almost as much as he did.

"You were afraid of what?" Edward asked from near the door. I hadn't realized he'd followed Donovan back in.

"Anita is like a new lycanthrope. It means her hungers are not under her control completely. Donovan may be powerful, but he's a prey animal, and her beasts smell that," Sylvie said.

I nodded from the bed, my hand falling to the white sheet. "What she said."

Donovan looked at me; his blue-gray eyes, as changeable as the sky, had gone to rainy gray. "Would you really tear my throat out?"

"Probably a gut wound, actually, soft underbelly."

He raised those soft, pale eyebrows.

"No oral sex," Sylvie said, and anyone else would have said it with humor; she was utterly serious.

The door opened behind them. I got a glimpse of some tall, dark-haired man who I didn't recognize. He looked too young to be standing there, but then there were a couple of other guards that I thought the same thing about. Then the doorway was full of people and I had to look at them, but I promised myself that I'd talk to Claudia about putting an age limit on the guards here. I'd voted out Cisco for being eighteen, but apparently I hadn't made it clear that it was the age, not Cisco himself, that was the problem. If we all survived today, I'd make that more clear. No, not if, when. When we survived. To think anything else, well, it had to be when.

I looked for Asher in the vampires who came first through the door, but he wasn't there. It was as if Requiem read my mind, or at least my face, because he said, "Oh, my evening star, you look eagerly past me, as if I am not here. Asher wakes seventh among us. When dawn comes he will die, but those who stand before you now have a chance to remain awake long enough to see this through." His face was a glimpse of white flesh between the black of his hooded cloak and the beard and mustache. His hair was lost in the blackness of the hood. The only true color to his face was the brilliant blue of his eyes, with that hint of green in them like sea water in the sunlight he would never see again.

London, with his short dark curls and black-on-black suit and shirt, came next. He always looked like a cross between an executive Goth and a movie hit man. His nickname for centuries had been "the Dark Knight." Yeah, long before Batman, there was London. He was also almost perfect food for the *ardeur*. Feeding me actually gained him power, instead of draining him. But like all the secondary abilities in Belle Morte's bloodline it was a double-edged blade. He was the perfect food, but he was also almost instantly addicted to the *ardeur*. One feeding had undone centuries of abstinence when he'd fled Belle's slavery. One feeding and he'd been more tightly bound to me than any civil ceremony could have made us. But feeding, even from London, wouldn't be enough for what we needed now. He smiled at me and came to take my hand. He knew he wasn't the love of my life, nor I his, and we were both okay with that. He would be the leading contender to be my *pomme de sang*, if only he were available in daylight. His hand was warm in mine, which meant he'd fed on some willing donor. So many people were willing to open a vein these days, there was no reason to force anyone. People lined up for it.

He raised my hand and laid a gentle kiss on the knuckles. "We are here to see that you do not eat the swan king for real." His smile widened and filled his dark eyes with happiness. Requiem and other vamps who had come from England with him said they'd never seen him this relaxed, and hadn't even known he could smile.

I smiled back at him and nodded. "That would be bad."

Jason peeked around the much taller man. He grinned at me, but there was a flinching around his spring-blue eyes, a hollow look that said he'd been crying. I held out my other hand to him. London moved out of the way so Jason could hug me. He practically climbed into the bed to do it. We were friends, and sometimes lovers, but his reaction surprised me. I patted the top of his short blond hair, sort of awkwardly, and it wasn't just the IV that made it awkward, though that pulled. That was sooo going to have to come out before I fed on Donovan.

"Jason," I said, "it's all right."

He shook his head against my shoulder and raised a tear-stained face. His voice was thick with tears as he said, "Liar." He tried to smile, but didn't quite make it.

I touched his face with my free hand. "Jason, I . . ." I didn't even know what to say. This reaction was more than a friend's reaction. Then I thought, maybe the grief wasn't for me. His Ulfric and his master were both near death. If they died, his world would never be the same. The next Master of the City might not have a use for him as a *pomme de sang*.

I tried to cup his face, but the IV caught again. "Can someone get this out of me? I can't feed the *ardeur* hooked up to tubes."

Lillian threaded her way through the growing crowd and took out the needle. I carefully looked away at the crucial moment. I was better than I used to be, but I still didn't like seeing needles go in or out of my flesh. It just creeped me.

Jason moved away enough for the doctor to work, but he kept my hand like it was a lifeline. Jason was usually so together that sometimes I forgot that he was only twenty-two. He was actually the same age as some of the werelion college students that Joseph had let me choose from. His excuse on the age had been that older lions had jobs and families. At the time I hadn't questioned, but now, well, I'd probably be questioning everything the lions did for a while.

"I'm your wolf in case your beast decides to rise," Jason said.

"I thought Sylvie . . ."

She spoke from in back of the crowd of shapeshifters. "With the *ardeur* raised in the room, I'm not staying. Nothing personal, Anita. I mean you're cute, but I don't do women, and with you this weak, and Jean-Claude out of it, I don't want to take the chance that this thing spreads through the room." She came to the bed and patted my shoulder, a little awkwardly. She wasn't much better at the buddy thing than I was. "The wolves will do everything they can to get you all through this."

"Better than the lions," I said.

"It's not their Rex in the next room, it's our Ulfric," she said, and there was a flare of her beast, like the hot breath of the monster in the dark. I shivered, and she shut the power down. "Sorry, I'm going." With that she went for the door. As she went out, someone else came in, and I cried out, "Micah!"

He didn't exactly run to me, but it was close. He was still wearing the dress shirt and slacks I'd last seen him in, but they were covered in dried stains. Blood dried to black and brick red. Maybe I stared at the bloodstains, because he unbuttoned it as he came and threw it on the floor. For once, seeing his chest and shoulders bare didn't make me think of sex. All I could think of was whose blood it was, Richard's or Jean-Claude's. Micah said, "Don't reach out to them with power, Anita."

"How did you know that's what I was thinking?" I asked.

He smiled, but his eyes were tired, relieved to see me up and around, but tired. "I'm your Nimir-Raj." That was often his answer to things when I asked how he read me so well. He was Nimir-Raj to my Nimir-Ra, and that seemed answer enough for him. He kissed me, and

I expected Jason to let go of my hand so I could hug Micah, but he didn't. Micah and I glanced at him, and I saw the fear naked in Jason's eyes for a moment. I'd never seen his eyes like that. That one look let me know how terribly close we'd come to dying, and how close we still were. One look, and I knew that we weren't out of the woods yet.

I looked up into Micah's chartreuse eyes. "It's not just the little vampires that the energy is supposed to save, is it?"

Jason's hand tightened on mine. Micah hugged me, and I put my free hand over that smooth, warm, permanently tanned skin. I breathed in the scent of his neck, so precious to me. "Tell me," I whispered.

He drew back enough to see my face. "When Jean-Claude dies at dawn he could take you and Richard with him." I searched his solemn face and found only truth there. Truth, and fear, behind his eyes, hiding better, but it was there.

I called out, "Lillian!"

She was there. "Yes, Anita."

"How likely is it that Jean-Claude will drag us with him?"

"Truthfully, we don't know, but it's a possibility, and we'd rather not find out." She touched my forehead the way a mother takes a temperature. "Feed on Donovan, Anita. Take the energy he offers so we don't have to worry about it."

"You're not sure this will work, are you?"

"Of course we are."

"I don't need to be a vamp or a shapeshifter to know that was a lie," I said.

She stepped back, suddenly brisk and all professional. "Fine, we aren't certain, but it will be enough energy to save some of you. Whether all of you will be saved, we just don't know. This is new science here, Anita. New metaphysical science, which is always an uncertain thing."

I nodded. "Thanks for telling me the truth."

"You asked," she said.

Edward came up through the crowd. "They told me it would work."

"We said it was the best idea we had," Lillian said. "That is not the same thing."

Edward nodded. "All right, I heard what I wanted to hear." He gave me a very serious look. "Don't die on me. The other bodyguards would never let me live it down."

I smiled. "I'll do my best to protect your reputation." I had a thought. "Now you get to wait outside."

"What?" he said.

"I don't think I can have sex in the room while you watch. Sorry."

He grinned at me. "I guess I'd have trouble in front of you, too." Then he did something that surprised me. He moved Jason away from my hand and took it, firm and certain, in his. He held my hand, and we looked at each other for a long moment. He opened his mouth, closed it, shook his head. "If you die, I promise the Harlequin will pay for it."

Apparently, the secret was out, and we were just calling a spade a scary shovel. I nodded. "You didn't have to say it, I knew you would."

He smiled, squeezed my hand, and left. I almost called him back. Surrounded by men I loved, and had sex with, but strangely I felt safer with Edward in the room. But the danger I was about to face wasn't his kind of danger. In the room or out of it, Edward couldn't help me now.

27

I DIDN'T SO much raise the *ardeur*, as simply stop fighting it. My control of it had grown to the point where I had to give it permission to feed. I had to unleash it. Maybe if the beasts inside me hadn't risen at nearly the same time, I wouldn't have thought of the *ardeur* as something on a leash. Something on a chain, yeah, a chain with a leather collar at the end of it. Yeah, something leather and metal studded, and tight.

I'd thought they had too many guards in the room, until I got close to Donovan Reece. Then part of me thought sex, and three or four other parts of me wondered what the flesh under all that skin would feel like between my teeth. Donovan had requested that the other men turn their backs and give us what privacy they could. They'd done it. Some had done it with a look that said it was silly, but they'd done it. Then Donovan took his clothes off. He stripped like a pale, white dream. The *ardeur* had made certain that his body was ready for me. He lay against the front of his body like something carved of ivory and blushed with the first pink of sunrise. He was as pale as a vampire, but he was dawn, he was sunlight on water, he was moonlight on wings. I heard the sound of birds calling in the night. I'd never known swans had a voice, almost like geese, but . . . no. No, not geese, swans.

Donovan's voice came strained. "You've undone my control of my power. Something about the *ardeur* has stripped me bare of more than my clothes."

I found I could still talk, above the feel of a night's sky and moonlight, though it was like seeing double, as if the vision in my head threatened to be more real than the man beside me. "My version of the *ardeur* gives you what you want most, sometimes." I leaned in beside his cheek and whispered into that perfect curve of ear. "What do you want most, Donovan Reece?"

He turned to me, and his eyes were a dull gray. "Not to be king." He rolled us over so that he was suddenly looking down at me. His body was still pressed to the front of mine, not inside, but the sensation of him hard and firm trapped between our bodies made me cry out. He leaned over me, pressing that weight against me. He wrapped his arms around me, which put my face into his chest. I'd have trouble breathing with him on top. But he seemed to realize it and raised his upper body enough to curl around me, until his face was next to mine. "Can you give me what I most want, Anita?"

"I don't know," I whispered.

"Try."

"It may not work the way you think it will." I tried to think past the *ardeur*, past the feel of his body against mine, tried to think past the warm scent of his skin. The *ardeur* had a mind of its own, and a funny way of granting desires. I didn't trust what would happen if that was what he truly wanted.

"Give me what I want, Anita." He raised his upper body above me.

"I can't control the *ardeur* that well, Donovan."

He raised himself so that his upper body was in a half push-up, which pushed his lower body harder against mine. I whimpered for him.

"Did I hurt you?" he asked.

I had to open my eyes to answer him. "Not hurt, no."

Something in my voice, in my unfocused gaze, made him smile. "No, not hurt," he said, smiling down at me. His eyes were bluer than I'd ever seen them, as if something about this moment had chased the gray from his eyes.

I realized that his request to not be king had made me tone back the *ardeur*. It scared me, because the *ardeur* was a power unto itself. It did things, decided things, that I didn't understand. If Jean-Claude had been able, I would have asked him. Of course, I had people I could ask.

It was just going to be awkward to ask. One of the other reasons that Requiem and London were in the room was that they had more centuries of experience with the *ardeur* than I did. As victims, true, but still they knew it in ways I'd only begun to glimpse.

I put a hand on Donovan's chest, to push him away, to give me breathing space. We were in a hurry, but we weren't in such a hurry, were we? I mean, if he were dead, he wouldn't be king. Sometimes the *ardeur* was a very literal thing. But I'd forgotten that the white hairs on his chest weren't hair, but feathers. The moment my palm touched the silk of the feathers and the heat of his chest, I forgot what I was going to ask. My hands found his body, and he was hot to the touch, as if his temperature had spiked.

"Your skin, it's hot."

"I told you, you took my control away." He leaned in as he said it, keeping his shoulders up, but lowering his head for a kiss. I could feel his heart thudding against the palm of my hand. I could feel it in a way that I hadn't been able to feel since the *ardeur* was new to me. I felt his heart like it was something holdable, as if I could reach into his chest and cup it, caress it. I was suddenly very aware of all the blood rushing through his body. I could hear it, feel it, like warm ribbons running just under his skin. I could smell it, hot, metallic, sweet. I had closed my eyes so I wouldn't see his face, watch him kiss me, but it wasn't the human part of me that was the problem. Closing my eyes didn't take away the feel, the weight, the scent of his skin, and of what lay so close under all that flesh.

He kissed me. He kissed me for the very first time, and I didn't care. I moved away from those soft lips, and kissed my way along the line of his jaw. Kissed my way onto his neck. He seemed to take it as an invitation, because the hard length of him pushed between my legs. I opened for him, but put my hand on the back of his neck, holding his neck close to my kisses. His hair was the softest I'd ever touched, but it meant almost nothing to me. I could smell what I wanted, smell it like candy just under his skin.

He pulled against my hand. His voice was strained as he said, "Anita, I need a better angle."

I kept my hand pressed into his neck, brushed by that soft hair, held him where a few kisses more would put me where I wanted to be. I felt him now, pushing against my opening, but not quite there. Normally, that distracted me from other things, but not tonight. Almost without thinking I moved my hips, my legs, angled my body for him. He entered me, and that did distract me. It made my eyes fly open wide, made me cry out and writhe underneath him. But I never let go of the back of his neck. I pressed my face in tight against his, as I raised my hips off the bed, my legs in the air so he could push himself in and out of me. I cried out under the strength of his body.

"Let me rise, Anita. Let me look at you."

"No," I whispered, "not yet."

He pushed against my hand at his neck again. I put my other hand on his back. I held him in place and kissed over the pulse in his neck. It jumped and beat against my lips like something alive. Like a trapped bird in a cage of flesh. I would set it free. I would let it pour into my mouth, and . . . There was a moment of sanity, a heartbeat of, no, then Jean-Claude's power breathed through me, his hunger, both his hungers, and there was no more doubt. There was only the press of Donovan's pulse against my mouth, his body thrusting inside mine, my hips rising to meet him, and my mouth on his neck.

I bit him and tried to be gentle, but gentle wasn't what I wanted, wasn't how I felt. The sensation of his flesh in my mouth, caught between my teeth, as I bit slowly down, harder, and harder, felt so good. But what I wanted to do was bite more, take more of his flesh into my mouth, into me. The fluttering heat of his pulse like a frightened butterfly beat against the roof of my mouth. It was like a caress, urging me on, begging me to free that dancing bit of life.

Donovan lifted me up off the bed, his arms locked around me as he went to his knees. The movement startled me, made me ease back from the biting.

His voice was shaky. "Too much teeth, Anita."

He knelt on the narrow bed, his arms wrapped around me, his body no longer inside me. My legs were wrapped around his waist. I must have done it automatically when he moved. He'd stopped making love to get me to stop trying to eat him.

His neck had a perfect impression of my teeth like a purplish-red bruise in the white perfection of his flesh. Blood traced down his shoulder and back where my nails had gone into that smooth skin. I could have said so many things, but the one thing I said was the one that amazed me most. "You broke the *ardeur*'s hold."

"I may not be a predator, Anita, but I'm still a king; that means I have to give myself to you. You can't just take it."

"I'm sorry," I said.

"It's all right, I'm not angry. Just don't tear my throat out, or carve my back up, okay?"

"I'm not sure she can help it," Micah said. I looked out from the man in my arms to find not just Micah but all the men crowded around the bed. Remus seemed to be arguing with Requiem and London. Too low to hear, but body language said it all. I met Micah's eyes and asked for help with a look. I'd thought of Donovan as just meat, just food. The sex hadn't been enough to distract me from blood, and meat.

Donovan asked, "What can I do to keep myself safe?"

Requiem came to the bed, his black cloak tight around him. "If you are strong enough to sit up with her as you did, then you are strong enough to hold her down."

"We can't guarantee your safety, Reece," Remus said.

Donovan looked at the guard. He shifted his grip from my waist to lower, but there was no wavering, as if he could have held me forever. It answered whether the swanmanes were stronger than normal humans; they were. "I know you cannot guarantee my safety."

"She could tear your throat out before we could move," Remus said.

"If it gets that out of hand, we interfere," Micah said.

"Interfere how?" Remus asked.

"Grab her, help Donovan hold her down."

"The *ardeur* will spread to anyone who touches her," Remus said.

Micah nodded. "I know."

Remus shook his head, a little too rapidly. "I can't do my job then. I can't keep Reece safe."

"Because you won't risk the *ardeur* spreading to you." Micah made it a statement, not a question.

"Yes," Remus said.

"Then leave," London said.

"We need a senior guard in here," Remus said. "Who do I send in my place? Bobby Lee is still in South America. Claudia, no. Who replaces me?" He sounded tormented, torn between duty and what? Duty and fear? Duty and the *ardeur*?

"We are out of time for niceties, Anita," Requiem said. "I speak for

the vampires. If the lesser among us are to be saved, it must be now."
There wasn't a poetic allusion in the statement. Things were bad when
Requiem stopped quoting poetry.

It was almost as if his words brought the *ardeur* crashing back. One
moment I was almost neutral in Donovan's arms, the next I was kissing him as if I'd crawl into his mouth. My nails just seemed to automatically dig into his back again. The feel of his flesh parting under
my nails made me cry out in pleasure, and him in pain. I tried to tone
down what I wanted to do to him. I tried not to bite at his mouth but
only kiss, but the effort had me making small frustrated noises against
his lips.

He pressed us back to the bed, his weight suddenly pinning me
down. My legs were still wrapped around his waist so his body was already pushing against my opening. I fought to concentrate on the sex
instead of flesh and blood. But the sex was tangled up with the feel of
my nails in his back, my mouth at his lips. I wanted that hard press of
flesh to shove its way inside me, but almost more I wanted to bite his
lips and draw blood. I wanted blood more than sex. I was feeding for
Jean-Claude, but the *ardeur* wasn't his first hunger.

I licked Donovan's lower lip, drew it into my mouth, so full, so rich,
so . . . I bit down on his lip, hard and sharp. Blood, sweet, metallic,
warm blood filled my mouth, and the world vanished in a dance of
light flashes and pleasure. It wasn't sex, or orgasm, but it was as if that
sip of blood ate the world in a red wash of pleasure. I'd had the world
go red from anger, but never from sheer joy. It was as if every piece of
my body filled with warmth and happiness all at once. It was orgasmic
and not, but whatever it was, it was amazing.

I was left gasping and almost limp underneath Donovan. It was as if
I'd lost time, because he had my wrists pinned, his body trying for the
right angle to enter me. I blinked up at him as if I didn't remember
how I got there. His chin was covered in bright, crimson blood; his
lower lip was shredded. Had I done that?

Then he found his angle and was pushing his way into my body. I
gazed down the length of our bodies to watch him plunge himself into
me. The sight of it made me cry out and raise my hips to meet his
thrust. His eyes fluttered shut, and he gasped, "You take all my control away."

"Fuck me, Donovan," I whispered.

He looked down at me, with blood spilling down his face, but his eyes filled with that look that a man gets. That look that says, *Mine, sex, more, less than that.* His eyes were bluer than I'd ever seen them as he began to shove himself in and out of my body. He found his rhythm, quick, fast, over and over. I watched all that pale, hard length plunge in and out of me. I felt the warmth begin to build. I whispered, "Soon."

"Your eyes," he whispered, "your eyes like blue flame."

I might have asked what he meant by that, but one last thrust and the orgasm hit me. I screamed and struggled underneath him. He fought to hold my hands down, fought to pin my lower body, fought to keep me where he had me, as his body thrust inside me in one last powerful movement that brought me screaming again, or maybe I hadn't stopped screaming from the first time. The *ardeur* fed, fed on his body plunged inside mine, fed on the strength of his hands on my wrists, fed on the heat of him, and then I felt the swans. The three women I knew in St. Louis were in a small bedroom. They stared up at me as if I were something they could see, something that had come to get them. Then other faces, more startled eyes; some cried out, some slumped on their couches, fell from chairs, others writhed on their beds. I fed, we fed, the *ardeur* fed. Dozens of faces, of bodies, and I felt Jean-Claude wake, felt it like a jolt through my belly and groin.

He took control of the energy and I might have tried to stop, but it was too late to stop. We fed on the swans, we fed on them all. So much power, so much life. We ate them down while they stumbled in mid-step, while they slid down walls, and none of them fought us. They just gave it up. An army of prey, an army of food; a glorious rush of power.

Richard woke; I felt his eyes flash open, felt him begin to choke and fight the tube in his throat. Jean-Claude drew me back from him, enough so I did not choke with him. I saw the white coats pile around Richard as he began to struggle.

Then it was night and moonlight and wings, strong wings beating against so much air. The *ardeur* hit those wings like an arrow through his heart. One pulse beat it was feathers and wings, the next pulse it was a man falling to earth. The *ardeur* took his power, drank down that pale body, that dark hair, the mix of pleasure and terror as he plummeted. Richard's power burst over me, through me, in a rush of heat and electricity. He reached out to the falling man, and simply thought—Change. He called the man's beast, called that energy and covered the flesh in feathers, turned the arms to wings in time for him to turn and skim over the treetops. I felt leaves brush our feet as wings beat frantically to gain height. But *frantic* didn't quite cover all that smooth, muscled power. When all we could feel was wind and space, we left him, and I had a moment of staring into Richard's face, a moment to see his chest covered in healing scars. Then I was back in the narrow bed with Donovan on top of me, his body poised above me, spine bowed, hands gripping my wrists as if I were the last solid thing in the world. His eyes were closed; blood dripped from his mouth onto my skin like red flowers exploding on my body.

I breathed his name. "Donovan."

He opened his eyes and they were solid black and no longer human. He threw his head back and screamed. The sound was high and piteous. The sound froze my heart in my throat. I had time to think, *I've hurt him*, and then that pale, perfect body began to thrust into me all over again, as if we hadn't just made love. But before he'd been gentle, careful. There was nothing gentle this time. He plunged into me as hard and fast as he could. He brought me screaming, writhing, underneath him. His hands bruised my wrists, held me in place as his rhythm became frantic, his breathing ragged, and feathers flowed around his body like a nimbus of white light. I had a second to think, *Angel*, and then all I could see was feathers, brushing me, covering me like a blanket. He cried out again and his body thrust into mine. He brought me one last time, covered in feathers, blinded by them, breathing them in. His hands vanished and I could move my hands, but all I could touch were feathers and bones too delicate to be human. Huge wings beat the air above me, and I could finally see a long graceful neck, the head, the beak. I was trapped at the center of a storm of wingbeats and feathers, as he fought for lift. I covered my face with my arms, because a swan can break the arm of a grown man with one blow. Then he was off, almost hovering, but the ceiling was too low. He crashed to the floor.

I was left buffeted, breathless, heart hammering in my chest. A single feather longer than my hand lay across my stomach. I managed to prop myself up, the feather fluttering down between my legs to land beside the condom that lay discarded on the bed. It had been the only clothes he'd been wearing.

Jean-Claude's voice eased through me. *"Je t'aime, ma petite, je t'aime."*

"I love you, too," I whispered.

Then dawn came, and I felt him die. Felt that wonderful person I loved go away. I heard the sound of a body hitting the ground. Requiem was a heap of black cloak. One of the guards had managed to catch London and was lowering him to the ground a little more gently. The vampires were dead for the day, all of them. We had hours of daylight to find the Harlequin and kill them. I'm not sure that's what Jean-Claude and the other vampires would have wanted, but the vampires were down for the count until nightfall. It was daylight, and the humans were in charge. Thanks to Jean-Claude I was the top human in our city. Thanks to Richard's self-loathing, the guards would listen to me instead of him. All right, except for the wolves. The wolves were his, but that was okay, I needed professionals, not gifted amateurs. I needed Edward and his backup. At that moment I would have welcomed any backup he thought could handle the job.

28

I WAS WRONG. I didn't want to welcome Edward's backup. One of them I wanted to send back to his mommy. The other I wanted to put a bullet in his brain, or heart. He was human, so either would do the job.

At least I was dressed for the fight. I never fight as well naked. I would so not have been comfy naked in front of Edward, let alone in front of his "backup." "What the fuck were you thinking?" I shouted at him. Yeah, it was one of those kinds of fights.

Edward's face was blank, empty, peaceful. It was one of the faces he killed with when he wasn't enjoying the kill. "Olaf is good backup for this, Anita. He's got the skills we need: a covert spook, any weapon you care to name, hand-to-hand, and better with explosives than I am."

"He's also a fucking serial killer, whose victims of choice are petite brunette women." I slapped my upper chest. "Sound like anyone you know?"

He let out a breath; if it had been anyone else I would have said he sighed. "He's a good match for this job, Anita, I swear that he is, but he wasn't my choice, not exactly."

I stopped pacing and came to stand in front of him. I'd kicked everyone out except Micah when he handed me the overnight bag full of clothes and weapons. I loved a man who knew how to pack for me. When I'd stepped out into the hallway and seen Olaf and

Peter, I'd gone back in the room, kicked Micah out, too, and invited Edward in.

"What does that mean, he wasn't your choice, exactly? You just said his skills match this job."

"They do, but do you really think I'd have brought him within a hundred miles of you, Anita? Olaf likes you, likes you in a way I've never seen him like a woman. He has whores and he has victims, but whatever he feels for you is different."

"Are you saying he loves me?"

"Olaf doesn't love anybody, but he feels something for you."

"He wants me to play serial killer with him, Edward."

Edward nodded. "The last time he saw you, you and he killed a vampire together. You decapitated it, and he cut out its heart."

"How do you know what we did? You were in the hospital trying not to die."

"I heard about it later from the local cops. They were creeped by the way you butchered the vampire. Said you were both real good at cutting up the body."

"I'm a legal vampire executioner, Edward. It's what I do."

He nodded again. "And Olaf has been a special-ops assassin for most of his adult life."

"I don't hold his day job against him, Edward; it's his damn hobby that I don't like."

"Hobby? You call the fact that he's a serial killer his hobby?"

I shrugged. "I think that's how he sees it."

He smiled. "I think you may be right."

"Don't you smile at me. Don't you fucking smile at me. You hinted that you didn't want to bring him on this job, so why did you?"

His face sobered. "He wanted to come to St. Louis to see you"—he put air quotes around the *see*—"on his own. I told him if he came near you I'd kill him. He believed me, but he said that if I ever got called to back you up again, I had to include him. If I didn't, he'd come on his own, and take his chances with me later."

"Later? Later, after what?"

Edward gave me a look out of those blue eyes that were some of the coldest I ever looked into. "So he's here to what, kill me?"

"He doesn't kill women, Anita. He butchers them."

I shuddered, because I'd seen Olaf at a serial-killer crime scene. Not his own work. He'd been helping Edward and me track down a different killer. But the victim had been just a pile of meat. It had been one of the worst things I'd ever seen done to a human being. Olaf had looked up from that pile of carnage, and the look in his face had been sexual. As if what lay on that table was the biggest turn-on he'd ever had. He'd looked at me, and he'd been thinking sex, yeah, but he'd been thinking sex not just without my clothes, but as if he wondered what I'd look like without my skin. Most humans didn't scare me anymore, but Olaf scared me.

Edward said, "Anita, you look like you've seen a ghost."

"I'd rather see a ghost than him."

He smiled again. "Rather see a ghost; I keep forgetting that you're not just a pretty face."

I frowned at him. "You're smiling. This fight isn't even close to over."

"I had to invite Olaf to play, Anita. This way I have his word that he'll behave himself."

"Define *behave himself.*"

"No serial killing on your turf, period."

"So I'm off the menu, too?"

"He wants to help you slaughter your victim of choice, vampires. He'll even help you kill men, he said."

I shivered, rubbing my arms, squeezing tight so the gun in its shoulder holster dug into my breast a little. I liked the discomfort. I wasn't helpless. It was just that Olaf was six feet plus of trained muscle. I was stronger and faster than a normal human thanks to Jean-Claude's vampire marks, but I still knew enough about physical potential to know that Olaf was a very dangerous man. He was crazy and trained to kill; that seemed an unfair advantage to me.

"You think he would have come on his own by now, if you hadn't given him your word?" I asked.

"Yes." He wasn't smiling when he said that last. He was as serious as I'd ever seen him. "I would never have invited him to that last case in New Mexico if I'd thought I would be needing your help. Please, believe that the last thing I wanted was for him to meet you. I knew it would be a disaster. I just didn't expect you to . . . charm him. I didn't know there was a woman on the planet that could have made him feel anything close to . . ."—he searched for a word—"he wants to help you hunt and slaughter these vampires."

"I don't want him here, Edward."

"I know, but this was the best compromise I could make with him, Anita. Actually I hoped he'd be out of the country, so far away that the fireworks would be over before he could get back to the United States. He took a job with a government agency to help train up some of their new antiterrorist infiltration groups. He took a job that he's qualified for—he speaks more Middle Eastern languages than I do—but it wasn't a job that let him exercise his urges."

"You mean he's not been allowed to kill anyone."

He nodded.

"Why would he take a job that didn't let him slaughter people?"

"Because he knew if he went out of the country, he'd never make it back in time to be in St. Louis when you needed me."

I stared at Edward. "Are you saying that Olaf took a job that he didn't want so he'd be closer to me?"

"That is exactly what I'm saying. This last year and some change is probably the longest he's ever gone without killing someone. If you'd asked me, I'd have said he couldn't go this long without killing someone."

"How do you know he didn't?"

"He's got a deal with our government. He doesn't play serial killer on American soil. They look the other way, as long as he abides by that."

I hugged myself tight again. "I didn't ask Olaf to be a good boy, Edward."

"I know you didn't."

"Why does the fact that he's behaved himself on the off chance that he can come play with me scare me?"

"Because you're smart."

"Explain to me why it makes my skin run cold that he's gone to this much effort for me?"

"He is crazy, Anita. Which means that you never know what will trigger him with a woman. He likes you as much as I've ever seen him like a woman. But he has high standards for women."

"What does that mean?"

"It means that when he saw you almost two years ago you weren't sleeping around. Now you are. I'm a little worried that that will change his opinion of you."

"He kills whores," I said, my voice flat.

"I did not call you a whore."

"You said I sleep around."

"You have half a dozen regular lovers, and you just had sex with a new one. Give me another way to say it."

I thought about it, then shook my head and almost smiled. "A full dance card. Oh, hell, Edward. Fine, I'm sleeping with a lot of men." Which brought me to another thought. "God, Peter was in the hallway while Donovan and I were in here . . ." I felt myself blush and couldn't stop it.

"I figured you for a screamer."

I gave him a very unfriendly look.

"Sorry, but Peter was embarrassed. What else do you want me to say?"

"Say why you brought him. Say why the hell would you involve him in this dangerous mess?"

"Short version, because we've only got a few hours to find these bastards."

"I agree we've got a ticking clock, but you have to explain Peter being here. I can't just let him go hunting vampires with us, Edward. He's sixteen years old, for God's sake."

"It was the phone call when you talked to him. He knew you were in trouble. Short version, he wanted to return the favor. You rescued him, he wanted to help rescue you."

"I don't need rescuing. I need people to help me kill other people. I don't want Peter to get better at killing people. I watched him kill the woman who raped him. I watched him blow her face to red sauce." I shook my head and started pacing the room again. "How could you do this to him, Edward?"

"If I had left him home he just would have followed me. He knew where I was going. This way I can keep an eye on him."

"No, you can't. We can't do this job and babysit at the same time. They almost killed all three of us: Richard, Jean-Claude, and me. We're kind of hard to kill, Edward. These guys are good, dangerous good. Do you really want Peter's first real job to be against something this scary?"

"No," Edward said, "but he was coming. I had the choice of bringing him with me, or letting him find his own way."

"He's sixteen, Edward. You're his father. You say no, and you make it stick."

"I'm not married to his mother yet, Anita. I'm not his official step-anything."

"He sees you as his dad."

"Not when he doesn't want to."

"What does that mean?"

"It means that I don't have the authority that a real dad would have over him sometimes. It means that I'll always wonder if he'd been mine from the beginning if he'd be different, or if we'd have ended up here anyway."

"He's out there in the hallway, armed. He's carrying more than one gun, and at least one knife. He's carrying them like he's done it before. What the hell have you been teaching him, Edward?"

"What any father teaches his son."

"Which is?"

"What he knows."

I just stared at him, knowing my face held a soft, growing horror. "Edward, you can't make him into a little you."

"He was scared all the time, Anita, after the attack. His therapist thought that martial arts training, training him to take care of himself, would help. It did. He stopped having the nightmares after a while."

"Training him to take care of himself is different from what's standing out in that hallway. There's a loss of innocence in his eyes. A . . . oh, hell, I don't know what is missing, or what's there that shouldn't be, but I know it when I see it."

"It's the look that you have in your eyes, Anita. It's the look that I have in mine."

"He is not like us," I said.

"He's killed twice."

"He killed the wereanimal that killed his father and would have slaughtered them all. He killed the woman who raped him."

"It's pretty to think that it matters why you take a life. I guess it does, but what the taking of a life does to you inside doesn't care why you did it. You either can kill and sleep nights, or you can't. Peter isn't bothered by the killing, Anita. He's bothered by what the bitch did to him. He's bothered by the fact that he couldn't protect his sister."

"No one sexually abused Becca," I said.

"No, thank God, but her hand is still stiff sometimes. She has to do hand-strengthening exercises. The hand works, but it's not a hundred percent."

"And the man who tortured her is dead," I said.

Edward gave me those cold blue eyes. "You killed him for me."

"You were a little busy," I said.

"Yeah, dying."

"You didn't die," I said.

"I came as close as I've ever come. But I knew you'd save the kids. I knew that you would see it right."

"Edward, don't do this to me."

"Don't do what?" he asked.

"Don't make me part of taking Peter's childhood away from him."

"He's not a child, Anita."

"He's not a grown-up either," I said.

"And how do you grow up if no one shows you how?"

"Edward, we're going up against some of the most dangerous vampires that you and I have ever faced. Peter can't be that good yet. He can't be up to that skill level, no matter how much you've taught him. If you want to get him killed, fine, he's your kid, but I will not be a part of it. I will not help you get him killed in some macho bullshit initiation thing. I won't do it. Do you understand me? I won't allow it. Maybe you can't send him home, but I can."

"How?" he asked.

"What do you mean, how? I tell him to go the fuck home before he gets himself killed."

"He won't go."

"I can demonstrate that he's out of his depth, Edward."

"Don't humiliate him, Anita, please."

It was the *please* that got me. "You'd rather he die than get humiliated?"

Edward swallowed hard enough that I heard it. He turned away so I couldn't see his face. Not a good sign. "When I was sixteen, I'd rather have died than have a woman I loved humiliate me. He's sixteen and male, don't do that to him."

"Wait, what did you say?"

"I said, he's sixteen and male, don't humiliate him."

I went to him, walked around so that he had to meet my eyes. "Not that part."

Edward looked at me, and there was real anguish in his eyes. "Jesus, Edward, what is it?"

"His therapist says that an event like what happened to him just as his sexuality was awakening can be a defining event."

"What does that mean?" I asked.

"It means that his view of sex and violence is all mixed up together."

"Okay, what does that mean, exactly?"

"It means he's had two girlfriends in the last year. The first one was perfect. She was quiet, respectful, pretty. They were sweet together."

"What happened?" I asked.

"Her parents called one night and asked what kind of monster our son was, that he'd hurt their daughter."

"Hurt her how?"

"The usual. She was a virgin and they didn't do enough foreplay."

"It happens," I said.

"But the girl claimed that when she told him it hurt, he didn't stop."

"Sounds like buyer's remorse to me, Edward."

"I thought so, too, until the second girl. She was rough trade, Anita. As bad as the first girl had been good. She slept around, and everyone knew it. She broke up with Peter, said he was a freak. This girl was a freak, Anita. She was all leather and spikes and piercings, and it wasn't just for show. She said he hurt her."

"What did Peter say?"

"He said he didn't do anything she didn't ask him to do."

"What does that mean?"

"I wish I knew."

"He won't tell you?" I asked.

"No," Edward said.

"Why not?"

"I think it's rough sex. I think he's embarrassed to talk about it, or what they did was bad enough that he thinks I will think he's a freak, too. He doesn't want me to think that."

I didn't know what to say, so I said nothing. Sometimes silence is the best you can do. Then I thought of something worth saying. "Liking rough sex doesn't make you a freak."

He looked at me.

"It doesn't," I said, and I felt myself begin to blush.

"It's not my thing, Anita. It just doesn't move me."

"Everyone has things that do it for them, Edward."

"Rough does it for you?"

"Sometimes."

"When a kid is abused, they can react a lot of different ways; two of the choices are that they identify with the abuser and become abusers, or they embrace the role of victim. He didn't embrace the role of victim, Anita."

"What are you saying, Edward?"

"I don't know yet. But his therapist says that he's also identified with his savior, you. He has another option besides just victim or abuser; he has you."

"What does that mean, he has me?"

"You saved him, Anita. You took off the ropes, the blindfold. He'd just had the first sex of his life, and he looks up and sees you."

"He was raped," I said.

"It's still sex. Everyone likes to pretend that it's not, but it is. It may be about dominance, and pain, but it's still sex. I'd take it away, make it so it never happened, but I can't. Donna can't. His therapist can't. Peter can't."

My eyes were burning. Damn it, I would not cry. But I remembered a fourteen-year-old boy who I'd had to watch be abused on camera. They'd done it so I'd do what they wanted. Done it to prove that if I failed them, I wouldn't be the one who suffered. I had failed Peter. I had saved him, but not in time. I had got him out, but not before.

"I can't save him, Anita."

"We already saved him, as much as we can, Edward."

"No, you saved him."

I realized in that one statement that Edward blamed himself, too. We'd both failed him, then. "You were saving Becca at the time."

"Yes, but what that bitch did to Peter is still happening. It's still inside him, in his eyes. I can't fix it." His hands clenched into fists. "I can't fix it."

I touched his arm. He flinched but didn't pull away. "You don't fix shit like this, Edward, not outside television sitcoms. In real life you don't fix this. You can make it better, you can heal, but it doesn't just go away. Real life doesn't fix that easy."

"I'm his father, or all the father he has. If I don't fix it, who can?"

"No one," I said. I shook my head. "Sometimes you just accept your losses and move on. Peter's scarred, but he's not broken beyond repair. I've talked to him on the phone, I've looked in his eyes. I see the person he's becoming, and it's a strong person, a good person."

"Good." He laughed and it was a harsh sound. "I can only teach him what I am, and I'm not good."

"Honorable then," I said.

He thought about that, then nodded. "Honorable. I'll take that, I guess."

"Strong and honorable is not a bad legacy, Edward."

He looked at me. "Legacy, huh?"

"Yeah."

"I shouldn't have brought Peter."

"No, you shouldn't have."

"His skills aren't a good match for this job," he said.

"No," I said, "they aren't."

"You can't send him home, Anita."

"You'd really rather see him dead than humiliated?"

"If you humiliate him, it will destroy him, Anita. It will destroy that part of him that wants to save people and not hurt them. If he gives up that part of himself, I'm afraid that all that will be left is a predator in training."

"Why do I feel like you're leaving out stuff?"

"Because this is the short version, remember?"

I nodded, then shook my head. "Jesus, Edward, if this is the short version, I'm not sure my nerves can take the long one."

"We'll keep Peter in the background, as much as we can. I've got more backup on the way, but I'm not sure they'll get here in time." He glanced at his watch. "We're running out of time."

"Let's do this."

"With Peter and Olaf?" He made it a question.

"He's your kid, and Olaf is good in a fight. If Olaf gets out of hand, we kill him."

Edward nodded. "My thought, exactly."

I wanted to let it go, God knew I did, but I couldn't. I was a girl and I couldn't let it go. "Did you say that Peter was in love with me?"

"I wondered if you'd heard that."

"I understand why he has a crush on me, I guess. I saved him. You hero-worship someone who saves you."

"It may be a crush, or hero worship, but remember, Anita, that it's the strongest emotion he's ever had for a woman. It may not be love, but if you've never felt anything stronger, how do you tell the difference?"

The answer was, you don't. I just didn't like that answer, not one little bit.

29

I HADN'T RECOGNIZED Peter at first, because he'd done that growth spurt thing that teenage boys do sometimes. He'd been a little taller than me when I last saw him. Now he was damn close to six feet. His hair had been chestnut brown last time I saw him; now it was darker, a brown that was almost black. It wasn't a dye job, just a child's hair darkening to the color it would be as an adult. His shoulders had broadened, and he looked older than sixteen if you looked only at muscle development, but the face, the face hadn't caught up to the body. The face still looked young, unfinished, until you hit the eyes. The eyes were young one minute and cynical and old as hell the next. It would have been unnerving enough to see Peter under these circumstances, but Edward's little talk hadn't helped my nerves at all. It made me look for signs that Peter was what Edward feared, a junior predator. If I hadn't had Edward's warning in my head, would I have noticed that look, that gesture? Would I have scrutinized him, trying to see the damage? Maybe. But I cursed Edward for oversharing, cursed him loud and long in my head.

Peter wasn't Peter Parnell, he was Peter Black. He even had ID to prove it. The ID said he was eighteen, too. The ID looked damned good. Edward and I were sooo going to talk about Peter's educational experiences if we could just avoid getting him killed here and now.

And that was the real danger to Peter being here. Edward and I needed to concentrate on the bad guys, but we'd both be worried about Peter, we just would. It was going to fuck with our concentration. Maybe I could persuade Peter to stay out of the action by telling him he might get us both killed. It might be the truth.

Olaf stood against the far wall in a ring of bodyguards. They hadn't disarmed him, yet, but my reaction to him coming through the door had made them not like him at all. Or maybe it was the fact that he was taller than Claudia, which put him perilously close to seven feet tall. He wasn't thin, but I'd seen him shirtless and knew that there was nothing but muscle under that pale skin, a lot of muscle. But it was lean muscle, muscle that could move fast. Even standing still, there was a potential in Olaf that just about raised the hairs on your neck. He was still perfectly bald, with a dark shadow of almost-beard on chin and jaws and upper lip. He was one of those men who needed to shave twice a day to stay perfectly shaved. His eyes were so deep set it was like staring into twin caves. Dark eyes, set deep in a pale face. His eyebrows were black above them. He was dressed in the same black I'd seen him in almost two years ago. Black T-shirt, black leather jacket, black jeans, over black boots. I wanted to ask him if he owned anything with color to it, but I didn't want to tease him. One, he didn't like to be teased; two, I wasn't sure if he'd think I was flirting. I just didn't understand Olaf enough to mess with him.

He was trying to be neutral in the circle of bodyguards, but there was something in him that was never truly neutral. Most serial killers make the neighbors say, *He was such a quiet man, a nice boy, so surprised.* Olaf had never been a nice boy. I'd seen him vanish into a nighttime field in plain sight, like magic. Not supernatural powers, but military training. Edward had called him a special-ops spook, and I'd seen it work. I knew that all that tall muscled violence could melt into the night. What I didn't believe was that it could pretend to be harmless and do undercover work. Edward did that kind of work, and was fabulous at it. But Edward was sane, and Olaf wasn't. Crazy people have trouble stopping the crazy long enough to blend in with the normals.

He put that cave-dweller gaze on me. I shivered, because I couldn't help it. He actually smiled. He liked that I was afraid of him. He liked that a lot. A part of me screamed, *Kill him now.* The rest of me really didn't disagree with that little voice.

"We need the muscle," Edward said at my side.

"You're reading my mind," I said.

"I know you."

I nodded. "Yeah, you know me." I glared at him. "And yet this is who you bring to my party."

"He had no choice," Olaf said in that deep, rumbling voice that seemed to come from the very center of that big chest.

"I heard that," I said.

Claudia said, "Anita, what is he?" She jerked a thumb at him.

"Backup," I said.

She gave me a look.

"He's given his word of honor that he'll behave himself while he's in our city."

"Behave himself how?" Remus asked.

I looked at Edward. "You explain it. I need to get some paperwork from Jean-Claude's room."

"Paperwork," he said.

I nodded. "I think I've got warrants of execution for the two vamps that fucked us earlier."

"I thought no one knew they were in town," he said.

"They've been setting up some of the vamps from the Church of Eternal Life."

"Busy girls," Edward said.

"They were women, these vampires?" Olaf asked. His voice was neutral, I'd give him that.

I hated to answer his question, because if the driver's license photos looked as much like the vampires Mercia and Nivia as I remembered, then I knew why two of Malcolm's people had been naughty. The Harlequin were spies and covert ops; a little play-acting was right up their alley. Was I certain that Mercia and Nivia had pretended to be Sally Hunter and Jennifer Hummel? No. Was I almost sure? Yes. Was I sure enough to use the warrants to kill them? Oh, yes.

"Yes, they were both female," I said, and I didn't look at him as I said it.

"Are we going to kill them?"

"Probably."

"What do they look like?" he asked, and his voice was losing its neutral edge.

"Why does that matter to you?" Claudia asked.

I forced myself to look up and meet Olaf's gaze. I fought to watch his face while I said, "They fit your vic profile, if that's what you want to know. One of them maybe a little tall, but the other one is juuust right."

The look on his face . . . such joy, such anticipation. It made me want to cry, or scream, or shoot him.

"Vic profile," Claudia said. "What are you saying?"

"Olaf is special ops. He's an assassin, and a soldier, and a spook, and he's good at all of it."

"Not just good," he said, "I am the best."

"I'll let you and Edward discuss that someday, but he's good, Claudia. He's backed my play before, and he was . . . useful." I licked my lips. "But no woman of any description is to be alone with him at any time."

"Why?" she asked.

"I gave my word," Olaf said.

"I'm going to treat you like a recovering alcoholic, Olaf. Let's just keep temptation out of reach, okay?"

"We are going to slaughter these two women together, correct?" he asked.

I licked my suddenly dry lips again, then nodded. "I think so."

"Then I will not be tempted elsewhere."

Normally, I'd have just used silver shot and blown holes through the vampires until I saw daylight. Or maybe a good old-fashioned staking. But they were Harlequin. I would have to treat them as if they were master vamps, heavy hitters. Which meant shoot them with silver shot, then decapitate them, take the heart out, and burn them both. You burn the body in a separate fire. Then you scatter the ashes in running water, different bodies of running water if you want to be truly paranoid. Was I paranoid, or just cautious? These two vampires had almost killed Jean-Claude, Richard, and me from a distance, using powers I'd never seen before. Paranoid it wasn't.

It was a messy, dirty job to decapitate and take a heart. There were vampire executioners who quit after having to do it a few times, just didn't have the stomach for it. Did I have the stomach for it? Yes. Would I let Olaf help me? Who the hell else would volunteer? Edward would do it if I asked, but truthfully, Olaf was better at taking the body apart. I guess practice makes perfect, and Olaf had had a lot of practice.

Claudia asked again, "What do you mean he's like an alcoholic?"

"You tell her, Edward. I'm going to go check my paperwork."

"Not without guards, you aren't," he said.

"Fine," I said. "Send guards with me."

"Where is the paperwork?" he asked.

"In my briefcase in Jean-Claude's place."

"You can't go to the Circus of the Damned without me, Anita."

"Or me," Olaf said.

"If I said 'or me,' would you get mad?" Peter said.

I frowned at him. "Yes."

He grinned at me. He was entirely too pleased to be here with his guns and knives strapped to his body. He was even wearing a black T-shirt, but at least his jeans were blue, though his leather jacket was black. The boots were brown and looked like Edward's, real cowboy boots, not boots you'd wear to go dancing like Olaf's. Though the fact that I thought Olaf's boots were club boots was probably a fact best kept to myself.

"I have to vote with them," Claudia said.

"No one asked your opinion, woman," Olaf said.

"Let's get this clear, right now," I said. "Claudia is one of our officers. You don't like it, I know that, but I trust her with my life."

"She nearly got you killed."

"Didn't I end up in the hospital a couple of times in New Mexico, when you were supposed to be watching my back?"

Anger flared across his face, thinning out his lips, making his eyes look even more cavernous.

"Don't bitch at Claudia, if you can't do better." The moment I said it, I knew I shouldn't have.

"I can do better than a woman."

"Shit," I said.

"Anita," Claudia said.

"Yeah," I said.

"Let me prove it."

I sighed. "As amusing as the thought of you and Olaf going at it is, please don't. I know where the two bad vamps are, and I have current warrants of execution."

"How do you know where they are?" Edward asked.

"I saw hotel stationery fall from a table in the vision. If they didn't wake up and move their asses, we got 'em." I looked at Olaf. "If you don't slow me down by picking fights with my guards, then we get to kill two vampires today. They're powerful enough that we'll have to take their heads and hearts."

"Like we did in New Mexico," he said, and there was an eager purr to that deep voice.

I nodded, swallowing past a feeling that might have been nausea. "Yes."

"To hunt with you again, Anita, I will let this one believe what she likes."

I understood what a huge concession that was for Olaf. Claudia said, "I don't believe it, big man, I know it."

"Claudia," I said, "please, oh, hell, just don't be around him, okay? He can't seem to help how he feels about women. Just don't crowd him and we'll get this done, okay?"

She didn't like it, but she nodded.

"Great. Edward, you fill in the guards on why Olaf isn't to be alone with the women. I want to see Richard alive, not just in a vision. When you're done telling everyone what a big, bad man he is, come find me, and you can drive me to the Circus of the Damned for the warrants."

"I don't want you going out of my sight without guards, Anita."

"Jesus, Edward, it's daylight."

"Yeah, and you know better than I do that master vamps have human servants, animals to protect them, and just plain human victims who will do anything they're told."

I nodded, a little too fast, a little too often. "Fine, fine, you're right. I'm tired, and I'm . . . oh, hell, just pick some guards so I can go see Richard."

I should have understood if he picked guards, who one of them would be. Just shadowing me to Richard's hospital room was an easy job, a safe job, or should have been. I went for the far door with one bodyguard in front of me and one behind. The one bringing up the rear was Peter.

30

OUTSIDE RICHARD'S ROOM I had a fight with my guards. The other
guard was Cisco, who was all of eighteen. I felt like a chaperone at a
prom. But the fact that they were both still teenagers didn't make
them less stubborn. Hell, maybe it made them more stubborn.

"Standing orders," Cisco said, "are that you are not to go anywhere
without at least one guard with you at all times." He ran his hand
through his carefully blond-tipped hair and frowned. He wasn't happy.

"I don't need an audience to see my boyfriend."

"Orders are orders," he said.

I looked up at Peter. I still wasn't used to having to look up at him.
I'd visualized him over the phone as my size, with that brown hair cut
in a standard short cut. But the brunette do was cut short but longer
on top, not exactly a skater's cut but close. It was more modern, more
teenager, less little boy. I didn't like it. "I need a little privacy, Peter,
you understand that."

He smiled and shook his head. "I'm not fourteen now, Anita."

"What does that mean?"

"It means I'm sympathetic, but not stupid. Edward gave the orders,
and Claudia and Remus backed them up."

They were both young enough that I thought I might be able to embarrass them into letting me talk to Richard alone. "Fine, which of you wants to see me get all emotional with Richard?"

They exchanged looks.

"How emotional?" Cisco asked.

"I don't know, maybe I'll cry, maybe we'll have a fight. You never know with Richard and me."

Cisco spoke to Peter like I wasn't there. "They are pretty weird around each other."

"Weird how?" Peter asked.

"I am standing right here," I said.

Cisco looked at me with those big dark eyes. "You and Richard are like scary weird together as a couple; come on, it's true."

I had to smile. "Scary weird, huh?"

Cisco nodded.

I sighed. "Fine, I guess so, but I would like privacy, come on. He almost died, and so did I."

"I'm sorry, Anita," Cisco said. "I can't do it. One of us has to be in the room with you."

"Don't I have any seniority here?"

"Claudia and Remus both made it really clear that if I fuck up again, I'm gone, like fired gone. I'm not going to fuck up again."

"What'd you do?" Peter asked, then actually blushed. "Sorry, sorry, not my business. Later."

Cisco nodded. "Later."

Cisco sniffed the air and turned toward the far end of the hallway. Soledad came around the corner. She saw us, and her face looked suddenly stricken. She dropped to all fours and started to crawl toward us. Not in that almost sexual way the lycanthropes could, but broken, as if it hurt her to move.

"What's up?" I asked.

Her voice came, as broken as her movements. "I shot Richard. I'm sorry."

"You shot Richard," I said. I looked at Cisco.

He shrugged and gave me a look as if to say, *Yeah*. "I think if she hadn't shot him, he might have just torn Jean-Claude's heart out."

"I'm sorry," Soledad said. "I didn't know what else to do." She had stopped a few feet from us, her hand held out in the air, her head down. I'd seen a similar gesture among the lions. It was a way of asking to come closer when you were pretty sure the dominant in question didn't like you.

I'd been told that a guard shot Richard, and that it had saved Jean-Claude's life, but no one had told me who had done it. I stared at the woman holding out that hand, asking for forgiveness. She'd done her job, sort of. What would I have done in her place? Frozen. I wouldn't have been able to shoot Richard to save Jean-Claude. I'd have frozen and Jean-Claude would have died. Which would have probably killed both Richard and me. Shit.

"They took her weapons," Cisco said, "until they review it all."

"Like when a cop is involved in a shooting," I said.

"A lot of us are ex-police now," Cisco said, and he gave me a look, as if to say, *Well, what are you going to do?*

What was I going to do? I sighed, hung my head, and started forward. Why was it that in the middle of every crisis I always seemed to be babysitting someone's emotions? Usually someone who was dangerous, armed, or should have been some kind of tough guy, or girl. The monsters were a lot softer than they seemed.

I went to her and gave her my left hand. Most people did it like they were shaking hands, but I kept my gun hand free; just habit. Soledad made a sound like a sob as she gripped my hand. I had a moment to feel how terribly strong she was as she crawled close enough to put her face against my hand. She rubbed her cheeks against my hand and lower arm, and murmured, "Thank you, thank you, Anita. I'm so sorry, so sorry." Her tears were cool against my skin. Funny, tears were always colder than blood; shouldn't they both feel the same? Her power flared across my skin like a giant's breath, so hot, and so everywhere. Any strong emotion can undo a shapeshifter's control.

She drew a shuddering sob and threw herself around my waist, her long arms clutching me. She was practically wailing. "I didn't know what else to do with Richard. . . ."

"It's okay, Soledad, it's okay." I patted her hair and started to turn in her arms. I didn't know her well enough to be this up close and personal, and the emotional content was a little much for near strangers. Hell, I wouldn't have wanted this much emotional content from close friends. I had actually turned around, with her hands only lightly on me, when she moved. She grabbed me around the waist, lifted me in front of her face and chest, and I blocked the clawed hand that had gone for my throat with my arm. Claws dug into my side just below the ribs. The pain was sharp and immediate, and I suddenly had two goals. I strained to keep her hand from my throat and gripped her wrist at my waist to keep her from slicing open my belly.

Her voice growled from behind me, "I'm sorry you have to die, Anita."

31

CISCO AND PETER both had their guns out. I'd have loved to go for a gun or a knife, but wrestling the weretiger took both my hands. She wasn't trying that hard to close on my throat, and the hand at my belly was almost immobile except for the fact that the hooked claws she'd conjured from her skin had pierced my side.

She called to the boys, "Don't yell for help or she's dead. I don't want her dead. Just let me leave with her and I won't hurt her."

"You've already hurt her, I can smell the blood," Cisco said. His gun was very steady on us, but she'd taken all his kill shots. If they only wounded her, she would have time to kill me before they could kill her.

"A little prick, that's all. She likes pricks, don't you, Anita?"

My voice was a little strained from keeping her hand from my throat. The claws weren't as big as they seemed, they only looked huge because the human flesh didn't cover the bone of the tiger claw. But they were plenty big enough to tear out my throat. I might survive the gut wound, but the throat would be fatal. I managed to say through gritted teeth, "If you're going to kill me, do it, but don't make fun of me, too."

She laughed, a throaty sound. Her power flared, hot, so hot, almost burning. Hot liquid burst over my back and hair. My first thought was blood, but I knew better. It was that clear liquid that shifters lost when they changed. When the change was smooth it was like heated water; when it wasn't smooth it was gelatinous and chunky. This flowed like water. She never hesitated, or stumbled, as her body re-formed around me. Fur and muscle flowed under my hands. Her power ran over my body like biting insects, so much power, it hurt. Had she thought I'd panic and let go? She had the wrong girl for panic. I kept my grip on her as fur replaced bare skin. I didn't let go even as my skin danced and jerked as if she'd laid a live wire against me. Jesus, the control she had, to be able to shift this smoothly. She was better than Micah, and that was saying something. It would have been impressive if I hadn't been wondering how close her new fangs were to my spine. Part of me noticed that her fur was the wrong color. She was striped pale lemon gold and white. Weren't tigers orange and black? If I lived, I'd ask someone.

"You're one of the Harlequin's animals to call," Cisco said.

She growled, "Yes."

"You'll never make it out of here if you hurt Anita," Cisco said.

"She knows where my mistress rests in the day; I can't let her share that knowledge, can I, Cisco?"

He flinched at her using his name. Always harder to kill someone you know.

"Because if your master dies, you die." Peter said it. He was pointing his gun at the floor, as if he knew he didn't have a shot he could take. Remus had told me that Cisco had some of the highest scores on the gun range of any guard. I was about to bet my life on his skill.

Her hand strained toward my neck again, and I put a lot of effort into holding it off. Her arm was a steady push; mine was shaking. "You belong to Mercia," I said.

"No," she growled, and eased a few sliding steps backward. Cisco and Peter moved the same space forward. It was like an awkward dance.

"Nivia," I said.

"How do you know the names?"

"Does it matter?" I asked.

"Yes," she whispered. "Tell me who's talked to you."

"Jesus, Soledad, don't make me do this," Cisco said.

Soledad stopped whispering to me and called to Cisco, "You're a good shot, Cisco, but are you that good? Are you sure you're that good?"

It was plain on his face that in that moment he wasn't sure. I guess I wouldn't have been either. I'd have given a great deal for Edward in that moment. Or Remus, or Claudia.

Peter said, "What's the rule?"

Cisco almost glanced at him, but remembered and kept his eyes on us, his gun steady, but he didn't have a killing shot and he knew it. Soledad began to back down the hallway with me in her arms. Just a few steps, but slow and steady.

Cisco and Peter moved with us. Cisco had his gun pointed, but frankly he was as likely to hit me as the weretiger. No, more likely. Peter's gun was still pointed at the floor. He didn't seem to know what to do.

Peter said, "The rule is that if they have a weapon and want to take you someplace else, it's so they can kill you slower." His voice was almost a monotone, as if he were reciting.

I thought I understood what he meant. I hoped I did, because I was about to encourage him. "You're right, Peter," I said.

He looked up. His eyes met mine. Cisco said, "God." I threw my head back, used all that long hair to cover her eyes for a second. Peter dropped to one knee and shot at her legs. The shots reverberated in the hallway. Soledad dropped abruptly to her knees, but claws curled deeper inside me, her other hand trying for my throat for real this time. I made a choice. I let go of the wrist at my stomach and used both hands to keep her from tearing out my throat. Two-handed to her one and I was losing. She clawed at my side and stomach. It felt like she'd hit me with a baseball bat, so much damage, like a blow. It stole my breath, or I'd have screamed.

Cisco and Peter were there, standing over us. There still wasn't a clear shot. She tried to crawl backward on her wounded legs, while I held on to her hand, and held it a fraction away from my throat. Cisco was still trying to find a shot. Peter threw himself onto us, he just jumped us, and we were all on the ground with her underneath us. She stopped trying for my throat and reached for Peter. I was suddenly trying to wrestle her hand away from him instead of me. Her hand wasn't on my stomach anymore. Peter's body reacted as if something hurt. But I kept her off his throat. It was all I could do. I had a moment of being pressed between them, and then the gunshots exploded just behind my head. It was insanely loud that close to me. I kept my grip on her as the inside of my head rocked with the sound of gunfire beside it. Her body jerked, and still she tried for my throat again. The change of angle startled me, and she might have nicked me, but I didn't feel it.

Peter kept firing; his gun must have been pressed into her head. We ended up on the ground in a breathless, deaf heap. He was up on one arm, his gun still shoved into her face. Peter's T-shirt was in rags over his stomach. Cisco was above us; his lips were moving, but I couldn't hear him. I rolled free of the pile. I had my gun out and pointed before my back hit the wall, before I could truly see what was happening.

Soledad's head was a red mass. There was no face left. Brains were leaking all over the floor, her brains. Even for a weretiger, this was dead. Peter was still over the body, his gun pumping into that mass of tissue. I think he was dry-firing by now, but I couldn't hear well enough to say. Cisco knelt beside him, his lips moving, but I couldn't make out the words. He got Peter to stop firing into the body, then tried to ease Peter off her. Peter let him ease him back onto his knees, then Peter popped his empty magazine out, put it in his left jacket pocket, got a spare clip out of his right-hand pocket, and reloaded. His stock was pretty high with me right then; the reload made it go higher. Maybe we wouldn't get him killed.

Cisco tried to get him to stand up and move away from the body. I think Cisco was worried about how Peter would react when the shock wore off. It made me think better of Cisco. Then a lot of things happened at once. I couldn't hear it, but I must have seen movement out of the corner of my eye, because I turned to see Edward and company come barreling down the hallway, guns drawn. The door to Richard's room was open, and he was leaning in it. His beautiful chest was a mass of scars on one side. He was pale as death, and looked as if the only thing keeping him upright was the doorway. The scars showed where the bullets had taken a chunk out of all that nice muscled flesh. Sometimes silver scars. He mouthed something, but I still couldn't hear anything but the ringing silence in my own head. Gunshot too close to the ear. I'd be lucky if my hearing wasn't permanently damaged.

I felt movement nearer to me, and turned, but I was slow. I think Peter wasn't the only one in shock. Cisco was pulling Peter to his feet by the collar of his jacket. Cisco was shouting something. I couldn't see what the problem was—there was nothing but Soledad's body. Then I looked at the body and realized that she was still in tiger form. Her body hadn't reverted to human form. Dead shapeshifters always revert to human form. I raised my gun and had it aimed, when the "body" sprang up and threw itself at Peter and Cisco.

32

CISCO FOULED PETER'S shot by throwing his body in the way of the claws. I got off two shots before the faceless body brought them to the floor. And I was suddenly having the same problem they'd just had, trying to find a place to fire into that fur that wouldn't hit the two boys underneath it. They had saved my life and I still thought, *Boys.*

Claudia and Remus got there first, because you just can't outrun a shapeshifter. Edward and Olaf were close behind, but they didn't get there first. It was Claudia and Remus who joined me around the struggling pile. A gun fired up through the tiger's chest. Claudia actually pushed me out of the way hard enough that I fell against the wall. Too many guns in too small a space; friendly fire was as dangerous to us as Soledad.

Whoever was shooting was trying to make a hole through her chest. Her body jerked and jumped with the power of it. She staggered to her feet. I swear that I could see the hallway through the hole in her lower chest. But even as I watched, the muscle began to flow like water, healing. Shit. It was Peter who had shot a hole through her. Cisco was trying to breathe through a throat that wasn't there anymore.

Edward and Olaf were beside each other, firing into Soledad's body like they were on a shooting range. So cool, so professional, so accurate. It was a little hard to miss her at this range.

Some of the guards had gone to their knees around Edward, Olaf, Remus, and Claudia, some standing, some kneeling so they wouldn't get in each other's way, a very organized slaughter. The tiger's body jumped and danced with the bullets like some sort of spasming puppet. But she didn't go down. I fired from the wall where Claudia had thrown me. I emptied my clip into Soledad and watched her body and fur flow over the wounds. It was fucking silver and she was treating it like it was ordinary bullets. I'd never seen a shapeshifter able to do that. Even fairies, once you opened a hole in them that big, didn't heal like this. I emptied my clip and did almost exactly what Peter had done earlier, except that my extra clip was attached to my belt. She wasn't acting like a wereanything. She was acting like a rotting vampire, that special kind of undead that were rare in the United States. Of course, her master wasn't from around here.

My hearing was coming back in my left ear, because I could hear screaming, distantly, as if they weren't all standing right next to me. My right ear was still a buzzing silence. I yelled, "Fire, we need to set her on fire!" I must have yelled it too loud because they all looked at me. I yelled, "Burn her!"

Olaf took off running back down the corridor. Seeing him run away actually distracted me enough that I jumped when the guns started firing again. I turned back to the action, and found the body up and moving again. The face had grown back, but the chest was a gaping wound. Her lungs had to be gone, but she moved; she jumped at me in one of those long arcs that made her body a golden smear of light. I fired at that blur until my gun clicked empty. I dropped the empty gun and went for a blade, and knew I'd never make it.

A second blur was in front of me, and we were crashing back into the wall, hard enough that I saw stars before I realized that the second blur was Claudia. She'd thrown her body in the way, and was slugging it out hand to claw. She must have been out of ammo, too. Those claws sliced up her chest, and she went into a defensive crouch, protecting herself as well as she could. The tiger screamed, or roared at us, and then turned and ran the other way. It was almost funny, because for a breath we all just stood there. Then almost as a mass we ran after her. My stomach didn't so much hurt as twinge, as if the muscles weren't working quite right. It made me stumble, then I found my feet, and I ran. If I could run, I couldn't be that hurt, right? I could feel blood flowing down the front of me, soaking into my jeans. If Soledad got out, she might move the vamps, or warn someone, or set up an ambush. We had to stop her, had to. But we couldn't run like the shapeshifters ran. Remus and the others passed Edward and me as if we were standing still.

They bayed her at the double glass doors. They bayed her within sight of the parking lot, in sight of freedom. Remus was cut up now, too. They formed a circle around her, double thick in front of the doors. She crouched in the center of that circle, snarling at them. She was all gold and white, and even after everything I could still see that she was beautiful. Graceful in that way that the cat lycanthropes seemed to be. Her tail twitched, tight and angry.

Edward popped a fresh magazine home. He pulled the slide back and put one in the chamber. The sound echoed around the circle. Not everyone had more clips; some, like me, were out, but enough of them did that it was eerie and businesslike.

Soledad snarled with her tiger fangs. "My death will not stop the Harlequin from killing you. My mistress's death will not protect you from the wild hunt that is coming."

"You didn't give us a black mask," I said.

Her orange-yellow eyes turned to me. She made a noise that was between a growl and a purr. The sound of it raised the hairs on the back of my neck. "You will die."

"The vampire council is all about rules, Soledad. It's against your own laws to kill us when you've only given us white masks, something about fair play and all that."

I wasn't great at reading even people I knew in animal form, but I thought she looked afraid. "If you kill us, the rest of them will hunt you down, Anita. It is against vampire law to slay the Harlequin."

"I'm not killing you as Jean-Claude's vampire servant. I'm killing you and your mistress as a federal marshal and a legal vampire executioner."

"I know your laws, Anita. You have no warrant for us."

"I have two warrants for two vampires that look a damned sight like your Mercia and your mistress."

Again there was that flinching through her alien eyes. I was just getting better at reading furry faces. Bully for me.

"The warrants list names of church members," Soledad purred.

"But the warrant is worded sort of vaguely. It states that I can kill the vampire responsible for the death of the victim, and that I can, at my discretion, kill anyone who assisted in that death. It also allows me to kill anyone who tries to impede me in carrying out my court-appointed duty." I looked into that strangely beautiful face. "Which means you."

Olaf was beside Edward. He had a can of WD-40 in his hand and a torch made of rags bound to what looked like the end of a metal mop handle. There was a sharp oily smell from it all. He said in that deep voice, "I was going to go for the ordnance in the car, but the janitor's closet was closer."

I almost asked what he meant by *ordnance*, but was probably glad I didn't know. Though maybe what they had in their car would have been quicker than what we were about to do to her. Olaf had Edward light the torch. Apparently he'd soaked it in something, because it burned clear and bright.

Claudia told the people on the far side of the room to clear a space. They parted like a curtain and left Soledad in a clear kill space. The guards formed two lines, one kneeling and one standing. They took their stances, and Edward joined them.

Claudia yelled, "Head or heart!"

Soledad leapt, not toward the double line of doors and freedom, or the firing squad, but the thinner line that led back down the hall. The guns all seemed to sound at once. That liquid leap of gold and silver crumbled to the floor. She could heal, but the initial injury was real. They fired into her until she twitched, but didn't try to rise again.

Olaf turned so I could see the gun tucked in the back of his belt. "Cover me."

I kept expecting my wound to catch up with me, but the adrenaline was carrying me. I'd pay for it later, but right now I felt fine. I wrapped my hand around the gun and pulled it free of the inner pants holster. I'd expected Olaf to go for something big, but it wasn't. It was an H & K USP Compact. I'd looked at one before I settled on the Kahr. I clasped it in a two-handed grip and aimed it at the fallen weretiger. "Ready when you are," I said.

Olaf glided into the circle with his torch and his squeezy can of accelerant. I didn't glide, I just walked, but I was at his side when he got to her. I was at his side when he sprayed accelerant over her ruined face and chest. The world suddenly smelled thick and oily. She reacted to the liquid or the smell, reaching out at us. I shot her in the face. The gun jumped in my hands, so it was pointed at the ceiling before it came back down to point at her.

"What the fuck is in this?" I asked.

He shoved the torch into the wound I'd made, and she started to scream. The smell of burning hair was strong and bitter. It began to overwhelm the scent of the accelerant. He set her afire. He covered her in the thick oily liquid and burned her. She was too hurt to do much, but she could scream, and writhe. It looked like it hurt. It smelled like burning hair, and finally, when she stopped moving, it smelled like burning meat, and oil. She made a high-pitched keening noise for a very, very long time.

Edward had moved up beside me to aim his gun with the one Olaf had loaned me. The three of us stood there while Soledad died by pieces. When she stopped moving, stopped making noise, I said, "Get an axe." I think I actually said it in a normal voice. I could hear out of one ear at least. The one that Peter had shot beside was still out for the count. It made sound echo oddly in my head.

"What?" Edward asked.

"She heals like one of the vampires that descends from the Lover of Death."

"I do not know this name," Olaf said.

"Rotting vampires, she heals like one of the rotting vamps. Even sunlight isn't a sure thing. I need an axe, and a knife, a big, sharp one."

"You will take her head," Olaf asked.

"Yeah, you can do the heart, if you want."

He looked down at the body. She was human now, lying on her back, legs spread. Most of her face was gone, and her lower chest; one breast was burned and blasted away, but the other one was still pale and perky. One side of her hair, the yellow of her tiger fur, was still there. There was no face, no eyes to stare up at us. I might have been grateful for that except that staring into the blackened, peeling ruin of her face wasn't really an improvement.

I swallowed hard enough that it hurt. My throat burned as if breakfast might be trying to come back up. I tried a deep breath, but the smell of burnt flesh also wasn't an improvement. I ended up breathing shallow and trying not to think too hard.

"I will find her heart for you," Olaf said, and I was glad my hearing wasn't quite working right. It made his voice sound flat and lose a lot of the inflection. If I'd heard all the longing in his voice that I saw on his face I might have shot him. I was betting his special ammo would have made a really big hole in a human body. I thought about it, I really did, but in the end I gave him back his gun. He extinguished his torch. Someone brought us an axe and a freshly sharpened knife. I was really missing my vampire kit, but it was at home, no, at the Circus.

Her spine was brittle from the fire, easiest decapitation I'd ever done. Olaf was having to dig in her chest to find the pieces of burnt and bloody heart. We'd made a mess of her. I kicked the head a little ways from the body. Yeah, I wanted to burn the head and heart and scatter the ashes over moving water, but she was dead. I kicked the head again, so that it skittered across the floor, too burned to bleed.

My knees wouldn't hold me anymore. I collapsed where I was standing with the axe still in my hands.

Edward knelt beside me. He touched the front of my shirt. His hand came away crimson like he'd dipped it in red paint. He ripped my shirt open to my chest. The claw marks looked like angry, jagged mouths. There was something pink and bloody and shiny bulging out of one of the mouths like a swollen tongue.

"Shit," I said.

"Does it hurt yet?" he asked.

"No," and my voice sounded amazingly calm. Shock was a wonderful thing.

"We need to get you to a doctor before that changes," he said, and his voice was calm, too. He wrapped his arms around me and stood, cradling me. He started back the way we'd come at a fast walk. "Does that hurt?" he asked.

"No," I said again, my voice distant and too calm. Even I knew I was too calm, but I felt sort of distant and unreal. Let's hear it for shock.

He started running down the hallway with me in his arms. "Does it hurt now?" he asked.

"No."

He ran faster.

33

EDWARD HIT THE door to the main trauma room with his shoulder. We were inside, but there was no one to pay attention to me. There was a white wall of doctors and nurses, and some of them in civilian clothes, but they were all around one gurney. Their voices held that frantic calm that you never want to hear when you're on your back looking up at doctors.

A spike of fear got through the shock—Peter. It had to be Peter. The adrenaline rush of it stabbed through my stomach like a fresh blow. Edward turned, and I could see more of the room. It wasn't Peter. He was lying on a different gurney, not that far away from the one that had everyone's interest. Who the fuck was it? We didn't have any more humans on our side.

The only person with Peter was Nathaniel. He was holding the boy's free hand. The other hand was hooked up to an IV. Nathaniel looked at me, and his face showed fear. Enough that Peter fought to turn and see what was coming through the door.

Nathaniel touched his chest, held him down. "It's Anita and your . . . Edward." I think he'd been about to say *your dad*.

I heard Peter's voice as we got closer. "Your face, what's wrong with them?"

Nathaniel said, "I didn't think there was anything wrong with my face." He tried to make a joke of it, but the noises from the other side of the room made humor sort of hard.

I couldn't see past all the white coats. "Who is it?" I asked.

Nathaniel answered, "It's Cisco."

Cisco. He wasn't hurt that badly. I'd seen shapeshifters heal throat wounds that bad. Were there more bad guys in here with us? "How did he get hurt?" I asked.

Peter actually tried to sit up, and Nathaniel kept him down with that hand on his chest, as if he'd been having to pin Peter to the gurney for a while. "Anita," Peter said.

Edward put me on the nearest empty gurney, and the movement didn't so much hurt as let me know that it was going to hurt. It was as if things shifted around that I shouldn't have been able to feel. I had a moment of nausea and knew that that was just me thinking too hard, or hoped it was. Edward moved me so Peter could see me without moving. It meant that I could see Peter. His jacket and shirt were gone, but bulky bandages were taped across his stomach; more of them were on his left shoulder and upper arm. His weapons and jacket and the remains of his bloody shirt were on the floor under his gurney. It'd be my turn next.

"What happened to Cisco?" I asked.

Peter said, "You're both hurt."

"I'm fine," Edward said, "it's not my blood."

Peter looked at me, his eyes too wide, face sickly pale. "He got his throat torn out."

"I remember, but he should be able to heal that," I said.

"Not all of us are that good at healing, Anita," Nathaniel said.

I looked at him now. The fact that I hadn't truly looked at him said clearly how much I was hurt. He was wearing one of his pairs of jogging shorts that left very little to the imagination. His hair was back in a tight braid. I met his eyes, and I still loved him, but for once my body didn't react to the sight of him.

Edward came to stand by Peter, and Nathaniel came to me, an exchange of emotional prisoners. Nathaniel took my hand and gave me as chaste a kiss as we'd ever exchanged. His lavender eyes held the worry that he'd been hiding from Peter, or trying to hide from him. He leaned over my body, and I heard him draw in a big breath of air. "Nothing's perforated," he whispered.

Until he said it, I hadn't thought about it. My intestines could have been perforated, or hell, my stomach. If I'd had to get clawed up, it wasn't a bad place for it. It wasn't a fatal hit, not right away, not if things weren't spilling out of me. They were bulging out, not spilling. There was a difference.

"Is Peter . . ."

"Not perforated either, you were both lucky."

I knew he was right, but . . . The voices had risen in pitch across the room. When the doctors start sounding that panicked, things are very bad. Cisco, shit.

It was Cherry who peeled away from the crowd around him and came to me. She had thrown a white coat over the usual black Goth outfit. Her heavy eyeliner had run down her face like black tears. She touched Peter's shoulder as she went past, and said, "Let the drugs work, Peter. You can't help him by fighting to stay awake."

"She was trying for me," he said. "She was reaching for me. He put himself in her way. He saved me."

She patted his shoulder and checked the IV almost automatically, but she also adjusted the little knobby thing on it. The liquid began to drip a little faster. She patted him again and came to the other side of the gurney so that she could look at Nathaniel across me, or maybe so she could keep an eye on what was happening to Cisco. There were so many people around him that it looked like they were getting in each other's way.

She said, "Nothing I can do over there." She said it almost to herself, as if she were trying to convince herself.

She put on a fresh pair of gloves before she looked at my stomach. There was blood on the sleeve of the white coat she was wearing. She seemed to see it at about the same time I did. She just stripped off the coat, tossed it in the little hamper they had for washables. Threw the clean gloves away, got another pair of clean gloves, and came back to me. Her eyes stared at the wound, not at me. Her face had gone to concentrating on her job. If she just concentrated on her job then she wouldn't fall apart. I knew the look, I had one like it.

I tried to do something else while she looked at the wounds. Somehow I didn't want to see my insides on the outside again. But it was like a train wreck; you couldn't quite look away. "What is that?" I asked.

"Intestine," she said, in a voice that held no emotion.

I heard someone shout, "Clear!"

The crowd around Cisco cleared, and I saw Lillian using the crash cart on his chest. She was about to try to jump-start his heart. Fuck.

Micah was in the crowd. He turned and looked at me, his mouth and chin covered in blood. As if Nathaniel read my mind, he said, "He was trying to call flesh and help Cisco heal the wound."

Micah could help a healing wound heal faster by licking it. He'd done it for me once. He wiped the blood off his face as he looked at me across the room. The look on his face was anguish. He'd tried.

Lillian hit Cisco's chest three times, four, but that high-pitched alarm sound just kept going. Flatline.

I didn't hear the door open, but Richard came through leaning so heavily on Jamil, one of his bodyguards, that he was being half-carried. Jamil put him by the gurney. Their bodies blocked me from seeing what was happening.

Cherry was swabbing my hand; she had a covered IV needle in her other hand. I looked away. Richard's power ran over my skin like heat. Nathaniel shivered where he held my hand. I glanced at him. His body was covered in goose bumps.

"You feel it?" I asked.

"We all do," Cherry said, and the needle bit home in my hand. I squeezed Nathaniel's hand hard and kept staring at Richard's broad back.

Micah came to stand at the head of my gurney. He'd wiped most of the blood off, but his eyes held defeat. If I'd had a spare hand I would have offered it. He laid his face against the top of my head. It was the best we could do.

Jamil stumbled away from Richard, leaving him to half-collapse across the gurney. Jamil's body exploded; one second he was tall, dark, handsome, the next he was the black-furred werewolf that had saved my life once. Lillian fell to the floor, her body writhing, twisting. She was suddenly gray-furred. She lay on the floor with her newly ratty face turned up to the gurney. The other doctors and nurses kept their distance. Richard was trying to bring Cisco's beast, trying to help him heal by forcing him to shift. But the alarm was still screaming, still letting us know that Cisco's heart wasn't beating.

Richard clutched at the gurney with one hand and Cisco with the other. His power spread through the room as if someone had forgotten to turn off some invisible hot bath, and it was filling up the room. Micah stood up, put his hand against my head. I felt his power spring to life, felt him throw it around the four of us like a shield, keeping Richard's power out. Most of the time Micah could protect the other wereleopards, but my ties to Richard were too strong. It worked today. Today, Micah held me in the calm of his power along with Nathaniel and Cherry.

Richard screamed, a long, loud, anguished sound. He collapsed to his knees, one hand still clinging to Cisco's arm. The arm flopped limp, dead. Richard's back rippled as if some giant hand were pushing out from the inside. He threw his head back and screamed again, but before the echo had died, the scream turned into a howl. Fur poured over Richard's body. It was as if his human body were ice, melting to reveal fur and muscle. His human form just melted into a wolf the size of a pony. I'd never seen him in full wolf form, only the half-and-half. The wolf threw its head back and howled, long and mournful. It turned a head as big as my entire chest to look at me. The eyes were all wolf, amber and alien, but the look in them was not a wolf's look. It held too much understanding of the loss that lay on the gurney.

One of the other white coats started turning off the machines. The scream of the alarm went silent. Except for the ringing in my one ear the room was deathly quiet. Then everyone began to move. The doctors and nurses started pulling things out of Cisco's body. He lay on his back, eyes closed. I remembered seeing spine in the throat wound; now the bone was covered. He'd been healing, but not fast enough.

Jamil climbed to his furry feet and put a half claw, half hand on the wolf's back. He said in a voice gone to growl, "I'll take us to feed."

One of the doctors helped Lillian to her feet. She seemed more shaken than Jamil was, but then I'm not sure she'd ever had someone rip her beast from her human form. Jamil had been on the wrong end of Richard's anger more than once. "Come with us, Lillian," he said, and the wolfish muzzle had trouble with the double *L* sound.

She nodded and took the hand he offered. The dark-haired man who had turned off the alarm said, "We'll take care of the other patients, Lillian."

Her own voice sounded high-pitched and nasal. "Thank you, Chris." The three of them walked out together, leaving the others to begin to clean up.

"Why did he die?" I asked.

"He bled out faster than his body could heal," Cherry said.

"I've seen you guys heal from worse," I said.

"You hang around with too many big dogs, Anita," Cherry said. "We don't all heal like Micah and Richard." She had the IV on its little metal hat rack. She reached up for the knob that would start the drip.

"Wait, will that put me out?" I asked.

"Yes," she said.

"Then I need to make some phone calls first."

"You're not hurting too much yet, then?" She made it half question, half statement.

"No, not yet. It aches, but it doesn't exactly hurt."

"It will," she said, "and when it does you'll want the painkillers."

I nodded, swallowed, nodded again. "I know, but we still have Soledad's masters out there. We need them dead."

"You aren't slaying any vamps today," she said.

"I know, but Ted Forrester still can."

Edward looked at me at the mention of his alter ego. His hand was on Peter's hair, as if he were a much younger boy and Edward had just come in to tuck him in for the night.

"I need you to take over my warrants," I said.

He nodded. His eyes weren't cold, they were rage-filled. I wasn't used to seeing this much heat from Edward; he was a cold creature, but what blazed in his eyes now was hot enough to burn a hole through me. "How is Peter?" he asked Cherry.

"Now that he's out, we'll sew him up. He should be fine."

Edward looked at me. "I'll kill the vampires for you."

"We will kill them for you." Olaf's voice from the door. He must have arrived in time to hear the last few comments. I hadn't heard him come in; not good. Not good that I hadn't heard Olaf, but not good that it could have been someone else, something else. I trusted Edward to see me safe, but I was usually more help to myself than this. Admittedly, I was having a bad day.

The dull ache in my stomach was beginning to have twinges of something sharp. It was like a promise of what the pain would be in a little while. I looked down my body; I couldn't help it. Cherry blocked my view with her arm, turned my face to her. "Don't look. You'll sleep.

The doctor will look at you. You'll wake up better." She smiled at me; it was a gentle smile, but it left her eyes haunted. When had Cherry gotten that look in her eyes?

Someone found a cell phone. I dialed Zerbrowski directly. The Regional Preternatural Investigation Team, RPIT, was who I should have called, and I should have probably started by talking to Lieutenant Rudolph Storr, but I just wasn't feeling well enough to argue with Dolph about who, and what, was or wasn't a monster. Zerbrowski answered with his usual, "Zerbrowski."

"It's Anita," I said.

"Blake, what's shaking?" There was a thread of laughter to his voice, the beginnings of his usual teasing. I didn't have time today.

"I'm about to get sewed back up."

"What happened?" The teasing note was gone.

I gave him the shortest version I could, and left out lots. But I gave him the important parts; two vamps, maybe with more servants, masquerading as two upstanding vampire citizens to get us to kill the two upstanding citizens. "They must have thought I was close, because they sent one of their animals to kill me."

"How hurt are you?"

"I'm not hunting any vampires today."

"What do you need from me?"

"I need you to get cops around the hotel. I need you to make sure these two don't get outside."

"Shouldn't they be dead to the world, no pun intended?"

"They should, but after what I saw in the servant, I wouldn't bet anyone's life on it. Call in Mobile Reserve; if it goes wrong you'll want the firepower."

Dr. Chris came to stand over me. He was a little under six feet but seemed taller because he was so thin, one of those men who just couldn't seem to put on muscle mass. I'd have called him willowy if he'd been a girl. He said, "Get off the phone, Anita. I need to look at your wounds."

"I'm almost done," I said.

"What?" Zerbrowski said.

"The doc's here. He's wanting me off the phone."

"Tell me who's going to be processing your warrants and do what the doctor says. You've got to be healed by the time we do the barbecue at my house. I finally got the wife talked into letting you bring both your live-in boyfriends. Don't make me waste all that persuasion."

I almost laughed but thought it might hurt, so I swallowed it. That sort of hurt, too. "I'll do my best."

"Off the phone, Anita," Dr. Chris said again.

"Ted Forrester will have the warrants," I said.

"We didn't know he was in town."

"Just got here."

"Funny how it all goes pear-shaped when he blows into town."

"I only call him in when it's already gone to hell, Zerbrowski; you're reversing cause and effect."

"Says you."

"He's a federal marshal, just like me."

A hand scooped the phone out of my hand. Dr. Chris was a lycanthrope, but still . . . I should have at least seen it coming. "This is Anita's doctor; she needs to go now. I'm going to put the other marshal on. You two play nice. I'm going to make Ms. Blake go night-night." He hesitated, then said, "She'll be fine. Yes, guaranteed. Now let me tend my patient." He handed the phone to Edward.

Edward put on his Ted Forrester good-ol'-boy voice. "Sergeant Zerbrowski, Ted Forrester here."

Dr. Chris shooed Edward farther away so I couldn't hear what he was saying. He turned the knob on the IV and said, "You're going to sleep now, Ms. Blake. Trust me, you'll enjoy the examination more that way."

"But . . ."

"Let it go, Ms. Blake. You're hurt. You have to let someone else hunt the vampires today."

I started to say something, probably to argue, but I never finished the thought. One minute I was staring up at Dr. Chris, the next— nothing. The world went *poof.*

34

I WOKE UP, which was nice. I was blinking up at a ceiling I'd seen before, but couldn't quite place. I was not in the room that I remembered last. This room was painted an off-white, and there were pipes in the ceiling. Pipes . . . that should have meant something, but I was still a little fuzzy around the edges.

"'She wakes; and I entreated her come forth, and bear this work of heaven with patience.'"

I knew who it was before he stepped beside the bed. "Requiem." I smiled up at him, and reached out to him with my right hand; the other one was full of needles. Reaching for him made my stomach ache a little, but not that bad. It made me wonder how long I'd been out, or what drugs were coming through the IV tube. Requiem took my hand in his and bent over it to lay a kiss on the back. I was happy to see him. Hell, I was happy to see anyone. "I don't know the quote," I said.

"The words of a worthless friar," he said.

"Sorry, still a little fuzzy," I said.

He held my hand underneath his cloak, against his chest. His blue, blue eyes glittered in the overhead fluorescents. "Perhaps this will help: 'A glooming peace this morning with it brings; The sun for sorrow will not show his head. Go hence, to have more talk of these sad things; Some shall be pardon'd, and some punished; For never was a story . . .' "

I finished with him. " ' . . . of more woe than this of Juliet and her Romeo.' "

He laughed then, and it transformed his face from a thing of cold beauty to something livable, lovable, more touchable. "You should laugh more often, it becomes you," I said.

The laughter leeched away, as if the two reddish tears that slid down the white perfection of his cheeks stole his joy away as they fell down his face. By the time the tears melted into the dark line of his beard, his face had its usual melancholy handsomeness.

I'd been happy to take his hand. Happy to touch someone I cared for, but there was something in the weight of that ocean-blue-and-green gaze that made me take my hand back. I had other lovers who would look at me that way, but the look in his eyes was one that Requiem had not earned, or that our relationship didn't deserve. He was Requiem, he wasn't a light comedic sort of person; no, he was definitely a lover of tragedies.

"Where's Jean-Claude?"

"Did you expect him to wait by your bedside?"

"Maybe."

"He and Asher are busy elsewhere, together. I was left to tend you while they had more important things to do."

I stared at him. Was it on purpose? Was he trying to make me doubt them? I'd nearly died, and was still hooked up to tubes; fuck it, I'd ask. "Are you implying that they're having sex together somewhere, and that that is more important to them than me?"

He looked down; I think he was trying to be coy. "They are off together, and they left me to tend you. I think the situation speaks for itself."

"You really shouldn't try to play coy, Requiem. You're not good at it."

He gave me the full weight of those blue, blue eyes, with that swimming shadow of green around the iris. Eyes you could sink into and swim away in, or be drowned in. I actually looked down, rather than meet his gaze. Normally he wasn't a problem, but I was hurt, weak, and I didn't like his mood.

"My evening star, you are thinking too hard. Let us rejoice that you live, that we all live."

That gave me other questions to ask; maybe since they weren't about Jean-Claude, he'd answer them. "Then Peter is all right?"

His face went blank, even that pressing need in his eyes fading away. "He is in a room nearby."

"Is he all right?"

"He will heal."

"I don't like how you're saying that, Requiem."

I heard the door open as a male voice said, "God, you are a gloomy bastard." Graham strode into the room.

I watched him for signs that the Harlequin were messing with his mind, signs of that panicked false addiction. He was his usual smiling self. Okay, his usual self when he wasn't feeling grumpy about me not fucking him.

"Are you wearing a cross?" I asked.

He drew a chain out of his shirt, and on the end of it was a tiny Buddha. I stared at it. "You're a Buddhist?"

"Yep."

"You do violence, you can't be a Buddhist," I said.

"So I'm a bad Buddhist, but it was still the way I was raised, and I do believe in the chubby little guy."

"Will it work if you're not following the tenets of the faith it represents?" I asked.

"I could ask you the same question, Anita."

Did he have a point, or not? "Fine, I just wouldn't have pegged you for a Buddhist."

"Neither would my parents, but when Claudia told us to get a holy item, I realized I didn't believe in the Jewish carpenter, never raised in that faith." He shook the little Buddha at me. "This I believe in."

I gave a small nod. "Okay, whatever works."

He grinned at me. "First, Peter will be fine, but he heals human-slow."

"How hurt is he?"

"About as hurt as you were, but not healing as fast."

Graham came to stand beside Requiem. He was still in the red shirt and dark pants, but somehow it didn't bug me now. Graham would answer questions better than Requiem. He also seemed to be himself, while the vampire was being weird even for him.

I started to ask how fast I was healing, but I wanted to know about

Peter before I asked questions about me. I felt amazingly well. "I'm going to ask this again, and I want a straight answer. How hurt is Peter?"

Graham sighed. "He got a lot of stitches—like the-doctor-lost-count stitches. He's going to be fine, honest, but he's going to have some manly scars."

"Shit," I said.

"Tell her the rest," Requiem said.

I glared at Graham. "Yeah, tell me the rest."

"I was getting to it." He flashed an unfriendly look at the vampire. Requiem gave a small nod, almost a bow, and moved back from the bed.

"Then get to it, Graham," I said.

"The doctors are offering him the chance for the new antilycanthropy therapy."

"You mean the inoculation they offer?"

"No, something brand new." He said "brand new" as if he had a bad taste in his mouth.

"How new?"

"St. Louis is one of only a handful of cities that are experimenting with it."

"They can't experiment on an underage kid."

"Underage?" He made it a question. "I thought Peter was eighteen."

Shit, I thought. Apparently Peter Black was holding up as a secret identity. "Yeah, I mean, shit, fine."

"If he's eighteen, then he can give permission for it." Graham gave me a funny look as he said it, as if he wanted to ask why I didn't believe Peter was eighteen, or maybe he didn't either.

"Give permission for what exactly?" I asked.

"They're offering him a vaccine."

"Like I said, Graham, they've been offering a vaccine against lycanthropy for years.

"Not the one that they used to offer in college. Not since that bad batch turned a lot of nice upper-class college students into monsters about ten years back." He said it without referencing Richard—who had been one of those college students. I wondered if Graham didn't know. Not my place to share, so I let it go.

"The vaccine's a dead organism now, not live and kicking," I said.

"Did you get it?" he asked.

I had to smile. "No."

"Most people won't volunteer for it," he said.

"Yeah, there's a bill wandering around Washington, D.C., right now to force inoculation against lycanthropy on teenagers. They claim it's safe now."

"Yeah, they claim." Graham's face said how much he believed in the "claim."

I shook my head, moved a little too much in the bed, and found that my stomach gave a twinge. However healed I was, it wasn't perfect yet. I took in a deep breath, let it out, and forced myself not to move around so much. There, that was better. "But Peter has already been attacked. The inoculation is only effective before an attack."

"They want to give him a live shot."

"What?" I said, and it was almost a yell.

"Yeah," Graham said.

"But that will give him whatever lycanthropy is in the shot."

"Not if he's already got tiger lycanthropy," Graham said.

"What?"

"Apparently, they had some people who were attacked by more than one beast in a single night. The two different strains canceled each other out. They came up clean and completely human."

"But it's not dead certain that he'll get tiger lycanthropy," I said.

"No, most of the feline strains are harder to catch than canine."

"You can't even reliably test for cat-based lycanthropy for at least seventy-two hours. If they give him this shot and he's not going to be a tiger, then he will be whatever the shot is," I said.

"And therein lies the problem," Graham said.

"Therein," Requiem said, his voice softly mocking.

Graham flashed him another unfriendly look. "I try to improve my vocabulary and you make fun of me; what kind of encouragement is that?"

Requiem gave a full bow, graceful, with one hand sweeping outward. That hand always seemed to cry out for a hat with a plume, as if the gesture was only half finished without the right clothing. He stood. "I beg pardon, Graham, for you are quite right. I do wish to encourage you in your improvements. It was churlish of me, and I apologize."

"Why is it that when you apologize, you never seem to mean it?" Graham asked.

"Back to the main problem, boys," I said. "What's happening with Peter?"

"Ted Forrester, federal marshal"—he said it the way you'd say "Superman, Man of Steel"—"is with him. He seems to be helping him choose."

"But he may be fine, and the shot will guarantee the very thing they don't want to happen."

Graham shrugged. "Like I said, it's a new thing."

"It's an experimental thing," I said.

He nodded. "That, too."

"What kind of lycanthropy is in the shot?" I asked.

"They don't want to say, but it's probably one of the cat-based lycanthropies, and it won't be tiger."

"Let's hope not," I said. "They make vaccines in big batches. Are they positive what kind of kitty they've got in the shot?"

Graham looked at me as if that hadn't occurred to him. "You aren't saying that they'd give him tiger twice? I mean, that wouldn't work at all. That would guarantee that he'd be tiger."

"Yeah. Has anyone asked them what flavor of kitty it is?" The look on Graham's face said no one had asked in his hearing. I looked at Requiem.

"I have been in attendance upon your bedside. I have not seen the boy."

"Graham, go ask, and make sure Ted knows I wanted to know."

Graham actually didn't argue. He just nodded and went for the door. Good. Because I knew where I was now. I was in the basement of what used to be a hospital, but the lower levels had been turned into a place where you kept suspected vampire corpses if you didn't think you'd get to them before nightfall, and where you held lycanthrope victims, or injured shapeshifters themselves until they were well enough to leave. Or you could force them into one of the government prisons—oh, "safe houses." The ACLU was about to be heard by the Supreme Court on just how many constitutional rights the "safe houses" violated. Being admitted was voluntary—if you were eighteen or over, anyway. They told shapeshifters that they'd let them out once they learned to control their beast, but somehow people went in and never came out. Most hospitals had an isolation ward for shapeshifters and vampires who got injured, but this was the place they sent you if they were truly worried. How the hell did we end up here?

"Requiem," I said.

He came to the side of the bed, his hooded cloak back to being tight around him. Only a pale glimpse of face was visible. "Yes, my evening star?"

"Why does that sound more and more sarcastic when you say it?"

He blinked so that those vivid blue eyes were shielded for a moment. "I will endeavor to say it as I mean it, my evening star." This time it was soft, and romantic. I didn't like that either. But I didn't say so out loud. I'd complain later when I figured out how to get any use out of it.

"I asked you once where Jean-Claude is; now I'll ask again. Where is he and what's he doing?"

"Can you not sense him?"

I thought about it and shook my head. "No, I can't." A spurt of fear ran through me like fine champagne. It must have shown on my face because Requiem touched my arm. "He is well, but he is shielding mightily to keep the Harlequin from reading him, or you, or the wolf king."

"So there were more than just the two of them in town," I said.

"Why would you assume only two?"

"It's all I saw," I said.

"Saw how?"

Again, I didn't like the question and how he asked it. "Does it matter?"

"Perhaps not, but yes, Jean-Claude has detected more than two in your fair city."

"I'm impressed that Jean-Claude can keep them out of us all," I said.

Requiem's hand tightened on my arm. "As are we all." He took his hand back, and it vanished under the black cloak again.

"Tell me what I've missed of the vampire end of things. Wait, how long have I been out?"

"It is only the night of the day you were injured. You have been out, as you put it, for only a few hours."

"A few hours, not days?" I asked.

"No."

I touched my stomach, and it didn't hurt the way it should have. I started to raise the hospital gown I was wearing. I hesitated, glancing at the man. He was my lover, but . . . there was always something about Requiem that made me less than perfectly comfortable around him. Micah, Nathaniel, Jean-Claude, Asher, even Jason, I would have simply looked at the wound. Richard, maybe I wouldn't have. But Requiem made me hesitate for different reasons.

"Look at your wound, Anita. I will not ravish you from the sight of your nakedness." He sounded like I'd insulted him. Since he was an old vampire, that I could hear that much emotion in his voice meant one of two things: either he allowed me to hear the emotion, or he was so upset he couldn't control himself.

I compromised. I raised the gown and kept the sheet over my lower extremities.

"I am not an animal, Anita; I can bear your nakedness without being affected." The anger and disdain were so thick in his voice that I knew it was lack of control.

"I never doubt your control, Requiem, but there's no way to be nude in front of you and have it be casual. I need to just look at my body and see what's wrong and right with the wound. I don't want to make a big deal out of it, or a romantic deal out of it."

"Would it not be a big deal if Jean-Claude were here in my stead?"

"Jean-Claude would concentrate on business and worry about the romance later."

"Is he that cold?"

"He's that practical," I said. "I like that in a man."

"I know you do not like me, my evening star." Again the emotion was thick on the ground.

I did the only thing I could: I ignored him. Once I saw my stomach it wasn't that hard to ignore him. I had pinkish scars where she'd clawed me open. It was weeks' worth of healing. I ran my hands over the skin, and it felt smoother, almost as if the shininess of it could be a texture. "How many hours?" I asked.

"It is now nine o'clock in the evening."

"Ten hours." I said it soft, like I didn't believe it.

"About that, yes."

"All this healing in ten hours?"

"It would seem so," he said. There was still a thread of anger to his voice, but it was less.

"How?"

"Should I quote to you, 'There are more things in Heaven and Earth, Horatio, than are dreamt of in your philosophy.' Or should I simply say I do not know?"

"The 'I don't know' would be fine, but at least I know you're quoting from Hamlet. Now tell me, what's been happening while I slept?"

He glided to the bedside, a slight smile curving his lips. "Your friends slew a member of the Harlequin while she slept. Though the tall one, Olaf, or Otto, complained that she was dead when they arrived. He wanted her to be squirming when they cut her up."

I shivered and put my gown back in place. I tried to ignore the whole creepy Olaf thing and concentrate on business. "There should have been two members dead."

"You admit it," he said. "You admit that you sent them to slay members of the Harlequin."

"Admit it, hell, yes."

"Jean-Claude is locked in arguments with the council, even now, on whether the Harlequin are within their rights to slay us all for what you have done."

"If they don't give a black mask first, but they kill, not in self-defense, then it's a death sentence for them."

"Who told you that?"

I debated on whether to admit it, but finally shrugged and said, "Belle Morte."

"When has our beautiful death spoken to you?"

"She came to me in a vision."

"When?"

"When the three of us were dying. She helped feed me enough energy to come back and keep us all alive."

"Why would she help Jean-Claude?"

If it had been Jean-Claude, I'd have told the truth, all of it, but it wasn't. Requiem was, well, being his usual weird self. I wasn't certain that Belle would want her reasoning blabbed around. "Why does Belle do anything?"

"You are lying. She told you her reason."

Great, he knew I was lying. "The shapeshifters say that I don't smell like I'm lying anymore; my respiration rate doesn't even change."

"I am not smelling or listening to your body, Anita. I simply feel the lie. Why do you not tell me the truth?"

"I'll tell Jean-Claude, and if he says it's okay to tell everyone, then I will."

"So you will keep secrets from me."

"You know, Requiem, we have a lot of bad shit happening, and you seem more interested in your own hurt feelings than in the life-and-death stuff."

He nodded. "I feel raw tonight, undone. I have felt that way since earlier in Jean-Claude's office."

"We were being messed with then," I said.

"But there is no holy object that I can wear, my evening star, no refuge that I can take from what the Harlequin have done to me."

"Are they messing with you now?"

"No, but they showed me certain truths about myself, and I cannot seem to unknow what I have learned."

"You don't sound like yourself, Requiem."

"Do I not?" he said, and again there was too much emotion in his voice. I wanted Graham back here, or someone back here. Requiem thought they weren't messing with his head, but I was betting the Harlequin were playing Scrabble with his thoughts right now.

He undid his cloak and flung it backward onto the floor. I'd seen him do a similar gesture on stage at Guilty Pleasures near the end of his strip act. He was fully clothed in elegant gray dress slacks and a shirt that was a clear cornflower blue that turned his eyes as blue as blue could be. I'd looked into a lot of blue eyes, but none quite the color of his. It was a startling blue, a color that had made Belle Morte try to collect him and add him to her collection of blue-eyed lovers. He flung his long straight black hair behind his shoulders.

"I would not have left your side for any business, my star. If you would but love me as I love you, nothing would be more important to me than you."

I called, "Graham!" It wasn't a yell but it was close to one. Was I afraid? A little. Maybe I could use necromancy to knock the Harlequin out of Requiem, but last time I tried I nearly got myself killed. I'd like to heal from one attack before I got hurt again—selfish, but there you go.

The door opened, but it wasn't Graham. It wasn't even Edward. It was Dolph, Lieutenant Rudolph Storr, head of the Regional Preternatural Investigation Team, and paranoid hater of all things monster. Shit.

35

REQUIEM DIDN'T EVEN turn around. He just said, "Leave us." But he said it in that "voice," that power-ridden voice that some vamps have. That voice that was supposed to bespell and bemuse.

I saw the flare of Dolph's cross around his neck. It made a halo around Requiem's body. I could see Dolph over Requiem's head, because he had eight inches on the six-foot-tall vampire. I didn't like the look on Dolph's face.

"He's my friend, Dolph, but the bad guys have him bespelled." My voice held more fear now than it had when I'd called for Graham. The look on Dolph's face made me afraid.

"One vampire can't bespell another," Dolph said. I saw his arms move, and knew before he moved around the vampire's body that he'd drawn his gun. He moved so that if he had to shoot, he wouldn't risk me. His cross stayed at a steady white light, not too bright—after all, the vampire who was being bad wasn't actually in the room.

"These vampires can, I swear to you, Dolph. Requiem is being controlled by one of the bad guys."

"Is that what is happening to me?" Requiem asked, and he looked confused.

"He's a vampire, Anita; he *is* a bad guy."

"They're brainwashing you, Requiem," I said, and reached out to him.

"Don't touch him," Dolph said, his gun up and pointed.

Requiem's hand closed over mine; his skin was cool to the touch, as if he hadn't fed. But he had fed; I'd felt his power. "If you shoot him now, like this, it's murder, Dolph. He hasn't done anything wrong." I drew a breath of my own power, my necromancy, and tried to "look" at Requiem, gently. If I had a repeat of being thrown across the room by metaphysics, I was afraid Dolph would blame Requiem and shoot him.

"You're the one who taught me that if my cross glows, they're fucking with me."

"They are fucking with you, and with Requiem. They're messing with you both."

"I'm still wearing a cross, Anita; my mind is my own. You taught me that, too. Or did you forget everything about monster hunting when you started fucking them?"

I was too scared to be insulted. "Listen to yourself, Dolph, please. They are messing with your thoughts." I traced my power over Requiem, as delicate a brush of power as I'd ever attempted. I felt the power, and I knew the taste of it. It was Mercia. If we all survived, I'd ask Edward how he managed to miss her. But it was like chasing a ghost; her power withdrew before me. She just gave him up and left. Maybe she didn't want to risk another metaphysical knockout.

Requiem swayed, grabbing the rail, and my hand, to keep from falling.

"Get away from her, now," Dolph said.

"The bad vamp is gone, Dolph," I said.

Requiem said, "Give me but a moment and I will do as you ask, officer. I am unwell." He kept his face averted from the cross that was still glowing soft and steady. It wasn't glowing because of Requiem.

Edward came slowly through the door. Olaf loomed behind him. "Hey, Lieutenant, what's going on?"

"This vamp is trying to mind-fuck me." Dolph's voice was low and even, with a thread of anger to it like a fuse waiting to be lit. He was holding a two-handed shooting stance; the gun looked strangely small in his hands.

"Anita," Edward called.

"Requiem is fine now. The bad vamps were messing with him, but it's over."

"Lieutenant Storr, we don't have a warrant of execution on this vampire. Kill him now, and it's murder." Edward's voice was his good-ol'-boy best, apologetic, somehow implying by tone that he thought it was a shame, too, that they couldn't just kill all the vampires, but shucks, it just didn't work that way.

Edward and Olaf eased into the room. Edward hadn't gone for a weapon. There was already one too many guns in this room. I had an idea.

"Dolph, this vampire messed with me while I wore a cross. She makes your feelings stronger. You hate vampires, and she's feeding that feeling. Requiem is jealous of Jean-Claude, and she was feeding that."

"There's nothing wrong with me," Dolph said.

"You're about to shoot an unarmed civilian," Edward said, in his good-ol'-boy voice. "Is that a good thing, Lieutenant, or a bad thing?"

Dolph frowned, and the tip of the gun wavered. "He's not a civilian."

"Well, now," Edward said, "I agree with you, but legally he's a citizen with rights. You kill him, and you're up on charges. If you're going to go down for killing one of them, why not make it one that's actually breaking the law? Lose your badge saving some innocent human from a bloodsucker about to munch on 'em. That'd be satisfyin'." Edward's down-home accent was growing thicker as he talked. He was also easing deeper into the room. He waved Olaf to stay near the door, then crept closer to Dolph.

Dolph didn't seem to notice. He just stood there, frowning, as if he were listening to things I couldn't hear. His cross kept up a steady white light. He shook his head as if trying to chase off some buzzing thing. His gun pointed at the floor, and he looked up. The cross faded, but it had never had the light it should have for such an attack. It was almost as if whatever Mercia's powers were, they somehow didn't set off holy objects as much as they should have. Dolph looked first at Edward. "I'm okay now, Marshal Forrester."

Edward, with Ted's smiling face, said, "If you don't mind, Lieutenant, I'd feel better if you came out of the room."

Dolph nodded, then put the safety on his gun and handed it butt first to Edward. Edward let his face show surprise. I didn't try to hide the shock I felt. No cop gives up his gun voluntarily, least of all Dolph. Edward took the gun. "You still not feelin' okay, Lieutenant Storr?"

"I'm okay at the moment, but if this vampire can get past my cross once, it can do it again. I almost shot him." He jerked a thumb in Requiem's direction. "I want to talk to Marshal Blake alone."

Edward gave him all the doubt on his face, and said, "I'm not so sure that's a good idea, Lieutenant."

Dolph looked at me. "We need to talk."

"Not alone," Requiem said.

Dolph didn't even look at him, but kept those dark, angry eyes on me. "Anita."

"Dolph, this bad vamp wants me dead. Even unarmed you outmuscle me. I'd rather we had company for the talk."

He pointed a finger at Requiem. "Not him."

"Fine, but someone."

He looked at Edward. "You seem to feel like I do about them."

"They're not my favorite thing," Edward said, and the good ol' boy was starting to fray around the edges.

"Fine, you stay." He looked at Olaf and the people in the hallway beyond. "Just the marshals."

Edward said something low to Olaf, who nodded. He started to close the door.

Dolph said, "No, the vampire leaves, too."

"His name's Requiem," I said.

Requiem squeezed my hand and gave me one of his rare smiles. "I take no offense, my evening star; he hates what I am, many people do." He raised my hand and gave it a kiss, then picked up his cloak from the floor and moved toward the door.

He stopped closer to the door and Edward, away from Dolph, but turned to the big man. "'Darkling I listen; and, for many a time I have been half in love with easeful Death, Call'd him soft names in many a mused rhyme.'"

"Are you threatening me?" Dolph asked, in a voice gone cold.

"Not you," I said. "I don't think he was threatening you."

"Then what did he mean by that?"

"He's quoting Keats. 'Ode to a Nightingale,' I think," I said.

Requiem looked back at me and nodded, making it almost a bow. He kept looking at me, and there was too much intensity in that gaze. I met it, but it took effort.

"I don't care what he's quoting, Anita. I want to know what he meant by it."

"What it means," I said, meeting Requiem's blue, blue gaze, "at a guess, is that he's half-wishing you'd pulled the trigger."

Requiem bowed then, a full-out sweeping movement, using his cloak as part of the theatre of it. It was a lovely, graceful show of body, hair, and all of him. But it made my throat tight, and my stomach jump. My stomach didn't like that, and I winced.

Requiem put his cloak on, drawing the hood around his face. He gave me the full force of that handsome face, those eyes, and said, "'I saw pale kings and princes too, Pale warriors, death-pale were they all; They cried, "La Belle Dame sans Merci Hath thee in thrall!"'"

Dolph looked at me then, then back at the vampire. Requiem glided out the door all black cloak and melancholy. Dolph looked back at me. "I don't think he likes you very much."

"I don't think that's the problem," I said.

"He wants to pick out curtains," Edward said from where he was slouched beside the door. He only slouched when he was pretending to be Ted Forrester.

"Something like that," I said.

"You fucking him?" Dolph asked.

I gave him the look the question deserved. "That is none of your damn business."

"That's a yes," he said, and his face was taking on that look, that disapproving look.

I glared at him, though frankly it's hard to glare in a hospital bed hooked up to tubes. It always makes you feel so vulnerable. Hard to be tough when you're feeling weak. "I said what I meant, Dolph."

"You only get defensive when the answer's yes," he said. The disapproving look was sliding into his angry look.

"My answer's always defensive when someone asks me if I'm fucking someone. Try asking if I'm dating him, or hell, even if he's my lover. Try being polite about it. It's still none of your business, but I might, *might*, answer the question if you weren't ugly about it."

He took in a lot of air, which with his chest was a whole lot, and let it out very slowly. Olaf was taller, but Dolph was bigger, beefier, built like an old-style wrestler before they all went to heavy bodybuilding. He actually closed his eyes and took another breath. He let that out and nodded. "You're right. You are right."

"Glad to hear it," I said.

"Are you dating him?"

"I'm seeing him, yes."

"What do you do on dates with a vampire?" It seemed to be a real question, or maybe he was just trying to make up for being pissy.

"Pretty much what you do on a date with any guy, except the hickeys are really spectacular."

It took him a second, and then he stared at me. He tried to frown, then laughed and shook his head. "I hate that you date the monsters. I hate that you are fucking them. I think it compromises you, Anita. I think it makes you have to choose where your loyalties lie, and I don't think us mere humans always win the coin toss."

I nodded and found that it didn't hurt my stomach to do it. Had I healed more in the little bit we'd been talking? "I'm sorry that's how you feel."

"You aren't going to deny it?"

"I'm not going to react all angry and defensive. You're being reasonable about your feelings, so I'll be reasonable back. I don't shortchange the humans, Dolph. I do a lot to make sure that the citizens of our fair city stay upright and mobile, the living and the dead, the furry and the not-so-furry."

"I hear you're still dating that junior high teacher, Richard Zeeman."

"Yeah." I said it carefully, trying not to act tense about it. To my knowledge the police didn't know Richard was a werewolf. Was his secret identity about to be revealed? I rubbed my hand over my stomach to give my eyes somewhere else to look and hoped that any tension in my body would be attributed to the wounds. Hoped.

"I asked you once if you were dating any humans, and you said no."

I fought not to look too relaxed, or too tense. This was Richard's world I was playing with. "You probably asked during one of our many breakups. We're pretty on and off."

"Why?"

"Why all the questions about my love life? We have a dangerous vampire out there to catch."

"To kill," he said.

I nodded. "To kill, so why all the questions about who I'm dating?"

"Why don't you want to answer questions about Mr. Zeeman?"

We were on dangerous ground. Dolph hated the monsters, all monsters. His son was engaged to a vampire, and she was trying to talk the son into joining her as undead. It had made Dolph's attitude toward the preternatural citizens go from cynical and dark to downright dangerous. Did he know about Richard, or suspect?

"Truthfully, Richard was who I thought I'd spend my life with, and the fact that we seem to be headed for the big breakup still hurts, okay?"

He gave me cop eyes, as if he were tasting the truth and weighing the lie. "What changed?"

I thought about how to answer that. The first time we'd broken up had been after I saw Richard eat someone. It had been a bad guy, but still, a girl's got to have standards. Or that's what I thought at the time. If I had it to do over again, would I have made a different choice? Maybe.

Dolph was beside the bed now. "Anita, what changed?"

"Me," I said softly, "I changed. We broke up, and I started dating Jean-Claude. I went back and forth between them for a while, and finally Richard just couldn't take me not deciding. So he decided for us, for me. If I couldn't choose, he'd take away one of my choices."

"He didn't want to share you."

"No."

"But he's dating you again, now."

"Some." I so did not like where this conversation was going.

Edward must not have liked it either, because he interrupted. "Not that this isn't fascinating, Lieutenant, but we still have a very powerful vamp out there. She's killed, or helped kill, at least two women that we know of: one Bev Leveto, and Margaret Ross." I think he used their names to make them more real to Dolph. Names have a way of doing that. "Shouldn't we be concentrating on catching the bad vampire, instead of quizzing the marshal here about her dates?" He said it all with a smile and a face full of down-home charm. I would never be the actor that Edward was, but damn there were moments when I wished I could be.

"How did you manage not to catch both of the vampires in the hotel room?" I asked. Maybe if we concentrated on crime-stopping, Dolph would let the other topic go.

Edward did his "aw, shucks" look, like he was embarrassed. The reaction wasn't his, but maybe the emotion was; it was incredibly rare for Edward to miss a target. He came to stand by the head of the bed.

One, so I could see him around Dolph's broad build, but two, I think, so Dolph wouldn't be able to scrutinize my reactions so damn closely.

"When we got to the hotel room there was only one vampire in the room. She was dead when we got there, but we took her head and heart, just like we're supposed to. I know that dead doesn't always mean dead for these guys."

"That must have been Nivia."

"How did you know her name?" Dolph asked.

I opened my mouth, closed it, and said, "An informant."

"Who, Anita?" he said.

I shook my head. "Don't ask, and I won't have to lie to you."

"You have someone who knows more about these murderers, and you won't bring them in so we can all question them. You, and just you, get to do the interrogation."

"It wasn't like that."

"You're good at your job, Anita, but you're not a better cop than I am, or Zerbrowski is."

"I never said I was."

"But you exclude us. You keep secrets from us."

"Yeah, just like you keep them from me. I know you don't call me in all the time anymore. You don't trust me."

"Do you trust me?" he asked.

"I trust you, Dolph, but I don't trust the hate in you."

"I don't hate you, Anita."

"No, but you hate some of the people I love, and that makes it hard, Dolph."

"I've never hurt any of your boyfriends."

"No, but you hate them, hate them for just being what they are, who they are. You're like an old-time racist, Dolph; your hate blinds you."

He looked down, took another deep breath. "I've been to the company shrink. I'm trying to come to an understanding with . . ." He looked at Edward, who looked innocently back at him.

"Your family," I finished for him so he wouldn't have to go into details.

He nodded.

"I'm glad, Dolph, really. Lucille's been . . ." I shrugged. What was I supposed to say, that his wife, Lucille, had been frantic, afraid for him and of him? His rages had trashed a room or two of their house, much like he'd done to an interrogation room with me in it, once. He'd manhandled me at a crime scene. Dolph was close to losing his badge, if he didn't get a grip.

"She said you've been helpful about it. Her."

I nodded. If Edward hadn't been in the room, I'd have said your son's fiancée. "I'm glad I could help."

"I will never be okay with you dating the monsters."

"That's fine, as long as you don't let it rain all over police business."

"Fine, police business." He glanced at Edward, then reached into his suit coat and got out his notebook. "What killed the vampire in the hotel room?"

"When her animal to call died, the master didn't survive it. It happens like that sometimes: kill one and they all die."

"The police have killed wereanimals that were guarding vampire lairs, and the master vampire didn't die."

"Most master vamps have an animal that they can control, but the phrase 'an animal to call' means it's the furry equivalent of a human servant."

"A human that's helping a vampire because of mind tricks?" He made it a question.

"I thought that once, too, but a human servant is more than that. It's a human with a preternatural connection, a mystical connection, with the vampire. Sometimes the vampire survives the death of its servant, but the servant usually doesn't survive the death of the vampire. I've also seen the body survive, but the human servant driven crazy by the master's death. But this weretiger had healing abilities that it shouldn't have had. It was almost like it had the best of both worlds on healing. The lycanthropy healing, and the rotting vampire's ability to laugh off bullets, even silver."

"I thought you just woke up?" Dolph said.

"I did."

"How did you know she rotted?"

"I didn't, but her animal healed like a rotting vampire, so I assumed she was one of them. But even if she was, her animal to call should not have had that close a tie with the vampire's powers. It's unusual, very unusual, as if the tie between master and servant was closer even than normal."

"She started to rot as soon as we took her head," Edward said.

"Ol . . . Otto must have been disappointed," I said.

"He was, but at least they don't smell like they look. Why is that?" Edward asked. "Not complaining, mind you, but why don't they smell like a rotting corpse?"

"I don't know, I think maybe because they aren't really rotting. It's like they, the vampires, went to a certain stage of rotting, then stopped. The smell is from decomposition. If the vampire isn't actually rotting, then no decomp, no smell." I shrugged. "Truthfully, that's just theory. I don't know for sure. I don't think I've seen more than a handful of them. It doesn't seem to be a common type of vamp, at least not in this country."

"They're all rotting corpses, Anita," Dolph said.

"No," I said, and met his eyes just fine, "no, they aren't. Most vampires, if you ever see them rotting like that, looking like that, they are well and truly dead. But the rotting ones can actually rot around you, then sort of heal themselves. They can go from looking like the walking dead to looking normal."

"Normal," Dolph said, and made a sound.

"Normal as they started," I said. I turned to Edward. "Do we know where the other vamp went?"

Dolph answered, "We know that a white male, late twenties, early thirties, brown hair, cut short, jeans, jean jacket, carried a large duffel bag out to his car and drove away while two uniforms watched."

"They watched," I said.

"Civilians who saw the incident said the man told the officers"— Dolph flipped back through his notebook, then read—"'You're going to let me go to my car, aren't you?' The policemen replied, 'Yes, we are.'"

"Shit, he pulled an Obi-Wan," I said.

"What?" Edward and Dolph said together.

"You know, from *Star Wars*, 'These are not the droids you're looking for.'"

Edward grinned. "Yeah, while Otto and I were taking the other vampire apart, the man pulled an Obi-Wan."

"He had to do it to several officers, or some version of it," Dolph said. "By the time he drove off there were police all over that hotel. I thought daylight wasn't good for vamps."

"I think the vampire was in the duffel bag. My guess, and it's only a guess, is that as the weretiger shared her master's healing ability, so the human servant of this other one shared her mind powers. I've never heard of anything like it, but it makes sense. If I think of another theory that makes more sense, I'll let you know."

"How did you know they would be at the hotel, Anita?" Dolph asked.

"I told you, an informant."

"Was the informant a vampire?"

"No," I said.

"No," he said.

"No," I said.

"Was the informant human?"

"I'm not giving you the name, so it doesn't matter, does it?"

"How many vampires are involved with these murders?"

"Two that I'm sure of."

"How close is your tie to your master, Anita?"

"What?" I just stared at him.

He looked at me, and there was no anger in his eyes, just a demand. He repeated the question.

My pulse was in my throat, and I couldn't help it. My voice was almost normal when I said, "Are we going to catch these bastards, or are you going to go back to obsessing on how up close and personal I am with the vampires? I'm sorry that I've disappointed you, Dolph. I'm sorry that you disapprove of my personal life, but we have dead on the ground. We have injured people. Can we please, please, concentrate on that instead of your obsession with my love life?"

He blinked, slow, over those cool cop eyes. "Fine, how did Peter Black get injured, and who exactly is he?"

I looked at Edward, because I had no idea what story he'd come up with. I doubted the truth, the whole truth, had been involved.

"Now, Lieutenant," Edward said, "I told you all this."

"I want to hear Anita's version."

"My version, like you know it's a version and not the truth," I said.

"I don't think you've told me the whole truth about anything since you started dating that bloodsucking son of a bitch."

"Politically, that bloodsucking son of a bitch is the Master of the City."

"Is he your master, Anita?"

"What?"

"Are you the human servant of the Master of this City?"

I'd outed myself once in front of Detective Smith. I'd done it to save the life of a vampire Good Samaritan. Apparently Smith hadn't ratted me out. I owed him a beer.

I needed a moment to think how to answer Dolph. Edward gave me that moment. "You know, Lieutenant, your persistent interest in Marshal Blake's personal life is a little disturbing. Especially as it seems to be distracting you from the investigation and capture of a double murderer."

Dolph ignored him and kept those cool cop eyes on me. If I'd been sure how the federal marshal program would have handled my being Jean-Claude's human servant I might have just said yes, but I wasn't sure, so I had to lie, or distract him. "You know, Dolph, I've tried to be professional here, but you've asked me if I've fucked someone, you've persistently asked personal and sexual questions. Did you miss the day they covered sexual harassment?"

"You are, you really belong to him, don't you?"

"I don't belong to anyone, Dolph. I'm so my own woman that I'm chasing some of them away. Requiem wants to own me; that's the vampire who just left, if you didn't catch his name. I don't want to be owned, not by anybody. Jean-Claude understands that better than any human I ever dated. Maybe that's what your son sees in his fiancée, Dolph. Maybe she understands him in ways you never will." That last was mean, and meant to be, but we had to end this conversation.

"You leave my family out of this." His voice was low and careful.

"I will if you will. Your obsession with vampires and my personal life started about the time your son got engaged to a vampire. It's not my fault. I didn't introduce them. I didn't even know he'd done it, until you told me."

"The Master of the City knew. He just didn't tell you," Dolph said.

"Is that what you've been thinking, that Jean-Claude somehow sicced a vampire on your son, so she'd seduce him?"

He gave me a look. "You're not the only vampire hunter in this country now, Anita. You're not even the only one with a badge. They tell me that the Master of the City has absolute authority. That no local vamp does anything without permission."

"If only that were true, but your son's fiancée belongs to the Church of Eternal Life. She's Malcolm's problem right now, not Jean-Claude's. The Church of Eternal Life is its own little universe in vampireland. Frankly, the other vamps are a little puzzled on how to deal with the Church when its members do stupid stuff like dating a policeman's son."

"Why was it stupid?"

"Because most police still hate the vampires. It's just better policy to leave the cops alone if you can. None of Jean-Claude's vampires have gone near a police person of any kind for anything."

"He's gone near you," Dolph said.

"I wasn't officially a cop when we started dating."

"No, you were a vampire executioner. He shouldn't have come near you, and you should have known better than to go near him."

"Who I date is not your business, Dolph."

"It is if it affects how you do your job."

"I do my job better because I'm up close and personal with the monsters." I struggled to sit up a little, tired of him looming over me. My stomach was tight, but it didn't hurt. "You count on me knowing more about the monsters. Hell, every cop that comes near me for help counts on me knowing more about the monsters than they do. How the hell do you think I found all that out? By keeping them at arm's length and hating them the way you do? They don't like talking to people who treat them like shit. They don't volunteer information to people they know hate them. If you want someone's help you have to reach out to them."

"How many have you reached out to, Anita?" Such innocent words, but he made it sound ugly.

"Enough so I could help you every time you called."

He closed his eyes then, balled his fist around his notebook until something in it ripped. "If I'd left you where I found you, raising the dead, Jean-Claude would never have met you. You went into his club on police business the first time. On my business." He opened his eyes and there was such pain in them.

I reached out to touch his arm, but he moved back, out of reach. "We did our jobs, Dolph."

"When you look in the mirror, is that enough, Anita? At the end of the day, is that enough, that we do our jobs?"

"Sometimes, sometimes not."

"Are you a lycanthrope?"

"No," I said.

"Your blood work says different."

"My blood work is puzzling the hell out of the lab, and it'll puzzle the hell out of any lab you send it to."

"You know you're carrying lycanthropy."

"Yeah, I'm carrying four different kinds of lycanthropy."

"You knew."

"I found out when I ended up in the hospital in Philadelphia, after that zombie case with the FBI."

"You didn't mention it to anyone here."

"You hated me for dating shapeshifters; if you found out I was carrying it"—I spread my hands—"I couldn't depend on how you'd react."

He nodded. "You're right. You were right not to tell me, but you could have told Zerbrowski or someone."

"It doesn't affect my job, Dolph. I've got a disease that I'm mostly asymptomatic for. It's no one's business unless it impacts the job." In my head I wondered what would happen if the almost-beasts that I carried inside me got out of control on a case. That would be bad. I almost had the *ardeur* under control, and now I had something else that might keep me from being able to do my police work.

"Anita, did you hear what I said?"

"I'm sorry, no, I didn't."

"I said, how do you know it doesn't affect the job? How do you know that your ties to the monsters don't color your choices?"

"I'm tired, Dolph. I'm tired, and I need to rest." Why hadn't I thought of that before? I was in a hospital, I could have just cried hurt. Damn, I was slow tonight.

He uncrumpled his notebook, tried to smooth it out as best he could. He tried to fit it back in his suit pocket, but he'd damaged it so bad it wouldn't fit. He finally just took it in his hand. "I'll want to talk to you when you've rested. There comes a point, Anita, when you have enough secrets from your friends that they begin to wonder where your loyalties lie."

"Get out, Dolph, just go."

"But he gets to stay," and he pointed at Edward.

"He hasn't insulted me. He's been nothing but professional."

"I guess I deserve that." He seemed about to say something else. He held his hand out. Edward hesitated, then gave Dolph back his gun. Dolph just left, closing the door softly behind him.

Edward holstered his gun and we waited a few seconds, then looked at each other. "You are not going to be able to avoid answering him for very long, Anita."

"I know."

"It's not just you that's going to be in trouble."

I nodded. "Richard."

"He was hinting."

"If he knew, he'd do more than hint."

"Lieutenant Storr isn't stupid."

"I never thought he was."

"His hatred makes him stupid in some ways, but it also makes him very determined. If that determination gets turned on you and your friends, well . . ."

"I know, Edward, I know."

"What are you going to do?"

"There isn't a law on the books that says I can't date the monsters. Legally it would be like telling a federal agent he can't date someone who's not white; it would be a public relations nightmare."

"But the human servant bit, that's an area they haven't covered in the federal regulations."

"You've checked?" I asked.

"Before I took the badge, yeah, I read up. Nothing says you can't be Jean-Claude's human servant and a federal marshal."

"Because the laws haven't caught up to themselves."

"It doesn't matter, Anita; it still means even if Dolph finds out, you're covered."

"I'm covered legally, but there are other ways to be gotten rid of, if cops want you gone."

"Like not calling you in on cases."

"Dolph's already doing that."

"Frankly, I think they see you sleeping with the enemy as being just as bad as any metaphysical stuff, or worse."

I thought about it. "They don't really understand the metaphysics, but they understand fucking."

"Your lieutenant seems almost as worried that you're sleeping around as who you're sleeping around with."

"A lot of police are prudes at heart."

"I think Lieutenant Storr would almost be as disappointed with you if you were just sleeping around with humans."

"I think he sees himself as sort of a surrogate father figure."

"How do you see him?"

"My boss, sort of. Once I thought he was my friend."

"You're sitting up—does it hurt?"

I thought about it, letting myself feel my body, sort of searching it for pain. I took a deep breath, all the way down to my stomach. "It's tight, but not painful. It has that tight feeling that it gets if you don't stretch the scar tissue out. You know?"

"I know."

"You don't have any scars as bad as mine, do you?"

"Only Donna knows." He smiled.

"How is Peter, really?"

"Brave."

"I meant, oh, hell, Edward, is he going to get the injection or not?"

"Still debating."

"You have to tell Donna."

"She'd take the injection."

"Legally, it's her decision."

"One of the reasons we kept him Peter Black was so he could make the decision. I've been talking to your furry friends. Tiger lycanthropy is one of the harder-to-catch ones. It's also one of the few that runs in families and can be inherited as well as caught."

"That's actually news to me," I said.

"Apparently the tigers keep it a close family secret. I've been talking to the only other weretiger in town."

"Christine," I said.

He nodded. "Did you know she ran to a town with no tigers to escape being forced to marry into a clan of weretigers?"

"I didn't know—wait, I remember Claudia saying that Soledad had come to St. Louis to probably escape an arranged marriage. Something about the tigers liking to keep it in the family."

"That was her cover story."

"How good was her cover?"

"It was good. I've seen her documents; they look real. They were excellent forgeries, and I know what I'm talking about."

"I'll just bet you do," I said.

He gave me a look. The real Edward began to peek out, Ted Forrester melting from the eyes outward. It was always his eyes that reverted back to real first. Sort of the way most lycanthropes shifted, interestingly enough.

"Thanks for sending Graham when you did. The shot they had was tiger. It's their standard because it's so rare. They're sending for a different batch, not tiger this time."

"Will he take the shot?"

"If you were him, what would you do?"

I thought about it. "I'm not the one to ask, Edward. I've been cut up a lot, and I've taken my chances. So far, so good."

"But the shot didn't exist last time. Would you have taken it?"

"I won't make this decision for you, or for Peter. He's not my kid."

"The other shapeshifters make weretigers sound like the last thing you'd want to be."

"How so?"

"Like I said, they try to force you to marry into the clan to keep everyone related. They'd find Peter and they'd offer him girls, try to lure him in. If he wouldn't be lured, they've been known to abduct."

"Illegal," I said.

"Most of them homeschool their kids."

"Very isolationist," I said.

"Peter doesn't like the sound of being a weretiger. He's not very big on other people telling him what to do."

"He's sixteen," I said. "No sixteen-year-old likes to be bossed around."

"I don't think he's going to grow out of it."

"He takes orders from you, and from Claudia."

"He takes them from people he respects, but you have to earn it. I wouldn't let some clan of weretigers take him, Anita."

"They can't force you, or Peter. Christine has lived in St. Louis for years and never been bothered that I'm aware of."

"Apparently, there're only four clans of tigers in the United States. They all keep to themselves. Their culture is also divided about purebloods, inherited lycanthropy, and attacks. Being given tiger lycanthropy is seen as a reward for a job well done. They think it's a sin to give it to someone you don't value."

"Sounds sort of vampirelike," I said. "They feel the same way about human servants and animals to call. But I've seen my share of both that were forced, and didn't go willingly."

"Were you willing?" he asked, and it was all Edward in those eyes now.

I sighed. "If I say no, are you going to do something stupid?"

"No, you love him. I see it. I don't understand it, but I see it."

"I don't get you and Donna either."

"I know."

"I wasn't willing at first, but somehow it just happened. Where we are now wasn't forced on me."

"Rumor has it that you're the power behind the throne, the one pulling his strings."

"Don't believe every rumor you hear."

"If I believed them all, I'd be too afraid to be alone with you."

I stared at him, trying to read that face, that unreadable face. "Do I want to know what people are saying about me behind my back?"

"No," he said.

I nodded. "Fine, get a doctor, see if I can get up and mobile."

"It's been ten hours, Anita, you can't be healed."

"Let's find out," I said.

"If you get out of bed this quick, some of those rumors are going to get confirmed."

"Are the police talking to you about me?"

"Not everyone knows that we're friends."

"Okay, what rumors?"

"That you're a shapeshifter."

"Some of my best friends are shapeshifters," I said.

"Meaning?"

"Meaning, get a doctor. I'm not going to stay in bed just to keep people from thinking what they already think. Truthfully, I've had actual shapeshifters think I'm one of them just from the way my energy feels."

"Would it hurt you to stay in bed?"

"Why do you care if people think I'm a shapeshifter?"

"I care because if Peter finds out you're already out of bed he'll feel weak. He'll want to be all macho, too."

"If the doctor tells me I'm too sick to move, I'll stay in bed. I'm not being macho."

"No, but Peter has similar injuries to yours, and he knows how he feels."

"His wounds aren't healing faster than normal?" I asked.

"They don't seem to be, why?"

"It's not a certainty, but often if a victim is going to get lycanthropy, wounds heal more than human-fast."

"Always?" he asked.

"No, but sometimes. Critical wounds that would cause death will heal faster. Smaller wounds sometimes heal faster, sometimes not."

"What do I tell Peter about the injection?"

I shook my head. "I can't make that call. I won't make that call." I looked at him, studied a face that didn't have the cheerfulness of Ted, or the coldness of Edward. There was real anguish there, guilt maybe. Since I thought he'd been foolish to bring Peter into this mess, I couldn't help him. Peter hadn't been ready for this much action. The shame of it was that in a few years he might have been.

"You're thinking I was wrong to bring him, that he wasn't ready."

"Hey, I told you that when I saw him. You don't have to read my mind, Edward. I'll usually tell you what I think."

"Okay, what do you think?"

"Well, shit," I said, and sighed. "Fine, fine. Of course you shouldn't have brought him. I was impressed with him in the middle of the fight. He held his ground. He remembered his training. In a few years, if he wants to follow in his father's footsteps, then fine. But he needs a few more years of practice and training. He needs a little seasoning before you throw him to the wolves again."

Edward nodded. "I was weak, I've never been weak before, Anita. Donna, Becca, and Peter, they make me weak. They make me back down. They make me flinch."

"They don't make you do anything, Edward. Your reaction to them, your feelings for them, has changed you."

"I'm not sure I like the change."

I sighed again. "I know the feeling."

"I let you down."

"I didn't mean that." I lay back down on the bed. Sitting up didn't hurt, but it didn't exactly feel good either. "What I meant was that loving people changes you. It's changed me, too. I'm softer in some ways, harder in others. I haven't compromised myself as much as you have."

"What do you mean by that?"

"I'm not trying to live with someone who doesn't know who and what I am. I'm not driving an eight-year-old to ballet class."

"My schedule's easier to move around than Donna's."

"I know. She runs her own metaphysical store. I remember, but that's not the point, Edward. The point is that I'm not trying to live a normal life. I'm not even trying to pretend that what I do, and what I am, is normal."

"If you had kids, you'd have to try."

I nodded. "The pregnancy scare last month made me have to look at that. I don't see myself ever getting pregnant on purpose. If it happens accidentally we'll deal, but my life doesn't work with babies."

"You're saying mine doesn't either." He sounded sad, and I hadn't expected that.

"No, I mean, I don't know. It doesn't work for me because I'm the girl. I'm the one pregnant, and, God forbid, nursing. Sheer biology makes it harder for me to combine gunplay and kids."

"I can't marry Donna, can I?"

The voice in my head screamed, *Nooo, you can't.* But out loud I said, "Again, I can't answer that. Hell, Edward, I have enough trouble with my own life, I can't run yours."

He gave me a look; it was an Edward look, but there was something in the eyes, something that wasn't cold, no, it was definitely warm, hot even. I watched the force of personality that could kill gather in his eyes. But what was it gathering for?

"Edward," I said, softly, "don't do anything right now that you'll regret later."

"We kill the vampire that caused this," he said.

"Well, of course," I said. "I meant don't make any hasty decisions about Donna and the kids. I don't know much, but I do know that if Peter does turn furry they'll need you more than ever."

"If he does turn furry, can I bring him up here to talk to your friends?"

"Yes, of course."

He nodded. He looked at me, his eyes softening a little. "I know you think I should leave Donna and the kids. You've always thought it was a bad idea."

"Maybe, but you love them, and they love you. Love's hard to come by, Edward; you should never throw it away just because it's a bad idea."

He laughed. "That made no sense at all."

"I'm trying here; what I meant to say was that you all love each other. If you can just make Peter stay home long enough to finish his training . . . I think in a few years, if he still wants to, he can join the family business, but he isn't ready now. Put your foot down and explain it like that and make it stick."

He nodded. "You think he can do it, what we do?"

"I think so, if this little adventure didn't take all the fun out of it for him."

He nodded again. "I'll go find a doctor." He walked out without a backward glance. I lay in the bed, listening to the sudden whispering silence of the room. I prayed that Peter wouldn't be a lycanthrope. I prayed that the council wouldn't let the Harlequin declare war on us. I prayed that we'd all survive. Well, I guess it was too late for Cisco. I hadn't known him that well, but he'd died defending me. He'd died at eighteen doing his job, defending the people he'd signed up to defend. It was an honorable death, a good death, so why didn't that make me feel better? Did he have family? Was he somebody's little boy? Someone's sweetheart? Who was crying right now for him? Or was there no one to mourn him? Were we, his coworkers and friends, all he had? Strangely, that thought made me more sad than any of the thoughts that had come before.

36

THERE WAS A soft knock at the door. Edward wouldn't knock, and if a doctor knocks it's followed with an opening door. Who knocks in a hospital? I asked, "Who is it?"

The answer came, "It's Truth."

A second voice called, "And Wicked."

They were brothers, and vampires, and had only recently joined Jean-Claude's group. The first time I'd met them, Truth had nearly died trying to help me catch a bad guy. They'd been warriors and mercenaries for centuries. Now they were ours. Jean-Claude's and mine.

Wicked came through the door first, in his pale-brown designer suit, tailored to the wide sweep of shoulder and the strain of muscles in his arms and legs. He actually went to the gym and had added some bulk to the muscles they'd both started with. His shirt was buttoned up tight, with an elegant tie and a gold tie clip. His blond hair was cut long enough to cover his ears, but still had a few inches to go before it reached shoulder length. He was clean-shaven so that the deep dimple in his chin showed. He was handsome, utterly masculine, and utterly modern from his haircut to his shined shoes. Only the sword hilt peeking from behind one shoulder spoiled the modern effect.

Truth followed at his brother's side as he usually did. He had the same half-growth of dark beard he'd had since I met him. It wasn't a beard, just as if when he'd died he hadn't shaved in a while, and he'd never gotten around to changing it. The almost-beard hid the clean, perfect masculine face, the dimple that they shared. You had to stare at them side-by-side for a while to realize how terribly much alike they looked. Truth's hair was shoulder length, a dark, nondescript brown that was almost black. The hair wasn't exactly stringy, but it was far from his brother's shining halo of hair. He wore leather, but it wasn't Goth leather. It was like fifteenth-century battle-hardened leather crossed with modern motorcycle leather. His boots were knee high, and they had a look about them that said they might be as old as he was, but they fit, they were comfortable, and they were just his boots. He liked them in the way that some men like that favorite chair that has molded to their bodies. So what if they were a little patched and worn; they were comfy.

Truth had a sword at his back, too. I knew they both were carrying guns—one hidden under the beautiful suit jacket, the other hidden under a leather jacket that had seen better days. The brothers were always well armed.

"Requiem said he didn't trust himself around you, so Jean-Claude sent us," Wicked said. He said it with a smile that filled his blue eyes with speculation.

"Why would Requiem say that?" Truth asked. His eyes were the mirrors of his brother's, but the expression in them was totally different. Truth was so sincere it almost hurt. Wicked always seemed to be laughing at me, or at himself, or the world in general.

"The Harlequin messed with his mind."

"So he didn't trust himself to keep you safe," Truth said.

"Something like that," I said.

There was another knock on the door, but Graham opened it and peeked through. "We've got company out here."

Wicked and Truth were suddenly on alert. It was hard to explain, but cops do it, too. One minute normal, ordinary, then suddenly they were on. They were ready.

"Who?" I asked.

"The lions' Rex."

I blinked at Graham. "You mean Joseph?"

Graham nodded.

"What's that bastard doing here?" Wicked asked.

"I think that's my line," I said.

Wicked gave me a small half-bow. "Sorry about that."

I said, "What does he want?"

Graham leaned the door closed and licked his lips. "I think he wants to beg your forgiveness, or something like that."

"I don't feel very forgiving," I said. I smoothed down the sheets on my hospital bed. No, I didn't feel very forgiving.

"I know," Graham said, "but he's out here alone. The lions left you and the vampires and our Ulfric to die. You don't owe them anything."

"Then why tell her he's outside?" Wicked asked.

Graham licked his lips again. "Because if I didn't tell Anita, and she found out later he'd come to see her, she'd be mad."

"Why would I be mad?" I asked.

"Because of what Joseph thinks is about to happen to his lions."

"His lions are no concern of mine anymore," I said, and I believed that down to the hard, cold feeling in my heart.

Graham nodded. "Okay, but don't say later that I didn't tell you, because I did." He moved away from the door so he could open it.

"Wait," I said.

Graham turned and looked at me, hand on the door handle.

"What do you mean, what's about to happen to the lions?"

"It's not our concern, you said so," Truth said.

I looked at the tall vampire, shook my head, and then looked back to Graham. "I feel like I'm missing something. Just in case I do care, a little, someone explain what I'm missing."

"Asher invited the lions from Chicago back," Graham said.

"When did this happen?" I asked.

"When you and Jean-Claude were dying," Truth said.

"And Richard," Graham added. "Our Ulfric was dying, too."

Truth gave a small bow from the neck. "I meant no offense, wolf."

Graham said, grudgingly, "It's okay."

"The vampires would not have listened to your Ulfric," Wicked said. There was something in the way he said it, the way he stood, that said he wanted a fight.

"Don't pick a fight, Wicked," I said.

He turned just enough to give me a little bit of his eyes. "That's not picking."

"I don't feel well enough to mess with it. I need everyone to be a grown-up, okay?"

Wicked gave me a look that wasn't entirely friendly, but he didn't say anything else. I'd take sullen silence. The brothers were an asset, the muscle we'd needed for a while, but they bothered me, too. There was always this feeling that they weren't quite the obedient little vampires they might have been. Maybe it was the fact that I knew they'd spent centuries with all vampires turned against them. They'd killed the head of their bloodline when he went crazy and sent his vampires out to slaughter humans. Their crime hadn't been slaying him, because the vampire council had decided he needed killing. Their crime had been surviving his death. Superstition said that lesser vampires died when the head of their bloodline died. Jean-Claude said it was true of weaker vampires, but it was supposed to be true of all vampires. I think it was a way to discourage palace coups. But Wicked and Truth were proof that it wasn't true, not if you were powerful enough. And of course, only the very powerful would attempt to overthrow their creator.

I had given the brothers shelter, a master to call their own. Truth would have died if I hadn't shared Jean-Claude's power with him. And where one brother went they both went, so Wicked was ours, too.

"Tell me about the lions," I said.

"Asher was in charge of the city as Jean-Claude's *témoin*, his second-in-command," Truth said.

"So?"

"He is not the second most powerful vampire in St. Louis. We thought"—and by *we* he always meant his brother and himself—"that sentimentality had clouded Jean-Claude's judgment. But there are other qualities in a leader than vampire powers. He was decisive, ruthless, and swift."

"What was he decisive, ruthless, and swift about?" I asked.

"We needed extra muscle," Graham said.

"You said that."

Graham nodded.

"Just tell me. I won't be mad."

Wicked laughed, a loud bray of sound that was nothing like the perfect masculine chuckle he usually allowed himself. "Don't promise until you know."

"I'll know if you tell me," I said, and already there was a thread of anger in my tone. Damn it.

"Asher called Augustine in Chicago. He asked for soldiers," Wicked said.

"He let Auggie send his werelions back into our territory," I said.

Wicked and Truth nodded. Truth asked, "Do you understand what that means for St. Louis's Rex and his pride?"

I lay in the bed and thought about it. I did know. "I sent Auggie's lions back to Chicago in November because they would have taken over Joseph's pride. He doesn't have anyone strong enough to protect them from the brutes that Auggie has."

"I'm not sure they'd like being called brutes," Wicked said, "but it's accurate." He smiled, a most unpleasant smile that turned his handsome face to something else. Something more basic, less practiced, more real. Wicked and Truth had honor; you could bank on that honor, trust it. If they'd been one inch less honorable, they would have been totally untrustworthy, and too dangerous to keep.

"Have they moved on Joseph's pride?" I asked.

"Not yet," Graham said. "I think they're waiting to talk to you first."

"Me, not Jean-Claude," I said.

"They talked to Jean-Claude. He's removed his protection from the lions."

"It's all up to you, babe," Wicked said.

"Micah is the head of the furry coalition," I said.

"Micah kicked them out, unless you make him put them back in," Graham said.

"When your Nimir-Raj found out what the St. Louis lions had done, he accused them of having broken the treaty with both the wolves and the leopards," Truth said.

Wicked continued the story. "Since they broke the treaty, they are no longer allies of the coalition. So the coalition members don't owe them anything."

"So when Auggie's lions attack, no one will come to their aid," I said, my voice soft.

"Exactly," Wicked said. He seemed pleased.

Graham said, "Joseph is outside, alone. He thinks you will be the weak link."

I looked at Graham, because it was odd wording. "You think I should let Joseph and his people fry."

"They betrayed us," Graham said. I saw something in his face then, a hardness that I hadn't noticed before. He could be a good bodyguard when he wasn't trying to fuck something, but he wasn't hard, or ruthless. Not until now.

I remembered what I'd said to Edward. I'd planned on taking revenge on the werelions. Edward was going to help me. But I'd met Joseph and his people, knew them. They were real, and they weren't all a waste of time. Travis and Noel had helped feed me for months while I tried to find a more permanent lion. They were too weak to satisfy my lioness, but they were good kids.

"Do I send him away?" Graham asked, as if that was what he wanted to do.

I thought about it. It would be so easy to just refuse to see him. Then I could be ruthless and hard-hearted, and not have to look the man in the face who I was condemning to death. I might be able to keep Auggie's lions from slaughtering all the pride, but one death would be an absolute must—Joseph's.

"Send him in," I said.

"You think that's a good idea?" Wicked asked. He managed to keep his voice neutral.

"It'd be easier not to see him," I said.

"Then why see him?" Wicked said.

"Because it would be easier."

"That makes no sense."

"It makes sense to me," Truth said.

I looked up at the other vampire. We exchanged a long look. He understood why I had to turn Joseph away in person: because if I couldn't look him in the eye and tell him the truth, then maybe it was the wrong thing to do. I had to see him, to know whether I could stand by and let nature take its course with the lions in our city. The lions weren't my problem, damn it. They had betrayed us. They would have let us all die. Their moral superiority had been worth more to them than the lives of our vampires. I wouldn't cause them harm, but I was done stepping in and saving them. Or that's what I told myself when I told Graham to open the door.

37

I WATCHED JOSEPH walk toward the bed. He was tall with dark blond hair cut short. He was dressed for a business meeting in a suit complete with tie. I was betting his wife, Julia, had picked the outfit. He started undoing the tie before he got to Wicked and Truth. They stopped him a little short of the bed. Normally, I might have thought they were being overly cautious, but my body agreed with them. I was healing, but only through a miracle of metaphysics; eventually you run out of miracles.

"Anita, how are you doing?" He tried for a neutral tone but it came out nervous.

"Ted Forrester has gone to find a doc. I may get out of bed today."

"That's great," and the relief chased over his face. His hands flexed and unflexed. "Julia said you'd be all right. She said that you'd find someone else to feed on. She said you would all be all right, and you are." He was talking a little too fast, as if even he didn't believe it.

"Who are you trying to convince, Joseph, me or you?" My voice was flat and my eyes empty. I'd had dinner with him at my house. I'd thought he was a good man. But in the end, he'd let us die.

"Anita." He tried to step closer to the bed, but the vampires stopped him.

"You're close enough," Wicked said.

"I would never harm her."

I raised the hospital gown, showed him the healing wounds that crossed my stomach and ribs. "The only thing that made me powerful enough to heal this was Donovan Reece's letting me feed on every swanmane in this country. He gave me the power to live through this."

Joseph's face had paled. "I'm married, Anita. Julia and I take our vows very seriously."

"If you were human that would be fine, Joseph, but you aren't human. You're a werelion. A werelion who owed allegiance to his allies. We needed you, and you failed us."

He went to his knees. "Do you want me to beg? I'll beg."

I shook my head. "My lioness has never wanted you, Joseph. Had you ever wondered why? Why wouldn't she want the strongest lion she could find? That's what she's programmed to do." I felt the lioness stir down that long dark tunnel in my head, or in my gut. I thought calm thoughts at her, and she stilled. I was almost surprised that it worked. I said a little prayer of thanks, and went back to paying attention to the lion in front of me.

"I thought you left me alone out of respect for my wife."

I looked at him. There was nothing wrong with him. He was good looking enough, if a little too masculine for my preferences, but he had never moved me. My lioness had never even tried for him.

"My lioness reacted to your lion the way she does to all the lions, but she was never drawn to you, the way she was drawn to some of the Chicago lions."

"You react to the Chicago lions because you slept with them. And their master vampire."

"Is that what everyone's saying?" I asked.

He looked puzzled. "It's the truth."

"No, it's half the truth. Augustine, yes, but I was very careful with his lions. I was careful because I didn't want to fuck up your lions. I left his lions very alone, because I was worried about you and yours."

"I knew you sent them back to Chicago, but I thought . . . I am grateful that you turned them down for us."

In my head, I could admit that it hadn't been entirely for Joseph and his people. The lion that most attracted my lioness had sooo been bad news.

"I did it because you were my ally, and I thought it was somehow my fault that the other werelions were going to come and take over your pride. I've learned since then that Augustine has had your pride

on his to-do list for a while now. Because you and your lions are too
weak to defend yourselves, and all the other lions know it."

"I kept my people safe," he said.

"No, I kept them safe. Jean-Claude kept them safe. Richard kept
them safe. The wererats have died keeping your city safe. The leopards nearly lost their queen. The swans risked everything. Where were
the lions while the rest of us bled and died?"

"If you had asked we would have fought for you."

"Why would we want the lions to fight for us, Joseph? You're too
weak. You don't train in combat, or weapons. You are werelions, so
fucking what? We're all wereanimals, but we offer more than just teeth
and claws. What do the lions offer us, Joseph?" The anger stirred that
place inside me, and I had to close my eyes and count, slowly, breathe,
slowly. The stirring eased again. Two times in a row the beasts had
quieted because I'd asked, or concentrated on being calm. Maybe I
was finally getting the hang of this.

"We are lions," he said, but his voice was soft.

"You are weak," and my voice was soft, too. Soft because I couldn't
afford the anger.

Joseph reached his hands out toward me, between Truth and
Wicked's legs. "Do not let them kill us."

"Am I your Rex? Am I your Regina?"

"No," he said, and his hands began to lower.

"Then why do you turn to me for help?"

"Because I have nowhere else to turn."

"Whose fault is that, Joseph? Whose fault is it that after this many
years your pride is so weak that you have to turn to humans and vampires, and other animal groups for safety?"

His hands were on his thighs now. "Mine," he said.

"No, not just yours. I'm betting your wife had something to do with
it. Every time someone remotely stronger than you and your brother
came along, she said no, didn't she? She said that you didn't need
them, didn't she?"

"Yes," he said.

"If you'd let some strength into your pride, you would have learned
how to be a better king."

"Or they would have killed me and taken the pride, taken . . ."

"Your wife," I said.

He nodded.

"I heard that some of the lion takeovers work like that. I can see where she wouldn't want to take the chance."

"Then you understand."

I shook my head. "I can't afford to understand, Joseph. I can't afford to let you hide behind my skirts anymore. Micah kicked you out of our alliance." I looked across the room to Graham by the door. "Graham, did the other animal groups vote with the leopards?"

"They said pretty much what you've said, that they have all lost people or had injuries and the lions just take resources and don't give anything back."

"I gave Anita the choice of all our unattached young men. I paraded them out for her like some kind of slave auction."

I'd been fighting off feeling bad about this decision, until that moment. "Slave auction, is that how you saw it?"

"You're picking men who will have to have sex with you. If you have no choice, then you're just a slave."

"I haven't fucked any of your young lions."

He looked at me like he didn't believe that at all.

"Didn't you ask them what they did for me?"

"We felt bad enough giving them to you. We didn't need to hear any details."

"You self-righteous prig. I didn't sleep with them because most of them are virgins, or damn close to it. Corrupting the young just doesn't appeal to me."

There was a knock on the door. Who could it be this time? Graham opened the door, and standing in the doorway was the reason for Joseph's fear, and the other reason for me sending the lions back to Chicago that first time. Haven, alias Cookie Monster, walked into the room.

38

HE WAS TALL, and a little slender for my tastes, but a leather trench coat gave him more bulk through the shoulders than I knew he had. His short, spiked hair was still shades of blue like Cookie Monster and spring skies. His eyes were still blue and laughing. He was still handsome. He was still dangerous.

Joseph got to his feet. Wicked and Truth put a hand on either of his arms. He didn't fight them about it. They just looked toward the other man. They were actually blocking my view at that point. I was okay with that. The less I saw of him, the better.

"It's against the rules for you to hold him for me." Haven's voice was pleasant, as if he were asking about the weather. He probably had a pleasant face to go with the pleasant voice. He could look pleasant and amused right up to the time he hurt you. He was a professional thug, and had been for all his adult life. He was a mob enforcer and a were-lion. Like I said, dangerous.

"I beat you last time," Joseph said. That was true.

"You got lucky," Haven said, and the voice was sliding down to something less pleasant.

"But I didn't even know you were here. I came to see Anita."

Truth and Wicked stepped aside, taking Joseph with them. I was suddenly lying there staring up at the other man. I had a moment of staring up into that deceptively blue gaze, such an innocent color, and then his gaze slid down my body. It wasn't sexual; I'd forgotten to lower my gown, so the wounds were still visible.

His face was very serious, and on the edge of that came a flash of anger through those sky-blue eyes. "Weretiger, huh?"

"Yeah."

He reached out, as if he would touch the wounds. I drew the gown back over my skin. He looked me in the face again. There was a look in his eyes that I couldn't decipher. It was a serious look, whatever it meant.

Something stirred inside me, something that flashed tawny and gold in the dark end of the tunnel. I suddenly smelled dry grass and heat so hot it had a smell to it. I smelled lion.

"I'm trying to be good here," Haven said. "If you go all lioness on me, I can't promise to be good."

"I appreciate that," I said out loud, but my hand ached to reach out to him. He was toning down his power level, and I was toning down mine, but the urge to touch him was still there. Micah had figured it out that my power wasn't seeking a lion to be another animal to call like Nathaniel. The power was seeking what Micah was to me, a Rex to my Regina. Chimera had been the same way, I guess; he'd been the dominant in whatever group he took over. The mix of panwere and Belle Morte's line of vamps seemed to have changed it from me trying to be dominant to everyone into trying to be a dominant couple with everyone.

"Take his hand."

I blinked up at them.

Truth repeated, "Take his hand."

"I'm not sure that's a good idea."

Haven reached out to me. I could have moved back, but I was just a little late in moving. Maybe it was a Freudian slip, or maybe it was an entire wardrobe.

His hand wrapped around mine with room to spare. His hands were as big as Richard's, the fingers longer, closer to the way Jean-Claude's hands looked, but the size was all Richard. The feel of his hand in mine made something tight in my chest loosen. I had enough men in my life, damn it. All I had to do was let go of his hand, but I didn't let go.

Haven was staring down at our clasped hands as if he didn't know what they were. He sounded distracted, like he was thinking about something very different from what his words said. "Your Nimir-Raj has kicked Joseph and his lions out of the coalition. I've checked with the wererats, the werehyenas, and your Ulfric. They're all cool with me doing what needs doing."

"It was good of you to check with everyone," Truth said.

"The animal groups in your coalition with Jean-Claude are still united. I didn't want to piss everyone off the first day back." He was rubbing his thumb across my knuckles as he talked. "I just need to ask you how you feel about it, and I can get started."

"Anita, please," Joseph said. He was still being held between the two vampires.

"No one in the coalition trusts you anymore, Joseph. I don't trust you either."

"So you won't care what I do?" Haven asked. He was looking at my face now. His face was more serious than I'd ever seen it.

"There are some lions in his group that are weak, but they're still valuable. Give them a chance to join you."

"Valuable how?"

"They have jobs. They bring income into the pride so that others don't have to work."

"Money won't be a problem. Auggie bankrolled us until things got up and running."

"And that's another thing; I'll try not to interfere in how you run the pride, but I can't let you bring new mob connections to St. Louis."

"You know that's one of the main reasons Auggie wanted us down here."

"I figured it was, but we've got enough crime without adding. I'll let the lions do what lions do, but the mob is human and I'm a federal marshal. Don't make me have to choose."

"I'll have to talk to Auggie." He was just holding my hand, not meeting my eyes again.

"I'll talk to him if you want, or Jean-Claude can."

"Jean-Claude probably can come up with a compromise that Auggie will listen to," Haven said.

"Remember the two lions you almost broke when you were here last time?"

"The college kids, yeah."

"They've helped me keep my beast under control. In fact, Joseph has a lot of young people in college. Let them finish their degrees, help bring in legitimate money."

His hand squeezed around mine, not hard, but firm. "Did you sleep with them?"

I started to ask why, but there was something about the way he was standing there, some quality of stillness that made me afraid to tease. I said the truth, "No."

"None of them," he said.

"No, but if you're not into sharing then you are holding the hand of the wrong girl."

"I know how many you got on your plate, but they aren't lions."

"And if I had slept with any of the other lions?"

He gave me a look; there was nothing comforting in that look, hell, there was nothing very human in that look. "I won't share with another lion."

"I'll need more than one of each of my beasts. You can't be with me twenty-four-seven."

He frowned. "No, I can't."

"Also, I've got Micah as my Nimir-Raj, then Nathaniel came as my leopard to call. It may work that way with all my animals."

"You only have the Ulfric."

"Not true," Graham said. "She sees a lot of Jason."

"He's Jean-Claude's *pomme de sang*," I said.

"That's why he's around a lot, but that's not why you do him all the time."

"Thanks for putting it that way, Graham." Funny how Graham reminded me often why he wasn't getting sex from me.

"He's also Nathaniel's best friend." Wicked added that.

"Can we please change the subject?" I said.

"But Jason isn't her animal to call," Truth said.

"Then why does she have a leopard but not a wolf to call?" Graham asked.

"We don't know," Wicked said.

"Guys, enough already," I said.

"She's right," Haven said. He looked at Joseph. "We can't settle this right now, so go. Go tell your pride that you failed them. Tell them that we'll give them tonight safe."

"What happens tomorrow?" Joseph asked.

Haven gave that unpleasant smile again. "Why, then you and I find out if you can get lucky again, or if your luck's run out."

"You will make him your Rex, Jean-Claude's Rex," Joseph said. He looked at the werelion. "Are you prepared to do what the Nimir-Raj and the Ulfric do?"

"What's that?"

"Sleep with her master. Sleep with Jean-Claude."

Funny how some rumors never die, no matter how many times you try to kill them. Before I could say anything, Haven answered, "Do you believe every rumor you hear?"

"They are not rumors, if they are true."

"You thought I was sleeping with your little lions, and I wasn't."

"You say you weren't."

"Get him out of here," Haven said.

The vampires looked at me. I nodded.

They started escorting Joseph to the door.

"You condemn me to death, Anita," he called back over his shoulder.

I didn't know what to say to that, so I said nothing. You can't save everybody, and we couldn't afford to have any ally that wasn't with us completely. It wasn't just the sex. There'd been no lion in his pride good enough to be a bodyguard. Not a single one. You couldn't be that weak and survive.

Wicked was saying something to Joseph, low and urgent. His grip on the man's arm was tight enough to show at a distance. Whatever he said quieted the protests and sent him out the door.

"What did you say to him, Wicked?" I asked.

"I told him that the werelion had given him tonight to be safe, but if he kept saying mean things about our masters, I'd just do him tonight."

"It's my fight," Haven said.

"I said that I'd do him, not that I'd kill him. After everything he'd just said, I figured rape would scare him enough to get him out of here."

"You don't like guys," I said.

"You don't know what I like. You've worked hard not to know. My pride's hurt, but I'll get over it. But Joseph would believe anything of Jean-Claude's people, even male-on-male rape."

"So there really is a rumor that no one gets to join Jean-Claude's kiss without fucking him."

"Or you," Truth said.

"I'm really disappointed that one isn't true, by the way," Wicked said, with a grin.

"Me, too," Graham said.

I gave them both the look they deserved.

"I do not wish to," Truth said.

They looked at him. "Why not?" Graham asked.

"Because I am already much in thrall to Anita. If I bedded her, I would be little more than the slave Joseph accused us of being."

"Trust me, guys, you're overestimating my appeal," I said.

"I don't know about that," Haven said. He spread my hand on his palm and touched my hand with the fingers of his other hand. "You have such small hands."

"Delicate and dangerous," Wicked said.

Haven started talking, almost as if to himself. "I'm not a complicated guy. I know that. I'm not stupid, but I'm not exactly a brain trust either. I know that, too. I like being a guy. I like being muscle. I like hurting people. I don't mind killing people. I like my job. I like drinking with the guys, a little poker, and strip clubs, fucking. It was a good life."

"You make it sound like it's over," I said.

"I went back to Chicago, to my life, but it didn't work anymore. I still liked hurting people, but I started wondering if you'd hate me for doing some of the stuff Auggie had me doing. I kept thinking, *What would she think?* Wondering what you'd think started getting in the way of my job. Auggie noticed it."

"I sent you back home, Haven. I didn't make you think about me." I tried to take my hand back, but he wrapped those long fingers around me, and I didn't fight it.

"Yeah, you did, Anita, maybe not on purpose, but you did. First it fucked up my job, then it fucked up my fun. I started looking at my friends and what we did, and thought, *She'd be disappointed. She'd think it was stupid.*" He shook his head. "Damn it, I've never let any woman mess me up like this."

"Haven, I . . ."

"Let me finish," he said.

I wasn't sure I wanted him to finish, but I let him.

"Women are just for fucking, or marrying so you can have kids if you want them. Women don't count, not in my world, not in Auggie's world. But you counted, to him, and to me. But especially to me. No matter what woman I was with, or how good the sex was, the moment it was over, it felt bad. It wasn't enough. Damn you, damn you, I started thinking about relationships. Having a girl to talk to. Stupid shit that I gave up before I hit fifteen, and suddenly it was all back. I was this kid again, thinking there was more to life than being muscle for Auggie. There isn't more to life, Anita. There isn't anymore." His voice had sunk to a low growl.

I didn't know what to say. *Sorry* seemed lame, and *It's not my fault* seemed worse. *I didn't mean to fuck up your life* seemed the most accurate. I finally settled for, "I didn't make you rethink your life, Haven."

"Yeah, you did. Auggie says you did. He says you didn't mean to do it, but you mind-fucked me just like Belle Morte does, or can. I'm your lion, Anita. I'm yours. Yours in a way I've never been anyone's. You make me want to be a better person. How fucking lame is that?"

Truth's quiet voice came. "A lady always makes a man want to be better than he is. Belle Morte did not make anyone want to be better. She made you obsess about her, follow her like a dog, but you did not think, *Will she think less of me if I do this awful thing?* She did things so much worse than anything we were willing to do; even Wicked found her immoral."

"Auggie said it was the same mind-fucking shit that Belle Morte did."

"Your attraction to Anita may have been vampire powers, but your reaction to her beyond that is not," Wicked said, and there was a note of almost sadness to his voice.

"What does that mean?" Haven asked, his voice irritated.

"It means, my good fellow," Wicked said, "you're in love with the woman."

"No," Haven said.

"Only love of a good woman will make a man question every choice, every action. Only love makes a warrior hesitate for fear that his lady will find him cruel. Only love makes a man both the best he will ever be, and the weakest. Sometimes all in the same moment."

I didn't know what to say. It seemed like I should say something. Maybe I wasn't in love with him. Or maybe it was just lust. Or . . . but one thing had to be clear between us.

"I appreciate all the honesty, Haven, really I do, but I need to be certain you understand a few things."

He gave me a look that was both angry and uneasy. "What things?"

"You've done good. You checked with all the other group leaders. That was great. But I haven't said I'd make you one of my boyfriends."

He squeezed my hand, traced his fingers across my wrist. I had to fight not to shiver under even that small touch. I knew this reaction. It was too close to how Micah had affected me, too damn close. But when Micah came into my life the *ardeur* was brand new, and so was having my own beasts. I wasn't new at controlling all of it now. Thank God.

"Your pulse speeds up just from that little touch. How can you say you don't want me?"

"I didn't say I didn't want you. But my life works, mostly. I like living with Micah and Nathaniel. I like bunking over with Jean-Claude and Asher. I don't need another man in my life who won't share. Frankly, I'm trying to thin down the number of men in my life. I really don't want another one."

"What are you saying?"

"I'm saying, don't come down here thinking it's a done deal between us. Don't take it for granted that you'll be able to fit into my life."

He let go of my hand, then, and the look was so cold. "I talk to you like I've never talked to another woman, and this is what I get?"

"Yeah, because my life works. The coalition works. The power structure in this territory works. I won't jeopardize it, not for lust, or even for love."

"Ask her how she feels about you," Truth said.

Haven shook his head.

"Tell him how you feel, Anita."

I didn't want to, but Truth was right. One, Haven had been honest with me. Two, a man's ego is a fragile thing sometimes. The toughest men sometimes are the easiest hurt, and hardest to heal. I didn't know what Haven and I would be doing with each other, but whatever we were going to do, it needed to be honest.

"I thought about you while you were in Chicago, but not to the extent you thought about me. I sent you away because I wanted to touch you. I wanted to be naked with you, and do all the things you do when the clothes come off."

"You're saying you wanted, like it's past."

"I still feel the attraction, trust me. But the initial attraction is the most overwhelming. It was like that with Micah, too. If I can get a little distance between me and the man, then, apparently, I get better control."

"I wonder how your control would be if I weren't shielding my lion from you? You're hurt. You need to heal, but when you're well, I want to see how your control holds up to my lion."

"Don't threaten me, Haven. I don't react well to that."

"It's not a threat, Anita. I am being so good right now. You have no idea how good."

"I appreciate that," I said.

"But I'm not good. I'm bad. I think like a bad guy. You keep pushing me away, and all my good resolutions will go out the window."

"What does that mean?" I asked.

"It means that once I kill Joseph and take over his pride, I'll be a permanent member of your coalition. I'll be the local Rex. Once I take over Joseph's pride, I can't go back to Chicago."

The human part of me, the commonsense part of me said, *Send his ass back home*. The coldly practical part said, *Who else is going to run the lions here?* There were no other candidates. The lioness in me wanted to know if he was as good as his brag. Not just about sex, but power. The lioness more than any other of my beasts wanted a mate that could protect her, keep up with her. None of my other beasts were as competitive as the lion. I got a distant swirl of tiger, like a dream of a dream. Tiger wanted to be left alone. Fine with me.

"I'm scared of you, Haven. Scared that you being my lion will fuck up my life. I know you're bad, and you've been bad your entire adult life. That's a lot of bad habits to break."

"I'm not sure I know how to be good."

"I know."

"Do I stay? Decide now, Anita, because once the pride is mine, the choice is gone."

I thought about it. I'd have been fine with him coming in as the new Rex, but coming in as a new boyfriend, well, that just had disaster written all over it. I opened my mouth to say *go*, but my lioness swiped a claw up inside me, like she was playing with my liver. It made me writhe on the bed and not in a good way.

I was suddenly getting asked by a lot of people, "Anita, are you all right?"

I nodded. I had more control over my beasts, I really did. But apparently, I didn't have complete control. Would the lioness let me send Haven back to Chicago, or would she tear me apart?

I don't know what I would have said to Haven, because I didn't get a chance. The door opened, and it was Dolph again, but with more police at his back.

"Everybody in here carrying a weapon, but not carrying a badge, out."

Since that was everybody but Graham, they went. Dolph was pissed that they'd managed to get past everyone in the first place. Apparently, heads were going to fly, at least figuratively.

Edward came back into the room while Dolph was giving each of the armed "guards" a police escort off hospital grounds. Dolph decided that Ted Forrester and his German friend in the hallway were enough muscle to keep me safe, so Graham didn't need to be here either.

"Dolph, Graham isn't even armed."

"You've got Forrester and Otto Jeffries to guard your back, or is there something going on in our city so dangerous that you need all this firepower?" He gave me those searching cop eyes that always seemed to see everything.

I shook my head. I told Truth, Wicked, Haven, and Graham to go with the nice police officers. They went. Because Dolph was right with Edward and Olaf, I was safe enough, at least from our enemies. I'd seen Olaf use a gun. I knew he was a good man in a fight, but somehow I just never felt entirely safe from Olaf with Olaf nearby. Funny, that.

39

THE DOCTOR TOLD me I could go. That if I exercised and didn't let the scar tissue harden up on me, I'd be fine. He also assumed I was a shapeshifter, a new kind of shapeshifter that could do different animals. He actually used the term *panwere*. It was the first time I'd heard anyone but a shapeshifter say it. The doctor had never actually seen one, until me. I told him he still hadn't seen one, but nothing I said persuaded him different, so I gave up. If people won't believe the truth, and you don't want to lie, then you're out of options. Chimera had been the real deal, a true panwere, and one of the scariest beings I'd ever met. I wondered what the doctor would have made of him?

I walked down the hall to Peter's room with Edward leading the way. Olaf brought up the rear. I didn't like him behind me, but he wasn't doing anything wrong. For him, he was positively being a good boy. The fact that I could feel the weight of his gaze on my back almost like a hand pressing between my shoulder blades wasn't something I could really bitch about. I mean, what was I supposed to say, *Stop looking at me?* It was a little too childish for me to say it out loud, no matter how true it felt.

It didn't help that Olaf and I were dressed alike, sort of. Edward was in his white button-down shirt and jeans, and cowboy boots. Ted Forrester dressed to be comfortable; Olaf dressed either to intimidate or because he liked the Goth assassin look. I hadn't picked my clothes, Nathaniel had. Black jeans tight enough that the inner pants holster dug in a little, but they tucked nicely into the lace-up boots. The black T-shirt was scoop-necked and the push-up bra that was under it made sure I had plenty of scoop to show. My cross sat on my breasts, rather than hanging in front of them. How did I know Nathaniel had packed the bag and not Micah? First, the panties and bra matched, and the panties were perfect for the lower waistline of the jeans; second, the shirt and bra showed a lot of cleavage; third, the boots. Maybe my Nikes were covered in blood, they probably were, and the boots were comfy and low heeled, but Nathaniel was twenty and male and often looked at clothes from the perspective of his job. Micah had a tendency to not match everything perfectly; he would have just put on an ambi-sexual T-shirt from the T-shirt drawer we shared. The outfit wouldn't have looked so terribly like an outfit if Micah had done it. I'd have to talk to Nathaniel about picking out things with this much cleavage when I was working with the cops. I had my backup shoulder holster instead of the custom-made leather one, which probably meant hospital efficiency had destroyed it. That would be the second or third one that had gotten cut to pieces in an emergency room.

I felt heat, or air movement, or . . . something. I turned and must have done it fast enough to catch Olaf in midmotion, pulling his hand back. He had almost touched me.

I glared at him, and he stared at me. Those dark, deep-set eyes stared at my face, and then his gaze slid down the front of my body in that way that men can do. That look that slides over you so that you know they're thinking about you naked, or worse. In Olaf's case it was probably worse.

"Stop looking at me like that," I said.

Edward was watching us both.

"Every man who sees you tonight will be looking at you like that." He made a gesture in the vague direction of my chest. "How can they not?"

I felt the heat run up my face, and spoke through gritted teeth. "Nathaniel picked the clothes to bring to the hospital, not me."

"Did he buy the shirt and the bra?" Olaf asked.

"No," I said. "I did."

He shrugged. "Then do not blame the boy."

"Yeah, but they're date clothes, and I don't think there's going to be time for a date tonight."

"Will we be hunting the vampire that escaped us?" he asked.

I nodded. "Yeah, if we can figure out where she and her human servant have gotten to, yeah."

He smiled.

"What?" I said, because the smile didn't match what we were talking about.

"If things work out as I hope, I may owe your boy a thank-you."

I shook my head. "I don't understand."

Edward touched my arm, and I jumped. "You don't want to understand." He led me down the hallway, his hand on my arm. Olaf stayed where he was, staring at us with that strange half-smile on his face.

"What?" I asked Edward.

He leaned in close, speaking low and quick, "While you were unconscious, Olaf came into the room. You were covered in blood and they'd cut off most of what you were wearing. He touched you, Anita. The doctors and guards chased him back, and I got him out of the room, but . . ."

I stumbled, because I was trying to stop, and he kept us moving. "Touched me where?" I asked.

"The stomach."

"I don't understand," and then I did. "The wounds, he touched the wounds."

"Yes," Edward said, and stopped us outside a door.

I swallowed hard; both my pulse and a certain nausea were trying to climb up my throat. I looked down the hallway where Olaf was still standing. I knew my face showed fear; I couldn't help it. He drew his lower lip under and bit it. I think it was an unconscious gesture. A gesture you make when you are moved to the point where you don't think about how you look, or who's looking. Then he moved down the hallway toward us like some black movie monster. The kind that looks human, and is human, but in their mind there's nothing human left to talk to.

Edward opened the door and drew me inside. Apparently we weren't waiting on Olaf. Fine with me.

I stumbled over the doorsill. His hand tightened, steadying me. The door closed on the sight of Olaf gliding up the hallway. He moved like all his muscles knew what they were doing, almost like one of the shapeshifters. He so needed killing.

I must have looked pale, because Micah came across the room and took me in his arms. He whispered against my cheek, "What's wrong?" He hugged me tighter. "You're shivering."

I wrapped my arms around him and pressed as much of me against as much of him as I could. It was one of those hugs when it feels almost like you're trying to meld yourself into the other person. Sometimes it's sexual, but sometimes it's because the world has gone too wrong and you need something to cling to. I clung to Micah like he was the last solid thing in the world. I buried my face against the curve of his neck and drew in the scent of his skin. He didn't ask again what was wrong; he just held me close.

Other arms hugged me from behind; another body pressed tight against me. I didn't need to open my eyes and see Nathaniel to know it was him. I didn't even need the faint hint of vanilla. I knew the feel of his body against mine. I knew the feel of them holding me together.

Another body came in from the side of us. I did turn to see, and found it was Cherry. She put an arm around both men. I realized with a start that she wasn't taller than Nathaniel now. "What's wrong?" she asked, dark eyes worried.

What did I say? That I was afraid of Olaf? That the thought that he'd caressed my wounds creeped me? That I wondered if he'd touched that bulge of intestine the way a man touches a breast? That I wanted to know, and didn't want to know?

The door opened behind us. Edward nodded at me and went to the opening door. He spoke softly, then walked out the door to talk to Olaf in private, or maybe to simply keep him away from me for a while. Whichever, I was grateful. Of course, that left me with Edward's other backup.

I looked past Micah's shoulder and Cherry's arm to the bed in the room. Pain had brought more of the shadow of that boy I'd first met into Peter's face. He looked pale and terribly young lying there hooked up to tubes and monitors. When I woke up, I hadn't been hooked up to anything that monitored my vitals. How much worse off was he than me?

I whispered, "I don't think I can explain what's wrong."

Cherry gave me narrow eyes.

"I'll try to explain later, promise."

She frowned at me, but stepped back as if she knew what I was going to do. Maybe she did. I'd probably made some small movement toward the bed, or turned my body as if prepping to move. Most people wouldn't notice, but a lot of the shapeshifters would.

I hugged Micah again, a little less intensely, and he kissed me. It was a gentle, lingering kiss. If Peter hadn't been watching I might have made it more, but he was, and Edward was taking care of big and scary in the hallway. That left me with not so big, but scary in a very different way. I leaned back to look over my shoulder at Nathaniel. He kissed my cheek, putting his hand against the other side of my face so he could press our faces together. I turned so he could get more of a kiss, but he gave me one of the most delicate, gentlemanly kisses he'd ever given me. I drew back, giving him puzzled eyes. His lavender gaze flicked across the room toward the bed. I got it, and didn't. Something about Peter watching made Nathaniel behave himself, but I didn't know why, or what. I mean it was a kiss, not making out. I pushed the thought away into the crowd of other confusing thoughts. There were so many of them, I felt like I needed a cage to hold them in, so that all the things I didn't understand wouldn't overwhelm me.

I got a better look at Nathaniel's clothes and realized he'd dressed himself almost exactly as he'd dressed me, except his T-shirt was a boy's, and he wasn't wearing any weapons. We looked like we should be going clubbing. Hard to complain about how someone dresses you when they're wearing the same outfit. The clothes were minor problems compared to what was waiting.

I took a deep breath and pushed out of the circle of comforting hands. I moved out of that circle of warmth to face the current confusing thought. This one was staring at me with brown eyes that looked like islands in the pale skin of his face. Peter wasn't naturally pale, not like I was, or Edward was, but he was pale now. Blood loss and pain will do that to you.

I walked toward the bed. In that moment I would rather have faced Peter than Olaf. Was I being a coward, or was Edward the one being the coward? I was betting that he'd rather face a thousand

Olafs than one almost-stepson right now. The look on Peter's face changed as I walked toward the bed. He was still hurt, but his gaze seemed to be drawn to something other than my face. By the time I got to the bedside he wasn't as pale; he'd found enough blood somewhere to blush.

40

"HEY, PETER," I said.

He turned his head so he was looking up at the ceiling. Apparently he didn't trust himself not to stare at my chest and wasn't sure how I'd react. I wasn't sure either. "I thought you were hurt," he said.

"I was."

He turned to look at me, frowning. "But you're up. I feel awful."

I nodded. "I'm a little surprised myself, truthfully."

His gaze had drifted down again. Olaf was crazy and mean, but he was right about one thing. Men would stare, some on purpose to be rude, but not all. Some like Peter, well, it was as if my chest were a magnet and their gaze iron; it just attracted it. I was sooo going to have to talk to Nathaniel about what clothes to pack next time. Next time I got so hurt I ended up unconscious in the hospital. I simply assumed there'd be a next time. Unless I changed jobs, there would be. The thought startled me. Was I thinking about giving up the vampire hunting? Was I really, truly considering it? Maybe, maybe I was. I shook my head and pushed the thought into that cage with all the other thoughts. The cage was getting awfully damn full.

"Anita?" Peter made it a question.

"Sorry, thinking too hard."

"What about?" He was managing eye contact. I felt like I should pet his head and give him a cookie, good boy. God, I was in a strange mood tonight.

"Truthfully, wondering if I want to keep hunting vampires."

His eyes went wide. "What are you talking about? This is what you do."

"No, I raise zombies; the vampire hunting is supposed to be a sideline. Sometimes the zombie thing gets me hurt, but the vampire and rogue lycanthrope hunting are more likely to put me in the hospital. Maybe I'm just tired of waking up with new scars."

"Waking up is good, though," he said, and his voice sounded fragile. He wasn't staring at my face or my chest now. He was looking into the distance, with that look on the face that says you're seeing something unpleasant, reliving it, just a little.

"You didn't think you were going to wake up," I said, and kept my voice gentle.

He looked at me, eyes wide, looking lost, frightened. "No, I thought this was it. I thought . . ." He stopped and he wouldn't meet my eyes.

"You thought you were going to die," I finished for him.

He nodded, then winced as if the movement hurt.

"I knew I wouldn't die, or you. Stomach wounds hurt like hell and they can take a lot of healing, but they're rarely fatal with modern antibiotics and prompt medical attention."

He looked at me, uncomprehending. "Were you really thinking all that as they put you under?"

I thought about it. "Not exactly, but I've been hurt a lot, Peter. I've lost count of the number of times I've lost consciousness and woken up in a hospital, or somewhere worse."

I thought his eyes were on my chest again, but he said, "The scar on your collarbone, what did that?"

Another interesting sideline of wearing this much of my chest in full view was that some of my scars were on display. I'd been more worried about my modesty than about the scars. "Vampire."

"I thought it was a shapeshifter bite."

"Nope, vampire." I showed him my arms with all their scars. "Most of these are from vampires." I touched one on my left arm: claw marks. "This one was a shapeshifted witch, which means her shapeshifting was a spell and not a disease."

"I didn't know there was a difference."

"Well, the spell isn't contagious, and it's not tied to the full moon at all. In fact, strong emotions don't cause you to shift, or any of that. You don't shift until you put on the item, usually a fur belt or something."

"Do you have any scars from shapeshifters?"

"Yes."

"Can I see?"

Truthfully, the most permanent scars were claw marks on my ass. They were almost delicate marks. Gabriel, the wereleopard who had done it, had considered it foreplay before he tried to rape me on film. He'd been the first person I'd ever killed with the big knife in its spine sheath. I was going to have to figure out a different way to wear the knife until I could get the shoulder rig remade. But I had new scars now, ones I was willing to show Peter.

It took a little work to get the T-shirt out of the pants, but somehow I didn't want to unbuckle or unzip anything. I got the shirt up and raised it over my belly, exposing the new wounds.

Peter made a surprised sound. "That can't be real." He whispered it. He reached out as if he'd try to touch, then drew his hand back, as if he wasn't sure what I'd say.

I stepped closer to the bed. He took it as the invitation it was, and ran his fingertips across the new pink scars. "The scars may disappear altogether, or they may stay. I won't know for a few days, or weeks," I said.

He drew his fingers back, then put his whole hand across the biggest wound. The one where it looked as if she had tried to take a chunk of flesh. His hand was big enough to cover the mark and leave his fingers splayed out beyond the scars. "You can't have healed this in less than, what . . . twelve hours. Are you one of them?"

"You mean a shapeshifter?" I asked.

"Yes." He whispered it as if it were a secret. He slid his hand along my stomach, tracing the ragged marks of claws.

"No."

He ran his hand over my skin until he came to the edge of the scars where they dribbled away just past my belly button. "They just changed my dressing. I look like shit. You're healed." He curved his hand around to the side of my waist that wasn't scarred. His hand cupped my waist, and his hand was big enough to do it. That one gesture caught me off guard. The only man I was dating whose hand was big enough to do that was Richard. It seemed wrong that Peter's hand was that big. It made me move back from him and let my shirt drop over my stomach. Which embarrassed him, which wasn't my intent. I just suddenly realized I probably shouldn't let him touch me that much. It hadn't moved me or made me uncomfortable until that moment.

He took his hand back, and again wasted blood that he didn't have in blushing. "Sorry," he mumbled, and wouldn't look at me as he said it.

"It's okay, Peter. No harm, no foul."

He gave me a quick upward glance of his brown eyes. "If you're not a shapeshifter, how could you have healed like that?"

Truthfully, it was probably because I was Jean-Claude's human servant, but since Dolph was wanting to know that, I just didn't want to share it with people who didn't know. "I'm carrying four different kinds of lycanthropy. So far I don't turn furry, but I'm carrying."

"The doctors told me you can't get more than one kind of lycanthropy. That's the point of the shot. The two different kinds of lycanthropy cancel each other out." He stopped at the end of the speech and took a deeper-than-normal breath, as if talking too much hurt.

I patted his shoulder. "Don't talk if it hurts, Peter."

"Everything hurts." He seemed to try to settle into the bed, then stopped as if that had hurt, too. He looked up at me, and the angry, defiant face was like an echo of almost two years ago. The kid I'd met was still in there, he'd just grown up. It made my heart hurt. Would I ever get to see Peter when he wasn't getting hurt? I guess I could just go visit Edward sometime, but that was just weird. We did not just visit each other. We weren't that kind of friends.

"I know it hurts, Peter. I didn't always heal this fast."

"Micah and Nathaniel have been talking to me about weretigers and being a lycanthrope."

I nodded, because I didn't know what else to say. "They'd know."

"Do they all heal as fast as you do?"

"Some, no. Some faster."

"Faster," he said. "Really?"

I nodded.

His eyes filled with something I couldn't decipher. "Cisco didn't heal."

Ah. "No, he didn't."

"If he hadn't thrown himself between me and the . . . weretiger, I'd be dead now."

"You couldn't have taken the damage that Cisco took, that's true."

"You're not going to argue about it. Tell me it wasn't my fault."

"It wasn't your fault," I said.

"But he did it to save me."

"He did it to keep both my guards alive longer. He did it to give us time for other guards to come and help us. He did his job."

"But . . ."

"I was there, Peter. Cisco did his job. He didn't sacrifice himself to save you." I wasn't entirely sure that was true, but I kept talking. "I don't think he meant to sacrifice himself at all. Shapeshifters don't usually die that easily."

"*Easily?* He had his throat ripped out."

"I've seen both vampires and wereanimals heal from wounds like that."

He gave me a disbelieving face.

I crossed my heart and gave the Boy Scout salute.

That made him smile. "You were never a Boy Scout."

"I wasn't even a Girl Scout, but I'm still telling the truth." I smiled, hoping to encourage him to keep doing it.

"Healing like that would be cool."

I nodded. "It is cool, but it's not all cool. There are some serious downsides to being a wereanimal."

"Micah told me some of it. He and Nathaniel have answered a lot of questions."

"They're good at that."

He glanced past me at the door. I glanced where he looked. Micah and Nathaniel had given us as much privacy as they could without leaving the room. They were talking softly together. Cherry had actually left the room. I hadn't heard her go.

"The doctors want me to get the shot," Peter said.

I looked at him. "They would."

"What would you do?" he asked.

I shook my head. "If you're old enough to have saved my life, then you're old enough to decide this on your own."

His face crumbled around the edges, not like he was going to cry, but as if the child was peeking out. Did all teenagers do that? One minute grown-up, the next so fragile like a dream of their younger selves? "I'm just asking your opinion."

I shook my head. "I'd say call your mom, but Edward doesn't want to. He says Donna will vote for the shot."

"She would." He sounded resentful, face sullen. He'd been pretty moody at fourteen; apparently that hadn't changed completely. I wondered how Donna was coping with this new, more grown-up son.

"I'll tell you what I told Edward; I won't give an opinion on this one."

"Micah says that I might not get the tiger lycanthropy even if I don't get the shot."

"He's right."

"He said fifty-five percent of the people who get the shot don't get lycanthropy, but that forty-five percent get lycanthropy. They get what's in the shot, Anita. If I get the shot and catch what's in there, it means if I'd just left it alone I wouldn't have gotten anything."

"I didn't know the stats broke down that nicely, but Micah would know."

"He says it's his job to know."

I nodded. "He takes his job at the coalition as seriously as Edward and I take ours."

"Nathaniel said he's an exotic dancer, is that true?"

"It's true," I said.

He actually lowered his voice to say, "So he's a stripper?"

"Yes," I said and fought not to smile. With everything that was going wrong in his life, he was weirded out that my boyfriend was a stripper. Then I realized that he might not know that Nathaniel was my boyfriend. No, we'd kissed when I came through the door. But then, Cherry had joined the hug. Oh, hell, now was not the time to try to explain my love life to him.

"Micah told me some of the jobs that other lycanthropes have. Nurses, doctors, but only if they don't find out. I might not be able to join the armed forces, any branch."

"They consider lycanthropy a contagious disease, so probably not." In my head I remembered a talk Micah and I had had about a rumor. A rumor about the armed forces looking into deliberate recruiting of shapeshifters. But it was a rumor. He couldn't trace anyone who had actually been approached. It was always a friend of a friend's cousin.

"Did you get the shot?"

"They didn't offer. It's too late for me, Peter. I'm carrying already."

"But you're not a shapeshifter?" He made it a question.

"I don't turn furry once a month, or at all, so no."

"But you're carrying four different kinds at once. The whole shot thing is based on the idea that that's impossible."

I nodded and shrugged. "I'm a medical miracle, what can I say?"

"If I could heal like that and not turn furry, that would be amazing."

"You still wouldn't pass blood screenings for some jobs. You'd still hit the radar as a lycanthrope."

He frowned. "I guess so." Then he gave me that young face again, that echo of before, and it was a frightened face. "Why won't you help me decide?"

I leaned closer. "This is what it means to be grown-up, Peter. This is the bitch of it. If you're playing eighteen, then you have to decide. If you want to fess up to your real age, then everyone will treat you like a kid. They'll make decisions for you."

"I'm not a kid," he said, and he frowned, going sullen on me.

"I know that."

His frown slipped to puzzlement. "What do you mean?"

"You stood your ground today. You didn't panic, or lose it. I've seen grown men lose it around lycanthropes when the situation wasn't as desperate. Most people are afraid of them."

"I was afraid," he said softly. "I've been afraid since I was a kid."

I had one of those moments of, *shit* and *aha*. "The attack on your father," I said. How could I have forgotten that this wasn't the first lycanthropy attack he'd survived?

He gave a small nod.

"You were what, eight?"

"Yes." His voice was soft, his eyes staring into the distance again.

I didn't know what to say. I cursed Edward for not being here. In that moment I might have traded a talk with Olaf for this talk with Peter. I could always shoot Olaf, but no weapon would help me deal with Peter's pain.

"Anita," he said.

I looked at him, met his eyes. His eyes reminded me of Nathaniel's eyes when I first met him. Eyes that were older than they should have been. Eyes that had seen things that older men would never see.

"I'm here, Peter," I said, because I couldn't think what else to say. I met his gaze and fought my face not to show how much it hurt me to see his eyes like that. Maybe they'd been that way years ago, but it took dating Nathaniel to teach me what eyes like that meant in a face that hadn't seen twenty yet.

"I thought if I trained with Edward that I wouldn't be so scared, but I was. I was scared just like last time. It was like I was little and watching my dad die again."

I wanted to touch his shoulder, take his hand, but wasn't sure it was what he needed me to do, so I kept my hands still. "I lost my mom when I was eight to a car wreck."

His eyes changed, lost a little of that awful look. "Were you there? Did you see?"

I shook my head. "No. She drove away and just never came back."

"I saw my dad die. I used to dream about it."

"Me, too."

"But you weren't there; what did you dream about?"

"Some well-meaning relative took me to see the car she died in. I used to dream about touching the bloodstains." I realized I'd never told anyone that.

"What?" he said. "What's wrong?"

I could have said so many things, many of them sarcastic, like *I'm talking about my mother's death, why wouldn't something be wrong?* I settled for the truth, which crosses the lips like jagged glass, as if you should bleed when you say it. "Just realizing I've never told anyone about that dream."

"Not even Micah and Nathaniel?"

Apparently, he did know they were my boyfriends. "No, not even them."

"Mom made me go to therapy afterward. I talked about it a lot."

"Good for Donna," I said.

"Why didn't your dad send you?"

I shrugged. "I don't think it occurred to him."

"I thought I could face my fears, and I wouldn't be so afraid, but I was afraid." He looked away from me again. "I was so scared." He whispered the last.

"So was I," I said.

He gave me a startled look. "You didn't look it."

"Neither did you."

It took him a moment, but he finally smiled and looked down in that pleased way that young men do. They seem to grow out of it, but it was strangely charming. "You really think so?"

"Peter, you saved me today when you jumped on us in the hallway. She was going to kill me as soon as she was out of sight of you guys."

"Edward told me that if a bad guy wants to remove you from the scene, and is already threatening or has a weapon, that most of the time they mean to kill you, but if you go with them, you die slower and more painfully."

I nodded. "I thought that's what you meant when you repeated the rule in the hallway."

"You understood," he said.

"I encouraged you, remember?"

He searched my face, as if trying to read something there. "You did, didn't you?"

"Edward and I know a lot of the same rules."

"He said you think like him."

"Sometimes," I said.

"Not always," Peter said.

"Not always," I said.

"I won't get the shot," he said, and his voice sounded firm.

"Why not?" I asked.

"Do you think I should get it?"

"I didn't say that, I just want your reasoning."

"If I don't get it, and I turn into a weretiger, well, then I did it saving you. If I don't get the shot, and I don't turn into a weretiger, then it's good. If I get the shot and I wasn't going to be a weretiger, I'll get whatever's in the shot, and I'll have turned into a shapeshifter because I was scared to be a shapeshifter. That sounds stupid."

"But if you are going to be a weretiger, then the shot would stop it from happening."

"You think I should take it," he said.

I sighed. "Honest?"

"Honest would be good," he said.

"I didn't like the way you said that if you turn into a weretiger, it's good because you did it saving me. I don't want you to think about me in this equation. I want you be a selfish son of a bitch, Peter. I want you to think about yourself and yourself alone. What do you want to do? What feels right to you?"

"Honest?" he said.

"Yeah, honest," I said.

"I think I've made up my mind, then I go back and change it. I think if I decided, and they had the shot here and ready, I'd just take it, but they won't bring it until I say so." He closed his eyes. "Part of me wants to call my mom and let her decide for me. Part of me wants someone to blame if it goes wrong, but a man doesn't do that. A man makes his own decisions."

"In this situation, yes. But don't imprint that whole lone gunman mentality too deep on your psyche."

"Why?" he asked.

I smiled. "I know from experience that it's hard to be part of a couple when you're so damned independent. I've had to learn how to share my decisions. Balance is what you're looking for."

"I don't know how to balance anything anymore," and his eyes were shiny.

"Peter, I . . ."

"Go, okay?" he said, in a voice that was too thick. "Just go, please."

I almost reached out and touched his shoulder. I wanted to comfort him. Hell, I wanted to go back in time and put his ass back on a plane home as soon as he showed up in St. Louis. I wished I had humiliated him and sent him packing. Wasn't a bruised ego better than this?

Hands came and touched me, drew me back from the bed. Micah and Nathaniel drew me away so Peter could cry without me watching. My throat was so tight it hurt to breathe. Fuck, fuck, fuck.

They got me outside in the hallway before the first tear slid hot and almost painful down my own face. "Damn it," I said.

Micah tried to hug me, but I pushed him away. "I'll cry if you hug me."

"Anita, just let it out."

I shook my head. "No, don't you understand. We have to kill her first. I'll cry when Mercia's dead."

"You blame her for Peter being hurt," he said.

"No, I blame me, and Edward, but I can't kill us, so I'll kill who I can."

"If you're going to talk about killing people, Anita, you might not want to do it in front of a policeman." Zerbrowski walked down the hallway with his usual smile. He looked as he always did, like he'd slept in his suit, though I knew he hadn't. His dark curly hair had more gray in it, but it was still the careless curls. Katie, his wife, hadn't made him cut it recently. He was cheerfully messy, and Katie was one of the neatest people I'd ever met. Opposites attract.

I had a horrible urge to hug him. He just looked so nicely normal coming down the hallway. Which made me turn to Micah and Nathaniel. If I was thinking about falling into Zerbrowski's arms, I was badly in need of a hug. All three of them had seen me cry before, including Zerbrowski.

I threw an arm around Micah, then held the other one out to Nathaniel. I let them hold me, but I didn't cry. My face felt hot, but no more tears came. I clung to them, let them hold me. I had this horrible urge to simply collapse, to just fall apart in their arms, but I couldn't do it. I couldn't let myself do it.

"I'll give you some privacy," Zerbrowski said.

I shook my head and drew back from the men. "No, we have to catch this bitch."

"No one's seen her, Anita. Her or the man who we assume is her human servant."

"He has to be her human servant to share her mind powers, Zerbrowski." I tried to move farther away, but Nathaniel's arm slipped around my shoulders, drawing me back. I patted his arm and said, "I'm okay now."

He whispered, "Liar, but maybe it's me who needs to touch you." He squeezed me tight, his other arm sliding around my waist. "You've got to stop almost dying, Anita; it's hard on the heart."

Somehow I didn't think he meant hard as in a heart attack. There were so many more ways for a heart to break. I let him press me back against his body. I stroked my hands down his arms.

Zerbrowski shook his head, smiled. "You know, Katie feels the same way after I get hurt, but she's too cool to do it in public."

I looked at him, and it wasn't an entirely friendly look.

He held up his hands. "It wasn't a criticism, Anita, Nathaniel. It's just, well, hell, I mean it's interesting watching people be as open as you guys are. Is it a shapeshifter culture thing?"

I thought about it. "Yeah, I guess it is."

"If we don't have to play human," Micah said, "we're very touchy-feely, and we tend to wear our emotions out."

Zerbrowski grinned. "Damn, that must have been an adjustment for you, Anita."

"What's that supposed to mean?"

"It means you're like most cops I know—you stuff your emotions. Does this mean if the boyfriends aren't around at a crime scene some night, I can look forward to you hanging all over me?"

"You wish," I said, and smiled at him. I patted Nathaniel's arm and took a step forward. He let me draw a little farther away from him, but kept my hand. I understood the need to touch and be touched. It wasn't just the normal lycanthropy stuff. I wanted to hug Peter as if he were a little boy, and tell him it would all be all right, but it was a lie. Even if he'd been a little boy, it would still have been a lie. I couldn't promise him anything.

"That's an awful serious face for a woman who just got a hug from her sweetie."

"I'm thinking about Peter."

"Yeah, you got cut up trying to save him."

I fought to keep my face neutral. If we were going to change the story for the police, then Edward should have told me. That he didn't tell me the "official" version, and I hadn't asked, said just how distracted the two of us were. Not good.

"You saved his life, Anita. That's the best you could do," Zerbrowski said.

I nodded, and went for a hug from Micah, partially to hide my face, because I still couldn't quite figure out how to look. My guilt was because Peter had gotten cut up saving me. He wouldn't even get credit for it from the cops. That seemed like insult to injury.

Micah kissed the side of my face and whispered, "Edward didn't tell you the official version?"

"No," I whispered back.

Micah spoke with me still in his arms. "I think Anita also blames herself because she was already hunting the vampires. She thinks they might not have reacted so violently if they hadn't known she was on their trail."

I turned, still half in Micah's arms. "When a person knows that they're being tracked by someone who can kill them on sight, Zerbrowski, what options does that leave them?"

"Are you saying you disagree with the execution order?" he asked.

"No, not in this case, but there are nights when I wish I had an option that was less than lethal force. I'd love someone to do a study and see if the vampires get more violent in trying to stay alive than in the crimes they were originally condemned for."

"Have you had that happen?" Zerbrowski asked.

"No, no, I guess I haven't. Most of them would have kept killing if we hadn't stopped them. But, still, the vamp we're hunting framed a vampire from the Church of Eternal Life. She helped frame two of them. If I had just followed the trail they mapped out for us, I'd have killed two innocent people."

"Isn't this the second time you've had the bad vampires frame the good vampires and try to use you as a murder weapon?"

"Yes," I said, "it is, and if it's happening to me, then it may be happening to other vampire executioners. But they may not be looking beyond the obvious."

"You mean because they aren't up close and personal with the vampires, they just accept that a good vampire is a dead vampire."

"Yeah."

Zerbrowski frowned at me. "Dolph isn't the only one who thinks you living with the . . ."—he made a vague gesture at Nathaniel and Micah—"compromises your ability to do your job. But I don't think it does; I think it makes you look at the vampires and shapeshifters the way the law says we're supposed to now. They're supposed to be legal citizens, people, and you see them that way. It's what makes it harder and harder for you to kill them, but it makes you a better cop. You look for the truth, catch the real bad guy, punish the guilty. The other executioners kill who they're told to kill. It makes them good killers, but I'm not sure what good cops they are."

It was a long speech for Zerbrowski. "You've put some thought into this."

He actually looked embarrassed. "I guess I have. I spend a lot of time defending your honor with the other cops."

"I can defend my own honor," I said.

He grinned again. "No, you can't. You can't explain that you see the monsters as people without implying that the bigoted bastard that just said the stupid thing doesn't see them as people. I can get away with it. I'm Zerbrowski, I can say a lot of shit and not make people mad. I go for the funny bone, you go for the jugular. It makes people pissy."

"He really does know you well," Micah said.

I drew away enough to look back at him. "What the hell does that mean?"

He grinned at me. I found Nathaniel fighting not to grin. They were all grinning at me. "What?"

My cell phone rang, and then I realized I didn't have it on me. It rang again, and it was the ring tone that Nathaniel had picked for my phone when I said I didn't care. It was "Wild Boys" by Duran Duran. I'd remember to care next time he asked. Micah fished the phone out of his pocket and handed it to me.

I didn't have time to ask when he'd picked up my phone. I just answered it. "Hello."

A male voice said, "I do not have much time." The voice was familiar, but it was a strange monotone that made it sound like someone I should recognize and a stranger all at the same time. "The Harlequin are at my church."

I started walking down the hallway away from everyone else. It was Zerbrowski I didn't want to overhear, not until I knew that I wanted the police to know. "Malcolm, is this you?"

The voice continued as if I hadn't spoken, "Columbine says she will blood-oath my congregation or she will battle me with vampire powers, for it is not illegal for a vampire to use vampire wiles on another vampire. She claims to have done nothing illegal in our country. She blames all crime on her dead partner. I cannot win against her, Anita, but I can give my congregation to Jean-Claude. Blood-oath them any way you like, but save them from the madness I sense in these two, Columbine and Giovanni. Give me permission to tell them they must duel Jean-Claude for these vampires, and not me."

"Malcolm, is this you?"

The voice changed, holding fear. "What's happening? Who is this?"

"Avery, Avery Seabrook?" I made it a question, though I was almost a hundred percent certain it was him. I could see his gentle brown eyes, the short hair, that young, unfinished face. He was in his twenties, but tasted too innocent for comfort.

"Anita, is that you?"

"It's me. What happened? What's happening right now?"

"Malcolm touched me and I don't remember what happened next. I just sort of woke up on my cell phone in the back of the church." His voice dropped to a whisper. "There are masked vampires here. I don't know them. Malcolm seems afraid of them."

"You're blood-oathed to Jean-Claude, they can't hold you."

"What is going on, Anita?"

What was I supposed to say, *You're such a weak vamp that Malcolm mind-fucked you like you were a human?* He sounded scared enough without me making him feel weaker. "Malcolm sent me a message."

"What?" Then there was noise on the other end. I heard Avery's voice, a little distant, as if he'd taken the phone from his mouth to talk to someone there.

"Avery?"

The voice that came on wasn't Avery, or Malcolm. "Who is speaking, please?" It was male, and I didn't know the voice.

"I don't answer your questions, you answer mine."

"Are you police?" he asked.

"Yes." It was the truth.

"We are breaking none of your laws."

"You're trying to take over the Church of Eternal Life here in my town. I'd say that's illegal."

"We have offered no violence to anyone. This will be a contest of wills and magical power. It is not illegal to use vampire powers on other vampires in your country. We will not use our powers on the humans here. I give you my word."

"How about the vampires? They're legal citizens of this country, too."

"We will offer them no weapon, no hand of violence. Your laws protect only humans from vampire powers. In fact, the law could be interpreted to exclude all supernatural citizens from the protection the law gives against vampire manipulation."

"Lycanthropes are still considered human under the letter of the law."

"If you say so."

"I say so. Give me your name," I said.

"I am known as Giovanni. I would like to know who I am speaking with."

Frankly, I wasn't sure that he'd treat me like a cop, or like Jean-Claude's human servant. I wasn't even sure which role would work best here. "I'm Federal Marshal Anita Blake."

"Ah, the Master of the City's human servant."

"Yeah, that, too."

"We have done nothing, my mistress and I, to anger you in either of your roles."

That was a little too close for comfort to what I'd just been thinking. Had he read my mind, and me not know it? Shit.

"If Columbine is your mistress, then yeah, she did piss me off."

"We read your laws, Marshal. Columbine used her powers on you, your master, and his wolf. She did not use her powers on humans."

"She and her friend Nivia framed two legal citizen vampires for murder, and two humans died to do that."

"Nivia did that on her own. My mistress was most upset when she found that Nivia had done these horrible things." He didn't even try to keep his voice from sounding fake.

He knew I couldn't prove beyond a shadow of a doubt that it hadn't been just Nivia, who was conveniently dead. It was her weretiger that had tried to kill Peter, a human. Again, conveniently dead.

"Son of a bitch," I said, softly.

"Excuse me, Marshal."

"I have a warrant of execution and it works just fine for you and your mistress."

"But if you use it knowing that we did not do these crimes, then you are a murderer. Perhaps you will never be tried as such, but you will know that you have abused your powers and simply killed to protect your master like a good human servant, but not a very good federal marshal."

"You've done your homework," I said.

Micah was beside me now. I held up a hand so he wouldn't try to talk to me. I glanced back and found Nathaniel still talking to Zerbrowski. Whatever he was saying had the sergeant's full attention.

"We know you are honorable, and your master is honorable. We will not harm Malcolm or his people. We will simply challenge him for them, and use only legal means to win the challenge."

"Avery Seabrook is already blood-oathed to Jean-Claude. He's off limits."

"Very well, but the others are no one's flock."

"Malcolm gave them to Jean-Claude. We haven't blood-oathed them yet, but they are ours."

"Lies do not become you, Marshal Blake."

"Can you taste a lie in my voice?"

"I have that ability."

"Fine, then listen carefully, Giovanni. Malcolm gave his entire congregation to Jean-Claude and me. They belong to the Master of the City of St. Louis now. You can defeat Malcolm with your vampire wiles, but it won't win you shit. By vampire law you have to defeat the master that owns them before you can oath them to you."

He was quiet for a second. I heard him breathing, which isn't a vampire thing. He was human, somehow; he was her human servant. He had more powers than most human servants, but then so did I.

"I hear truth in your words. But I heard truth in Malcolm's speech to my mistress only moments ago. She forced him to tell truthfully if Jean-Claude had a claim to his congregation. He said Jean-Claude did not."

"You underestimated Malcolm's powers, Giovanni. He got a message to us, and you have a church full of legal American citizens with rights. You have a church full of vampires who belong to the Master of the City of St. Louis, and they have rights under vampire law, too. You've been very careful that my status as a police officer isn't invoked here. I'll hold you to vampire law just as tight as human law. You break either of them, and I will rain all over your parade."

"But as the laws constrain us, they also constrain you, Anita Blake."

"Yeah, yeah, you and the horse you rode in on."

"I don't understand. We have no horses."

"Sorry, it's slang. I mean that I understand what you said, and I'm not impressed."

"Malcolm used your young vampire here to somehow give you this message, didn't he?"

"I don't have to give you information, not by either set of laws."

"True," he said, "but if my mistress blood-oaths enough of these vampires, then she will have enough power to defeat Jean-Claude."

"You're Harlequin. You can't kill anyone without giving them a black mask first."

"We are not attacking as Harlequin. My mistress has grown weary of being a tool for the council. She wishes to have her own lands in this new country of yours. Jean-Claude was harder to destroy with vampire powers than she anticipated."

"You're supposed to give a formal challenge before you start battling to take over."

"Did Jean-Claude give a formal challenge to Nikolaos, the old Master of the City, before you slew her for him?"

I took a breath, then didn't try to say anything. Truthfully, I hadn't realized that killing Nikolaos would make him master. I'd just been trying to stay alive and keep her from killing other people. But it had opened the way for Jean-Claude to own the city. Saying it had been an accident would make us sound weak. So I shut my mouth and tried to think.

Micah was on his own cell phone. I heard him say, "Jean-Claude." Had Micah heard enough to tell Jean-Claude what he needed to know?

"I'll take that as a no," Giovanni said.

"I thought the Harlequin couldn't have a territory of their own. They're supposed to be neutral."

"We grow weary of this wandering life. We wish for a home."

"You could petition Jean-Claude to join his kiss."

"My mistress wishes to rule, not to serve."

I started walking toward the exit. Whatever we were going to do, we needed to be at that church. We needed to stop whatever they had planned. Somehow I didn't think they were done with their bid for power in St. Louis.

"The council has forbidden war between master vamps in America right now."

"Only if the fight cannot be kept secret. My master is confident this will be settled tonight, quietly."

"Overconfidence, Giovanni, it'll get you killed."

Nathaniel was alone at the end of the hallway. I didn't know where Zerbrowski had run off to, but it was just as well. I wasn't sure what my face looked like, but I knew I didn't look happy. I didn't want to lie to him, and so far this was a party for monsters, not cops.

"We will try our powers against each vampire here in turn. Those that cannot withstand us will be blood-oathed to Columbine."

"You can't blood-oath someone else's vamps, it's against the rules."

"Think of it as the beginning of the duel between your master and mine." The phone went dead.

"Shit," I said.

Micah handed me his phone. "It's Jean-Claude. I've told him it's the Harlequin, and it's the church."

I took the phone and started talking. Jean-Claude listened and asked a few questions here and there. Maybe he felt my urgency over the phone, or maybe he'd spent too many centuries dealing with exactly this kind of shit.

"Will you bring human police?"

"I'll bring Edward and Olaf, but I don't know about the rest. I can't prove they've broken any human laws."

"I will leave it to your discretion whether a lie would be useful here."

"You mean use the warrant even if I'm not certain she did it?"

"It is your honor that is at stake, not my own. I will call the were-animals and my vampires. Be careful, *ma petite*."

"You, too." He hung up.

I stopped walking. My pulse was suddenly in my throat. Panic screamed through me. I was sure, certain, I would get everyone killed. If I took the cops, they'd die. If I didn't invite the cops, my other friends would die. I couldn't do this.

I looked at Micah. "This could turn into a hostage situation, and I'm not trained for that. They've got a few hundred people in there; what if I get them killed? What if I make the wrong choice?"

Micah searched my face with his gaze. "First, you need to shield better, because this kind of self-doubt isn't like you. Second, she doesn't want them dead. She wants to blood-oath them, and that means she wants them healthy."

I nodded. "You're right, you're right." The tremble of panic in my gut was still there. He was so right. I'd had vampires mess with my mind before in all sorts of ways, but Mercia's power was almost the most awful. Because it made you have to feel your own emotions intensified until you almost couldn't stand it. I think I'd have rather dealt with a good old-fashioned attempt to control me with her thoughts than this emotional rape.

"Why isn't it affecting you?" I asked.

"I don't think she's targeted me yet."

"She targeted Graham. How did she know to target him?"

"Soledad scouted for her, maybe," he said.

I nodded. "Right, right."

Nathaniel came up to us, alone. I asked, "Where did Zerbrowski go?"

"I got him talking about the party at his house. I asked what food his wife wanted us to bring. I think he's more worried about you bringing us both to the party than he admits, because it distracted him from your super-secret phone call. What's really happening?"

I told him. "I'm afraid no matter what cops I send in, she'll mindfuck them. It's so subtle, she just emphasizes what you're already feeling. It seems not to activate the holy items."

"Because she's not adding anything," Nathaniel said.

"What?" I asked; we all looked at him.

"She's not putting power into you, she's giving more power to what's already inside you. Maybe that's why the holy objects don't go off?"

I smiled at him. "When did you get so smart?"

He shrugged, but looked pleased.

"What if we call out Mobile Reserve and she fucks their minds? I can't guarantee that she won't turn them against each other, or more likely the congregation, and once I call them, they sort of take over. I'll lose control of the situation."

"I'm not sure you have control of the situation now," Micah said.

"Thanks," I said.

He touched my shoulder, gently. "Anita, what you're really trying to decide is, is it the police you need to be backup, or is it Jean-Claude's vampires and our shapeshifters?"

I nodded. "You're right, you are exactly right. That is what I'm trying to decide."

"Won't Zerbrowski and the rest of the uniforms suspect something when you run out of here?" Nathaniel asked.

"I have nearly total discretion on how any warrant of execution is served. I don't have to include any other police. But the Harlequin have fixed it so that the warrant really isn't in effect here."

"It's a shame you can't deputize civilians, like in the old movies," Nathaniel said.

I had the grace to look embarrassed. "I was sort of disappointed I couldn't do that, too. It would have been so damn convenient."

"Whatever you are going to do, it has to be done now," Micah said.

I felt paralyzed. I couldn't decide. It wasn't like me in an emergency. I stepped away from both of them so they weren't touching me. I took a deep calming breath, and another. All I could think about was how I'd almost gotten Peter killed. He might be a lycanthrope, at sixteen. Would I get Malcolm killed? I didn't want to risk anyone else. I couldn't bear the thought of Zerbrowski dead and having to face his family. I couldn't . . .

Hands grabbed me, and I was suddenly staring up into Nathaniel's face. "I can feel it," he said. "She's shoving doubt into you." His hands gripped my arms tight, his face was so intense. I was suddenly filled with certainty. A certainty built of unshakable faith. He believed in me. He believed in me utterly and completely. I tried to be frightened that anyone would believe so perfectly in me, but the fear could not last on the tide of his belief. He simply knew that I would do what was right. He knew that I would save Malcolm. He knew that I would punish the bad and save the good. He simply believed. It was one of the most comforting things I'd ever felt. There was a small part of me that screamed in the background, *His faith isn't in God, it's in you.* Again, I tried to be afraid, or struggle against it, but I couldn't. I felt his certainty, and there was no room for doubt in it.

I stared up at him and smiled. "Thank you," I said.

He gave me that smile, the one that he might have had if his life had been gentler. It was a smile that he'd only found in the last few months. I'd helped him find that smile. Me, and Micah.

Micah came to stand close to us but made no move to touch. "The power is coming off you in waves. It feels similar to what happens when you touch Damian, sometimes."

I nodded and looked back at Nathaniel. I'd never wondered what I'd gained from Nathaniel being my animal to call. Damian, as my vampire servant, gave me his control, honed over centuries of being at the mercy of one of the most sadistic vampire masters I'd ever heard of, which was saying something pretty terrible. I'd never thought to ask what Jean-Claude gained from Richard. From me, a certain ruthlessness; we sort of doubled our natural practicality. When we'd all survived tonight, I'd ask what he gained from Richard. But in that moment, I simply kissed the man in my arms. Kissed him not for lust, though that was always there, but because no one else could have made me believe in myself.

41

I THOUGHT I'D have trouble ditching the police, but no one wanted to play with me. I got nervous glances from some of them, or ignored, or even downright hostile stares. No one questioned where I was going with Micah and Nathaniel. None of the officers were ones that I knew well, but it was still unnerving. Helpful, in that moment, but it didn't bode well for future police work.

"They think you're one of us," Micah whispered.

"And it makes that much difference to them?" I said.

"Apparently, yes," he said.

Nathaniel hugged me one-armed as we walked past the people who had come here because a cop had been hurt. They'd come because I was one of them. The looks on their faces said, clearly, that I wasn't one of them anymore. Did it hurt my feelings? Yeah, it did. But I'd worry about my reputation later; right now there was a fight to finish.

I realized I was about to walk out without the only police backup I'd be taking: Edward and, oddly, Olaf. I didn't want to be in a car with Olaf. The space was too small to share with him. As if I'd thought too hard about him, he walked through the doors of the exit. Edward was right behind him, but for a moment Olaf looked at me. For a moment I saw his eyes bare, no hiding. The look in his eyes, on his face, stopped my breath in my throat. There were so many things to be afraid of tonight, but in that instant I was afraid of Olaf, truly and completely afraid.

Micah started to step in front of me, doing that guy-protection thing. With almost anyone else, I'd have let him do it, but not for Olaf. I moved so that Micah was beside me, where he'd started. I stepped out in front of both my men, so that the only target for Olaf's eyes was me. Me, he liked; he didn't like my boyfriends. They were just in his way. Call it a hunch, but I was betting that people who were just in Olaf's way didn't last long.

His eyes changed from that look that would haunt me to something that was almost, almost, admiration. In some strange way I understood him better than most. Edward understood him, too. It should have worried both of us that we understood someone like Olaf.

Edward hurried to get ahead of the bigger man. He was talking as he walked. "I think you need to get out there and rescue your friend from the lieutenant."

"What friend?"

"Graham," he said, and Edward's eyes melted around the edges, showing me the anger that was underneath. Anger about Peter, anger about Olaf, anger about what? I couldn't ask, and when I got a chance later, he'd probably lie anyway.

Edward took my arm, something he had never done that I could remember. He took me by the elbow like I was a girl and needed to be led. I might have protested, except I caught sight of Olaf's face. He watched Edward touch me, touch me like I was a girl, which he'd never seen before, because it wasn't how Edward touched me, ever. I was a lot of things to Edward, but I was never a girl. Edward led me past the looming presence of Olaf. Micah and Nathaniel trailed us. Olaf watched us with a considering look on his face. I was through the doors and into the cold of the parking lot beyond before I realized that Edward had done what I wouldn't let Micah do: he'd protected me, put himself between me and Olaf. It hadn't been as obvious as Micah's attempt, but I didn't pull free of Edward even after I figured it out. Of all the men I knew, Edward could handle himself, even against giant-sized serial killers.

Graham was a big guy, knew it, liked it. But standing beside Dolph, he looked small. It made me wonder for a second how tiny I must look standing beside Dolph. Edward let go of my elbow as we got to the argument. It wasn't quite a fight, yet, but it had the feel of something that might turn into one. We didn't have time for this shit. Jean-Claude and his vampires were on their way to the church. We had to go.

"Since when does a federal marshal need a bodyguard?" Dolph asked, his voice deepening with anger. His big hands were already curled into fists.

The energy of Graham's beast was trailing the air like tiny, searching hands. Pats and tickles of energy touched my skin. Nathaniel shivered beside me. Micah would control it better, but he'd feel it, too. The fact that it was only small touches of power meant Graham was really fighting to control himself. I wasn't so sure the same could be said of Dolph.

Edward let me walk a little ahead of everyone so that I stood just out of reach, but close enough to be heard by Dolph and Graham.

"Hey, Dolph, I'll take Graham off your hands."

Dolph gave me a glance, but didn't seem to want to look away from the man in front of him. I'd seen him try to pick a fight once with Jason. It hadn't worked, because Jason didn't get upset that easily. Graham did.

Detective Smith walked up beside me. He was rubbing his arms, as if he were cold. It was December, but it wasn't that kind of cold. Smith was psychically gifted, no specific ability that I knew of, but he sensed lycanthropes and other otherworldly stuff. Standing out here with an arguing werewolf had probably not been comfy for him, but Smith was a good sport.

"Lieutenant, I think Marshal Blake is leaving. She'll take her guard with her, and that way you won't have to worry about what he's doing here." Smith made his voice light, trying to sound harmless. He was pretty good at harmless, not much taller than me, blond hair, young for his age. He was the newest detective on the squad. Where was Zerbrowski? He was the best at managing Dolph's moods.

"I want to know why a federal marshal needs a bodyguard," Dolph said through gritted teeth.

Graham looked at me. The look said, *What do I say?*

Unless I was willing to fess up to being Jean-Claude's human servant or Richard's lupa, I didn't know what to say. I seldom lie well if I don't see the lie coming a long way off.

Micah stepped into the charged silence. "It's my fault, Lieutenant. I love her, and she almost died. I'm sorry if my hiring Graham to be by her side upset you, but I know you're married. I'm sure you understand how frightened I was when I saw her lying in that bed." Sometimes I forgot how smoothly Micah could lie. Of course, the only real lie in the mix was that he had hired Graham personally. The rest was probably true.

"You aren't married to Anita."

"Micah's been living with me for seven months."

"Talk to me when you've made a year," he said.

"You were always onto me to find a steady boyfriend who had a pulse. I found one, so now what's your problem?"

"When did humans stop being good enough for you, Anita?"

I shook my head and made a push-away gesture. "I'm not having this fight tonight, Dolph. Come on, Graham, let's go."

We went. Dolph didn't have any reason to hold us, except his hatred of the monsters. But being hated isn't against the law. Good to know.

42

EDWARD DROVE INTO the parking lot of the Church of Eternal Life, with Olaf riding beside him. I'd opted to sit in the middle seat with Micah and Nathaniel. Graham was in the back by himself. Edward hadn't even questioned why I let Olaf ride shotgun. I think he didn't want to watch Olaf stare at me either. It takes a lot to creep out Edward, but whatever Olaf had done while I was cut open had done it.

The parking lot was so full that we had to park illegally, close to the small green area with its benches and growing trees. In the December cold it was a bleak little space, or maybe my reaction was partly that the last time I'd stepped on the church's grass I'd shot a vampire to death with a handgun. It takes longer with a handgun. They tend to squirm and cry. Not one of my best memories. I shivered in the short leather jacket that Nathaniel had brought for me. The jacket would have been warmer if I'd been willing to zip it up, but I wanted to be able to get to my weapons more than I wanted to be warm.

You could tell who was carrying weapons by whose coat was flapping open in the winter cold. Nathaniel was zipped tight, but he'd continued his matching theme with his short leather jacket, so we still looked like we were going to a Goth club prom. The disturbing part was that Olaf matched us: black on black, leather jacket, boots.

Nathaniel had zipped up, Olaf hadn't. Micah had belted his lined trench coat. Graham's leather was fastened tight, too.

The church rose above us white and bare. The lack of decoration always made the church seem unfinished to me. No holy objects allowed when most of your congregation are vampires.

We walked up those wide, white steps to the double doors. Graham insisted on opening the doors for us. I didn't have patience to argue, and I was pretty certain Edward didn't argue because he knew cannon fodder when he saw it. He was hard-to-kill cannon fodder, but Graham wasn't armed, and I wasn't in love with him. From Edward's point of view it changed how he would treat him. Truthfully, me, too. I wanted everyone to come out alive tonight, but if it came to choices, who you loved counted. If you're not willing to admit that out loud inside your own head, then you should stay out of firefights and keep your family at home. Be honest, who would you save? Who would you sacrifice? We let Graham swing wide those double doors. He didn't even try to take cover. He stood framed in the light, his body dark with that nimbus of brightness around it. He turned back to me with a smile, as if he'd done a good thing. I said a prayer that Graham didn't get himself killed tonight. Yeah, we were supposed to be doing metaphysical battle, no weapons, but there were ways to kill with metaphysics. I'd seen it done. Hell, I'd done it a time or two. Illegal, that, if it's a human that dies. I won't tell if you won't.

Nathaniel reached for my left hand. He was warm, warmer than he should have been, fever warm, but there was no sweat on his palm. It wasn't nerves. It was power. It climbed up my arm, across my body in a wave of heat that made my skin dance in goose bumps. I made a small stumble on the steps. Micah grabbed my arm. He meant it to be helpful, but the power leapt from me to him. And it wasn't a power meant for him. Damian was meant to be on the other side of me for this. He was meant to cool this fire, but Micah's was never a magic that cooled me down. The power found the only thing it could recognize. It found his beast. I could actually see his leopard roaring up inside him like a black flame, roaring to life, spilling upward inside him. Micah could control it, but the velvet pouring of his beast brought mine. I was caught between two wereleopards. There was no other animal to distract my beasts.

I almost screamed it. "Not now!"

Olaf's deep voice said, "What is that?"

I didn't have time to look around and see if there was something else coming. Edward would take care of it. I believed that.

Micah managed to tear himself away from my arm. He went to his knees on the steps, as if he were having more trouble than normal controlling his own beast. It wasn't close to full moon. It shouldn't have been such an effort.

Graham was coming toward us. He was coming in a blur of speed, but my leopard was rising faster. It was tearing its way up through my body. I needed to cool this heat. I almost reached for Jean-Claude. He was vampire. He was the chill of the grave, but he never affected me that way. He was always passion to me. I needed to think. I reached for my other vampire. I reached out to Damian. I reached out with desperation. I screamed in my head, *Save me, save us, kill this heat.*

I felt him stagger when my call hit him. I knew someone grabbed his arm to keep him from falling. But my power hit him, and he gave me what I demanded. He gave me that coolness. That utter control that he had learned in years of servitude to the master that created him. He gave me the control that had helped him survive, and betray nothing by thought, word, deed, or glance. He gave me that control in a sweep of cold, steely willpower.

The visual in my head was of my leopard finding a metal wall in her path. She snarled at it and reacted like any self-respecting leopard would if a giant wall suddenly appeared in the forest path. She ran. The leopard ran back the way she had come, to hide in that empty, full, dark place where all the beasts seemed to wait inside me. It was like the blackness of space before the light found it, except it was inside me somewhere. I don't explain the show, sometimes I just watch it.

A woman's voice, half singing, beautiful and pure and strangely joyous, spoke from inside the open doors. "Let it begin at last, our contest, Jean-Claude. Your servant has struck the first blow."

I yelled, "It was an accident." But it was too late. I had done metaphysics. Either she didn't realize how little control I had over some of my powers, or she was using it as an excuse to start the fight. Either way, shit.

Graham offered me his hand, and I took it. He dragged me and Nathaniel up off the steps. His hand in mine was just a hand, just warmth. Maybe he wasn't armed, and maybe he didn't understand how to take cover, but in that moment no one else with us could have dragged me to my feet without complicating things. I looked up and found Edward with his hand on Olaf's stomach, or lower chest. Olaf would have helped me off the steps, and Edward had stopped it. He looked at me, and the look was enough. They weren't psychic enough to tell the difference between beasts rising and the *ardeur* rising, not in its early stages. Edward didn't want to have it spread to him, and he was going to make certain it didn't spread to Olaf. I pushed the thought away, into that crowded cage that all the other thoughts had gone into for the last few days and hours. *Think about it later.* We were running up the steps. Graham had my right hand, but we weren't supposed to be pulling guns tonight, right?

43

FACES TURNED TO us as we stumbled through the door. There was no vestibule, so the three of us were just suddenly in view of the crowd. Nathaniel and I were breathing as if we'd run a mile. Only Graham was calm at my side. Edward and Olaf fanned out to either side of us. Micah moved wide around us all. Was he still fighting off his beast? I trusted him to handle it. I had to trust him, because there were things happening that I didn't trust anyone else to handle.

The area behind the pulpit had become a stage. There were three people on stage in masks. What could only be Columbine and Giovanni were to the left. She was elegant in a skintight version of the Harlequin's motley, all red, blue, white, black, and gold with a short half skirt to pretend at modesty. A gold tricorn hat had multicolored balls to echo the colors of the rest. Her mask left a white chin and crimson mouth bare. The man beside her was much taller than she was, dressed in a white mask like the one they'd sent us in the first box. His face was an empty blankness trapped in the black hooded cloak that covered him to his ankles. A black tricorn hat completed the outfit. They stood in a contrast of bright and dark, color and not.

The third masked figure was on our side of the stage, standing beside Jean-Claude and his vampires. Damian and Malcolm were close at his side, behind Asher. But the last masked figure wasn't a vampire.

He looked more like he was about to do bondage than go to Carnival. The mask was leather and hid most of the face, covering even the back of the head, a hood instead of a mask. It was the broad shoulders framed by the leather vest, and the slightly paler version of his summer tan, that let me know it was Richard. He'd come to stand at Jean-Claude's side after all. Jake and some of the other bodyguard werewolves stood behind him.

Asher stood on the other side of Jean-Claude, his hair catching the lights like spun gold. Remus and a handful of other werehyenas stood behind him. Most of Jean-Claude's vampires were scattered around the stage. But Elinore and a few others weren't there because Jean-Claude had made them stay away. If we died tonight and managed to take the Harlequin with us, he trusted Elinore to rebuild the city's vampires. Truth and Wicked were there, along with Haven and his werelions. Rafael and his wererats were there, on the stage. There was an ocean of wereanimals around our side of the stage. The two Harlequin looked so outnumbered. Part of me was sad that it wasn't going to be a stand-up fight. It looked like we might win that kind of fight. Of course, the Harlequin standing in the church had scouted us; they knew our resources. Maybe there was more than one reason they'd offered a metaphysical fight instead of a physical one.

My pulse had started to slow. We started up the aisle, Graham a little ahead of us all, Nathaniel and I still hand in hand. Micah was still giving us room. I'd have loved to touch him, but he was right. We didn't need another visit from our leopards. Edward and Olaf brought up the rear. I thought we'd get to the stage. I thought I'd get to touch Jean-Claude, and Damian, but Columbine thought otherwise.

Her power poured over the congregation like invisible smoke. My breath caught in my throat. I felt her power touch some of the vampires. They were choking on her power. I was choking on her power. I dropped Nathaniel's hand and grabbed for the back of a pew. Whatever was happening, I didn't want it spreading to Nathaniel.

"Anita," he said, "what's wrong? I feel power, but . . ."

I shook my head. I couldn't talk past the feel of her power. It was almost delicate, like choking on feathers; light, airy, and deadly. Vampires were standing in the pews or falling to the floor. I fought to stand and stared at the vampire in her colored clown outfit. If something that elegant could be called a clown. I realized I wasn't choking. It wasn't death the power offered, but it was the end of free will. Her will was so large, so powerful, that it would be slavery. I could feel it. She would control us as surely as I could control a zombie that I had raised. Her power was something close to mine. She could control vampires, so why was it hitting me this hard?

Her power was a dainty fingertip sticking into my mind, pushing against my will. "Be mine," it whispered. "Be mine."

Nathaniel touched me. His power shivered over my skin, chasing back that cold touch. I could think again, feel again, take a deep breath again.

My own power roared to life. My necromancy, and something else, something that was necromancy, and not. I thrust that power into the delicate, coaxing touch. There was nothing delicate about what I did. I smashed into her power with a hammer, straight through that deceptive softness. Hit it, and found the steel nail underneath the lie of gentleness. It was all lies. There was nothing gentle, nothing kind. *Submit*, the power breathed. *Be mine, I'll take care of you, I'll take away all your problems, be mine*. I screamed down those lying words. I drowned her voice in my head in sheer power, like dynamiting a hotel because you didn't like your room. Her power collapsed, retreated, and I was suddenly standing in the aisle when I hadn't realized I'd moved.

I was standing with Nathaniel's hand in mine. I could taste pulses, blood flowing sluggish in a dozen veins. Vampires turned and looked at me, because they had no choice. I'd smashed her power and replaced it with my own. The dozen vamps hadn't fed yet tonight, so slow the beat, so sluggish the pulse. We needed food.

Nathaniel's hand convulsed around mine, bringing me back from that thought. Had he shared it? I could suddenly smell their skin, half a dozen different perfumes, someone's sweet shampoo, the sharp scent of cigarettes, aftershave. I could smell their skin as if I'd put my face just above their arms, their necks. Jean-Claude had kept me from drowning in the sensations of them last time I'd come to the church. Why wasn't he helping me now? I turned to the stage and found him looking, not at me, but at Columbine and Giovanni. Something was happening. Were they talking? I couldn't hear them. It was as if all my senses were narrowed down to scent and touch and vision.

I felt her power draw inward, like you'd take a breath before blowing out a candle. Except this candle was a few hundred vampires. That power spilled outward, and it was like water moving around the rocks of the vampires that Nathaniel and I could sense. We could save them, but the rest . . . the rest were lost.

Damian cried out, in my head, a scream. Nathaniel and I turned and found Malcolm wrapped around Damian, Malcolm's mouth shoved into Damian's throat. Malcolm shoved his power into the less powerful vampire, but taking his blood meant he was blood-oathing to him. It made no sense. Then the power hit us. Hit me.

It was like a door blew open inside my head. Nathaniel cried out, and I echoed him. My power, our power, blew outward over the other vampires. Malcolm had created almost every vampire in here. He had trusted no one else. Now he blood-oathed himself not to Damian, but to me. He was using his power to send mine over the rest of his flock. He was giving them all to me to keep Columbine from taking them. But I think Malcolm didn't understand what blood-oathing to me could mean. Maybe he thought that blooding himself to me and not Jean-Claude would make it a weaker bond, but I'd never blood-oathed someone without Jean-Claude's guidance. I only knew one way to do anything, and that was all the way.

In one of those moments that lasts forever, and is the blink of an eye, I saw inside Malcolm's mind. He had thought me the lesser evil. He had thought he could control me and retain some control of his people. It wasn't words, but more pictures, like some dream short-hand, if dreams could slap you as they ran across your mind. I'd always wondered if Malcolm's motives were as pure as they seemed. I'd assumed it was a bid for power; all vampires wanted power. But I saw him holding his people, cradling them while they wept. I saw him plunging fangs into their throats to give them that third bite. I felt him treat it as a holy thing, a ceremony as pure in his own heart as the marriage of a nun to God. It was his fault that the joining was so complete, his power thrusting into mine, and not understanding that my necromancy was like the biggest gravity well that any vampire would ever touch. It sucked him in, and I could not stop it.

But I was of Belle Morte's line, and all our talents are double-edged blades. I felt his power dive as deep inside me as mine in him, and I couldn't keep it out. And it wasn't just my mind. Nathaniel's and Damian's memories flooded to the surface. Nathaniel as a little boy, a man holding his hand, food for a hungry stomach, then hands where . . . Malcolm broke the memory before he went further. He understood that I could not steer us through these waters. He couldn't break what was happening, but his centuries of being a master helped us skim along the surface and not drown. Damian on the deck of a ship in the sunlight; the wind was so fresh, the sea smelled so good. The darkness of his creator's dungeon. That dark stairway, the screams, the smells. Malcolm drew us away from it. My mother's funeral, and I drew us away from that. It was like blinking; you see something you don't want to see, and you blink, and look away. You look away, and there's another picture.

Malcolm thought of his congregation, and just like that we had images to go with the scents and tactile explosion in our heads. I knew that the girl who smelled of soap and some sweet shampoo wanted to go to college, but was fighting to get enough nighttime classes to complete her degree. I knew that the family of vampires was trying for a house in a neighborhood that did not want them. I knew that the "child" was the master of the house. Malcolm gave us the problems and hopes. What we gave him back was the scent of their skin, the finger brush along a collar, a dozen different aftershaves, twenty different perfumes, from powdery sweetness to an herbal cleanness that was almost bitter. We gave him back sighs, as our power swept over them. We gave him back upturned faces as they shivered at the touch of power that was more sensuous than anything Malcolm had shown them. It didn't have to be sexual, but it was a dance of the senses. To be touched by Belle's line of vampires was to understand that someone's breath against your arm, just your arm, could cover your body in shivers.

Malcolm drew back from Damian's neck like a drowning man surfacing. We all came to the surface of that binding. Nathaniel and I ended in a heap on the carpeted aisle. Hands had to catch Damian or he would have fallen.

"You have not saved them, Malcolm. When I wrest them from you, you will come with them like a dog on a leash." The voice was clear and bell-like, echoing to the ends of the big church. I didn't think it was vampire powers. It was more like a voice that had been trained centuries before microphones existed.

Jean-Claude touched Malcolm to keep the other vampire from answering. He answered with a voice that sounded almost ordinary compared to Columbine's. It was as bland and empty as his voice got, but somehow it filled the room. "We bargained that you would duel the first to use magic. *Ma petite*, my servant, did not know these rules."

"We also promised not to use our servants to bolster our powers," she said.

"So I was not allowed to contact her mind-to-mind."

"You might have plotted behind my back."

"But you did not attack *ma petite*, you struck at the congregation. That seems as if you have broken the bargain first." His voice held a shiver at the end, and the entire congregation reacted to it, shuddering. They began to gaze at him, some reluctantly, but they heard him now, felt him now. In that moment I understood that Malcolm had been right in one thing. Blood-oathing to me was blood-oathing to Jean-Claude. Blood of my blood and all that.

"Your servant was using her leopards and her vampire. I could have reached out to my servant, Giovanni, but I kept to our bargain. But if she was allowed to gain power from others, then it seemed fair that I could do the same."

"You can feed off the combined power of all the vampires." Jean-Claude made it a statement.

"Yes," she said, and sounded pleased with herself.

Edward and Olaf were standing on either side of us like good bodyguards. It was Micah who knelt and asked, "Are you safe to touch?"

I knew what he meant: Will whatever metaphysical crap is happening spread by touch? "I think I'm safe to touch."

He grabbed my elbow and lifted, effortlessly. Graham offered Nathaniel a hand. We both swayed a little, but we were upright. Yea.

Columbine had meant to own the congregation and use them like a battery to make her own powers greater. Great enough to win a fight with Jean-Claude, maybe. But now they were mine, and through me, Jean-Claude's.

"You are too late," Malcolm said. "I have given them to my master."

"Oh, such bonds, when fresh, are not so firm," she said.

"Bold words, Columbine," Jean-Claude said, and his voice slid over my skin. Nathaniel shivered beside me. I felt two hundred vampires, or more, react to that voice. One vampire cried out, "Malcolm, save us from this lecher and his whore."

I turned and found the man who had spoken. He was staring at

Malcolm, his hand out, beseeching. I started to be angry, but then sensed a thought, and I could feel his fear. Jean-Claude's voice had made this heterosexual man's body react. Just the voice, ordinary words; Jean-Claude wasn't even trying, not yet. How would I feel if it were a female vamp? The thought made me think of Belle Morte. She'd done a lot more than use voice powers on me. The thought brought heat in a rush up my face. I burned at the thought of her body, her hands on me. Then I could taste her mouth, the sweetness of her lipstick. The silk of her skin clung to my fingertips, so that I rubbed them against the leather of my coat to get some other sensation, but it didn't help. The feel of her skin clung to my fingers like a cobweb that I could not brush away.

Nathaniel started to touch me, but I jerked back. I was shaking my head. I held my hands out to all of them, and was backing down the aisle. I needed Jean-Claude, or Asher. I needed someone who understood her power better than I did. Maybe it was just a reaction to what she had done to me in dream, but I couldn't count on that. If she was going to try to take me over, I needed to be near someone who could help me fight.

I don't know if Columbine understood what was happening, or thought it was the *ardeur*, but she seemed to think it was an opening; a weakness. She attacked the congregation again, but what she'd done before had been a feint. She'd just been pretending to try. Her power cut through the vampires like a burning sword. Where it touched, they screamed, and the ties that bound them to me, to Jean-Claude, seared away. It was as if she literally could cut the metaphysical bonds like rope that was too fragile to hold.

One of the vampires she cut free stumbled into the aisle and fell on all fours at my feet, shrieking. I couldn't feel what she was feeling, but apparently it hurt. A man reached out, gray eyes wide. He screamed, "Master, help me!" He didn't reach toward Malcolm, or Jean-Claude. He was inches away, and he reached for me.

I took his hand. I didn't even think about it. His hand was bigger than mine, so it was his hand that encircled mine, but the moment he touched me, he stopped screaming. He came out of the pew and wrapped himself around me. He held me as if I were the last safe thing in the world. I hugged him back, tight, and the feel of Belle Morte's skin faded under the muscled realness of the man in my arms. The girl on the floor crawled to me, touched my leg. She stopped screaming.

She wrapped herself around our legs, the nameless vampire and me. I was of Belle Morte's line. I knew how to stop the pain. I knew how to bring them back and make them mine.

I raised my face to the gray-eyed man. He bent toward me, folded his tall frame downward. I held his face in my hands and went up on tiptoe. His mouth found mine, and we kissed. His lips were dry, nervous, afraid, but I did something I'd never been able to do before: I was able to draw a little bit of the *ardeur*. I understood, as if the light had finally dawned, that the *ardeur* didn't have to be an ocean. It could be a single drop of rain, to wet the lips. I gave that tiny bit of power to him, breathed it into his mouth. I found the broken piece inside him that Columbine had cut. She had cut it with pain and force, and offered them a warning. She had showed them torture, fire, to burn and destroy them, if they refused her. I offered a kiss. I offered gentleness. I offered love. If I hadn't tasted Malcolm's power only moments before, maybe I couldn't have done it, but his intent was so pure, so unselfish, that it was like the *ardeur* had learned a new flavor. I offered that flavor to them. I offered them a choice. I gave them cool water and safety. She offered terror and punishment. She was threat. I was promise.

I won them back with a kiss, a touch. They poured from the pews, and I moved among them. Damian and Nathaniel helped me, moving into the crowd, touching, a kiss here and there. There was a gentleness to the *ardeur* that I had never felt before. Columbine's power died under a wave of kindness. A wave of touch, and chaste kisses. A wave of offering help. *We will save you. We will take away your pain.* She should have remembered that people have given everything they own, everything they are, to be taken care of, and to have their pain gone. It's the lure of cults: the promise of a good family; it's what people think love is, but love isn't absence of pain, it's a hand to hold while you're going through it.

Columbine screamed her frustration, and she broke the pact. She reached out to Giovanni. I felt her touch him. Not the hand that she took, but her power. The power that we had been pushing back suddenly took a leap. I felt it like a huge tidal wave rising above us. I turned and looked up as if there should be something to see, but there was nothing. Then that nothingness hit. It was like standing in the middle of a whirlwind of fire. Every breath was agony, death, but you had to breathe. Power seared down my throat, and I fought to scream, but there was no air. There was nothing but pain.

A voice came out of that pain and said, "I will make the pain stop. Be mine, and it will stop." I screamed my defiance to that voice in my head, but it was the kind of pain that eventually would break you. Eventually, you'd simply say yes, anything, everything, just to make it stop.

Vaguely, I felt the carpet of the floor underneath me. I knew I was writhing on it, but the pain ate all other sensations. My vision ran in streamers, sliding images, as if my eyes could not see past the pain. Hands tried to hold me down, but my body wouldn't be still. It hurt too much to be still.

The voice in my head said, "Let go, and it will feel so good. Just let go. Let go. They are strangers to you; let me have them, Anita. Let them go."

I didn't even know who "them" was. There was nothing but the pain, and some part of me that would not give in. It was as if everything underneath my skin had turned to fire and was trying to burn its way out.

Hands held me down, and there were enough hands that I had to feel them. They were firm and real, and it was like an anchor in the pain. I could feel the hands, feel that they were real. Which meant . . . Light, burning light, the sun dazzled my eyes, and I burned.

I screamed, and something covered my mouth. Lips, a kiss, and down that kiss was the sweet musk of leopard. My leopard rose to that scent. The sun was warm, and good, not a burning thing. I rose with Micah's beast, two black furred creatures that writhed and danced, and rose up and up, toward the light. The pain fell away as I remembered fur and claw, and teeth, and meat. I wasn't a vampire, not really. I was nothing that she could make burn. Her power only worked on the dead. I was reminded that I was very much alive.

I blinked up into Micah's face from inches away. He was lying on top of me, his hands trapping my face between them. I couldn't turn my head to see who was leaning weight on my arms and legs, but there were a lot of hands. I smelled wolf and hyena and human. I scented the air before I tried to see who was holding me down.

Micah stared down at me with his leopard eyes. "Anita?" He said my name like a question.

"I'm here," I whispered.

Micah crawled off of me. I could see Edward on my right arm now. Olaf was on my right leg, and Remus was on my left leg. Graham was on my left arm. I turned back to the men who were still pinning me. "You can let me up now."

"Not yet," Edward said. I realized he was up on all fours, putting his full body weight on just the one arm. I wondered how hard he had had to work to hold me down.

"You acted as if you were about to shift," Remus said, from where he had my left leg pinned.

"If there is another animal left, we cannot let go," Olaf said. The big man, almost as big in human form as Graham's animal form, seemed very serious about holding my leg down. I think the strength had impressed even Olaf. What the hell had I done?

I wanted to argue, but the looks on everyone's face said that I had scared them, or at least impressed them all. Impressed in a bad way. Nothing I could say would make them let up, but I so did not want to be spread-eagled on the ground, held down, sort of helpless in the middle of a fight.

"Our servants have fought, Jean-Claude, and mine is still standing."

"But *ma petite* won, Columbine. She withstood Giovanni's power. All the pain you caused her, and she did not let you use her to own the other vampires. They are still mine. You cannot feed upon their powers, as you had planned."

I could turn my head and see Jean-Claude on the stage, but Columbine was just a voice out of sight. I needed to be at his side. Call it a hunch, but bad things were coming. You could feel it in the air.

"Someone has talked out of turn," she said.

"I felt your power, Columbine, felt it forming them into a great fire to feed your power. No one had to bear tales for me to understand what you meant to do. You can take other vampires and make of their powers one great weapon."

"Yes," she said.

"But *ma petite* stopped you from taking these little vampires and forming them into your army, your source of power. What will you do now that you cannot win power in this way?" His voice breathed through my head, "You beside me would be well, *ma petite*."

I whispered, "Trying. Let me up, boys."

Power breathed through the church. It sought to feed your doubts, no, to feed on them. I'd met vampires who could feed on lust, on fear, but never one who fed on doubt. Dear God, she fed on it, and she could cause it, just like the vamps who fed off lust and fear. I was suddenly overwhelmed with the certainty that we would lose. Everyone was going to die, and there was nothing I could do about it.

\ "God." Remus almost moaned it. He had his head in his hands. Edward and Olaf seemed the least affected. Micah reached out to me. I let him draw me into the circle of his arms, let myself sink into the strength of him, but the doubts didn't go away. I was suffocating in my doubts. People cried out, some begged for it to stop. I heard one man say, "Anything, anything, just stop it, stop it." There was more than one way to win this fight.

Nathaniel crawled to us. He reached out, head hanging down. I touched his hand and a surge of power knocked back the doubts. He raised his face and gave me the full look of those beautiful eyes. His face brightened like the sun coming from behind a cloud. He said, "I believe in you."

I drew him into the circle of Micah's body. "You make me believe in myself." As it had earlier, Nathaniel's touch chased back the doubts. His unwavering certainty kept us both safe from her. Even sitting in the room with her, her doubts could not get past the certainty that Nathaniel gave me.

Damian crawled to us. I think partially the doubts assailed him, but also he was a vampire. The burning illusion of being consumed by the sun had hit him, too. I could feel his pain, and the double pain of the memory of watching his best friend die in the sunlight. His tie to me let him be in sunlight and not burn, but the terror of the light made him unable to enjoy it. Sunlight was death, period, end of story. He was remembering watching his friend's skin peel away under the heat of a summer day.

Nathaniel grabbed his wrist, I took his hand, and we pulled him into the circle of our arms. The moment we touched him, he shuddered, but raised a tear-stained face. "Her power is terrible. You would do anything to make it stop."

I nodded. The crowd was still crying for help, for it to stop. If they'd set up similar rules to the last challenger Jean-Claude had had, then it was winning over the crowd that would decide it. An actual member of the vampire council had come to town. He was the Earth-mover, he could cause earthquakes with his power. To save the city and keep the destruction to a minimum, Jean-Claude had gotten him to agree that they would fight with less destructive powers, and one of the tests would be which one could sway the audience at the Circus of the Damned. If victory was in getting this crowd on our side, we were about to lose.

I tried to feel Jean-Claude through his own marks, but he kept me out. I got one hard glimpse of him drowning in doubt. But they weren't his doubts, they were Richard's. Poor Richard, he'd come to support Jean-Claude, but he was so full of self-doubt that he was hurting him, hurting them both. Jean-Claude shielded so I wouldn't feel it. That left him and Richard trapped in Richard's version of hell.

I got to my feet, still holding on to Nathaniel and Damian. Micah stood with us, but let his hands fall away. I told him, "I love you."

"I love you, too, now go. Go to Jean-Claude."

We started hurrying toward the stage. Jean-Claude needed to touch someone who had no doubts about him, or themselves. With Nathaniel's hand in mine, I had enough certainty to share.

44

WE HIT THE stage at a run, and I fell into Jean-Claude's arms. I fell into his arms with Nathaniel in my right hand, and Damian in my left. Jean-Claude staggered under the combined weight, or the momentum. Asher helped steady him, hands on his back to help him stay upright. Richard was on all fours, head down. He never looked up as we stumbled into Jean-Claude's arms, and Asher held us all for a moment.

Jean-Claude wrapped his arms around me. I felt Asher's strength at his back, at our backs, helping us, steadying us. I looked up into Jean-Claude's face, into those midnight blue eyes. Nathaniel wrapped his arms around Jean-Claude, me, and Asher. I think Asher would have moved back, but there was no time. Damian kept my hand but knelt by Richard. He touched the fallen man's shoulder. Nathaniel and I gave Jean-Claude certainty, a rock to build upon. Damian shared his coldness with Richard, his utter control. I felt both emotions in a rush of power that danced through my body, and into Jean-Claude's, and Asher's behind him.

Richard cried out, his head coming up, his hand grabbing Damian's arm like a drowning man taking the last help offered.

I felt Damian's coldness rush over Richard's panic and turn to a wall of ice. He gave Richard defenses to hide behind. He pulled Richard to his feet, and they stood there, hands on each other's arms, like a version of the guy-greeting that friends use sometimes when a handshake won't do but they're too manly to hug. Damian kept my hand in his, but he and Richard were outside the circle of everyone else's arms.

They were relieved to be outside the circle of the other men. Richard's fear flared. He wasn't just afraid of Columbine and her servant. He was afraid of Jean-Claude and me, and Asher. It was one of those too-close glimpses that we sometimes got into each other's minds. It was Damian who cut off the sensation, Damian who blocked the fear with his own iron self-control. He'd had centuries of learning to control fear when he was the plaything of a master vampire who could raise fear in another and feed on it, as Columbine fed on doubt.

"We must win the crowd, *mes amis*."

"Like when the Earthmover came to town?" I asked.

He nodded, arms tightening around me. I knew why the hug. The Earthmover had won. Only his trying to make me his human servant, trying to make me kill Jean-Claude for him, had given me the chance to kill him instead. I pressed my face against the stiffness of Jean-Claude's lacy shirt. I'd almost broken him of the old-fashioned lace, but tonight he'd dressed as I first found him, all frothy white lace and black velvet jacket; only the leather pants showed he knew what century he was in. I pressed my free hand against his side, underneath the jacket, held the line of his body and was afraid.

"I don't know who the Earthmover was," Nathaniel said, "but just tell me what to do, and I'll do it."

"If more of us were submissive, things would go so much faster," Asher said.

It made me smile, though the smile was lost against Jean-Claude's shirt.

"You aren't one of us," Richard said, and his voice was hostile.

"We must unite, Richard, or we will lose this night," Jean-Claude said.

"He is not your animal to call, or your servant. I don't have to play nice with him."

Asher started to move away, but Nathaniel tightened his arm, held him in place. "Don't go."

"Let me go, boy. The wolf is right, I am no one's darling." His voice held sadness, like the taste of rain on your tongue, lifetimes of sorrow in that one tone.

"Our certainty does not travel outside our triumvirates," Jean-Claude said. "Even our wolf is drowning. How can we save all the others if we cannot even save ourselves?" His voice was an echo of Asher's, full of sorrow, so that my throat closed with it, and I thought I'd choke on unshed tears.

"Fight, damn you!" Claudia came up to the edge of the stage. Tears stained her face. Her emotions were so raw, it looked like physical pain. "Fight for us! Don't just roll over and give that bitch your throat."

Malcolm came to stand on the other side of Richard. "Fight for us, Jean-Claude. Fight for us, Anita." He looked directly at Richard. Richard suddenly looked wrong in the leather mask. He didn't look cool in the leather outfit, he looked like he was doing exactly what he was doing. He was hiding. The rest of us stood there in plain view. Only the bad guys, and Richard, were hiding who and what they were from the world. Malcolm gripped his shoulder. "Fight for us, Ulfric. Do not let your fears and doubts destroy us all."

"I thought you, of all people, would understand why I don't want to be touching them when they raise the only power we have to fight these things."

"I felt what Anita and her triumvirate raised earlier. It was friendship, love as pure as any I've known. I begin to believe the *ardeur* is a jewel with many facets, but it needs light to shine, Ulfric."

"What the hell does that mean?" Richard asked, and his voice was angry and frustrated. He shoved Malcolm's hand away and looked at Damian. "You're keeping the worst of it out, aren't you?"

Damian just looked at him.

"To reap the benefits, I have to take the bad with the good. I can't do it. I can't." He looked at me. "I'm sorry, but I can't go where this is heading."

"What do you think we're going to do, Richard?" I asked.

"What you always do, fuck everything."

"It was not sex she offered to my congregation, only friendship."

"But it won't stay that way, it never does," Richard said. He looked at Malcolm and said, "You're asking me to do something that you would never do yourself."

Malcolm nodded. "You're right"—he nodded again—"you are absolutely right. I have stood on my moral high ground and been so certain. So certain that I was right, that Jean-Claude was not only wrong, but evil. I have said such hateful things to Anita, called her *whore* and *witch*. I have called all Jean-Claude's people that and worse to my congregation, but all my righteousness could not protect them."

Richard nodded. "I know. Anita saved my mother and brother, saved their lives, but she did terrible things to get there in time. Things I still think are immoral, wrong, and I have to live every day with the knowledge that if I had been there I would have stopped Anita from torturing that man. I wouldn't have let her dehumanize him, or herself. I would have stood on my moral high ground and my mother and my brother, Daniel, would both be dead." Tears shimmered, edged by the leather. "I used to be so sure of so much. Raina didn't shake my faith. She made me more certain. Only Anita, only Jean-Claude, only they have made me doubt everything."

I drew a little away from Jean-Claude, still touching, because I was afraid to stop touching him. If the doubts were this bad touching, I couldn't imagine what they'd be like if we weren't touching. We'd just die. "My cross still works for me, Richard. It still burns with holy light. God hasn't forsaken me."

"But he should have," Richard said. "He should have, don't you see? If what I believe is right, if what you say you believe is right, then your cross should not burn. You have broken so many commandments. You've murdered, tortured, fucked, but your cross still works. I don't understand that."

"You're saying I'm evil, so God should have turned his back on me?"

Even with most of his face hidden, I saw his face convulse with emotion, tears finally falling. He nodded. "Yes, that's what I mean."

I just looked at him, and knew that it was partly vampire powers messing with his head, but that perhaps Columbine's powers only brought out what was already inside you. Some part of Richard believed what he was saying.

"*Ma petite . . .*"

"No," I said, "no, it's okay." My chest felt like a piece of it had been carved out, not bloody and warm, but cold and icy. As if the piece had been missing a long time, but I hadn't wanted to see it, feel it, know it. "Maybe God isn't the sex police, Richard. Sometimes I think Christians get all hung up on the sex thing because it's easier to worry about sex than to ask yourself, *Am I a good person?* If as long as you don't have sex with a lot of people you're a good person, that's easy. It's easy to avoid that. It's easy to think, *I'm not fucking anyone, so I'm good.* It makes it easy to be cruel, because as long as you're not fucking around, nothing you do can be that bad. Is that really all you think of God? Is he just the sex police for you and Malcolm? Or is it that sex is easy to worry about, easy to avoid, and the whole love-your-neighbor-as-you-love-yourself thing that's hard? Some days it's so hard, I feel like trying to take care of everyone in my life will break me apart. But I do my best. I do my best for everyone in my life every damn day. Can you say that, Richard? Do you do your best for everyone in your life every damn day?"

"Do you include yourself and Jean-Claude on that list?" he asked, his voice so quiet, so full of emotion that it was strangely empty.

"Do you not include us?" I asked. I could feel the tears pushing in my throat, at the back of my eyes like heat. I would not cry for him.

Those true brown eyes stared at me. I watched the pain in them, but finally, he said, "No, I don't."

I nodded, a little too fast, a little too rapidly. I fought to swallow past the tears. I thought I'd choke on them. I cleared my throat twice, so sharp it hurt. I wanted to accuse him, say, "Then what were you doing in my bed today? Why did you sleep with Micah, Nathaniel, and me? Why did you have sex with me today? If I'm not a person in your life, then . . ." I swallowed the words, because they didn't matter. He'd have had some answer for everything I said, or he'd have felt bad about it. Either way, I didn't want to hear it, or see it. I didn't need to hear more explanations from him. I didn't need to see him agonize over his moral quandaries anymore. I was done.

"I'm not angry, Richard. I don't hate you. I'm just not going to do this anymore. You think I'm evil. You think Jean-Claude is evil. You think what we do to keep everyone safe is evil. Fine, fine."

"I didn't mean . . ."

I held up a hand. "Just stop, don't. The hand on your arm that's keeping the doubts from eating you alive was forged through sex, Richard. That calm was won through centuries of pain and sex and servitude. Jean-Claude, the evil bastard, saved Damian, ransomed him from hell. They didn't even like each other, but Jean-Claude wouldn't leave anyone with her, not if he could save him. Evil bastard."

"Anita," Damian said, and his face held—fear, something, as if he knew what was coming.

` "You benefit from our evil, Richard. You count on us being willing to do your dirty work. Hell, I'm the Bolverk for your clan. Literally, I am your evildoer. I do what the Ulfric will not. So fine, fine, I will be your Bolverk, but we are not in the lupanar this night. We are not lupa and Ulfric this night. This night is vampire business. This night I am Jean-Claude's human servant. I am Nathaniel and Damian's master. That is the power you are hiding behind right this second. You think we're evil, fine." I looked at Damian; I gave him a look to let him know I meant what I was about to say. "Damian, let him go."

"You wouldn't," Richard said.

"You can't have it both ways, Richard. You're right, the *ardeur* will have to rise. You don't want to be touching any of us when that happens, do you?"

He just looked at me.

"If you mean what you say, if you truly believe it's wrong, evil, then let go of Damian's arm. Let go, and stand on your moral high ground. If Jean-Claude and I mean nothing to you, then stand by yourself, Richard, stand on your own two feet."

He stared at me as if I'd said something terrible. He stood there clinging to Damian's arm. "Don't do this, not now."

"I think now is perfect, Richard. I think now is great. We need to raise the *ardeur*, so let go."

"Jean-Claude," he said, and looked at the vampire.

"It is a strange night, my Ulfric. I should be arguing your case. I should fight to keep you with us, but I don't seem to want to. I, like *ma petite*, grow tired of being judged by someone I care for. It cuts deeper tonight, and I know that is Columbine. She is laughing at us, even now. She has stopped attacking the congregation. She has put all her power upon us, because she found our weakness. The weakness that has always been there, from the first."

"You mean me," Richard said.

"I mean our triumvirate. It is flawed, and I do not know how to fix it. I feel what Anita has forged with her servants. The two of you are more powerful; my triumvirate should be the stronger of the two, but it is not."

"Because of me," Richard said.

"No, because of who we all are, *mon ami*. But whatever the cause, I grow tired of this fight." He leaned back against Asher, rested his head against the other man's face. "I have rejected those I do love to save your sensibilities, and Anita's."

"You're all lovers," Richard said. "Don't tell me otherwise."

"We will have to raise the *ardeur*, Richard," Jean-Claude said. "Let go of Damian's hand or you will be dragged into what is about to happen. If it is evil, and you would escape it, let go. Let go of us, Richard, let go of us all."

"This is vampire trickery," Malcolm said. "Do not let her force you into something you will regret later."

"It is vampire trickery, but as Richard said things he truly believed, so I think Anita and I have come to an understanding. We are tired of this, Ulfric. We are tired of you making us the villains. If we are the villains, then let go. If we are not the villains, then hold on, but either way, you know what I must do now. If you do not wish to be part of it, then you must separate from us."

"Let go, Richard," I said.

He looked at Jean-Claude, then turned to me. "Is this what you want?"

"Is it what you want?" I asked.

"I don't know," he said.

"Then let me go, Richard, let me go."

He let go.

45

RICHARD FELL TO his knees. His head bowed toward the floor, his hands rising to his head, as if he could shut out the doubt in his own mind. Alone, he could not fight Columbine's power. He was alone, but we weren't.

Damian's hand in mine drew him into the circle of our power. He had some of the same issues with the other men that Richard had, but Damian was a more practical creature. With him pressed against me, so that Jean-Claude had to move his arm to let the other vampire in closer, I heard, or felt, Damian's thoughts. It wasn't a fate worse than death, no matter what happened with Jean-Claude and the rest of the men; nothing that we would do with him would be half so awful as what he'd endured at her hands. The other thought, before Jean-Claude grabbed the reins of all our minds, was that Jean-Claude and I were good masters, kinder than any he'd known; we were worth fighting for. Then Jean-Claude settled into the driver's seat of our metaphysical bus, and calm, we were all suddenly so calm.

I stood with my back pressed against Jean-Claude. When he'd drawn Damian and me in, he'd turned us, like a dance movement, smooth and inevitable, so that we stood in the circle of his arm. Jean-Claude held us both. My hand had just slid around Damian's waist and drawn him in against the side of my body as if we fitted together from shoulder to hip. His own arm traced my shoulders, his hand cupping my arm, and again we fitted together in a way I didn't remember. Jean-Claude's arm was around Damian's shoulders, his other arm encircling Nathaniel, who was cuddled against his side, so that one arm traced the front of my body. I wasn't sure where Nathaniel's other arm was, but I knew that Asher was still at Jean-Claude's back.

Columbine stood just on the other side of the pulpit in her motley clothing, all red, blue, white, and black, edged with gold. Her tricorn hat was gold, with only a cluster of multicolored balls to echo the colors in her clothes. Her human servant stood at her back, all in black. He looked like a shadow beside her brilliance.

"You are very good, Columbine," Jean-Claude said. "I did not even feel you roll our minds. Your magic is very subtle."

"Such a pretty compliment, thank you." She gave him a low curtsey, holding the small half-skirt of her pants outfit to the side as if it were a much longer piece of cloth.

I should have been nervous, at the least, but I stood there in the circle of everyone's arms, and was so relaxed. It was a little like you feel when they give you drugs before an operation, calm, almost a liquid warmth, as if you could float away on it. Part of me thought, *It's what they do to you just before something really painful happens.* But the thought just drifted away on the warm calm.

"You attacked the audience as a diversion," Jean-Claude said in that voice that could make your skin shiver, but it didn't make me shiver. It was as if whatever he'd done to us, the people he was touching, protected us from that voice.

She laughed, but it had none of the touchable quality of Jean-Claude and Asher's laughs. Even through the near anesthetic haze that he had created around us, the laughter felt flat, human even. Or maybe the reason it sounded flat was the anesthetic haze. I couldn't tell whether I was still able to sense a little through what Jean-Claude had done, or if his power was protecting me from her.

The laughter died abruptly on that crimson mouth. She stared at us with eyes that were gray and as serious as death. "Oh, no, Jean-Claude, it wasn't a diversion, but I admit that I may have underestimated you, and your servant. If I could have won the audience from her, then I would have had enough power to defeat you easily."

"And now?" He made it a question, with a lilt of his voice.

"I think a more direct assault on you, personally, is needed."

"If you are too direct, then you will simply be executed," he said, his voice mild.

"My power can be subtle, but do not be deceived. I too can be direct. As direct as the power you hold in your arms with your raven-haired servant."

She gestured with one slender hand, and the man behind her stepped forward. He took off one glove and laid his bare hand in hers. "You are not the only master whose touch awakens more power in their servant, Jean-Claude," she said.

"I did not think I was," he said. His voice was as mild as her own, but his power was not mild. His power riffled through us, as if we were cards in his hand. What should he play? I'd had Jean-Claude drive the metaphysical bus before, but I'd never felt it like this, never been so aware of how terribly aware he was of his power, of my power, of the power we all offered him. He was vampire, which meant he was a cold power, a thing of logic, because emotions do not trouble the dead. He shifted through our talents, like Edward would have looked through his gun safe. Which gun will do the job? Which will make this shot? I had a moment to feel a thrill of fear, a thread of real doubt. He squashed it, shut it tight away from me, from us, because it wasn't just my mind that had felt it. I knew that Damian and Nathaniel had thought it, felt it, too. He feared that we had no weapon to protect from this. We had already nearly been destroyed by her power without her servant's touch. He shut the doubts away, but they were there. It wasn't the coldness of vampire I was feeling, it was the coldness of necessity. Doubt was her weapon. You do not arm your enemy.

Her power hit us, staggered us, as if emotion could be a great wind to blow your world apart. It was like having your mind and heart ripped open, wide, so you had to feel, know, how you truly felt. Most of us live because we don't shine the light too brightly inside ourselves. Suddenly, Jean-Claude, Damian, Nathaniel, Asher, and I, were at ground zero of the brightest light in the world.

Columbine specialized in doubt and pain, but Giovanni, her man, he gave her a wider range. Loss, that choking sense of loss, when you think you'll die with the person who was buried. Somehow she knew that we had all suffered losses, and she made us suffer them all over again. But it wasn't just our personal losses; Jean-Claude had bound us together, so that instead of one loss, we got them all. I heard Julianna scream as the fire consumed her. I heard her scream Jean-Claude's name as she died. Asher screamed in the here and now, and Jean-Claude joined him. We stood before a pyre of cold ash and knew that it was all that was left of the woman who had been our heart. Damian watched his brother burn to death again. His screams haunted us. Damian fell to his knees as if he'd been hit. We were small again, and Nicholas was dying. The baseball bat made a sickening sound as it hit his head, a wet, crunching sound. He fell on the floor, reached out to us. Blood was everywhere, and the man like some dark giant above us. Nicholas said, "Run, Natty, run!" Nathaniel screamed, *"No!"* in the here and now.

As a child, he had run. He raised his face up, but he was a child no longer, and said, "I won't run." I looked into his eyes, those lavender eyes; they were real, not this memory of pain and death. Tears stained his face, but he whispered, "I won't run."

I was eight again, and my father was about to say the words that would destroy my life. My mother was dead. But I hadn't run then. Nathaniel had run because his older brother told him to run, but he wasn't little anymore. It had been my father who had collapsed. He had wailed her loss, not me. I did not run. I did not run then, and I would not run now.

I found my voice, and said, "We won't run."

Nathaniel shook his head, still crying. "No, we won't."

Jean-Claude and Asher had slid to the ground with Damian, crushed under the weight of sorrow. No one else was close to us on the stage. The guards, even Richard, had fled from us. Fled from the weight of horror and loss. Fled so it did not spread to them. I guess I couldn't blame Richard, but I would later, I knew I would. Worse yet, later he would blame himself.

I caught movement in the aisle close to us. Micah was the closest, the only one brave enough or stupid enough to get close to the emotional thermonuclear bomb that had just been set off. Then I caught movement just behind Micah. Edward was there. More surprising was that Olaf was beside him.

Nathaniel touched my arm. He smiled at me; with tears still wet on his face, he smiled. It made my heart hurt, but not in a bad way, in that way that sometimes happens when you love someone, and you just suddenly look up and realize just how much. Love, love to chase back the pain. It washed over my skin like a warm wind, love, life, that spark that makes us get back up. It poured down the metaphysical links between Nathaniel and me, and the other men. Love, love to raise their faces and make them look at us. Love to help them to their feet, love and our hands to steady them, to help dry their tears. We finally stood, perhaps a little shaky around the edges, but we all stood and turned to Columbine and her Giovanni.

"Love conquers all, is that it?" she said, her voice thick with disdain.

"No, not all," I said. "Just you."

"I am not conquered, not yet." The lights seemed to dim, as if something breathed in the light, ate it. Twilight filled the church, a soft edge of darkness, spread out from the Harlequin on the stage.

"What is that?" Micah asked. He was beside the stage now.

Jean-Claude, Asher, and Damian said, "The Mother of All Darkness."

Nathaniel and I said, "Marmee Noir."

That which we call the Mother of All Vampires, by any other name would be fucking dangerous.

46

THE VAMPIRES IN the audience made a panicked run for the far doors. It was as if even Malcolm's tame vamps understood what was coming. Their screams let me know that the doors wouldn't open. I guess I shouldn't have been surprised; the Queen of All Darkness was coming to eat us. What was holding shut one door to everything she could do?

Micah leapt upon the stage like grace over muscles, proving that he didn't have to be in leopard form to be inhumanly graceful. He touched my arm, and the emotion we'd raised to save ourselves leapt to him. He was no one's servant, no one's master, but the love spread to him in a warm rush.

Jean-Claude looked at us with tears still painting faint pinkish streaks on his face. "You love him."

Even with all the good feelings, I frowned at him. "Yes, I do."

Jean-Claude shook his head. "I mean, *ma petite*, that your love for him . . ." He waved a hand and let me see inside his head, so much quicker. Because I loved Micah, Jean-Claude could feed off the energy of that love. It was as if his powers through Belle Morte's line had found a new way to think. She and her vampires were all about lust, love, but no one had ever been able to use love like fuel, the way the *ardeur* could use lust. It was like an intuitive leap in math, or science. You start with this bit of reality and suddenly you understand how to make a leap to a larger reality. Love, love was power in more than just a metaphorical way.

"Love won't conquer her." It was Richard from behind us. He'd come back to the stage.

I looked at him and wasn't sure I wanted him to touch me in that moment. Would the love spread to him, or would it not? Had he finally hurt me enough that he'd killed my feelings for him? If he had, then he would be no help here. He'd hurt me, hurt this soft new magic.

"You'll need a wolf, like last time," he said.

He was right, but . . . He held out his hand.

The dimness breathed around us, as if the room had taken a breath. He reached for me, grabbed my hand. His hand was warm in mine. It was still Richard, every gorgeous inch of him, but the power did not travel from my skin to his. He stood there holding my hand, and his touch did not move me. I'd never had him touch me where it didn't move me. The other men, even Damian was like a press of tenderness at my back, but Richard was cold to my heart.

"Anita . . ." He whispered it.

What could I say? "You said we were nothing to you. You said you didn't want the *ardeur*."

"This isn't the *ardeur*," he said.

I nodded. "Yes, it is, Richard. You never understood that for me the *ardeur* wasn't just about sex. This is the *ardeur*."

"I can smell the edge of it, it's as if love had a scent."

"It's the *ardeur*, Richard, what it's become."

"If I'd stayed by your side, you'd be spilling love all over me?" He made it a question.

"I don't know."

"*Ma petite*, could we discuss this later?"

We looked at him, still hand-in-hand. "Sorry," I said.

Richard scented the air, and for a moment I thought he really was trying to scent what love smelled like. "It doesn't smell like her."

I scented the air, too. "No, she smells like jasmine and rain, and night. There's no scent to this." The darkness wasn't growing . . . darker. It should have been. It was twilight, and power breathed through the room, but it wasn't quite enough power, not for her.

I turned back to Columbine and her servant. "Belle Morte said that the Harlequin are the servants of the Dark Mother. Did she mean that literally?"

"All of us bear a piece of the orignal darkness inside us, little girl. Feel the power of the night given human form and know true terror."

I shook my head and said to Richard, "It's not her."

He moved up beside me, as close as the other men would allow. We were getting to be quite a crowd again. "If I hadn't been in your dream with the real thing, this might be scary."

I nodded. "But we've felt the real deal, and this ain't it."

"This isn't the Mother?" Asher said. He'd gotten to his feet, scrubbing at tears on his face.

"No, it's a shadow of her, barely that," I said.

Nathaniel drew in a large breath. "I smelled her once in the car. She smelled like something cat, and jasmine, and so many things. This has no scent, it's not real."

The darkness began to press down like a shadowy hand, but it was only a shadow. The little vampires huddled and, beating at the doors, screamed louder. It had cleared the pews out so that there was no one but our guards in the aisles. The guards, and our vampires.

"The Dark Mother will consume you all, unless you lay down your arms and submit to us."

The shadow of dark tried to crush us. Damian made a small sound. "Don't be afraid," I said. "It's barely a shadow of her power. It can't hurt us."

Columbine gestured as if she were crushing something invisible in her hand. The shadowy darkness tried to squeeze down around us, but I thought, *Love, warmth, life*, and the shadows shredded. The lights began to grow brighter again.

Requiem spoke from a small distance away. "This is not the darkness that hunted my master in England. This is smoke and mirrors compared to what came for him in the end."

"Smoke and mirrors," I said, softly, "misdirection like a magician's illusion. How do we know you're the real Columbine, a real Harlequin? All vampires know the rules, the masks. Anyone could pretend," I said.

"You uppity little bitch," she said. "How dare you?"

"That would explain them breaking the rules," Nathaniel said. "They tried to kill you guys without giving you a black mask first."

"Are you truly asking us to prove we are of the Harlequin?' Columbine asked.

"Yeah, I am."

"Jean-Claude, does she do all your talking for you?"

"I am happy to have *ma petite* do my talking for me." Which wasn't always true, but tonight, I was doing okay.

"I wanted to own you, not destroy you, but if you insist," she said. A piece of blackness unwound itself from near the ceiling. It had to have been there all along, but none of us had noticed it. It was like some large black snake, if snakes were formless and could float. Oh, hell, it wasn't a snake, but I didn't know what else to call it. It was a ribbon of blackness that moved, and where it touched the lights, the lights went out, as if the light was eaten by the coming dark.

"It smells like night air," Micah said, in his growling voice.

"It does," Nathaniel and Richard said at the same time. They didn't even look at each other. The three wereanimals seemed intent on something I couldn't hear, or see, or smell. Then I felt it, a cool line of wind, and I did smell it, night air, damp, but not rain. Damp, but not rain. I drew in a deep breath. "Where's the jasmine?"

Half the lights on one side of the church had been engulfed by the sinuous stream of living darkness. The vampires and humans of the congregation had made a huddle of themselves on the other side of the church, as far from the dark as the closed doors would allow.

Requiem had pulled his cloak up around his face, but he was beside the stage now. "This is the darkness that killed my master."

"How did it kill him?" Micah asked.

"The darkness covered him, hid him from sight, he gave a terrible cry, and when we could see again, he was dead."

"How exactly, Requiem?" I asked.

"His throat had been torn out as if by some great beast."

We had two lights between us and the consuming dark. "I smell wolf," Micah said.

I shook my head. "The Mother of All Darkness doesn't do wolf, she does cats, lots of cats, no doggies."

Nathaniel and Richard sniffed the air, too. "Wolf," Richard said. Nathaniel nodded.

Edward called to me. "Can bullets hurt that thing?"

I shook my head.

"Let me know when you find something I can shoot."

"We can shoot," Claudia called.

The darkness was almost to the stage, but it didn't feel like her. It didn't feel like Marmee Noir. I closed down the warm fuzzy love flavor of the *ardeur* and reached out with my own power, my necromancy. I reached out not toward the coming dark, but toward the spot near the ceiling where it originated. Marmee Noir wasn't shy. If she'd been there, she'd have let us know. So what, or who, was it? Who held a piece of the dark inside them?

I searched the rafters near the high, vaulted ceiling. I almost heard a voice, almost a loud whisper, "Not here. Not here. I'm not here." I actually started to look away, then realized what I was doing. Something was in the corner of the ceiling, someone was there.

The darkness curled along the edge of the stage and began to eat the bright lights that usually spotlit the pulpit. Columbine laughed, a high, joyous, cruel sound. "The darkness will eat you all."

"You're not causing the darkness, Columbine, you or Giovanni," I said.

"We are Harlequin," she said.

"Tell your little friend hanging near the ceiling to show himself or herself."

Her body went very still. It was better than any human facial expression. There was someone there, and she hadn't thought any of us would know. Great, now how did it help us?

The darkness was almost here. A darkness that smelled like damp night, and earth, and wolf, like something acrid on my tongue. It wasn't wolf as I knew it. But I was out of time to analyze it.

I yelled, "Edward, shoot into that corner there." I pointed at the corner where I knew the vampire was hiding.

Edward and Olaf drew their guns, aimed. The darkness swirled toward us, toward Jean-Claude. I drew my gun and moved in front of him. Remus was beside me. "You're supposed to have bodyguards, remember?"

Haven came to my other side in a blur of movement. "Finally, something to shoot."

"Not yet," I said. "He's not here yet."

"Who isn't here?" Remus asked.

Edward and Olaf's guns fired, and darkness swallowed the world, black, moonless night. "Shit," Haven breathed.

They both moved in closer to me. I put my free hand on Remus's shoulder so I'd know where he was. I moved my leg to brush against Haven's, but his free hand found my back. At least we wouldn't shoot each other. We stood, pressed close in the utter dark, guns out, but nothing to see. How do you shoot if you can't see what you're shooting at?

Edward yelled, "Anita, can you hear me? We've got blood on the wall, but we can't see what we hit."

I yelled back, "I hear you."

"We're coming," he said.

I don't know what I would have yelled back, *Come, Don't come*, because Remus said, "Wolf."

Haven said, "Close."

There was a wet, thick sound, almost soft, like a knife being pulled out of flesh. If I hadn't been straining my ears like a son of a bitch, I might not have heard. But it would have been okay, because Remus and Haven turned like one person, and moved me with them, almost like you move a partner on the dance floor. We fired into that sound, that smell of bitter wolf. We fired until it hit us back.

"Claws," Haven yelled.

Remus was suddenly standing in front of me, enfolding me with his body. I felt him jerk, hard. I yelled, "Haven!"

"Anita," he yelled, and he was still on my right. I put my gun around Remus's body and fired into the body on the other side of Remus. I fired until my gun clicked empty. But Haven was there now, his gun shooting into what was on the other side of Remus. Remus's body jerked, and for a moment I thought Haven had shot Remus by accident, then I heard a sound, a ripping, meaty, wet, horrible sound. Bones cracked, and Remus screamed. Liquid ran hot across my skin. I screamed. Claws grabbed at my shirt. I drew a knife, because it was all I had left. A claw cut across my breast. I cut the claw back. Remus's arms had tightened around me, pressing me into the claws. I couldn't see what was happening, and what I was feeling made no sense. Where the hell was the claw coming from?

Haven wasn't touching me anymore. I heard fighting. "Get away, Anita, get away from him," Haven said.

"Get away from who?" I asked. I stabbed the claw that wasn't Remus. I cut it up, but it cut me up, too. I screamed more in frustration than anything. Remus whispered, "I'm sorry." His arms slid away from me and his knees buckled, but he didn't fall. I grabbed him, trying to support him, and that was when I realized where the clawed hand was coming from. I had to be wrong. I screamed, "Remus!"

There was movement, sound, fighting. I heard a sound I didn't recognize, grunts of effort. What the hell was happening? Remus suddenly fell forward. I tried to catch him, but it was too sudden and he outweighed me by a hundred pounds. I fell to the ground with him on top of me. He wasn't moving. The darkness vanished. I could see again.

There was a severed arm sticking out of Remus's back. I screamed. I couldn't help it. More guards were there, picking him up, getting him off me. They couldn't roll him onto his back, because the arm had pierced his chest. The hand looked human now, but my chest and Remus's said it hadn't been human when it went through. His eyes were closed, and he was so still, terribly still.

"Get that thing out of him," Claudia said.

Fredo was suddenly at her side with a knife the size of a small sword. He raised it up, and I looked away before he brought it down. I saw Wicked and Truth, with bare swords pointed at the throat and chest of a fallen Harlequin that I had never seen before. He was dressed all in black, even his mask. He was missing an arm. Edward and Olaf and more of the guards had Columbine and Giovanni at gunpoint. Jean-Claude, Asher, Requiem, and most of our vampires were gathered around them. I think with the real master Harlequin down, they'd been able to take the other two. Good that something had worked out. Haven was kneeling between the two groups, bleeding, but he'd live. I turned back to Remus. I wasn't so sure about him.

They had the arm out now, in two pieces, but there was a hole in his chest that I could see through like some sort of cartoon cannon shot. "Fuck," I said softly, "his heart."

Claudia looked at me, tears drifting silently down her face. "Bastard had silver bracers on his forearms. Silver, fucking razor wire as fucking jewelry."

"This one is healing," Wicked called. "How do we stop him from doing that?"

"Is Remus . . ." I couldn't say it.

"Dead," Claudia said, in a voice that was hard and cold and didn't match the tears.

"Yeah," I said.

She just nodded.

"He died saving me," I said.

"He died doing his job," she said.

I watched her tears and wondered if he had been more than just a friend to her. I hoped not. In that moment, I hoped not. I got to my feet and fell back down. Richard was beside me, holding me. "You're hurt."

"Remus is dead," I said, and pushed him away.

"Anita, please."

I shook my head. "Either help me walk over to Wicked and Truth, or go somewhere else."

"Can I at least see how badly you're hurt first?"

"No!"

"Do you want Remus to have died for nothing, is that what you want?"

Micah was on my other side. "Let us see, Anita, then we'll take you to Wicked and Truth."

Nathaniel was there, too. "Please, Anita."

I nodded and let them wipe away some of the blood with a cloth that someone gave them. The scratches weren't that deep, deep enough that if I'd been a little more human I might have needed stitches, and seeing that they were across the mound of one breast I should have been more worried about that whole cosmetic thing, but strangely, I wasn't.

"Take me to them," I said.

Richard took one arm and Nathaniel the other. They lifted me to my feet and helped me walk where I wanted to go. Micah followed us, carrying bandages. Maybe I'd even let him use them on me eventually. Remus was dead, and I wanted to know why. Or maybe, how? The thing that had come out of the darkness had been a vampire that smelled like a wolf and had claws like a powerful shapeshifter. Impossible. But Remus was dead, so it had to be possible.

"Who are you?" I asked.

"I am Harlequin."

"One of, or the?" I asked. My voice sounded strangely distant inside my own head, as if the distance was greater than it should have been.

"I am Pantalone, once Pantaleon. I was one of the first children of the dark."

"You didn't send us a black mask, Pantalone, but you tried to kill us. That's against council law. Hell, that's against the Mother of All Darkness's law."

"You know nothing of our mother, human. You are not vampire, or succubus. You are a necromancer, and our laws say you can be killed on sight."

I smelled jasmine. Nathaniel said, "Flowers."

Richard said, "What is that?"

I felt the rain on the edge of a wind that hadn't existed for a million years. I tasted jasmine on my tongue, sweet and cloying. I wasn't afraid this time. I welcomed it. Because I knew I wasn't the one she was pissed at. Though *pissed* was too strong for the feeling I got as she breathed closer. *Pissed* was too human an emotion, and as she'd said herself, she'd lost the knack of being human.

"Marmee Noir," Nathaniel answered Richard. I'd forgotten he'd asked a question.

"Anita," Richard said, "fight it, fight her."

"If you aren't going to help me do this, then get away from me."

"Do what, let the Mother of All Vampires possess you?"

I screamed at him, "Get away from me, Richard, *now*!" A cut opened on his arm like a red mouth. It wasn't Marmee Noir; I'd done that a couple of times before under stress. I couldn't do it dependably, but . . . "That's not her, that's me. Help me, or get away." I fought to keep my voice even, because my emotions were dangerous, apparently.

"Don't let her inside you."

"Micah, take my arm."

"Don't let her do this," Richard said to him.

"We are still in danger here, Richard," Micah said. "Don't you get that? We have to finish what we started."

"You mean kill them?"

"Yes," I said, "yes, kill them. Kill them all!" Another cut opened on Richard's arm. He let me go, as if I were something hot that had burned him. Micah slid furred arms around me. He and Nathaniel led me forward, so I could do what needed to be done. No, truth, what I was going to do. Not need, want. I wanted him dead. He'd killed Remus, and Remus had died because the vampire on the ground had meant to kill me. Remus had given his life to save mine. I'd pay my debt, now, tonight, in the blood and pain of his killer. It sounded like such a good idea.

The smell of jasmine was everywhere. I could taste rain on my tongue. The wind was cool and fresh against my face, and the wind was coming from me.

47

"TAKE OFF HIS mask," I said, but the voice held an echo of a different voice.

"If you see my face I will be forced to kill you all," he said.

I laughed, and the laughter made the wind play around the room, patting with cool, damp hands at people's hair, their skin. "You are going to die tonight, Pantalone. Your mask can come off now, or after your corpse lies stretched at my feet. I prefer now, but I guess it really doesn't matter." The wind eased back. I was drowning in the scent of rain and jasmine.

He struck at me with his own power. It was like some spirit wolf, a great dark beast that rose from him and came at me, huge jaws agape. Micah and Nathaniel pulled me backward, but though it looked like a shadow, it hit me and pulled us all to the floor. People were running from everywhere, but Marmee was already there. The shadow wolf spilled into me; she absorbed it like something melting into the snow. With the touch of his power came a memory.

A snowstorm, so cold, the wind howling, so that he thought he heard voices on the wind. He'd found a cave, buried in the snow. Shelter, he thought. Then he'd heard the growl, low and too close. Something else had taken shelter from the storm. Then a woman had stepped into the light of his fire. A woman with a spill of dark hair and eyes that glittered in the firelight. He had smelled death on her and tried to fight. I felt his body run hot and spill bone and muscle and flesh from human to wolf. But a wolf like none that still walked today. She had turned into a huge striped cat, the color of a lion, but striped like a tiger, bigger than both. She'd nearly killed him, but when pain and injury had turned him back to human, she'd fed on him. She fed on him for three days until the storm stopped, and when the fourth night rose, they went out together, to hunt.

I came back to the here and now and found that Wicked and Truth had pierced his heart and neck with their swords. He cursed them, and writhed, but he wasn't dead. I knew, I just knew that swords would not kill him. He was old blood. Blood when vampire and shapeshifter could be one, back before the blood weakened. We could take his head and heart and burn the pieces separately, but didn't I want answers? Yes, I did.

I sat back up with Micah and Nathaniel's help. "Your actions could get the entire Harlequin disbanded; don't you care?"

"Kill me, if you can, but I will not answer questions from you."

The darkness inside me thought otherwise. "Fredo," I called.

The slender knife-wielding man was just beside me. "Can you get enough help and enough knives to pin him to the floor?"

"We can pin him, but unless we're leaning on the knives, they won't hold him."

"Then pin him with your bodies, I don't care how. I need to touch him."

"Why?"

"Does it matter?"

"Tonight, yes," he said.

I looked up into his dark eyes. I saw pain there. I answered that pain. "The darkness can make him talk, and then I'm going to kill him."

Fredo nodded. "Good plan." He went around getting volunteers to hold the vampire down. There were a lot of volunteers.

Jean-Claude came to me while they were wrestling him into place. "I feel her all around you, *ma petite*."

"Yeah," I said, but I wasn't looking at him. I was watching them pin the big vampire.

"Look at me." He touched my chin and turned me so that I would look at him. I didn't fight him, but I didn't seem to care whether I looked at him or not. "There is a light in your eyes that I do not know."

I half-saw, out of the corner of my eye, a dark figure form. She formed of the dark, and she looked vaguely like she had in my dream, all-black cloak, a small female figure. But this was no dream.

Screams again from the vampires. The ones with Asher, standing guard over Columbine and Giovanni, held their ground, but no one was happy.

Pantalone himself screamed, like a girl. It made it harder for the guards to wrestle him into submission. Oh, well.

The figure spoke, and the smell of jasmine and rain was in her voice, or on the wind, or the wind was her voice. I wasn't sure which. "Did you think my laws were superstitions, Jean-Claude? You were supposed to kill her when you knew what she was. Now it is too late."

"Too late for what?" he said, and he wrapped his arm around me, drew me in against his body, and we both looked up as my nightmare damn near materialized in front of us.

"She's a necromancer, Jean-Claude, she controls the dead, all the dead. Don't you understand yet? Some of the Harlequin think I woke because I want to steal her body, ride her as the Traveller rides other vampires. I had that gift once, to travel from body to body, but that is not why I woke."

"Why did you wake?" he whispered.

"She attracts the dead, Jean-Claude, all the dead. She called me from my sleep. Her power called to me like the first ray of sunlight after a thousand years of night. Her warmth and life called to my death. Even I cannot resist her. Do you understand now?"

"You are so not under my power," I said.

She gave a low, dry chuckle. "Legend says that necromancers can control the dead, and that is true, but what legend does not say is that the dead give necromancers no peace. We pester the poor things, because they draw us like moths to the flame, except with vampires and necromancers it is a question who is flame and who is moth. Beware, Jean-Claude, that she does not burn you up. Beware, necromancer, that the vampires do not put you in your grave."

"Your law," Pantalone yelled, "your law says she must be put to death."

The dark figure turned toward the struggling pile of people. "Do not dare speak to me of my laws, Pantalone. I made you. I gave you a piece of myself, that is what made you one of the Harlequin. I have been listening to vampires that dwell closer to my physical form. You have been assassinating vampires for council members. You are neutral. You take no sides. That is what makes the Harlequin!" Her voice rose as she spoke until the wind held not just rain but the promise of storm. "I will take back what I gave you. What you used to make these pale imitations of my Columbine and her Giovanni. These are not my Harlequin."

"Columbine died. I had to make a replacement, and you were not here to guide me."

"Then the mask should have been retired, and the name with it. That was my will, and our way, once." She began to walk toward them. I could almost see her foot, dainty in a slipper edged with white pearls.

Jean-Claude called, "Do not look upon her face. For fear of sanity and life do not meet her eyes, any of you."

"I am not the Traveller, to need to steal bodies to walk. I did need flesh once, but I am the darkness made flesh, Pantalone. I am she who made you, made you all! Killing the necromancer will not put me back to sleep again. It is too late for that."

It was Jake who knelt beside me, and Jean-Claude. Jake whispered, "She's using your energy to manifest, Anita. You have to shut her down before she's solid here. You do not want her in America in flesh and bone."

I looked at him, and I knew. "You're one of them."

Jake nodded.

"You saved *ma petite*, when you could have let her die in the bathroom at the Circus," Jean-Claude said.

"The Mother was always going to wake again, nothing would prevent that. Some of us believe that Anita is our only hope of controlling her. Prove my master right by shutting down the power you're feeding her."

"I don't know . . ."

"She's feeding on your anger, your rage."

"I don't know how to stop that."

"If she feeds on Pantalone, one of the oldest of us, she may have enough power to be permanent flesh."

The black-cloaked figure was standing at his feet. The guards were looking at me. I said the only thing I could think of: "Get away from him."

Some of the guards hesitated, but most of them glanced toward the dark figure and moved a discreet distance.

"Anita," Jake said, "help us."

I turned to Jean-Claude and said, "Help me think of something besides my anger."

The black figure was spreading into what looked like a piece of the night sky, like some beautiful and frightening cloak of stars and darkness. Pantalone shrieked, as if whatever he saw in that piece of darkness was something terrible to behold.

"Hurry," I said.

Jean-Claude raised the *ardeur*, in a breath, in the feel of his mouth on mine. He raised the *ardeur* and stripped away my sorrow in a rush of skin and hands. I hadn't fed the *ardeur* in over twelve hours. I was suddenly starving.

Marmee Noir screamed, "No!" Her rage cut through me, and a sharp pain laced my back. I felt blood a second later. The *ardeur* was gone in a rush of fear and pain. I turned, and Jean-Claude caught my face, forced my eyes against his velvet jacket. "She is fading, *ma petite*."

Her voice came in a rush of rain and wind. "I know who your master is, wolf. You have betrayed me, and I will not forget it."

When I could no longer smell jasmine or feel rain against my skin like some invisible presence, I asked Jake, "How do I keep her from popping in to see me?"

"There's a charm for that."

I gave him a look.

"People used to think she was a demon, but whatever they thought she was, one human witch made a charm a very long time ago, and it works."

"Is it a holy symbol?" I asked.

He smiled. "No, it's magic, not faith."

"Isn't all magic faith?" I asked.

"No, sometimes it's just magic."

The concept was too hard for me. "You got one of those charms on you?"

"Always, but I'll get one for you. We should be safe for the rest of tonight."

"I hope those aren't famous last words," I said.

"What do we do with them, Anita?" Truth asked.

I looked at Jake. "He broke your laws more than mine."

"Kill him under your laws, we won't argue. We suspected one of us was being paid as an assassin, but we didn't know who. Then Pantalone volunteered to come check out Malcolm's church. It was just a visit, and a report back to the council. He usually only takes killing jobs, so we were suspicious. If Columbine had won Jean-Claude's lands, it would have been Pantalone who ruled here. We are allowed to leave the service of the Mother now, because she sleeps. Once she wakes, all that are in her service will be trapped there."

"So you came to spy," I said.

"And to help keep you alive."

"Thanks for that." I glanced back toward Remus's body. "I wish everybody were still alive."

"I'm sorry about that, truly. He was a good man."

I turned back to Wicked and Truth. "Did you guys wade into the dark and cut off his hand without being able to see anything?"

"Yes," Wicked said.

"Of course," Truth said.

"Then take his head."

Pantalone, with a missing arm, stabbed, shot, moved in a black blur. Truth was his own dark blur, his sword so fast it looked like lightning. He took him through the heart again, except spitting him this time the way Pantalone had spitted Remus. Wicked's blade glittered outward and the head went spinning. It wasn't just impressive. It was lovely in a macabre sort of way.

"Someone put the head in a sack. We'll burn it later, separate from the body."

"We should take the heart, too," Olaf said.

I nodded. "You're right. We'll do that after we take care of the other two."

"You killed our master," Columbine said.

"I would ask, does that frighten you, but I can taste your fear in your words. It tastes good. I'm going to ask you some questions. If you answer me truthfully, then you die quick, fairly painless. You fuck with me, lie to me, try not to answer the questions and I'll make your death something to write home about. I'll give you to Olaf. He's the big guy."

Olaf glanced back at me, gun still trained on them. "Do you mean it?"

"Right this minute, yes. She's a petite dark-haired woman, she even fits your victim profile. If she doesn't answer my questions, never say I didn't give you a good present."

"No," Columbine said, "please."

"You tried to kill me and the people I love. Your master killed my friend. *Please* isn't going to have much effect on me right now, not from you."

"Please," Richard said, "don't do this."

I shook my head. "Go home, Richard."

"Isn't there any other man in your bed who agrees with me, that there are some things you don't do, for any reason?"

Jean-Claude stood and went to Richard. He began to try to soothe him. It reminded me of when you gamed and you had to send the Paladin around the hill so you could loot the dead.

Nathaniel and Micah came to my sides. "You want to get closer to her?" Micah asked.

I nodded. "You don't think I'm a bastard for offering her to Olaf?"

"They've nearly killed you three times, Anita. You're my Nimir-Ra; I'll carve out her heart and serve it to you on a platter." The threat seemed more real with him in his kitty-cat form.

"I'm your submissive, I don't argue," Nathaniel said.

"Submissive when it suits you, lately."

He smiled at me. "I won't carve her up, but I might watch Olaf do it. She almost killed you, and Jean-Claude, and Richard."

I nodded. "And Peter."

"And Cisco," Nathaniel said.

I nodded, and started to turn back to look at Remus. Micah kept me moving forward. "Let's go ask your questions."

We went to ask my questions. Olaf was whispering to her as we came up, what he'd do to her, what he wanted to do to her. "Please, don't answer the questions. Vampires die so much slower than humans."

Guess what, she answered every question first time out. She and Nivia had killed the humans and tried to frame the church members. It had been to get leverage to try to force Malcolm to simply give the Church to them. Then I'd gone and spoiled it by killing Nivia. I didn't tell her that I wasn't even certain why Nivia had died, or what I'd done to cause it. Maybe Jean-Claude could help me figure it out later. Columbine was going to be the beard, the stalking horse, for Pantalone. Once he ruled here, even the Mother of All Darkness couldn't force him to abandon his territory. All of them, Pantalone, Nivia, Soledad, and Giovanni had all taken assassination jobs. The only question she hesitated on, even for a second, was, "Which council members did you work for?"

"They'll kill me."

"You don't have to be afraid of them anymore, Columbine."

"You'll protect me?"

"In a way. You don't have to be afraid of the council killing you later, because we're going to kill you tonight, remember? All we're negotiating on is whether you die easy, or hard. Your choice."

She shook her head.

"Olaf."

"Yes."

"We have to cut her heart out anyway. Want to do it first?"

He stared at me as if wondering if I was kidding. I remembered Remus's body in my arms. I knew now that I'd felt his body jerk as Pantalone had forced his arm through his chest, through his heart, dug his way through, and killed him. I could still hear his last whispered "I'm sorry." Not "help me," or "God, it hurts," but "I'm sorry."

"Do it," I said.

They held her down, and they held Giovanni down, and Olaf ripped her costume open, bared her breasts to the room, and began very slowly to carve out her heart. He didn't get very far before she gave up the names. Master of Beasts and the Lover of Death.

Olaf didn't stop when she gave up the names. He'd gone to his happy place. It was like trying to argue with an autistic child; he just didn't hear us.

Columbine screamed, "I answered your questions. In the name of the dark, kill me."

I told Wicked to behead her. He did, one clean blow that scarred the wood underneath her. I could never get a head to come off in one blow. Olaf looked up as the blood poured out of the neck in a crimson fountain. "I wasn't finished."

"She gave the information up a while ago. I promised her a quick death if she told me what I needed to know."

He gave me a look that wasn't friendly at all.

"You can still cut out her heart," I said.

"It's not the same," he said, and the look on his face was nothing I understood, or wanted to understand.

I started to apologize for not letting him cut out her heart while she was still alive, then I caught myself. Fuck, the shock was beginning to leave and I was wondering what the hell I'd been thinking. Legally, everything we were doing was A-okay. I had a warrant of execution, it covered a multitude of sins.

He did finish cutting out her heart. I had Wicked behead Giovanni. I was really going to see if he and his brother could teach me the beheading-a-person-with-one-blow technique. I could never manage, not even with a sword. Maybe it was a leverage thing?

I took Giovanni's heart myself, with one of Fredo's knives that was better for carving open a person's sternum than anything I had on me. I was tired, and the shock was wearing off, which made me clumsy. I was nearly elbow deep inside Giovanni's chest. I just couldn't seem to get the heart out of the ligaments that held the pericardial sac in place. I'd pierced the sac, but it was as if I'd gotten something tangled. I was so tired, and numb, and not numb enough.

"May I help?" Olaf was kneeling beside the body. His hands were bloody, too, but only one of them looked like he was wearing a red glove.

"Yeah, it's tangled. I think I'm just tired."

He slid his hand inside the hole I'd made, so that his arm slid up alongside mine in the chest cavity. It wasn't until his hand cupped mine, pressing both our hands into the still warm heart, that I looked at him. We were both leaning over the body, our faces inches apart, with our arms up the much longer torso of the male. He looked at me over the body, our hands around the heart, blood everywhere. He looked at me as if it were a candlelit dinner and I were wearing nice lingerie.

I thought very clearly in my head, *I will not scream.* I would be calm. Fuck, but I would be. Besides, he'd enjoy it if I screamed. My voice was only a little strained as I said, "I think it's just past my fingertips. Can you reach the ligament there?"

He slid his hand over mine, farther up the heart. He caressed my hand while he reached for the piece of the heart I couldn't reach. I started to slide my hand out as I felt him grab the piece of muscle or ligament. He laid the other heart on the dead vampire's groin and grabbed my arm before I could pull it out of the chest cavity. He held my hand inside so we'd be touching the heart together. If I struggled, he'd like it. I could yell for help, but he almost had it loose, and it would be over. I hesitated. He pulled the heart free of whatever had been holding it in place, and it spilled into both our hands. He kept his free hand on my arm, controlling how slow we eased out of the chest cavity. He made it last, and he stared at my face while we did it. I normally don't have much problem fishing around inside dead bodies anymore, but the sensation of our hands holding the heart, our arms pressed together as we slid out of the thick, bloody muscle, was too strangely intimate. For the last few inches of arm he looked down at the wound and not at my face. He watched our arms emerge from the bloody hole just under the sternum. He kept his hand on my arm and forced our hands upward, so that for a moment we held the heart together, and he looked at me over that bleeding muscle.

I knew I went pale. I couldn't help it. I knew he would enjoy my fear, and I couldn't stop it. Then he leaned in toward me. He leaned in over the bloody heart, the body, our bloody arms. He leaned in for a kiss.

I whispered, "Don't."

"You don't want me to kiss you," he whispered back.

"I don't want you to touch me," I said.

He smiled then. "Perfect."

He kissed me.

I had Fredo's blade going for a different chest when Olaf pulled back, out of reach. He laughed, a rich, deep laugh. A happy sound that didn't match anything we were doing. He'd left me with the heart in one hand and the knife in the other. If my hands hadn't been full I might have gone for my gun. Surely I could claim temporary insanity.

He wiped his bloody hands on his clothes, not just on his shirt, but wiped his bloody hands down his body, showing off all that muscled chest, stomach, and finally groin. He massaged his groin with his bloody hands, and looked at me while he did it.

That was it. I set the knife and heart on the floor and tried to run for the bathroom and never made it. I threw up in front of the door to the recreation hall. I threw up until there was nothing left. I threw up until my head was pounding and I was spitting up bile. Micah laid a cool and human hand against my forehead while I was sick. Nathaniel held my hair back, because my hands were still covered in blood.

Olaf left town. I've got a new recurring nightmare to add to the list. It's Olaf and me cutting up the body, except in the dream it's bloodier, and Giovanni is screaming, and I kiss Olaf back. Maybe the temporary insanity was not to shoot him.

Peter didn't take the injection, and he didn't catch lycanthropy. He's back home recovering, human-slow, but he's sixteen and in good shape. He'll heal, but he's going to have some seriously macho scars. I have no idea what Edward told Donna. I'm not sure I want to know.

Doc Lillian sewed up the marks on my breast. She said, "Unless you don't care if it scars?" I guess I did care. I asked her why the breast would scar when the stomach and side healed clean. They were more serious wounds. What the doc and the other doctors think happened is that the feeding on the swans gave enough energy not only to save everyone, but also to heal the injuries completely, and even faster than a normal lycanthrope could have done it. I'm not sure what a "normal" lycanthrope is, but Lillian has warned me to be more careful. "You can't find an entire animal group to feed off every night." She has a point.

Jean-Claude sent Sampson home to Cape Cod before the fight. He didn't want to get his friend's son killed. Sampson left without having sex with me. His mother's plans spoiled by the Harlequin's arrival.

There's a tiger inside me now, thanks to Marmee Noir and Soledad. We're trying to find some tigers willing to come to St. Louis. Though, strangely, something about what happened seems to have given me more control over the beasts. Or, at least, they haven't tried to tear me apart recently. In fact, letting out one beast seems to content the rest. No one seems to know why it's working this way now. I'm not sure I care why, as long as it stays this calm.

Haven stayed in town with his new lions. Joseph, his wife, and his brother all vanished. Most of the pride was offered a chance to join Haven's new pride. Some accepted. Haven and his fellow enforcers seem to be trying to live by my rules. I've managed to keep Haven out of my bed for now. The lioness seems strangely okay with that. Again, part of me wishes I knew why the beasts inside me are suddenly so reasonable, but most of me doesn't want to poke at the miracle too much. I'm just glad something is getting easier to deal with, instead of harder.

Richard had left the church before I threw up. He never saw me have my moment of conscience, or panic. Whatever. We aren't dating anymore, again. This one may stick, and the thought doesn't upset me, which is why it may stick.

Jake left town. Strangely, some people remember he was a Harlequin, and some don't. He and his master are worried that Marmee Noir will come back and try and use me again. He gave me a pendant made of a metal so soft I can bend the edges. It's carved with symbols I don't know. I'll have my metaphysical therapist, Marianne, look at it when I see her next weekend. Jake has made me promise to wear it always. After seeing Marmee Noir's slippers with little pearls, so real in the church, I'll wear the amulet, always. Small price to pay to avoid the Marmee Darling.

I found a priest to hear Malcolm's confession. I think it took like three days, with food breaks, to hear it all, but he had been saving up for centuries.

Remus and Cisco are still dead. Nothing changed that. I could bring them back as zombies, but that wouldn't be bringing them back at all. Remus's last words keep coming back: "I'm sorry." Sorry about what? Sorry he thought he'd failed to protect me? Sorry that he was dying? Sorry in general? I was the one who was sorry. I'd gotten him killed.

Peter calls me sometimes and we share our survivor's guilt. This isn't the first time people died and I lived, but it's the freshest. Peter still wants to grow up and be like his soon-to-be stepdad. If Cisco's death, and almost dying, couldn't cure him of wanting to play mercenary, then I'm not going to be able to talk him out of it.

Talking about things I'm not going to be able to talk people out of . . . I need to try to meet Nathaniel's needs, all his needs. I discussed with Jean-Claude that Byron had offered to teach me how to dominate Nathaniel. Jean-Claude agreed that I needed a teacher if I was serious about topping our pussycat. But Jean-Claude suggested a different teacher, one who was most certainly a top and not a bottom. Asher would be more than happy to teach me about BDSM, if I truly wanted to learn. Honestly, I'm not sure I do, but for Nathaniel's sake, I've got to at least try. Don't I? If I try and can't do it, then I've at least tried. If I don't try and we break up, then it's all my fault. I don't want to feel like any of my breakups are my fault anymore. There had to be a point with Richard, early on, where I didn't compromise. Maybe if Richard had agreed to sleep with me when I first asked, there would have been no room for anyone else. Maybe, if . . . I don't want to look back at Nathaniel and say *Maybe*, or *If only*. I'll compromise; I'll bend, though it's not one of my best things. Sometimes it feels like when I bend, that I'll break. Will letting Asher teach me how to make Nathaniel happy break me? I hope not.

A LICK OF FROST

The heat is on once again as America's only native-born faerie princess, Meredith Gentry, returns—and her sexy, suspenseful saga continues—in the brand-new adventure, *A Lick of Frost*. Leaving behind the faerie court, Merry plunges into her Los Angeles life as a private investigator, only to have faerie intrigue reach out to her yet again. Still, her coterie of handsome bodyguards are close at hand, and her erotically charged efforts to conceive an heir must go on . . . or else. When federal charges are levied against her bodyguards, human and faerie justice come into conflict. Between the two worlds lies territory fraught with dangers neither a princess nor a private eye can anticipate. At every turn Merry's tangled web of family and politics threatens to bring her face-to-face with a fate much worse than death.

Look for Laurell K. Hamilton's new Meredith Gentry novel, *A Lick of Frost*, coming October 30, 2007 from Ballantine Books.